ROGUE SQUADRON

THE KRYTOS TRAP

ROGUE SQUADRON

THE KRYTOS TRAP

MICHAEL A. STACKPOLE

NEW YORK

2022 Del Rey Trade Paperback Edition

Published in the United States by Del Rey, an imprint of Random House,
a division of Penguin Random House LLC, New York.

DEL REY and the CIRCLE colophon are registered trademarks of
Penguin Random House LLC.

Originally published in hardcover in the United States by Bantam Spectra,
an imprint of Random House, in 1996.

ISBN 978-0-593-49734-0
Ebook ISBN 978-0-307-79623-3

Printed in the United States of America on acid-free paper

randomhousebooks.com

2 4 6 8 9 7 5 3 1

Book design by Edwin Vazquez

To the memory of Patty Vardeman

THE ESSENTIAL
LEGENDS COLLECTION

For more than forty years, novels set in a galaxy far, far away have enriched the *Star Wars* experience for fans seeking to continue the adventure beyond the screen. When he created *Star Wars,* George Lucas built a universe that sparked the imagination and inspired others to create. He opened up that universe to be a creative space for other people to tell their own tales. This became known as the Expanded Universe, or EU, of novels, comics, videogames, and more.

To this day, the EU remains an inspiration for *Star Wars* creators and is published under the label Legends. Ideas, characters, story elements, and more from new *Star Wars* entertainment trace their origins back to material from the Expanded Universe. This Essential Legends Collection curates some of the most treasured stories from that expansive legacy.

DRAMATIS PERSONAE

ROGUE SQUADRON

COMMANDER WEDGE ANTILLES (human male from Corellia)
CAPTAIN TYCHO CELCHU (human male from Alderaan)
CAPTAIN ARIL NUNB (Sullustan female from Sullust)
LIEUTENANT CORRAN HORN (human male from Corellia)
LIEUTENANT PASH CRACKEN (human male from Contruum)

OORYL QRYGG (Gand male from Gand)
NAWARA VEN (Twi'lek male from Ryloth)
RHYSATI YNR (human female from Bespin)
ERISI DLARIT (human female from Thyferra)
GAVIN DARKLIGHTER (human male from Tatooine)
RIV SHIEL (Shistavanen male from Uvena III)
ASYR SEI'LAR (Bothan female from Bothawui)
INYRI FORGE (human female from Kessel)
M-3PO (Emtrey; protocol and regulations droid)
WHISTLER (Corran's R2 astromech)
MYNOCK (Wedge's R5 astromech)

ALLIANCE MILITARY

ADMIRAL ACKBAR (Mon Calamari male from Mon Calamari)

ALLIANCE INTELLIGENCE

GENERAL AIREN CRACKEN (human male from Contruum)
IELLA WESSIRI (human female from Corellia)
WINTER (human female from Alderaan)

CITIZENS ON CORUSCANT

FLIRY VORRU (human male from Corellia)
DIRIC WESSIRI (human male from Corellia)
BORSK FEY'LYA (Bothan male from Bothawui)
HALLA ETTYK (human female from Alderaan)
QLAERN HIRF (Vratix from Thyferra)

CREW OF THE *PULSAR SKATE*

MIRAX TERRIK (human female from Corellia)
LIAT TSAYV (Sullustan male from Sullust)

IMPERIAL FORCES

YSANNE ISARD, DIRECTOR OF IMPERIAL INTELLIGENCE
    (human female from Coruscant)
KIRTAN LOOR, INTELLIGENCE AGENT
    (human male from Churba)
GENERAL EVIR DERRICOTE (human male from Kalla)

ROGUE SQUADRON

THE KRYTOS TRAP

1

Commander Wedge Antilles would have preferred the ceremony to be private. Rogue Squadron had come to mourn the passing of one of its own on the week anniversary of his death. Wedge wanted the gathering to be small and intimate, with Corran Horn's friends all being able to share remembrances of him, but that was not possible. Corran's death had come during the liberation of Coruscant. That made him a hero from a company of heroes, and while a small memorial might have been what Corran himself would have wanted, it was not *heroic* enough for a figure of his posthumous stature.

Even though Wedge had known things would not go quite the way he wanted, he had not anticipated how out of control they would get when he requested permission to hold the ceremony. He had expected a number of dignitaries would come to the pseudogranite barrow that marked where Corran had died when a building collapsed on top of him. He even anticipated people lining the balconies and walkways of nearby towers. At the very worst he imagined people might gawk from the beds of hovertrucks.

His imagination paled beside that exercised by the bureaucrats who organized the memorial service. They took a ceremony based on heartfelt grief and made it into the focal point of mourning for the entire New Republic. Corran Horn was a hero—this they proclaimed loudly—but he was also a *victim*. As such he represented *all* the victims of the Empire. It didn't matter to them that Corran would have rejected being labeled a victim. He had been transformed into a symbol—a symbol the New Republic needed badly.

Rogue Squadron likewise underwent iconization. The unit's pilots had always worn orange flightsuits in the past, or, as supplies became harder and harder to find, whatever had been handy. Corran's flightsuit had been green, black, and grey, since he'd brought it with him from the Corellian Security Force. In homage to him, that color scheme was used to create new uniforms for the squadron: evergreen overall, with dark grey flank panels, black sleeves, leg stripes, and trim. On the left sleeve and breast rode the Rogue Squadron crest. It had also appeared on the evergreen hawkbilled caps designed by a Kuati, but Wedge had vetoed their addition to the uniform.

The makeup of the Squadron had also been adjusted. Asyr Sei'lar, a Bothan pilot, and Inyri Forge, the sister of a dead squadron member, had both been added to the squadron. Wedge would have gladly welcomed them, and they *had* been crucial to the success of the mission to liberate Coruscant, but they had been pressed upon him for political reasons. Likewise, Portha, a Trandoshan, had been made a member of the squadron despite his inability to fly. He was attached to the unit as part of a previously nonexistent security detail. Each of them was appointed by bureaucrats as a reward to various constituencies in the New Republic, and Wedge hated their objectification.

The ceremony grew out of all proportion until special grandstands had to be grafted to the nearby buildings and color-coded for the various levels of access people were to be accorded. Holocams had been stationed at various positions so the ceremony could be recorded and replayed on countless worlds. Despite the very real fears about contracting the highly contagious Krytos virus, the stands were packed to overflowing.

He looked up from his position on the reviewing stand and out at Rogue Squadron. His people were bearing up well despite the bright sunlight and unseasonably warm weather. The recent rains had raised the general level of humidity until clothing clung and the very air lay like a smothering blanket over everyone. The thick air seemed to deaden sounds and suppress emotions, and Wedge was tempted to allow himself to imagine that Coruscant somehow also mourned Corran's passing.

In addition to the members of Rogue Squadron, Corran's other friends stood on the platform nearest the barrow. Iella Wessiri, a slender, brown-haired woman who had been Corran's CorSec partner, stood next to Mirax Terrik. Despite being the daughter of a notorious Corellian smuggler, Mirax had managed to become friends with Corran. Mirax, who had known Wedge since they had both been kids, had tearfully confided in him that she and Corran had planned to celebrate the liberation of Coruscant together. He could see she'd fallen hard for Corran, and the lifeless expression on her face made his heart ache.

The only one who is missing is Tycho. Wedge frowned. Captain Tycho Celchu was a long-standing member of Rogue Squadron who had served as the squadron's executive officer. He'd surreptitiously joined the mission to Coruscant at Wedge's request and had been instrumental in bringing the planet's defenses down. His action was the latest in a string of heroic missions Tycho had carried off during his Rebel career.

Unfortunately, Alliance Intelligence had developed evidence that indicated Tycho was working for the Empire. They blamed him directly not only for Corran's death, but for the death of Bror Jace, another Rogue Squadron pilot who had died early on in the Coruscant campaign. Wedge had not been fully apprised of what the evidence was that they had against Tycho, but he did not doubt the man's innocence for a second. *Still, his innocence might mean nothing in the long run.*

In spite of the liberation, Coruscant was not a pleasant or stable world. A hideous epidemic—the Krytos virus—was ravaging the non-human population of the planet. It had struck at the non-humans in the Rebellion and was hard enough on some species that even coming down to the planet was an act of extreme bravery. Bacta, as usual, could cure the virus, but the Rebellion's entire store of bacta was insufficient to cure everyone. This resulted in panic, and resentment against humans for their apparent immunity to the disease.

The memorial service had become an important event because Coruscant's population needed something to unite them and to get their minds off their suffering, even if only for a moment. The fact that Rogue Squadron had humans and non-humans working together in it showed the strength of unity that had allowed the Rebellion to prevail. Non-humans coming together along with dignitaries from various other worlds to mourn a dead human acknowledged the debt the Rebels owed humans. Speakers devoted themselves to exhorting their fellows to labor together in building a future that would justify the sacrifices made by Corran and others. Their words raised things to a philosophical or metaphysical level meant to soothe away the anxieties and worries of the citizens.

Those were noble messages, to be certain, but Wedge felt they were not the right messages for Corran. He tugged on the sleeves of his uniform jacket as a Bothan protocol subaltern waved him forward. Wedge stepped up to the podium and wanted to lean heavily upon it. Years of fighting and saying good-bye to friends and comrades weighed him down—but he refused to give in to fatigue. He let his pride in the squadron and his friendship with Corran keep him upright.

He looked around at the crowd, then focused on the mound of pseudogranite rubble before him. "Corran Horn does not rest easy in that grave." Wedge paused for a moment, and then another, letting the silence remind everyone of the true purpose of the ceremony. "Corran Horn was never at ease except when he was fighting. He does not rest easy now because there is much fighting yet to be done. We have taken Coruscant, but anyone who assumes that means the Empire is dead is as mistaken as Grand Moff Tarkin was in his belief that Alderaan's destruction would somehow cripple the Rebellion."

Wedge brought his head up. "Corran Horn was not a man who gave up, no matter what the odds. More than once he took upon himself the responsibility of dealing with a threat to the squadron and to the Rebellion. Heedless of his own safety, he engaged overwhelming forces and by sheer dint of will and spirit and courage he won through. Even here, on Coruscant, he flew alone into the heart of a storm that was ravaging a planet and risked his life so this world would be free. He did not fail, because he would not let himself fail.

"Each of us who knew him has, in our hearts, dozens and dozens of examples of his bravery or his concern for others, or his ability to see where he was wrong and correct himself. He was not a perfect man, but he was a man who sought to be the best he could be. And while he took pride in being very good, he didn't waste energy in displays of rampant egotism. He just picked out new goals and drove himself forward toward them."

Wedge slowly nodded toward the rubble pile. "Corran is now gone. The burdens he bore have been laid down. The responsibilities he shouldered have been abandoned. The example he set is no more. His loss is tragic, but the greater tragedy would be letting him be remembered as a faceless hero mouldering in this cairn. He was a fighter, as all of us should be. The things he took upon himself might be enough to crush down any one person, but we all can accept a portion of that responsibility and bear it together. Others have talked about building a future that would honor Corran and the others who have died fighting the Empire, but the fact is that there's fighting yet to be done before the building can begin.

"We have to fight the impatience with the pace of change

that makes us look nostalgically on the days of the Empire. Yes, there might have been a bit more food available. Yes, power outages might have been fewer. Yes, you might have been insulated from the misery of others—but at what cost? The security you thought you had froze into an icy lump of fear in your gut whenever you saw stormtroopers walking in your direction. With the liberation of Coruscant that fear can melt, but if you forget it once existed and decide things were not so bad under the Emperor, you'll be well on your way to inviting it back."

He opened his hands to take in all those assembled at the monument. "You must do what Corran did: fight anything and everything that would give the Empire comfort or security or a chance to reassert itself. If you trade vigilance for complacency, freedom for security, a future without fear for comfort; you will be responsible for shaping the galaxy once again into a place that demands people like Corran fight, always fight and, eventually, fall victim to evil.

"The choice, ultimately, devolves to you. Corran Horn will not rest easy in his grave until there is no more fighting to be done. He has done everything he could to fight the Empire; now it is up to you to continue his fight. If he is ever to know peace, it will only be when we *all* know peace. And that is a goal every one of us knows is well worth fighting for."

Wedge stepped back from the podium and steeled himself against the polite applause. Deep down he would have hoped his words had been inspiring, but those gathered around the memorial were dignitaries and officials from worlds throughout the New Republic. They were politicians whose goal was to help shape the future others of their number spoke about. They wanted stability and order as a foundation for their constructions. His words, reminding everyone that fights were yet to be waged, undercut their efforts. They had to applaud because of the situation and who he was, but Wedge had no doubt most of them thought him a politically naive warrior best suited to being a hero who was feted and used in holograph opportunities to support this program or that.

He could only hope that others listening to what he had to say would take his message to heart. The politicians required stability, and the way they *acquired* stability was to ignore *instability* or patch it over with some quick fix. The citizens of the New Republic would find their politicians as distant as the Imperial politicians before them. With their new-won freedom, the people would be able to let their leaders know what they thought, and might be tempted to protest if things did not move swiftly enough in the direction the people wanted.

A rebellion against the Rebellion would result in anarchy or a return of the Empire. Either would be a disaster. Fighting for progress and against reactionary forces was the only way to guarantee the New Republic would get a chance to flourish. Wedge dearly wanted that to happen and hoped the politicians would look past their efforts to gather power to themselves long enough to take steps to provide real stability and a real future.

Over at the grave site an honor guard raised the squadron flag, then backed away and saluted. That signaled an end to the ceremony, and the visitors began to drift away. A cream-furred Bothan with violet eyes crossed to where Wedge stood and nodded almost graciously. "You were quite eloquent, Commander Antilles." Borsk Fey'lya waved a hand toward the departing masses. "I have no doubt quite a few hearts were stirred by your words."

Wedge raised an eyebrow. "But not yours, Councilor Fey'lya?"

The Bothan snorted a clipped laugh. "If I were so easily swayed, I could be convinced to back all sorts of nonsense."

"Like the trial of Tycho Celchu?"

Fey'lya's fur rippled and rose at the back of his neck. "No, I might be convinced that such a trial was not necessary." He smoothed the fur back down with his right hand. "Admiral Ackbar has not convinced you to abandon your petition to the Provisional Council about this matter?"

"No." Wedge folded his arms across his chest. "I would have

thought by now you would have engineered a vote to deny me the chance to address the council."

"Summarily dismiss a petition by the man who liberated Coruscant?" The Bothan's violet eyes narrowed. "You're moving into a realm of warfare at which I am a master, Commander. I would have thought you wise enough to see that. Your petition will fail. It must fail, so it shall. Captain Celchu will be tried for murder and treason."

"Even though he is innocent?"

"Is he?"

"He is."

"A fact to be determined by a military court, surely." Fey'lya gave Wedge a cold smile. "A suggestion, Commander."

"Yes?"

"Don't waste your eloquence on the Provisional Council. Save it. Hoard it." The Bothan's teeth flashed in a feral grin. "Use it on the tribunal that tries Captain Celchu. You'll not gain his freedom, of course—no one is *that* eloquent; but perhaps you will win him some modicum of mercy when it comes time for sentence to be passed."

2

HIGH UP IN A TOWER SUITE, up above the surface of Imperial Center, Kirtan Loor allowed himself a smile. At the tower's pinnacle, the only companions were hawk-bats safe in their shadowed roosts and Special Intelligence operatives who were menacing despite their lack of stormtrooper armor or bulk. He felt alone and aloof, but those sensations came naturally with his sense of superiority. At the top of the world, he had been given all he could see to command and dominate.

And destroy.

Ysanne Isard had given him the job of creating and leading a Palpatine Counter-insurgency Front. He knew she did not expect grand success from him. He had been given ample resources to make himself a nuisance. He could disrupt the functioning of the New Republic. He could slow their takeover of Coruscant and hamper their ability to master the mechanisms of galactic administration. A bother, minor but vexatious, is what Ysanne Isard had intended he become.

Kirtan Loor knew he had to become more. Years before, when he started working as an Imperial liaison officer with the Corellian Security Force on Corellia, he never would have dreamed of finding himself rising so far and playing so deadly a game. Even so, he had always been ambitious, and supremely confident in himself and his abilities. His chief asset was his memory, which allowed him to recall a plethora of facts, no matter how obscure. Once he had seen or read or heard something he could draw it from his memory, and this ability gave him a gross advantage over the criminals and bureaucrats with whom he dealt.

His reliance on his memory had also hobbled him. His prodigious feats of recall so overawed his enemies that they would naturally assume he had processed the information he possessed and had drawn the logical conclusions from it. Since they assumed he already knew what only they knew, they would tell him what he had not bothered to figure out for himself. They made it unnecessary for him to truly think, and that skill had begun to atrophy in him.

Ysanne Isard, when she summoned him to Imperial Center, had made it abundantly clear that learning to think and not to assume was the key to his continued existence. Her supervision made up in severity what it lacked in duration, putting him through a grueling regimen that rehabilitated his cognitive abilities. By the time she fled Imperial Center, Isard had clearly been confident in his ability to annoy and confound the Rebels.

More importantly, Kirtan Loor had become certain that he could do all she wanted and yet more.

From his vantage point he looked down on the distant blob of dignitaries and mourners gathered at the memorial for Corran Horn. While he despised them all for their politics, he joined them in mourning Horn's loss. Corran Horn had been Loor's nemesis. They had hated each other on Corellia, and Loor had spent a year and a half trying to hunt Corran down after he fled from Corellia. The hunt had ended when Ysanne Isard brought Loor to Imperial Center, but he had anticipated a renewal of his private little war with Horn when given the assignment to remain on Coruscant.

Of course, Corran's demise hardly made a dent in the legion

of enemies Loor had on Imperial Center. Foremost among them was General Airen Cracken, the director of Alliance Intelligence. Cracken's network of spies and operatives had ultimately made the conquest of the Imperial capital possible, and his security precautions had given Imperial counterintelligence agents fits for years. Cracken—or Kraken, as some of Loor's people had taken to calling the Rebel—would be a difficult foe with whom to grapple.

Loor knew he had some other enemies who would pursue him as part of a personal vendetta. The whole of Rogue Squadron, from Antilles to the new recruits, would gladly hunt him down and kill him—including the spy in their midst since Loor presented a security risk for the spy. Even if they could not connect him with Corran's death directly, the mere fact that Corran hated him would be a burden they'd gladly accept and a debt they would attempt to discharge.

Iella Wessiri was the last of the CorSec personnel Loor had hunted, and her presence on Imperial Center gave him pause. She had never been as relentless as Corran Horn in her pursuit of criminals, but that had always seemed to Loor to be because she was more thorough than Horn. Whereas Corran might muscle his way through an investigation, Iella picked up on small clues and accomplished with élan what Corran did with brute strength. In the shadow game in which Loor was engaged, this meant she was a foe he might not see coming, and that made her the most dangerous of all.

Loor backed away from the window and looked at the holographic representation of the figures below as they strode across his holotable. The ceremony had been broadcast planetwide, and would be rebroadcast at various worlds throughout the galaxy. He watched Borsk Fey'lya and Wedge Antilles as they met in close conversation, then split apart and wandered away. Everyone appeared more like toys to him than they did real people. He found it easy to imagine himself a titanic—*no, Imperial*—presence who had deigned to be distracted by the actions of bugs.

He picked up the remote device from the table and flicked it on. A couple of small lights flashed on the black rectangle in his left palm, then a red button in the center of it glowed almost benignly. His thumb hovered over it for a second. He smiled, but killed the impulse to stab his thumb down and gently returned the device to the table.

A year before he would have punched that button, detonating the explosives his people had secreted around the memorial. With one casual caress he could have unleashed fire and pain, wiping out a cadre of traitorous planetary officials and eliminating Rogue Squadron. He knew, given a chance, any of the SI operatives under his command *would* have triggered the nergon 14 charges—as would the majority of the military command staff still serving the Empire.

Loor did not. Isard had pointed out on numerous occasions that before the Empire could be reestablished, the Rebellion had to die. She had pointed out that the Emperor's obsession with destroying the Jedi Knights had caused him to regard the rest of the Rebellion as a lesser threat, yet it had outlived the Jedi *and* the Emperor. Only by destroying the Rebellion would it be possible to reassert the Empire's authority over the galaxy. Destroying the Rebellion required methods more subtle than exploding grandstands and planets, accomplishing with a vibroblade what could not be done with a Death Star.

Rogue Squadron could not be allowed to die, because they were required for the public spectacle of Tycho Celchu's trial. General Cracken had uncovered ample evidence that pointed toward Celchu's guilt, and Loor had delighted in clearing the way for Cracken's investigators to find yet more of it. The evidence would be condemning, yet so obviously questionable that the members of Rogue Squadron—all of whom had indicated a belief in Tycho's innocence at one level or another—would decry it as false. That would increase the tension between the conquerors of Imperial Center and the politicians who slunk in after the pilots had risked their lives to secure the world. If the heroes of the Rebellion could doubt and resent the government of the New Republic, how would the citizenry build confidence in their leaders?

The Krytos virus further complicated things. Created by an Imperial scientist under Loor's supervision, it killed non-humans in a most hideous manner. Roughly three weeks after infection, the victims entered the final, lethal stage of the disease. Over the course of a week the virus multiplied very rapidly, exploding cell after cell in their bodies. Their flesh weakened, sagged, and split open while the victims bled from every pore and orifice. The resulting liquid was highly infectious, and though bacta could hold the disease at bay or, in sufficient quantities, cure it, the Rebellion did not have access to enough bacta to treat all the cases on Coruscant.

The price of bacta had shot up and supplies dwindled. People hoarded bacta and rumors about the disease having spread to the human population caused waves of panic. Already a number of worlds had ordered ships from Imperial Center quarantined so the disease would not spread, further disrupting the New Republic's weak economy and eroding its authority. It did no good for human bureaucrats to try to explain the precautions they had taken for dealing with the disease since they were immune, and that immunity built up resentment between the human and non-human populations within the New Republic.

Loor allowed himself a small laugh. He had taken the precaution of putting away a supply of bacta, which he was selling off in small lots. As a result of this action, anxious Rebels were supplying the financing for an organization bent on the destruction of the New Republic. The irony of it all was sufficient to dull the omnipresent fear of discovery and capture.

There was no question in his mind that to be captured was to be killed, yet he did not let that prospect daunt him. Being able to turn the Rebels' tactics back on them struck him as justice. He would be returning to them the fear and frustration Imperials everywhere had known during the Rebellion. He would strike from hiding, hitting at targets chosen randomly.

His vengeance would be loosely focused because that meant no one could feel safe from his touch.

He knew his efforts would be denounced as crude terrorism, but he intended there to be nothing crude about his efforts. Today he would destroy the grandstands around the memorial. They would be nearly empty, and all those who had left the stands would breath a sigh of relief that they had not been blown up minutes or hours earlier; but everyone would have to consider congregating in a public place to be dangerous in the future. And if he hit a bacta treatment and distribution center tomorrow, people would also have to weigh obtaining protection from the virus against the possibility of being blown to bits.

By choosing targets of minimal military value he could stir up the populace to demand the military do something. If the public's ire focused on one official or another, he could target that person, giving the public some power. He would let their displeasure choose his victims, just as his choices would give direction to their fear. Theirs would be a virulent and symbiotic relationship. He would be nightmare and benefactor, they would be victims and supporters. He would become a faceless evil they sought to direct while fearing any attention they drew to themselves.

Having once been on the side attempting to stop an anti-government force, he could well appreciate the difficulties the New Republic would have in dealing with him. The fact that the Rebellion had never resorted to outright terrorism did not concern him. Their goal had been to build a new government; his was merely to destroy what they had created. He wanted things to degenerate into an anarchy that would prompt an outcry for leadership and authority. When that call went out, his mission would be accomplished and the Empire would return.

He again took up the remote control and returned to the window. Down at the memorial he could see small pinpricks of color that marked passersby on their way to and from other

places. He glanced at the holograms striding across his holotable and saw that none of the people were of consequence.
He followed the course of one woman, allowing her to clear the
blast radius, then pressed the button.

A staccato series of explosions went off sequentially around
the memorial. To the south the grandstands teetered forward
and started to somersault their way into the depths of Imperial
Center. A half-dozen people who had been seated on them fell
like colorful confetti. One actually grabbed the edge of the
platform next to the barrow and hauled himself up to safety,
but a subsequent blast tossed him back into the pit from which
he had narrowly escaped.

Other explosions twisted metal and shattered transparisteel
windows in the surrounding buildings. Grandstands clung to
the sides of buildings like mutilated metal insects with bleeding, moaning people clutched in their limbs. Dust and smoke
cleared to show the central ferrocrete ring around the memorial
had been nibbled away, with a huge chunk of it dangling peril-
ously by a reinforcement bar or two.

Loor finally felt the blast's shockwave send a tremor through
his tower. The hawk-bats flapped black wings to steady themselves, then dropped away from their perches. Wings snapped
open, sending the creatures soaring into a slow spiral that
would take them down to the blast site. Loor knew enough of
them to know the hawk-bats would first look to see if the holes
in the buildings revealed previously hidden granite slugs, but
when deprived of their favorite prey, they would settle for the
gobbets of flesh left behind by the victims.

"Good hunting," he wished them, "eat your fill. Before I am
done there will be more, much more for you to consume. I shall
let you feast on my enemies, and together, here on a world they
call their own, we shall both thrive."

3

I T SEEMED TO Wedge that the mood of the Provisional Council was as dark as the room in which they met and as sour as the scent of bacta in the air. The dimly lit chamber had once been part of the Senatorial apartments Mon Mothma had called home before the Rebellion and her role in it forced her to go underground. It had been redecorated in garish reds and purples by Imperial agents, with green and gold trim on everything, but the paucity of light quelled the riot of color.

A desire to hide signs of Imperial occupation of the apartments was not the reason for keeping the room dim. Sian Tevv, the Sullustan member of the Provisional Council, had been exposed to the Krytos virus. While there was no evidence he had contracted the disease, he had undergone preventative bacta therapy and had some residual sensitivity to bright light. The Council made a concession to him by lowering the light, and another to the non-human members of the Council by circulating a light bacta mist through the air to prevent possible contagion. This increased humidity seemed to please no one, save perhaps Admiral Ackbar, but he looked grim for his own reasons.

Primarily because I'm actually here. Wedge knew his petition was doomed to fail—Borsk Fey'lya had said as much at the memorial ceremony, and various other councilors had repeated the warning in the two days since then, including Admiral Ackbar and Princess Leia Organa. In fact, Wedge knew, the only reason he was being given a chance to address the Council was because of his status as a liberator of Coruscant.

The Council had arranged three long tables in a half-hexagonal formation, with Mon Mothma in the middle, flanked by Princess Leia and Corellia's Doman Beruss. Ackbar and Fey'lya anchored the far ends of the two angled tables. This left Wedge to stand in the open area before the Council, as if he were on trial. *This is exactly what Tycho will face if I do not succeed here today; therefore, I must succeed.*

Mon Mothma inclined her head toward him. "I need not introduce to you a man who has appeared before this Council previously and who has been so instrumental in the New Republic's success. Because Commander Antilles may end up discussing highly sensitive material, this will be an executive session of the Provisional Council. Everything said here is confidential, and reporting of it will result in possible criminal charges."

Doman Beruss smiled. "Ah, to have cases before we have a Judiciary, now that is civilization!"

Even Mon Mothma smiled at the remark, then set her face again into a mask of solemnity. "Please, Commander, speak your mind."

Wedge took a deep breath, then began. "I have come here today to ask you to prevent a gross injustice from being enacted. Captain Tycho Celchu has been arrested and will be tried on murder and treason charges. The evidence against him— what little of it I know about—is circumstantial and weaker than the defenses Ysanne Isard left behind here. Tycho is a hero of the Rebellion. If not for his efforts, we would not be here right now, and I would be dead. The man he's accused of killing is someone whose life Tycho saved on numerous occasions—

Corran would have long since been dead if Tycho wanted him dead. Tycho is innocent, and to put him through this trial after all he has endured would be cruelty on a truly Imperial scale."

Mon Mothma nodded slowly. "I appreciate your frankness, Commander, and have no doubt you believe everything you've told us. Before we can make any sort of decision, it would be useful for us to have a better grasp of the facts surrounding the situation." She pointed to a green-eyed man whose hair had shifted from its original red to mostly white. "If you would, General Cracken, please bring the Council up to date with what you have learned concerning Captain Celchu."

Cracken walked over to stand next to Wedge. "I hope Commander Antilles will forgive my contradicting him on a couple of points. Some of this information has been developed recently, and because the circumstances surrounding the investigation are tricky, I have not had a chance to brief him on them."

Wedge dropped his voice to a whisper. "Nice ambush."

"That's the last thing I want to do, Commander." Cracken cleared his throat. "Tycho Celchu is a native of Alderaan who graduated from the Imperial Naval Academy and was made a TIE fighter pilot. Subsequent to the destruction of his homeworld—which he had the misfortune of witnessing via holonet communications with his family—he defected from Imperial service and joined the Rebellion. He joined us just after the evacuation of Yavin 4, served with distinction at Hoth, and accompanied Commander Antilles on the assault on the Death Star at Endor. He is one of a handful of pilots who entered and escaped the Death Star.

"Slightly less than two years ago Celchu volunteered for a covert scouting mission to Coruscant. On the way back out, he was captured and sent to Ysanne Isard's Lusankya facility. Little is known about this prison, except that people who have come from it have routinely been brainwashed into becoming Imperial agents who commit acts of murder and mayhem when bidden to do so by Isard. Tycho is unique among those who have been to Lusankya in that he retains some memories of having been there. Prior to his appearance, former inmates revealed their connection to this place only after they had been activated, done their damage, and were captured by our forces."

Wedge shook his head. "I'm sure General Cracken will not mind my pointing out that Tycho did not escape from Lusankya. Isard transferred him to the penal colony at Akrit'tar, and he escaped from there to return to us."

"Thank you, Commander, I was just getting to that." Cracken's expression betrayed neither amusement nor irritation, which somehow made Wedge think things were not going to go well for Tycho. "Upon his return, Captain Celchu was debriefed, and his debriefing, in fact, indicated he recalled almost nothing of his time at Lusankya. We could find no indication he had been brainwashed by Isard. However, we had never detected brainwashing in any of her other little bio-weapons. We were left in the unenviable position of having to assume the worst about Captain Celchu. Commander Antilles, believing then as he does now in his friend's innocence, struck a bargain with his superiors to get Celchu assigned as his executive officer. Security was maintained, for the most part, and the incidents where it was not betrayed no Imperial leanings on the part of Captain Celchu."

Cracken frowned. "Unfortunately we have developed evidence that suggests Celchu has betrayed Rogue Squadron and the New Republic. In the case of Corran Horn, Tycho Celchu had access to the command code for the Headhunter Horn was flying at the time of his death, *and* Celchu had gone over the fighter, without supervision, just prior to Horn's flight. Horn confronted Celchu before they headed out; Horn threatened to uncover his treason, so Celchu had him killed. He waited until after the shields had been brought down, but we have pretty well determined Isard wanted us to take the planet and inherit the virus, so killing Horn *after* her goal was accomplished only makes sense.

"The Horn case is not the only death to which we can link Captain Celchu."

Wedge's jaw dropped in surprise. "What? You can't mean Bror Jace?"

"Indeed I do."

"Nonsense. The Empire killed him."

Cracken nodded. "Agreed, but the way they got him was unusual. Previously we believed he happened to have been trapped by an Interdictor Cruiser out looking for smugglers. However, we have been forced to amend that view following the defection of the Imperial Interdictor Cruiser *Black Asp*. Captain Iillor indicated in her debriefing that the *Black Asp* was directed to go to specific coordinates to intercept Bror Jace as he headed back to Thyferra. He was a bit late in arriving, but showed up exactly where he was expected to. They tried to capture him, but his ship exploded during the fight. The arrangements for Jace's journey home, including the plotting of his course, were made by Captain Tycho Celchu."

"By my order."

"Yes, Commander, by your order—which does not mean Isard could not have warped Celchu enough to make him betray your people."

"But, again, that's circumstantial."

"We have more." The Alliance Intelligence chief shrugged. "Horn told you, Commander, that he'd seen Celchu here on Coruscant talking with a known Imperial operative, Kirtan Loor. Horn had worked with Loor for years on Corellia, so the chance of a mistake in his identification are minimal. In backtracking Celchu's time here on Coruscant—granting that you ordered him to come here, Commander—we have periods of time for which we cannot account. Moreover, we have uncovered a number of banking accounts in which large numbers of credits have been accumulated. These accounts add up to approximately fifteen million credits, which means Celchu was being paid by the Empire."

"What?" Wedge couldn't believe what he was hearing. There was no way, just no way Tycho was an agent in the pay of the

Empire. "If he was one of Isard's sleeper agents, why would she be paying him?"

"Commander, for years I've been trying to fathom her mind, and I have been unable to do so. If I had to guess, however, I would say that creating those accounts was a precaution to let us uncover Tycho at some point or, as it stands now, a means to guarantee he will be tried for his crimes."

"But she has no interest in seeing justice done, which underscores how ludicrous all these charges against Tycho are." Wedge brought his head up. "If Isard wants a trial, you know conducting it will be to her benefit, which is yet one more reason not to go ahead with it."

Borsk Fey'lya tapped a talon against the tabletop. "Or is she providing more evidence than we need to convict so we will be convinced Celchu is being framed? If we *are* convinced he is innocent, we could exonerate him, raise him into a position of trust, and find ourselves again fodder for her schemes."

Wedge winced. He hated Fey'lya's wheels-within-wheels reasoning because it came down to a core problem with Tycho's case: either he was innocent and being made to look guilty, or he was guilty and being made to look innocent through a clumsy frame. The evidence served both explanations well, and sorting good data from bad was a task that could easily defy completion. Everyone could agree something was not right in the whole situation, but assigning blame and assessing truth was not going to be easy.

And no matter what happened, Tycho would end up being stigmatized, reviled, and ostracized. He would be destroyed by it all, and that was something he did not deserve.

For Wedge it was simple to separate fact from fiction, but he knew that was because he was starting from a deep belief in Tycho's innocence. Wedge didn't have a Jedi's insight through the Force—he just knew Tycho. They'd fought side by side through some of the most harrowing battles the galaxy had ever seen. They'd shared hardships that others could not have even imagined, and they shared good times that others could only envy. Wedge knew Tycho could no more betray the Rebellion than he himself could, but looking around at the Council, he realized that even *his* conduct might not be seen as above reproach.

"I still do not believe the evidence General Cracken's people have gathered is anything more than circumstantial." Wedge studied the members of the Council. "For any trial to go forward, especially as quickly as this trial is being pushed, is reckless and negligent. I know we all want swift justice if Tycho is guilty, but trying him on these charges right now can only hurt him and, ultimately, the New Republic."

Doman Beruss, her light eyes glinting coldly in the dimness, opened her hands. "Your opinion, Commander Antilles, is respected but not universally held. The evidence is sufficient in any jurisdiction of the galaxy to call for a trial."

Wedge's eyes narrowed as he sensed a transparisteel barrier descending between his argument and the Council's willingness to act. He knew he had to do something to get them to open their eyes, so he decided to take a chance. "This evidence may demand a trial, but at least delay it until there is time to scrape things down another layer or two and find out what's really going on. I think it is the minimum courtesy you owe someone like Tycho Celchu, and that's an opinion I do not need to keep private."

Borsk Fey'lya's head came up and his fur rippled like a storm-wracked ocean. "Are you threatening to use your status as hero to oppose *us*?"

Ackbar answered for Wedge. "He was doing nothing of the kind. Because Captain Celchu is facing a court martial, the trial and everything surrounding it is a military matter, and Commander Antilles knows unauthorized discussions of same violate regulations and oaths he took when he became an officer."

"Begging the Admiral's pardon," Wedge growled, "I *was* threatening to go public with my feelings about the trial. I still am. And if expressing my opinion about an injustice is not allowed in the Alliance military, I can always resign my commission."

That bombshell certainly had an effect, but not entirely the one he expected. While Ackbar looked disappointed, Borsk Fey'lya smiled victoriously. The other councilors reacted with horror or a grim acknowledgment of his bold stroke. If they had thought his speaking out against Tycho's treatment would attract attention, his resignation because of it would undoubtedly be an action with a much higher profile.

Leia leaned forward. "Chief Councilor, I suggest we recess for an hour. I would like a chance to speak with Commander Antilles, if I might."

"Please." Mon Mothma stood and gave Wedge a look that combined pride with frustration, anger with sympathy. Wedge felt not exactly pitied, but as if there was more going on than he had access to. He knew that was true, of course—he was just the leader of a fighter squadron, and these were the leaders of a new nation. But he hated to think their perspective could somehow justify what they were going to do to Tycho.

General Cracken left the room last and closed the doors behind himself, leaving Wedge alone with Princess Leia. In all the time he'd known her, she'd never looked so saddened. "If you want to convince me to save my career, I appreciate the effort, but I'll stand by what I said just now. You can't talk me out of it."

She remained seated and slowly shook her head. "I know that, so I'm not going to try. It's important to me that you know I think Tycho is innocent, too. I've known Winter for as long as I can remember, and she's terribly fond of Tycho. If she can remember nothing that's the least bit ambiguous about him, then I can't imagine there's anything sinister to uncover. You and I both know that the trial will be rough on Tycho, and unfair."

"Then help me convince them to stop it or delay it."

"I would if I could, but I can't." A deep frown creased her brow as she plucked at the fabric of her pale green gown. "The reason I asked for the recess is so I can tell you what's going to happen after someone here decides that we have been suitably courteous in listening to you and that we need to move on to new business."

Leia chewed on her lower lip for a second. "Mon Mothma will thank you for coming to us, but she will point out that Tycho is being tried in a military court. The Provisional Council has no authority to interfere with the way the military deals with violations of the code of military justice. Until there is a conviction, and punishment is decided upon, there is nothing the Council can do, and even at that point it is an open question whether or not we can interfere."

"But there has to be a chance to appeal a conviction. . . ." Wedge hesitated, then nodded. "Councilor Beruss's comment about a lack of a Judiciary . . . that was meant to forestall this argument, yes?"

Leia nodded. "In simple terms, yes, but we haven't yet had time to make decisions concerning the structure of such a body, much less its jurisdiction and duties. For example, would an appeal go to the New Republic courts first, or would it be sent to the courts on the defendant's homeworld, or the victim's homeworld? Putting together a government is not easy, and the process is not pretty or without pain. There are casualties all over the place."

"And Tycho will be one of them."

"Unfortunately, yes, he may be." Leia's shoulders slumped with fatigue. "You may not realize how fragile the New Republic is right now. With her Krytos virus Ysanne Isard has succeeded in driving a wedge between the human and non-human members of the New Republic. There have been accusations that some of us knew the virus was here and encouraged people to return to their native worlds specifically to spread the disease and kill off whole planetary populations. There are others who accuse us of not doing enough to get bacta to those who need it. If we do try to get as much as possible here to save as many people as possible, we drain the military of their supply. If Isard hits back, or Warlord Zsinj decides to strike at us, we can be devastated. Trying to buy up supplies of bacta has driven the price higher than ever before, and to make matters worse, the Ashern rebels on Thyferra have managed to damage production, limiting the supply at a time when the demand couldn't be higher."

She looked up at him. "It's a good thing we don't have a Treasury Ministry in place, because they'd tell us we're bankrupt."

When Wedge realized his mouth was hanging open he clicked it shut. "I had no idea. . . ."

"Of course not. Nor does anyone else outside the Council. Things are so dire that I'll be heading off to try to open relations with Hapes and ask them for help—and that's something that's so secret I'll deny even knowing you if it gets out."

Wedge nodded. "Already forgotten."

Leia mustered a weak smile. "Frankly speaking, there is a remote possibility that we can secure enough bacta to save many of the people who are afflicted by Krytos, but not all. Even if we cure 95 percent of the cases, those we don't cure will amount to millions of fatalities—non-*human* fatalities. The resentment against the government will rise until the Alliance falls apart. When that happens, someone like Warlord Zsinj or Ysanne Isard or who knows who else is lurking out there can come in and sweep up the pieces."

She shrugged her shoulders. "That shouldn't have anything to do with Tycho, but it does because Tycho is a *human*, accused of a heinous crime against a fellow Rebel and a man who is now a hero. If we do not bring him to trial quickly and let the trial take its course, we will be accused of favoring a human. People will suggest that were Tycho a Gotal or Quarren, we'd have tried, convicted, and executed him inside of a day. That charge is baseless, but it's critical we avoid any appearance of favoritism."

"So Tycho gets offered up as a sacrifice to keep the Alliance together?"

"I would have preferred being able to put Ysanne Isard on trial for having the Krytos virus created and spread, but she got away—how, I don't know, but she did. We probably could scoop up a double-handful of Imperial bureaucrats and put them on trial for past activities, but then the entire Imperial bureaucracy would go into hiding and any chance we had of trying to govern the galaxy would go away."

That comment brought Wedge up short. The notion of using the enemy to administer the territories of the new government struck him as wrong, but then he realized the Alliance military had always welcomed defectors from the other side into its ranks. Experience was enough to forgive past sins, especially when things were so critical. "You're right, creating a government isn't easy or pretty."

"But it's what we have to do."

The logic of her argument was inescapable, but Wedge bristled at it and didn't want to back down. "Perhaps resigning is something I *have* to do."

Leia shook her head. "No, no it's not. You're not going to resign, Wedge."

"Why not? The war's over. There have to be a half-dozen fueling depots I could buy and operate here on Coruscant or back on Corellia." He knew he was letting himself be a bit petulant, but to acquiesce seemed like abandoning Tycho. *I won't do that without sufficient reason.*

"You won't resign, dear heart, because of the same sense of responsibility that makes you threaten to resign." Leia smiled at him. "Cracken's people have been doing more than looking into Tycho's activities. Turns out that Warlord Zsinj hit a Thyferran bacta convoy and stole a fairly big shipment. An Ashern rebel was on the convoy and got word out to us about the location of the space platform where Zsinj has the convoy docked. The bacta will save a lot of people, but getting our operatives in and back out means someone very good is going to have to be flying cover for our strike. Rogue Squadron will be leading the way."

Wedge nodded. "Resign and doom millions, or stay and watch a friend be destroyed. Not much of a choice."

"Not so, my friend, it is indeed quite a choice. Not an easy one."

"Oh, the choice is easy, Leia, but living with the result will not be." Wedge swallowed past the lump choking him. "You'll let the Council know I've reconsidered my resignation."

"I'll tell them that you meant the suggestion as a way to underscore your concern for Captain Celchu." Leia nodded solemnly. "According to Cracken you'll be briefed inside a week and then head out. May the Force be with you."

"I'll save the Force for Tycho." Wedge's eyes became slits. "No matter what sort of reception Zsinj has for us, what Tycho's going to face will be a million times worse."

4

THE PRISON UNIFORM Tycho Celchu had been given looked enough like a flightsuit that Wedge Antilles could almost imagine his friend being free again. The black jumpsuit had red sleeves and leggings that started at elbow and knee respectively. They also ended well shy of wrist and ankle so the fabric would not interfere with the operation of the binders Tycho wore.

Wedge shuddered with anger and embarrassment. *I will see you free again, my friend.*

Tycho looked up and smiled. A bit taller than Wedge, but with the same lithe build, Tycho was a handsome man whose blue eyes appeared brighter than Wedge would have thought possible. Tycho held his hands up in greeting to Wedge and Nawara Ven, and almost made it seem as if the binders were not hampering him. He waited patiently as a guard in a control room opened the transparisteel barrier separating him from the visitation center, then shuffled in past his escort.

Wedge rose and started across the sparsely furnished white room, but Tycho's guard brandished a Stokhli Spray Stick. "Keep away from the prisoner, Commander."

Wedge felt a hand on his left elbow and turned back to face the Twi'lek who had accompanied him to the detention center. "Commander, we're not allowed physical contact with Tycho—no one is allowed to touch prisoners. It's security."

Wedge frowned. "Right."

Nawara Ven skewered the guard with a pink-eyed stare. "You've done your duty here, now I require you to leave us alone with my client and my droid here."

The heavyset guard's eyes narrowed, then he tapped the Stokhli Spray Stick against the palm of his other hand. "I'm going to be right out there. Anything funny happens, and you'll be spending a lot of time with this traitor." He turned and headed back out to the far side of the transparisteel barrier.

Wedge dropped into one of the four chairs around the table in the middle of the room. "How are you doing? Is that guard causing you trouble? Because if he is, I'll do something about it."

Tycho sat across from him and shrugged. "Voleyy isn't so bad, he just doesn't like things to get odd on his watch. Other guards are worse, and if I weren't in solitary confinement, I think the general population would have already tried and executed me."

"What?" Tycho's comment caught Wedge by surprise. "What do you mean by that?"

"I thought it was rather self-explanatory." Tycho shook his head, then smiled up at his friends. "You have to remember, I've been charged with murder and treason. There are guards here who are just waiting for an excuse to show the New Republic how deep their patriotism runs. Some of the prisoners think they could win a pardon by saving the Republic the cost of a trial. I shouldn't think that would come as a surprise to you, Wedge."

"No, I guess it doesn't, but your reaction to it does. If I were in your boots, I'd be angry and outraged."

"That's because you've never been a guest in the Empire's correctional system." Tycho sighed and Wedge read weariness in the way his shoulders sagged. "All the anger and outrage I can muster won't get me out of here any faster, *and* it could get me in trouble."

"But aren't you angry about being imprisoned for something you didn't do?"

"Yes."

Wedge opened his hands. "Then why don't you show it? You can't keep it bottled up inside. It'll tear you apart."

Tycho took in a deep breath, then let it out slowly. "Wedge, you've always been my friend and you've supported me with no questions asked, but what I'm enduring now is really no different from what I endured while being under house arrest. Sure, I can't go flying, can't head out to Borleias with Mirax to save Corran's tail, and I'm not free to walk the streets of Coruscant as your hole card, but nothing has really changed. Since my capture by the Empire right here on Coruscant I've been their prisoner. I've never really escaped the Empire because they managed to make others suspicious of me. I was outraged then and have been since, but protesting wouldn't do me any good. The only way I can be free, truly free, is for the Empire to be destroyed. I know, as it falls apart, someone somewhere will have the information that will set me free."

"And if they don't?"

Tycho cracked a smile. "You figured out a plan to take Coruscant away from the Empire. Springing a friend from prison shouldn't be that hard for you to manage."

Nawara Ven cleared his throat. "Let's not be adding conspiracy to the charges against you."

Tycho nodded. "As you wish, Counselor. How's my defense going?"

"Good and bad." Nawara Ven sat at the end of the table and a little green and white R2 unit rolled up beside him. "The best thing we have going for us right now is that Whistler here has joined our defense team."

"But I'm accused of killing Corran Horn. He and Corran were partners. Why would he want to help defend me?"

The droid keened a reply.

Wedge smiled. "Ah, he did know Corran well."

The Twi'lek nodded. "Well enough to decide Horn was wrong about you, Captain Celchu. If Horn was wrong about your being a traitor, that means someone else killed him. Since you've been framed for the murder, if Whistler does nothing to help you, he's ensuring that his friend's murderer is getting away. Having Whistler on the team is unbelievably useful because of the specialized circuitry and programming he has. It allows him to wade through a lot of law enforcement data, including Imperial files."

Tycho shifted around in his chair, making his binders click against the edge of the table. "I hope the bad news doesn't obliterate the good."

Nawara's braintails twitched lethargically. "Corran had reported to Commander Antilles that he saw you in the Headquarters talking to Kirtan Loor. You said you were speaking with," Nawara glanced at his datapad, "a Duros Captain Lai Nootka."

Tycho nodded. "Right. He flew a freighter called *Star's Delight*. I was negotiating with him for spare parts for the Z-95 Headhunters I'd bought."

"Well, no one can seem to find him or his ship. The prosecution can introduce ample evidence that Kirtan Loor was here on Coruscant, that Corran would have recognized him, and that knowing you were exposed, you had to take steps to cover yourself."

Wedge frowned. "If the only way out of that trap is to find Nootka, we'll find him."

Whistler tooted a dour message.

Rogue Squadron's commander rubbed his eyes for a moment to ease their burning. "Fine, fine, there are 247 unidentified bodies of Duros here on Coruscant, and the possibility exists that the Imps caught him, killed him, and dumped him so we'll never find him. We can still try to find the ship. The log might have an entry in it about the meeting."

Tycho gave Wedge a smile. "You're more nervous than I am, Wedge."

"That's because I don't think you understand what's at stake here, Tycho." Wedge got up and began to pace. "Your trial is going to go forward and go forward quickly. It's going to be used to show that the New Republic can be just as hard on humans as the Empire was on non-humans. I have to tell you, if Nawara here weren't already a lawyer, I'd be looking for the best non-human counsel I could find for you. The judges here are going to feel pressure to convict to seem fair; I want the fact that your defender is non-human to make them worry about how your being found *guilty* will look."

"Captain, you might want to look into more competent counsel than me."

Tycho shook his head. "No, Nawara, I want you. I've read your file and I know you. This is going to be hard enough without having a lawyer who wants the case for the notoriety."

"Tycho's right, we need you. The squadron is behind Tycho, and having you represent him means the rest of us don't feel entirely impotent." Wedge's dark eyes narrowed. "Do you see a problem with defending him?"

The Twi'lek hesitated for a moment, then answered. "I've defended a lot of people in criminal cases, but the stakes have not been this high before, nor the opposition so tough. Emtrey knows all the regulations, so having him in court with me means I'll have a good grasp on the differences between military law and civil law, but it would be better for you to have someone who doesn't have to rely on a droid for that stuff. The fact that I was down with the first stages of Krytos during the alleged murder means I can't be called as a witness of fact in the case—at least, *I'd* not call me, but the prosecution might have other ideas."

He tapped a button on his datapad. "The prosecutor is Commander Halla Ettyk. She's 34 years old and from Alderaan. She had gained quite a reputation as a prosecutor there and happened to be off Alderaan to depose a witness in a case when Alderaan was destroyed. She joined the Rebellion and was part of General Cracken's counterintelligence staff. She may not have prosecuted any cases over the last seven years, but that's not going to dull her skills. Captain, you don't happen to know her or have a family vendetta with her family or anything that could let me suggest she has a conflict of interest, do you?"

"Nothing, sorry."

"What about the tribunal?" Wedge stopped pacing, crossed his arms, and looked down at the Twi'lek. "The subpoena I was served with yesterday indicated General Salm, Admiral Ackbar, and General Crix Madine were going to serve as judges. Salm has never liked Tycho. Can't you get him removed?"

"Trying to get him replaced is tricky. If he does not recuse himself, he clearly thinks he has no conflict of interest. If we suggest he does and we fail to remove him, we've poisoned him. The other thing to keep in mind is that Salm was present at the first battle of Borleias and saw Tycho flying an unarmed shuttle and rescuing pilots, including me. He's got to weigh what he remembers against the evidence he hears, and we'll be sure to remind him of Borleias."

Tycho nodded. "I'm willing to take my chances with Salm. What do you think of the other two?"

The Twi'lek shrugged. "Ackbar agreed to have you serve as Rogue Squadron's executive officer and has remained neutral regarding this prosecution. Crix Madine came over from the Imperial side around the same time you did, Captain. Given his work planning covert missions for the Empire, I would have to guess he has met Iceheart and is aware of the work she has done. He knows of your reputation and, being a Corellian like Commander Antilles, has an appreciation of bravery and audacity."

"You're forgetting, Counselor Ven, that Corran Horn was Corellian, too."

"No, Commander, I've not forgotten that fact. I'm counting on it to motivate General Madine to seek the people truly responsible for Corran's death."

Wedge nodded. "So that's the line of defense: Tycho's been framed?"

"The truth always is the best defense. Their evidence is all circumstantial, so we can slip someone or several someones in to raise doubt about who actually committed the crime." Nawara Ven pressed his hands flat on the table. "This trial will be played as much to public opinion as to the judges. It's going to do no good if the people think Captain Celchu is guilty while the court lets him off. Everyone knows how twisted and full of plots the Empire was. The mention of Kirtan Loor and Lusankya allows us to bring up Ysanne Isard. I can show that Captain Celchu's pattern of activity is all wrong by showing what Isard does do with her people. I can even point to the bombing as likely residue of her evil. If we have public opinion looking at Captain Celchu as the last victim of Imperial intrigue, a Rebellion hero being destroyed by a bitter and vengeful Empire, we have a lot of maneuvering room in the aftermath of the trial."

Nawara Ven's explanation made sense to Wedge, but he didn't like all it entailed. Fighting enemies who were shooting back was one thing. Winning a court case was quite another—one akin to politics, and Wedge knew he'd utterly failed in that arena at the Council meeting. Waging a public relations war to win the hearts and minds of a planet for a man who was already being entered into the pantheon of evil with Darth Vader, Prince Xizor, Ysanne Isard, and the Emperor himself—well, that was a battle no one could consider easy.

Wedge nodded toward the lawyer. "What happens if Tycho is found guilty?"

"Hard to say. There's no clear appeals system set up. Unless the judges reverse their decision, he'll be stuck."

Tycho raised an eyebrow. "What do you mean by stuck?"

"This is treason, Captain, and murder." Nawara Ven shook his head as Whistler moaned. "Given the mood of the people and the nature of your crime, if we lose, the New Republic will put you to death."

5

As WEDGE ENTERED the darkened briefing room, the pilots of Rogue Squadron broke from the knot surrounding Nawara Ven and took their places. Some of their expressions were difficult to read. Riv Shiel, the Shistavanen wolfman, wore his perpetual impenetrable frown. Gavin Darklighter, the youngest of the pilots in Rogue Squadron, seemed fairly cheerful, but the hardness of the flesh gathered at the corners of his eyes betrayed the pressure most of the rest of the unit felt.

Wedge stepped behind and past Aril Nunb, then paused with the holoprojection table in front of him. "I appreciate your getting here so quickly. I had hoped we'd get at least a week's liberty after the conquest of Coruscant. . . ."

The fiery-haired lieutenant in the front row, Pash Cracken, shrugged. "We've not had that much to celebrate, sir."

"I know." Corran's death, then Tycho's arrest, had undercut the Rogues when they should have been enjoying their greatest triumph. While everyone else on Coruscant was jubilant about the world's liberation, the Rogues felt still enslaved by Tycho's plight. The contrast between the congratulations they got from others and the way they felt inside remained sharp enough to slice them up emotionally. To save themselves, the squadron members had rallied around Tycho and were determined to prove his innocence. That provided them a sanctuary and sense of control, though it did nothing to endear them to others who thought Tycho's guilt was indisputable.

"The one thing we do know, people, is that the source of our problems lies on the Imp side of things. We should also realize that what we're suffering is nothing compared to what hundreds of thousands of people out there are suffering." Wedge pointed a finger toward Nawara and Riv Shiel, then glanced back at Aril Nunb. "Three of our own came down with this Krytos virus, but they got quick treatment with enough bacta to knock it out. Bacta is in high demand right now, but supplies are very short."

Erisi Dlarit, the dark-haired pilot from Thyferra, pressed a hand to her own sternum. "I know the cartels are producing as much as they can—at least the Xucphra group is. I have personally sent messages to my grandfather to let him know of the need for bacta here."

"Thanks, Erisi, every bit of help we can get is vital." Wedge folded his arms across his chest. "Warlord Zsinj hit a bacta convoy heading out from Thyferra. I believe it was from the Zaltin group, Erisi, not your family's corporation. Zsinj took the bacta to a storage facility, but a member of the Ashern rebel group . . ."

"Terrorists!" Erisi spat.

". . . happened to be crewing aboard the Zaltin ships. He managed to get a message out concerning the location of the space station Zsinj is using." Wedge nodded toward Aril, and the Sullustan punched up a holographic image of the station on the holoprojector. The station consisted of a central disk with thick expanses of living quarters above and below the horizon. Slender towers rose from the middle of the disk, suggesting the station had been impaled on spears. Three wedge-shaped launch-and-recovery causeways stabbed out into space from the central disk like spokes meant to connect up with a nonexistent rim.

"This is an *Empress*-class space station located in the Yag'Dhul system. Basic armament is ten turbo-laser batteries and six laser cannons. It also has the capability of housing up to three squadrons of TIEs, though the usual complement is only two dozen fighters. The bacta is being held here, and we're going to get it away from them."

As Wedge continued his briefing, little glowing icons appeared to hover around the station. Each represented a ship and entered the display as its part in the operation was explained. "We will be leading two squadrons from General Salm's Defender Wing to pull a quick strafing run on the station and get them to scramble their fighters. The squadrons we'll have with us are Warden and Champion—you remember them, they saved us at Borleias."

The Gand toward the back raised a three-fingered hand. "As Ooryl remembers it, Commander Antilles, Defender Wing flies Y-wing fighters. Provoking TIE fighters to come out and attack Y-wings would seem to Ooryl as potentially dangerous for Defender's pilots."

"Your concern is noted, Ooryl, and has been taken into account. Guardian Squadron, the third of Defender Wing's component parts, has been refitted with B-wings. This adds considerable firepower to the wing. We'll pull the TIEs out and away from the station and the B-wings will drop on them and help us kill them. The Y-wings will continue in toward the space station and start working on its defenses with their ion cannons.

"Following us in will be a half-dozen assault shuttles and then enough bulk-cruisers to haul the bacta away. This is a hit, hold, then run operation."

Gavin smiled. "Sounds like a dew-run."

"Maybe." Pash Cracken leaned forward in his chair. "Where's the *Iron Fist* supposed to be?"

Wedge shook his head. "I've been given no data concerning the *Iron Fist*." Warlord Zsinj's flagship was one of the *Super*-class Star Destroyers created by the Kuat Drive Yard's ship-works before the Empire collapsed. The ships were, for all intents and purposes, fleets unto themselves. They carried 144 fighters, had a crew of over a quarter of a million people, and bristled with over a thousand missile launchers, ion cannons, and turbolaser batteries. Though the Rebel fleet had managed to destroy the *Executor* at Endor, everyone knew that ship had died because of luck, not skill.

If the *Iron Fist* showed up at Yag'Dhul, the operation was doomed. Wedge knew it, as did all of the pilots in the room. "While I am as concerned about the appearance of *Iron Fist* as any of you, I know the bacta is too valuable to risk on an operation that could be so easily jeopardized. I have to assume that Intelligence has the *Iron Fist* located and that it won't interfere with the mission. If it does show up, all we can do is pull out." *And hope no one gets left behind.*

Rhysati Ynr, the blond woman sitting next to Nawara Ven, raised her hand. "Do we just fly cover when the assault shuttles go in, or are we going to land and go in-station, too?"

"Right now we're just flying cover. If things change, you'll be the first to know." Wedge sighed. "We're heading out in twelve hours, so you're now all under security quarantine. Report to your quarters, get your gear, and go to the hangar. Once there you'll get a more specific briefing and run through a basic simulation of the exercise before we leave. Any other questions?"

Gavin looked around nervously, then nodded. "Sir, won't Nawara's heading out on a mission compromise Captain Celchu's defense? I mean, shouldn't Nawara be here setting things up?"

A question I asked myself. "Your concerns, Gavin, are valid, but not terribly important in the face of what we're doing here. We're already one pilot light because of Corran's death, so we need everyone we can get. The fact is that obtaining the bacta is far more important to the future of the New Republic than Tycho's trial, so that is our priority."

"Besides, I have Whistler and Emtrey doing a lot of computer fact-finding for me right now." Nawara sat forward and slapped Gavin on the shoulder. "The lawyering part of all this comes later. It occurs to me that if we do get the bacta and things begin to calm down, someone might start listening to reason instead of political pressure, and this case will be dumped in some black hole, where it deserves to be."

"May the Force be with you in that regard." Wedge smiled openly. "If that's it, get going. Everyone should be in the hangar in an hour at the very latest."

As the pilots started to leave the room, Wedge caught the eye of a black-and-white-furred Bothan female. "Sei'lar, if I could have a moment of your time."

"Yes, Commander."

He watched Asyr as she waited for the others to leave, then walked toward him. There was no overt challenge in her stride, though the fire in her violet eyes did reveal a strong streak of Bothan pride running in her. Splotches of white fur covered her from throat to belly, gloved her, and slashed down from her forehead over her left eye to her cheek. They almost succeeded in diluting the predatory power in her petite frame. She stopped before him and snapped to attention.

"At ease, Sei'lar."

"Thank you, sir."

"You might want to reserve your thanks until you've heard what I have to say." Wedge looked down on her and saw her fur ripple with irritation. "Two things I want to discuss. The first is Gavin."

Asyr blinked with surprise that flowed out into her fur. "I was under the impression that pairing among members of the squadron was not prohibited. Nawara and Rhysati, and Erisi and Corran . . ."

"I'm not under the impression anything was going on between Erisi and Corran."

"But her reaction to his death . . ."

"They *were* close, but not in that way, as I understand it." Wedge frowned for a moment. Mirax Terrik had been crushed by Corran's death and had confided in Wedge that she and Corran had chosen to begin dating once the conquest of Coruscant had been accomplished. Though Corran had never revealed his feelings about Erisi or Mirax to Wedge, Corran's attraction to Mirax had been fairly easy to spot, which led Wedge to believe Erisi was out of the picture.

"Regardless of what was or was not happening between Erisi and Corran, or what is or is not happening between Rhysati and Nawara, the big difference between those situations and *your* situation with Gavin is that Gavin's barely seventeen years old. He's very young and hasn't had the experiences that your education at the Bothan Martial Academy has afforded you. He's not a stupid young man—he's actually fairly intelligent—but his upbringing on Tatooine has left him a bit idealistic."

Asyr's violet eyes sank into crescents. "Are you ordering me to stop seeing him?"

Wedge laughed. "No, not at all. You've only been out twice—"

"Have you had someone watching us?"

"No, and that's just the point." Wedge opened his hands. "Gavin is so taken with you that his enthusiasm isn't always kept under control. While he remains very circumspect about private moments you have shared, he is very happy to let others know how much fun you're having together doing all the things you have done. It's all very innocent and natural, but it's also a sign of his falling in love with you. He may not quite be there yet, but he'll be hurt badly if you pull away from him abruptly after too much longer. I don't want to see him hurt, so if you don't really care for him, let him down easy and now, please."

Asyr's chin came up and defiance blazed in her eyes. "What makes you think I might be toying with him?"

"The second thing I want to discuss with you does, Sei'lar. I wonder if you don't have another agenda that you're working on." Wedge met her hot stare unflinchingly. "You graduated near the top of your class from the Bothan Martial Academy but never formally entered the military. Your records are decidedly sketchy, but I would imagine, given your age, that you were recruited into the Martial Intelligence Division of the Bothan military in an effort to replenish the supply of spies who died securing the plans to the second Death Star. The fact that you were already here on Coruscant when our operation arrived suggests the Bothan government had its own goals here on Coruscant."

"But you forget, sir, that I did help organize and participate in the operations that cleared the way for the Rebel Alliance to take the planet."

"I never accused you of being stupid, Sei'lar. Quite the contrary, I think you are very intelligent. You saw an opportunity that *had to* succeed and you did your best to make it succeed." Wedge let a smile tug at the corners of his mouth. "That selfsame intelligence is why I want you in this squadron.

"The fact is, Sei'lar, who and what you are makes you very valuable and desirable. I want you here in Rogue Squadron. I think you are an incredible asset to the Rebellion. Flip a bit, though, and it's easy to see that your Bothan masters also find you quite useful. That means, sooner or later, you're going to have some decisions to make."

Asyr glanced down. "Decisions about Gavin."

"And about your loyalties to your planet and your nation."

"Or my squadron."

"Exactly." Wedge nodded slowly. *The pressure is not on you right now, but it will come. Borsk Fey'lya likes having a Bothan in Rogue Squadron, but at some point he'll want to exert control over you.*

Her head came back up. "Do you want me to make those decisions right now?"

"I want you to make them when you feel they need to be made. I trust you, and I want to continue to trust you. If you find you can't be part of the squadron, you can walk away and I'll have been proud to have had you as one of us."

Asyr arched an eyebrow. "No threat of retribution if I betray you?"

Wedge shook his head. "If you decide to betray us, I can't imagine we'll survive long enough to avenge ourselves on you. On the other hand, Rogues tend to take a lot of killing, so you can't be sure of how things will turn out."

"I'll keep that in mind." Asyr smiled and Wedge took it for a good sign. "And, Commander, concerning Gavin, there is no hidden agenda. His wide-eyed way of looking at everything is refreshing and, perhaps, even energizing. I've lived a long time in the shadows, so moving into the light feels very good. I'll do nothing to hurt him."

"Good." Wedge waved her toward the door. "Go get your stuff and get to the briefing. I'm trusting you'll see the holes in this plan and help us plug them before Zsinj accomplishes what the Empire could only dream about: the destruction of Rogue Squadron."

6

CORRAN HORN LET his joy at again being in the cockpit of a starfighter consume him. It did not matter to him that he did not know how he'd gotten into the ship. He did not let the fact that he was flying a TIE Interceptor concern him. He thrust aside anxiety born of his ignorance of his location. None of those things were germane to his present situation.

The only relevant facts in his life were these: he was flying and, he knew, if he flew well enough he would be allowed to fly again. He had no idea how he knew his performance would be rewarded with more flight time—that fact seemed as fundamental to him as his need for air and food and sleep. His desire to continue flying blazed hot in his gut and burned from him the annoyance at the squint's inefficient controls and sluggish reaction time.

"Nemesis One, report."

It took Corran a moment to realize the comm unit call had been directed at him. He glanced at his scanner windows. "One is clear."

"One, we have two eyeballs vectoring in on a heading of 239

degrees at a range of ten kilometers. They are hostiles. You are free to engage and terminate them."

"I copy. Nemesis One outbound." Corran hit the left rudder pedal and swung the ship around onto the proper heading. The starfield whirled around him, then froze in place again. He could recognize none of the constellations, but that did not concern him. His mission was to destroy the enemy, and that he would gladly do no matter where he found himself.

His breathing reverberated loudly in the full helmet he wore. The sound came rhythmically. It betrayed no nervousness. It was not the quickened breathing of prey, but the strong steady respiration of a predator on the hunt. He had already killed more TIE starfighters than he cared to remember; these would just be two more.

And yet, in the back of his mind, he knew he could not actually remember his previous kills, and this amnesia began to nibble away at his emotional well-being.

With a thumb he flicked the Interceptor's quad lasers over to dual-fire mode, then pulled back on the steering yoke and brought the ship up in a slight climb. A quick starboard snap-roll onto his head turned the climb into a dive, and suddenly he was upon the eyeballs. His index finger tightened on the trigger and a stream of verdant laser-bolts sliced through the lead eyeball.

Because of his angle of attack, the bolts scored black furrows in one wing, then pierced the ball cockpit from the top. On the other side they freed the wing, but the ship's explosion shattered the hexagonal panel. It blasted debris into the flight path of the second TIE, causing it to roll to starboard and dive. The maneuver succeeded in saving the second ship from a collision with its dying wingman, but dropped it straight into Corran's sights.

Corran cut the throttle back by a quarter, matching speed with his prey. The pilot he hunted juked right and left, but made none of the hard breaks and sharp turns needed to shuck Corran from his tail. Without remorse, but full of contempt, Corran flicked the squint's lasers over to quad-fire, then impaled the TIE fighter on his crosshairs and hit the trigger with a delicate twitch of his finger.

The four green laser-bolts converged and merged into one a nanosecond before they burned the top from the cockpit, sheering it off just above the engine assembly. Corran imagined he could see the pilot's blackened body in silhouette for a second, then the eyeball exploded and seared that image into his brain. Exultation at having been victorious swept through Corran, though in its wake came the feeling that those two pilots had been so inexperienced that he had not really fought them, but had just slaughtered them.

"Nemesis One, we have two uglies at five kilometers, heading 132 degrees. They are hostile. Engage and terminate."

"As ordered." Corran brought the squint up and around, then punched the throttle to full power. He wanted to close quickly so he would be able to get a look at the ships he faced. Uglies were hideous, hybrid spacefighters cobbled together from various salvage parts. Smugglers and pirates used them fairly often. He couldn't pinpoint how he knew that, but he did know he'd fought uglies before. Given that he was alive, he assumed they had not proved too much of a problem for him.

Something about that assumption niggled in the back of his mind. He knew it was not incorrect. He was a good pilot and he knew it, but his assuming superiority seemed wrong. He hadn't made the assumption on the basis of the fact that uglies seldom had the performance characteristics of the fighters from which they were created. He realized he'd assumed anyone flying uglies would be pirates or smugglers, and had instantly assumed they were his inferiors. While he could find no facts to dispute his assumption about his foes, he knew there was something wrong with his having made it.

A warning klaxon blared in the cockpit, alerting him that one of the uglies had gotten a torpedo lock on him and had launched a proton torpedo. Corran banished thoughts about his enemies' combat-worthiness, rolled the ship up onto its port wing, then dove. His abrupt maneuver hurled his ship onto a course at right angles to the one he'd been traveling previously. The proton torpedo, which was traveling roughly twice as fast as he was, shot past his starboard wing and started on a long loop to head back at him.

A proton torpedo has thirty seconds of flight time. I can't outrun it, but I can out-maneuver it. Corran smiled. *Or deal with it more directly!*

He reversed the squint's thrust and hit the port rudder pedal. This threw the Interceptor into a flat spin that brought the nose around to face back along his flight path. Where the proton torpedo had been coming straight at his back before, now it was coming straight in at his cockpit. He killed the thrust and glanced at his scanner monitor—*750 meters and closing fast.*

At 400 meters he flicked the lasers over to dual-fire and tightened his finger down on the trigger. Pairs of laser-bolts burned green through space seeking the torpedo. One bolt hit the torpedo at 250 meters out. It failed to destroy it, but did melt its way into the body and ignite a fuel cell. The subsequent explosion pitched the torpedo off course. When the onboard computer calculated the torpedo would not hit its target, it detonated the warhead, but the Interceptor remained a hundred meters outside the blast radius.

Switching thrust forward again, Corran throttled up to full and punched up profiles of the uglies. One was an X-TIE. It had the body of an X-wing fighter with the hexagonal wings from a TIE starfighter. Corran found the ship hideous to look at and would have dismissed it immediately except it had launched the proton torpedo.

The other ship looked fairly ridiculous. It mated a TIE's ball cockpit with the engine pods from a Y-wing. This particular hybrid was rare because it combined the TIE's lack of shields with the Y-wing's lumbering, slothful handling. Corran knew this type of ugly was often referred to as a TYE-wing, though DIE-wing was a common nickname for it as well.

Corran put his Interceptor on a course that shot him past

the X-TIE, then broke on down into a series of maneuvers, twisting and turning, that left the TYE-wing far behind. The X-TIE hung with him long enough for Corran's scanners to pick out details. X-wing fighters had two torpedo launching tubes in the nose and four lasers, one mounted on each end of the stabilizers that supplied the ship with its name. Lacking those S-foils, the X-TIE had replaced one proton torpedo launch tube with what Corran guessed would be a laser cannon.

Undergunned and overmatched. Corran rolled his way down through a corkscrew dive that lengthened his lead on the X-TIE and the TYE-wing. The X-TIE's pilot began to pull the fighter's nose up, as if he intended to return to his wingman's side and the safety the TYE-wing would provide him. Corran watched him turn away, then inverted and pulled the Interceptor through a tight turn and shot back up and in at the X-TIE's exposed aft.

Clearly unaware of Corran's maneuver, the X-TIE's pilot inverted and headed back toward the TYE-wing. Corran saw the pilot's head come up as he scanned space for signs of the Interceptor. Coming in from behind made spotting the squint difficult. The pilot never managed it, though Corran did see the R5 unit's head swivel around and spot him.

Corran hit the trigger and walked laser fire from stern to nose on the ugly. Two bolts blew the R5's flowerpot head off, then two more punctured the cockpit, exploding it into a cloud of transparisteel and duraplast fragments. The last bolts hit forward and touched off a proton torpedo's fuel cells. The fuel's detonation filled the slender craft with fire and sent the nose spinning wildly off into space.

Pulling back on the yoke, Corran brought his nose up and spitted the DIE-wing on the crosshairs. The ugly began a roll, so Corran matched him and tightened up on the trigger. Green laser-bolts slashed at one of the Y-wings, but the ugly flashed on past beneath him. Corran prepared to invert and loop, but a hail of angry red laser-bolts sliced across his flight path.

"What? Who?" He kicked the squint up on its right wing, wrenched the wheel right, and tugged back on the yoke. The maneuver pulled him sharply out of line with his previous course, but he wasn't content with just doing that. He broke again, to port and up, then searched his scanner monitor for whomever had shot at him.

The scanners reported two ships, both of them X-wings. "What's going on here?"

"Nemesis One, we have two hostiles. X-wings. It was an ambush. Engage and terminate."

Ambush me, will you? Corran translated his outrage into fluid maneuvering. Cutting and jumping, he bounced his Interceptor through a series of jukes that shook the X-wings from his tail and brought him around on the DIE-wing. Without really thinking about it, he pumped laser-fire into the ugly's ball cockpit, then pulled up and away as the misbegotten fighter exploded.

Two on one—same odds I've had all day. Despite that hasty assessment, he knew the odds were actually quite different in this battle. The squint's speed and maneuverability gave it an edge over the X-wings, but they had shields. They could take more damage than he could, and the ability to survive damage had a very direct relationship with the ability to survive in combat. More importantly, the two X-wing pilots seemed determined to operate together. They flew in tight formation and seemed familiar enough with each other that he wasn't so much fighting two foes as one meta-foe.

The X-wings came around on a vector that brought them straight at him. Corran knew head-to-head passes were the most deadly in dogfighting, and given the enemy's superiority of numbers, he had no intention of engaging in such a duel. He cut his throttle back and dove at a slight angle so he would pass beneath their incoming vector. They made a slight adjustment in their courses, apparently content to get a passing deflection shot. Corran then goosed his throttle forward, forcing them to sharpen their dives, yet before they could get a good shot at him, he had passed beneath them and had started up again.

One X-wing inverted and pulled up through a loop to drop on Corran's tail while the other broke the other way. The second X-wing looped out and away from the Interceptor, momentarily splitting the two fighters. Corran knew the second pilot had made a mistake and instantly acted to make the most of it. Cutting his throttle back, he turned hard to starboard and then back again to port.

Corran's sine-wave maneuver brought him back on course, but the X-wing that had been following him now hung up and out in front of him. The X-wing's pilot had continued on his course, assuming the Interceptor had been trying to evade him. It wasn't until he shot past the Interceptor and it dropped into his aft arc that he realized his error.

Corran throttled up and closed with the X-wing. *You're mine now, all because your buddy made a mistake.* He pushed the Interceptor in to point-blank range and started to fire— then he saw a blue crest on the X-wing's S-foils. It appeared to be the Rebel crest with a dozen X-wings flying out away from it. Though no words accompanied the crest, Corran knew they should have.

Rogue Squadron!

The second he recognized the crest, his finger fell away from the trigger. He didn't know why he didn't fire. Fear crystallized in his belly at the sight of it, but he knew he wasn't afraid of the Rogues. It was something else. Something was wrong, hideously wrong, but he could not pierce the veil of mystery surrounding that sensation.

Suddenly something exploded behind him, pitching him forward. He slammed hard into the steering yoke, crushing his life support equipment and driving the breath from his lungs. His chest burned as he tried in vain to catch his breath. He caught the fleeting scent of flowers, then a painful brilliance filled the cockpit. He waited for the pain in his chest and the fire in his lungs to consume him, but those sensations dulled, and his ability to focus on them or anything else eroded.

A woman's voice spoke to him. "You have failed, Nemesis One. You are weak." Her words came tinged with anger, bitten off harshly and clearly meant to hurt him. "Had this been other than a simulation, your atoms would be floating through space and the rabble would be laughing at you. You are pathetic."

Corran's right hand rose toward his throat and pressed itself against his chest. The shattered remains of his life support gear prevented him from touching his breastbone, but he knew something was missing, something that should have been laying against his flesh. He did not know what it was, but he knew he would draw comfort from it.

In its absence, despair flooded through him.

"I had thought you worthy, Nemesis One. You told me you were, didn't you?"

Though he recalled no such declaration, he confirmed it. "I did. I am."

"You are *nothing* unless I say you are something. Now I say you are *nothing*, nothing but a *failure*!" In the light he saw the silhouette of a tall, slender woman. The sight of her made him shiver more than her words. He knew he feared her, but he also wanted to please her. Pleasing her was very important to him, the only thing that was important in the world. "You have failed me and yourself."

"Please," he croaked, but her silhouette gave no indication she had heard him.

"One more chance, perhaps."

"Yes, yes."

"If you fail again . . ."

Corran shook his head adamantly. "I won't, I won't."

"No, for your next failure will be your last, Nemesis One." The silhouette folded its arms together. "Disappoint me again and what is left of your life will be spent in agonizing atonement, disgrace, and, after a long time, death."

7

T HE REVERSION TO REALSPACE brought Wedge and the Rogues out into a situation that just seemed like another simulator run, with one minor variation. As he expected, Wedge saw the space station slowly revolving in a star-stained void. Way off toward the right, closer to the yellow star burning at the center of the solar system, sat Yag'Dhul. The planet's grey cloud cover made it only slightly more colorful than the Givin who called it home.

The only variation from the opsims was the appearance of a flight of four TIE starfighters patrolling the area around the space station. Mynock, the R5 unit in Wedge's X-wing, immediately screeched out a warning when he noticed them off to port. Wedge glanced at his monitor, noted how the TIEs moved into an attack formation, and smiled.

Action beats inaction every time. He keyed his comm unit. "One flight, on me. Rogue Twelve, take the Defenders in."

"As ordered," Aril Nunb replied.

Committing only one flight of fighters against an equal number of TIEs, especially when he could have had two dozen Y-wings and seven more X-wings join the fight, might have seemed the height of arrogance, though Wedge knew it was quite the opposite. While TIE pilots seldom managed to amass the experience of their Rebel counterparts, they were quite competent, and more than capable of killing in a dogfight. Warlord Zsinj's pilots had proved to be good fighters in the past, and Wedge expected them to be nothing less in this engagement.

The reasons he only pulled one flight from his formation to deal with the TIEs were twofold. First, and most important, their operation demanded that the threat to the station caused it to scramble its fighters. The X- and Y-wings were to draw the TIEs out and away from the station to a point in the system where the B-wings would come in. The B-wings were in hyperspace, already on their way, so if surprise were to be achieved, Zsinj's troops had to be lured into position in a timely manner.

The second reason to match forces with Zsinj was because having too many fighters involved in a battle tended to wreak havoc on the efficacy of the pilots. The difference between a good pilot and a bad one, all other things being equal, came down to situational awareness. A pilot who could handle more variables, and keep track of more ships in his mind would do better in combat than one who could only deal with less in the way of distractions. Wedge had seen statistical analyses that showed that kill ratios fell as the number of fighters in a dogfight increased; so by keeping the fight small, he made it easier for his people to grasp all the aspects of the fight.

"Three, you and Four have the trailers. Two, I have lead. Target the second TIE."

"As ordered, Rogue Leader." Rhysati Ynr led Erisi Dlarit in a dive and sweeping turn that brought them around toward the following pair of TIEs. Rhysati's attack vector was intended to push the TIEs farther from the space station and the rest of the Rebel force. Wedge saw the TIEs begin to react to her maneuver, but they seemed content to let her dictate the direction of the fight.

Wedge flipped his weapon's controls over to lasers and set

them for dual-firing. He pumped his shields up to full and picked the lead eyeball as his target. They started to close, coming head to head, with their wingmen off starboard and hanging slightly back, each formation being the mirror image of the other. He smiled. *Just where I want him.*

"Rogue Two, do you have your target?"

"Confirmed, lead." Asyr's voice came through the comm unit cool and steady.

"Get ready. On my mark, I'm going to foul your target. Shoot immediately after that with a proton torpedo."

"As ordered."

"Three, two, one, mark!" Wedge rolled the X-wing up and over in a barrel-roll to port. His target did the same thing, sweeping his fighter across his wingman's flight path. That momentarily blinded the second TIE and caused him to shy. Wedge glanced at his monitor and saw a report of a proton torpedo launch, then touched the starboard rudder pedal a second before inverting the X-wing and making his pass on the TIE fighter.

Before Wedge applied rudder, the two ships had been heading straight at each other. The rudder drifted the X-wing's nose about ten degrees to starboard, pulling him out of line with the TIE. The inversion flopped the starfighter, bringing the nose back into line with the TIE. Before Zsinj's pilot could react, Wedge's fighter streaked in at him and started shooting.

The first pair of red laser-bolts missed low, but the next two pairs swept up and across the ball cockpit. One of the TIE's lasers died in a cloud of duraplast mist. Wedge's third shot lanced through the transparisteel viewport, igniting and melting all manner of components and equipment. The TIE starfighter rolled up on the starboard solar panel, then tightened down into a screw-spiral before exploding.

A second later a blue proton torpedo slammed into the port wing on the second TIE. The black solar panel closed around the torpedo like cloth around a thrown stone. The torpedo itself punched through the panel and penetrated the fighter's hull before detonating. The blast ripped the back half off the cockpit pod, freeing the engines to soar further in-system while the shattered husk of a fighter tumbled on through the void.

"Nice shot, Deuce."

"Thanks for the setup, lead."

Wedge brought the X-wing up and around to the original heading and saw a proton torpedo from Erisi's ship finish off a TIE. Farther along he saw streams of green laser-bolts spraying out from the space station. At the extremes of range the fire did not seriously threaten the incoming fighters, but it did keep them away long enough for the station to scramble its TIEs. Zsinj's fliers boiled up and out from the station and rose on an intercept course with the Rebel fighters.

"Lead, I have a dozen Interceptors and eight starfighters."

"I copy, Twelve." *That should be everything they have, unless they're holding something back.* Keeping ships in reserve made little or no sense to Wedge, but he'd long since learned that warfare and tactics seldom make a lot of sense to the opposition. *I just hope our run away from the station looks believable.*

Aril Nunb led the Rogues and Y-wings up and away from the station. The squints and eyeballs came on in pursuit, hot to thin the ranks of the Y-wings. The Interceptors opened a lead on the TIE starfighters and started to close fast with the Y-wings. Aril brought her X-wing over, and the rest of the Rogues followed her through a loop that took them back toward the Interceptors while the Y-wings continued heading away from their pursuers.

As the X-wing and Interceptor formations began to spread out into clouds, the B-wings burst into realspace and shot straight into the gap between the squints and the eyeballs from the station. Wedge marveled at how each cruciform ship flew with its wings and fuselage whirling around to keep the cockpit stable despite a wild series of maneuvers and course corrections. Having flown a B-wing a few times, he could appreciate the ship's firepower, but the way it moved and flew made him feel less like a pilot than a *driver*.

The B-wings slashed in at the Interceptors. Half of them seemed content to attack using lasers or blasters, while the other half employed ion cannons to take the squints out of the fight without killing them. Blue ion-bolts caught Interceptors in full flight, sending electricity skitter-jagging over the hulls. Laser and blaster fire ripped into other Interceptors, burning holes through solar panels and cockpits.

The B-wing ambush scattered the Interceptors, but the X-wings coming in at them did not break off in pursuit. They left that to the B-wings. The Rogues pushed on through the crumbling Interceptor formation, shot past the B-wings and, as One Flight reunited with the squadron, sailed on in at the eyeball formation.

The first pass came head to head. Static hissed through the X-wing cockpit as TIE lasers stung his forward shields repeatedly. Wave after wave of green light washed over the shields, but Wedge ignored it. He concentrated instead on his monitor and shifted the X-wing a bit to starboard, trapping a TIE fighter in the center of his targeting crosshairs. He tightened down on the trigger, pulsing kilojoules of scarlet energy into an eyeball's cockpit.

A roiling explosion shredded that ship. Wedge kicked the X-wing up onto the starboard S-foil, then climbed up and away from the expanding ball of gas. Letting his roll continue over the top, he dropped the X-wing into a dive, then rolled out to port and came around on an arc between the cloud of fighters and the station. He glanced off to starboard and saw Asyr still with him, which prompted him to toss her a salute. "Glad you stayed with me."

"That's my job."

From his vantage point at the periphery of the battle he could see a number of things that impressed him. The Rogues had hit the eyeballs very hard, but Zsinj's people regrouped in good order instead of scattering. Without shields, the TIE starfighters were really no match for the X-wings, but remaining together made them far more dangerous than individual ships fleeing. Whoever the leader of that squadron was, he was sharp enough to keep his people together and head them out and away from the fray.

"Rogue flights Two and Three, leave the flight of eyeballs alone and join the Y-wings. One flight, we're watching the eyeballs." Wedge hit two buttons on his flight console. "Mynock, see if you can get me a frequency for the comm unit communications between the eyeballs."

The droid hooted his understanding of the order.

While Wedge waited for the droid to get him that information, he watched the B-wings finish off the squints and head in toward the station. Wedge's monitor showed seven Interceptors hanging dead in space. That number was impressive, even in spite of the ambush, because blowing ships up was far easier than taking their electrical systems down. While he appreciated the fact that the pilots had not been killed when their ships had been stopped, he knew the choice to use ion cannons on them had been made for practical rather than altruistic reasons.

Each of those pilots will be debriefed, and what they know will be added to our store of information concerning Zsinj. It is entirely possible some or all of them served on the Iron Fist, *and learning about the ship's condition is of vital importance. It represents the core of Zsinj's might, and will let us determine how truly dangerous he is.*

The Rebel fighters all converged on the *Empress*-class space station with the Y-wings in the lead. While ungainly, the Y-wings were still not easy targets to hit. The station's weaponry sent energy beams shooting out at the attackers, but the incoming fighters supplied three targets for each weapon system, overwhelming the crews defending the station. Added to that was the ability of fighters to approach while using part of the station to shield them from many of the lasers. Using targeting data supplied by other ships, the fighters were able to pop from cover and fire at targets that had previously been unseen.

The swooping, diving, rolling, and climbing cloud of fighters boiled around the station like insects around a bright light. Direct hits on a fighter would make the craft break off and loop away until its shields were recharged, then head back in. The battle to defend the station was lost from the very start, but the fear Zsinj inspired in his people clearly kept them fighting long after it made sense for them to do so.

Mynock beeped, and Wedge saw a comm unit frequency come up on his monitor. He punched the number into his comm unit and keyed his microphone. "Starfighter flight, this is Commander Antilles of the New Republic Armed Forces. If you power down your weapons, we'll consider you noncombatants. The same offer goes for the people on the station."

"I copy, Antilles." The voice coming back to Wedge through the comm unit had the metallic echo commonly injected in speech by Imperial equipment. "My flight is disarming itself. I'll pass your message on to the station chief, Valsil Torr."

"Obliged, starfighter." Wedge checked his sensors for hostiles as he waited for a return message.

"Antilles, Torr has the message and is powering down his weapons. The station is yours. Be careful, though, he's a wily old Twi'lek."

Wedge smiled. Though the communications gear had robbed the voice of any humanity, it couldn't kill the personality in it. He might have been amazed that someone who had just been shooting at him and his people would so quickly offer helpful advice, but he'd long since learned that warriors from all sides of any conflict had more in common than not. "I copy the advice. I appreciate it."

"One thing, Antilles."

"Yes?"

"If we surrender to you, will you haul us out of here?"

"Don't want to be around when the *Iron Fist* gets here?"

"Not especially."

No surprise, that. Unlike the starfighters the Rebellion used, the TIE fighters were not equipped with hyperdrives. TIEs traveled between battles in the bellies of ships like the *Iron Fist*. The flight of starfighters was trapped unless Wedge arranged transport for them out of the system. Zsinj had a reputation for being short-tempered, so leaving them behind was tantamount to murdering them, and Wedge had no desire to have their murders on his conscience.

"Starfighter, surrendering to me means you'll lose your ship."

"That's a problem, Antilles. We're all mercenaries. We lose our ships and we starve." The TIE pilot fell silent for a moment, then continued. "Of course, no reason to eat and live if you can't fly."

"I understand, starfighter." Wedge thought for a moment. "I have an idea. If you hire on as guards to fly cover for one of the freighters coming in, you can get out of here and be free."

"Freighters?"

"Coming for the bacta."

"Bacta. So that's what we were guarding."

"And you can continue guarding it all the way to Coruscant, where it's needed. Give me your word you won't fight against the New Republic in the future, and you've got a deal."

"You have it, Antilles."

Right on cue, a dozen and a half bulk freighters and specialty haulers started coming out of hyperspace and cruising in toward the space station. Most were blocky, squared-off craft that had seen better days, but a few were more elegant ships whose very designs were tributes to the romanticism of space travel. One, a converted *Baudo*-class yacht, glided through the void like a metal simulacrum of the Corellian sea creature that gave the ship her name.

"Starfighter, the *Baudo*-class yacht there is the *Pulsar Skate*. I'll have the captain contact you on this frequency. Stand by."

"I copy."

Wedge opened a channel to the *Skate*. "*Skate*, this is Rogue Leader."

"Mirax here, Wedge. We're fourth in line to head in. What can I do for you?"

"We have a flight of four eyeballs orbiting. They've left Zsinj's service and need a ride out of here. Will you?"

"Sure. Not the first time I've hauled a ship for you."

No, the first one was Corran. "Thanks, Mirax. Mynock is sending you their comm unit frequency, so I'll leave the arrangements to you."

"It will give me something to do while I'm waiting."

"I copy." Wedge glanced at the Chronographie display in the corner of his monitor. "When we get back home, you and I will sit down and talk, yes?"

Weariness washed through Mirax's voice. "I'll have to offload the cargo first. Then maybe I can sleep. Haven't been doing much of that lately. I will call you when I'm functional again."

"Promise."

"I promise."

"And keep that promise, or I talk your father into coming out of retirement by telling him you're moping over the death of his worst enemy's son."

"Oh, Wedge, that's cruel." Light static hissed in Wedge's ears as Mirax's voice broke. "There's no reason I shouldn't mourn for Corran."

"Agreed, but you don't have to do it alone. That's a burden we all share, got it?"

"I copy." Resignation tinged with relief flooded her words. "See you back on Coruscant."

"I am counting on it." Wedge looked out at the station and his squadron patrolling around it. *And, miracle of miracles, it looks like everyone is going to make it back home again.*

8

CORRAN KNEW THAT once again being in the cockpit of a fighter should have made him happy, but it did not. He could find no fault with the fighter nor with being given a patrol mission. He'd done enough of those to expect boredom, and yet even that wasn't giving him a problem. Just to be flying again was enough to override boredom.

The fact was, he realized, that he was unhappy. Something was gnawing away at him inside. Something was wrong, and there was no way he could ignore it. It created an anxiety in him that was out of all proportion with what he was doing. It felt as if he weren't involved in a patrol at all, but in some other mission with a hidden agenda he knew nothing about.

"Nemesis One, report."

"One is clear, Control."

The voice coming through the comm unit betrayed no hint of deception or urgency, but Corran couldn't shake the sickening feeling that he was being manipulated. He had a natural aversion to being used, and he could feel unseen hands all over himself, pointing him in a certain direction, for reasons he could not fathom. He was surprised to find himself less resentful of their agenda—whatever it was—than of being manipulated.

I'm reasonable. I don't shy away from difficult tasks. I do what I am asked to do, within reason. Didn't I do that . . . ? His thoughts dead-ended as he realized he couldn't summon up specific memories to back up his argument. He *knew* he had performed many dangerous missions, but he couldn't pinpoint them. His inability to do so wouldn't have concerned him, and in fact almost did not, except that he kept feeling like a hologram being processed by someone else's computer.

"Nemesis One, we have two contacts on the heading of 270 degrees. They are ten kilometers distant. They are hostile. You are free to engage and terminate them."

"As ordered." Corran punched up the data on the incoming ships and displayed it over his monitor. *Two TIEs*. The starfighters inspired no fear in him, and he would have viewed them with utter detachment except that a random thought shot off through his brain.

Two TIEs aren't nearly as deadly as a single Tycho. The connection seemed entirely logical to Corran: the similar sounds created a link. The fact that Tycho Celchu had been an Imperial pilot who flew TIEs reinforced it. Corran knew Tycho had betrayed Rogue Squadron, and Corran had been determined to see him pay. *If I weren't here, I'd be* there, *taking care of Tycho*.

Before he could begin to wonder where *there* was, Control's voice came through the comlink again. "We have additional information on the incoming ships. Transmitting now."

The image on the monitor shifted from a TIE starfighter to an X-wing. An additional line of data beneath the fighter's image informed Corran the ship was flown by Captain T. Celchu. A jolt of adrenaline pulsed through his body, then slammed into his brain. He couldn't believe his luck—the coincidence of being able to fly against Tycho and avenge Rogue Squadron was incredible. *And I will make the most of it*.

Corran inverted the TIE Interceptor he flew and dove. The X-wings started to come after him, vectoring in on his belly, so he inverted again, then pulled through a climbing loop to starboard. He soared as the X-wings dove, neither side wasting laser energy when the chances of hitting were so small. Corran kept tightening the loop into a spiral that emphasized the squint's greater maneuverability, then streaked away to underscore its superior speed as well.

A light flicked on within the head's-up display, indicating one of the X-wings was trying for a proton torpedo target lock, but a quick climb, roll, and twisting dive broke the lock and brought Corran out on a vector toward Tycho's X-wing. Corran sideslipped the Interceptor to starboard, then rolled up on the left wing and climbed in toward Tycho. He flipped his lasers from quad- to dual-fire, assuming he'd have to use multiple shots in multiple passes to bring Tycho down. He led the X-wing, anticipating Tycho's break, then hastily snapped off a shot that splashed energy over Tycho's shields as the Interceptor overshot its target.

No reaction. That isn't like Tycho at all. Corran rolled up on the right stabilizer, climbed into a loop, then rolled over and out to port. Another inversion took him into a dive, but his scanners showed the X-wings hadn't stayed with him past the first maneuver, much less through the second.

Corran shivered. *They're handling like TIE starfighters, not like X-wings, and the pilot flying that first one isn't Tycho.* He switched his targeting computer over to the second ship and saw that X-wing was listed as being flown by Kirtan Loor. An immediate desire to vape that ship filled him, but it did not deflect him from thinking. In fact, the vehemence of his feelings about Loor swept him past the fact that Loor and Tycho had been in collusion on Coruscant.

It carried him far enough that he recalled Loor didn't know how to fly any space ships at all, much less starfighters.

Loor can't be there. The chance that Tycho and Loor would show up where I could attack and kill them is unbelievable. Whereas before he had taken great delight in the coincidence, now it became evidence that he was being manipulated. The

link between a TIE and Tycho had been made in his mind before Tycho showed up as a pilot. While he knew inferring cau-
sality from that relationship was not strictly logical, his being
manipulated meant it was more than possible.

*Tycho is an enemy, so he was placed in one fighter. Another
enemy was plucked from a list of my enemies and placed in the
second fighter.* More anger flared through Corran and battered
aside the blockages in his brain that had kept him thinking of
nothing outside the cockpit. The apparent insertion of personal enemies into his situation told Corran two things. *First
off, I'm in a simulator, and second, someone knows enough
about me to know who my enemies are. Pitting me against my
enemies gives me some wish fulfillment, which is a good thing.
It rewards behavior, but I have to ask myself, is flying an interceptor against X-wings behavior for which I want to be rewarded?*

His stomach shrank and hardened into a rock that threatened to explode volcanically. *I'm flying an Imp ship against
Rebels. I don't want to do that.* Corran immediately realized
that only his enemies—the remnants of the Empire—would
want him to feel good about attacking Rebels, yet few Imps
would take the time or make the effort to manipulate him that
way. Some would imprison him and the rest would just kill him.

Except one.

Ysanne Isard.

Injecting her into the jumble of thoughts bouncing around
his brain immediately started to impose order on his mind. She
was known and feared for her ability to warp Rebels and turn
them against friends and family. She had been successful with
Tycho Celchu, and he was not the only success story to come
out of her Lusankya prison. Her altered agents had wrought
havoc among the Emperor's enemies, and his death had done
nothing to cause Iceheart to curtail her operations.

The fog in Corran's brain began to evaporate. He remembered having met Isard after his capture. She'd vowed to transform him into a tool of the Emperor's vengeance. This simulator

run—*and the one before it*—clearly was designed to get him to attack Rebel symbols. Subsequent sessions would further crush his resistance, training him to greater and greater levels of efficiency while turning him against everyone he knew, loved, and respected.

She would make me over into the human equivalent of the plague she unleashed on Coruscant.

Corran shook his head, then raised his hands from the simulator's steering yoke and yanked his helmet off. Electrodes taped to his head pulled away rather abruptly, taking some hair with them, but he ignored the pain. *The electrodes fed my brain wave patterns to a computer. The patterns were compared to data gathered from interrogations, so the computer could recognize what I was thinking about and project the proper clues into the simulation. Very good.*

He pulled the respiration mask from his face and let it dangle against his chest. "This is Nemesis One. The game is over. I won't betray my people."

The star field on the screen in front of Corran vanished. In its place he saw Ysanne Isard's head and shoulders. Her mismatched eyes, the left one a fiery red and the right one an ice blue, added venom to the woman's steely expression. Her sharp, slender features might have made her seem beautiful to some, but the fear her anger stabbed into his heart made her more than ugly to Corran. Her long black hair had been pulled back into a ponytail, yet she had let her white temple-locks remain unbound as if that girlish affectation would somehow soften her image.

"You are under the impression, Corran Horn, that this little victory is significant and hampers my efforts in some way. It does not." An eyebrow arched over her arctic eye. "You worked with the Corellian Security Force, so you can understand how powerful certain interrogation techniques can be. What you have endured so far is little more than testing."

"And I passed."

"From your perspective that might seem true." Her eyes

sharpened. "From mine it merely means you have reclassified yourself. You will require more time than others I have worked with in the past, but here at Lusankya, time is abundant."

Corran shrugged. "Good, then I'll have abundant time to plan my escape."

"I doubt it." She sighed as if what she was about to say hurt her in some way. "Were you easy to train, you would find your stay here pleasant. As you are difficult, the next step is for me to determine if you know anything I consider valuable. Unfortunately this means sifting through a lot of things I don't want to know. I hope your life has been interesting, because my technicians have been known to resort to cruelty when they are bored."

"They'll learn nothing from me."

Isard frowned. "Please, Horn, skip the bluster. We will start with a level four narco-interrogation and work our way down to level one if we must. You know you'll tell us whatever we want to know."

Sheer terror froze the lump in Corran's stomach solid. With a level four interrogation session he'd be remembering things his *mother* had forgotten while she was carrying him in her womb. *I will have no secrets.* Hundreds of images flitted through his mind as he sorted valuable memories from the casual ones.

This process, while agonizing, also brought a smile to his face. Gil Bastra, the man who had created a series of identities for Corran to use after he fled from Corellia, had made sure the identities took Corran out into the outlier worlds. *From Loor they know everything about my days with CorSec. Thanks to Gil there's very little valuable information I can give her. I was out of circulation until I joined Rogue Squadron, and I don't know enough about the Rebellion to hurt it.*

"I see your smile, Horn. You may feel bold enough to smile now, but things will change." Isard herself smiled, and Corran found it a most forbidding thing. "When we are finished with you, smiles will be but a memory, and a painful one at that."

9

WEDGE LAUGHED ALOUD, telling himself he was laughing at the irony of feeling nervous, not because of *being* nervous. Here he was, a celebrated hero and the sole survivor of both Death Star runs, conqueror of Coruscant and leader of the most feared fighter squadron in the galaxy, and at Iella Wessiri's door he felt nervous. Enough ice water ran in his veins, so the rumors went, to replenish Coruscant's polar caps, yet he found himself clearing his voice and hesitating before he pushed the buzzer button at her door.

On the way over from squadron headquarters he had convinced himself he wasn't going to be asking her out on a date, really. He'd spent the previous hour being harangued by Erisi Dlarit concerning the Vratix terrorist and his whereabouts after the raid on Warlord Zsinj's bacta store. He'd done his best, over and over again, to explain to her that he had no reports about the Thyferran native, but promised to pass notice of her interest up to General Cracken. That really was all he could do, but Erisi took a lot of convincing on that point.

The experience had been draining. There had been moments when he considered just cutting her off and ordering her out of his office, but he could tell her concern about the Vratix was based on her conviction that the insectoid creature was a terrorist and a potential hazard to anyone who came in contact with it. He thought Erisi's reaction might have been born from her frustration at not having been able to do anything to prevent Corran's death. By making the terrorist her responsibility, she might prevent another tragedy, thereby atoning for her lack of action in Corran's case. Wedge found her motive noble, but her insistence exhausting. Corran's death and the misery of millions on Coruscant had everyone in the squadron worn thin, and being dismissive of Erisi's concerns would not help the situation.

Corran's death had likewise affected Iella deeply. She had been Corran's partner in the Corellian Security Force and had fled Corellia at the same time he had. Her flight had brought her to Coruscant, where she joined up with the Rebel underground. Her reunion with Corran had been a joyous occasion. It had been easy for Wedge to see how they complemented each other and must have worked well as a team.

Those qualities that made her well-suited to working with Corran were qualities Wedge found attractive. She was thoughtful and stable, yet possessed of a good sense of humor and a fierce loyalty to her friends and to justice. Unfortunately, her loyalty made her most zealous in helping the prosecution find evidence against Tycho Celchu, but she approached the search so openly that Wedge couldn't find fault with her in doing her duty as she saw it.

He pressed the door buzzer, then tugged at the cuffs of his jacket sleeves. *I'm not asking her out. I'm just here as a friend visiting a friend.* Wedge shook his head. For the past ten years, since the death of his parents and through his association with the Rebellion, he'd really given little thought to romance and relationships. He'd certainly found companionship with a number of Rebel women, but he'd not found a single companion, a partner, the way Han Solo or Tycho Celchu had. He couldn't explain why not, nor did he let it bother him—the nature of the Rebellion and his assignments meant planning for anything long-term was silly, and avoiding relationships meant the chances of getting hurt when the unspeakable happened were much less.

He'd seen Leia over the time Han Solo had been encased in carbonite. She had been driven almost to the point of reckless-ness in her attempts to free her beloved. He laughed. *Entering Jabba's palace meant she was driven* beyond *recklessness*. While he envied Han Solo the passion with which he was loved, he dreaded the idea of being plagued by the pain Leia had known.

The door to the apartment slid open and Wedge's nervous-ness slackened when Iella smiled. "Wedge. This is a surprise."

"A pleasant one, I hope." He glanced down at his hands for a moment, then back up into her brown eyes. "I should have called before heading over, but I was going to get something to eat and I thought, well, I hate eating alone and . . ."

The brown-haired woman's smile widened for a moment and carried on up into her eyes, then shrank as if the corners of her mouth had slammed into walls and were rebounding. "I think you'd better come in." She turned away from the door, and he followed the lithe woman down a short corridor to a modest-sized parlor. The door closed automatically behind him, cutting off the brightest source of light and sinking the room into a grey gloom.

The man sitting in the corner chair looked every bit as if he were constructed from shadow-threads and slivers of grey. The sharpness of his features accentuated the gauntness of his frame. His shoulders and knees poked like knobs against the grey fabric of the jumpsuit he wore. A few strands of black hair wove through the white and grey combed over his largely bald head but did nothing to disguise the shape of the skull beneath it. In fact, were it not for the spark of life burning in the man's brown eyes, Wedge would have believed him to be a mummified worker resurrected from some tomb in the bowels of Corus-cant.

Iella folded her arms across her chest. "Commander Wedge Antilles, this is Diric Wessiri. He is my husband."

Husband! Wedge covered his surprise by taking a step forward and extended his right hand toward Diric. "My pleasure, sir."

Diric inclined his head forward and shook Wedge's hand with a long-fingered grip that was firm and even strong, though the strength faded quickly. "The honor is mine, Commander. Your exploits bring glory to your world and fellow Corellians."

"Glory wasn't our goal, sir."

"Nonetheless . . ." The man smiled, then let his hand drop back toward his lap. "Forgive me, Commander. At another point I would engage you in a lively discussion, but now I am somewhat fatigued."

"I understand."

Iella walked to her husband's side and gently rested a hand on his shoulder. "The Imps caught Diric up in a sweep about a year ago. They interrogated him, broke his identity, then imprisoned him. Six months ago or so they set up a bio-research project and made Diric part of the slave-labor force. They only used humans because the lab produced what we know to be the Krytos virus." She gave his shoulder a squeeze. "General Cracken's people had Diric in quarantine, then debriefed him. I only learned he was alive when they brought him here four hours ago."

"I should be going, then, and leave you two alone."

"No." The old man raised his right hand and gently patted Iella's hand. "I have long been among Imperials and other slaves. It is good to have normal people here to ease me back."

Wedge coughed lightly into his hand. "I don't think you'll find my life normal at all."

Iella laughed politely. "Nor mine."

"How fortunate. Normal can be quite boring." Diric's head came up and he fixed Wedge with a steady stare. "And I want you to know, Commander, if anything has happened between you and my wife, I bear neither of you malice. I have been dead for a year. While I dreamed of being alive again, I do not bear a grudge against those who lived while I was dead."

Wedge held a hand up. "First, no titles."

"Where they kept me, we joked that titles were for when we were once again people. I use it to remind me I am again a man. And I use it out of profound respect for what you have done."

"Don't. I'm just Wedge. Nothing I've done is the equal of your enduring Imperial captivity, so titles don't apply here. Second, Iella is intelligent, a wonder to work with, a joy to be around, and above all else, loyal to her friends. In fact, save one thing, she's just the sort of woman I could see myself growing old with. That one thing is this: she's married to you. Her loyalty to you, her fidelity, has never been in question. You are undoubtedly one of the luckiest men on this planet."

As he spoke, his mind raced on through thoughts and dreams of what he might have had with Iella had Diric not reappeared. It seemed as if the life they would never share was flashing before his eyes even as his words killed it. The romantic in him just wanted to hold on to how wonderful it would have been, but the pragmatist knew from just looking at Diric that things would have fallen apart in the end. Iella had chosen Diric because he was a sanctuary. No matter what her life held in store for her, he was someone who would always be there to share her joys and ease her disappointments. Wedge realized that he could not have given her what Diric provided. It might have taken a long time for their relationship to destroy itself, and they might have overcome the difficulties, but Wedge knew he could never have been as perfect a match for her as Diric was.

Someday I'll find someone. Wedge smiled. *When I'm ready to settle down.*

Diric mirrored Wedge's smile and let his head sink back contentedly against the chair's padding. "I am glad Iella found friends as generous and honorable as you are, Wedge. I do feel quite fortunate."

"And I bet you're happy to be free."

"Happy? Yes, though captivity wasn't as brutal as imagined. They can only control your body, not your mind." Diric shrugged slowly as if the effort were all but beyond his ability. "I knew I would be free someday."

"That's what Tycho says."

"Who?"

Iella looked down at her husband. "The man who killed Corran."

"The man who is *on trial* for killing Corran," Wedge corrected her. "Your wife is working with the prosecution team."

"Working to find the truth, mind you." Iella gave Wedge a frank glare. "There's ample evidence to bind him over for trial and to convict him."

"And blasted little uncovered, so far, to acquit him." Wedge held his hands up. "However, discussing that case was not my purpose for coming over here."

Diric's bushy brows met over the bridge of his hooked nose. "You think this Tycho is innocent?"

"I know it. Tycho Celchu is as much a victim of the Empire as you were."

Iella gave Diric's hand a gentle squeeze. "Tycho was once captured by the Imps. He's been working for them since his supposed escape, though Wedge would tell you he's been neatly framed."

Diric looked up at her. "And you know Wedge is wrong?"

Her immediate response died in a moment of open-mouthed hesitation. Iella's gaze flicked up at Wedge, then back down again. "We have found a lot to indicate Captain Celchu was an Imperial agent of extreme resourcefulness."

"But there are gaps in the evidence." Wedge smiled slowly. "Everything that condemns Tycho is available, but those things that would acquit him have vanished. Given the timing, the only force that could provide with one hand and take away with the other is the Empire."

Diric disengaged his hand from Iella's and pressed it, fingertip to fingertip, against the other hand. "This Tycho must be something to earn such loyalty from you."

"I feel about Tycho what Iella feels about Corran."

"Hence the impasse between us."

"Impasse, indeed. Still, Captain Celchu sounds fascinating." Diric's voice became wistful and Iella straightened up.

"Don't even think it, Diric."

Wedge raised an eyebrow. "What's the matter?"

Anger creased Ieila's brow and put snap into her voice. "He's going to meddle."

The older man wheezed out a laugh and punctuated it with a wet cough. "Meddle, is it? You see, Wedge, my vocation in life is to seek out people who fascinate me. I study them. I try to understand them. I share what understanding I have with others."

Ieila's brown eyes narrowed. "On Corellia he found a defendant in a case *fascinating*. He got to know her and decided she was innocent."

"Was she?"

Diric nodded solemnly.

"He kept after Corran and me, constantly asking us little questions that forced us to look beyond the scope of our investigation. She had been framed, but we got the guys who were responsible in the end." She frowned at her husband. "That was a different case, it wasn't on Coruscant, and you weren't weak as an Ewok cub at the time. You need to recover."

"I will, dearest."

Wedge smiled as he heard all manner of meaning in those words. Ieila's sigh meant she heard at least some of them and knew nothing short of house arrest would keep Diric from meeting Tycho. *Diric will make sure Iella doesn't let her desire to avenge Corran stop short of discovering the truth of what caused his death.* "Having a hobby *will* likely speed your recovery."

"A hobby, very good."

"This man's hobby is going to be *my* nightmare." Iella shook her head. "Antilles, didn't you say something about food when you arrived here?"

"I did indeed." Wedge jerked a thumb up toward the ceiling. "There is an Ithorian tapcaf about thirty levels up that is supposed to offer some fairly exotic vegetable matter and then . . ." He stopped as a tone sounded from the comlink clipped to the collar of his jacket. "Hang on a second."

He pulled the comlink free and flicked it on. "Antilles, go ahead."

"Wedge, it's Mirax."

"Finally awake?" Wedge nodded toward Iella. "It's Mirax."

"Ask her if she wants to join us for food."

"Will do. Mirax, I'm at Iella's apartment. She wants to know . . ."

"I heard, but it'll have to be another time." Mirax's tone dripped seriousness. "I have a problem. It's on the *Skate*, and I need you to get down here. Just you."

Wedge frowned. *Those fliers for Zsinj should have been taken into custody a long time ago.* "How bad is it? Are your riders back and causing trouble?"

"No, no, not that. *That* I could handle." Mirax sighed. "Look, you know I usually haul rare items for folks, right?"

"Right."

"Well, at the station I picked up something that's very rare, and as near as I can tell, if I don't get rid of it in the right way, the New Republic will shake itself apart and a scant few people will be alive to start rebuilding the future."

10

GAVIN DARKLIGHTER FELT his gorge rising as the miasmal stench from the darkened hovel stabbed through his nostrils and into his brain. He reeled away from the doorway and fell to his knees, puking up what felt like every last bit of food he'd eaten since his return to Coruscant. His stomach muscles clenched again and again, wringing his guts empty, but doing nothing to soothe the prickly sensation in the back of his throat that prompted him to heave once more.

A piercing wail from a female Gamorrean drilled through his skull and reminded him where he was and why he was there. Gavin coughed once and spat, then croaked a command to the black M-3PO droid behind him. "Emtrey, don't let them go in there. Tell her I'll do all I can."

Gavin wiped his mouth with his hand, then weakly crawled up the hovel's exterior wall. He pressed his back against the ferrocrete and slowly straightened up. He coughed again and his body tried to make him heave yet again, but he clenched his jaw and refused to vomit. *Never seen one that bad before*. Though he hoped he never would again see such a case, he knew that was one hope that had no chance of becoming reality.

The M-3PO droid succeeded in guiding the Gamorrean female and her tusky children to the other side of the walkway, then turned back toward Gavin. The droid's nonstandard clamshell head—a refit from a spaceport control droid—canted slightly to the left. "Is there anything I can do for you, Master Darklighter?"

"I'll be fine in a minute, Emtrey. Just keep them back." Gavin again spat, trying to rid his mouth of the sour taste. "Ask her when she last heard from her husband."

The protocol droid swiveled his head around and grunted the question out to the Gamorrean female. She replied in subdued and broken tones, which Emtrey translated for Gavin. "She says she and the children had been visiting kin elsewhere. The last time she spoke to her husband it was by comlink. He had sniffles, but was not alarmed. I'm gathering, from the words she's using, sir, that there was some domestic discord, which is why a lapse in communication would not be surprising."

"Got it, Emtrey. How long was she gone from here?"

"A standard month, sir—she left well before the liberation."

Gavin nodded. A month meant the chances she'd been infected by her husband were nil—if she had been, she'd already be showing signs of the Krytos virus. "Tell her to get to a bacta center for evaluation. She doesn't want the kids sick."

"I've told her, sir. She wants to know if Tolra will recover."

Gavin sighed and pushed himself away from the wall. "Tell her he's very sick. The prognosis is not good, but we will do what we can. Then call Asyr and tell her we'll need a clean team here." He forced himself to smile. "And, Emtrey, tell Tolra's wife she did the right thing. Tolra was brave and smart, and together they saved many people."

The words rang hollow in his ears, but he knew they would not in hers. What he said was correct: when the Gamorrean in the hovel recognized how sick he had become, he sealed his home's entrances and scrambled the lock-codes, preventing anyone else from getting in and becoming infected. In that he had indeed saved many lives.

Except for his own. Gavin forced his fists to unclench. Had the Gamorrean used his comlink to summon medical help, he might have been saved. That he was lucid enough to entomb himself meant that he was not so far gone that bacta therapy couldn't have helped him. He needn't have become what Gavin had seen in the shadows.

The pilot realized the blame lay not entirely with the Gamorrean himself. The black-market price for bacta was astronomical, so far out of reach for the average citizens that they could not imagine there was any bacta available for them. Those who did summon help, or had it summoned for them, were often so far gone that no therapy could help, so they never returned. As a result, other citizens saw the medivac units as thinly disguised extermination units that took the sick away and destroyed them.

Ignorance is killing these people.

Gavin forced himself to step forward and reenter the Gamorrean's hovel. The fetid stink returned to his nose and found accompaniment in the horrible sights and sounds that greeted him. The single-room hovel itself was scarcely larger than his own room in the squadron headquarters—and he found that a bit cramped for one. It had two doors—the one he'd opened using a lock-descrambling unit and a back door. A heating plate and water spigot to the left of the doorway marked the extent of the dwelling's kitchen facilities. The refresher station stood farther along that wall, in the corner.

Spattered blood covered all of it, sprayed along the floor, up the walls, and across the ceiling. It had dried and taken on a black hue, making the room look as if a shadow had exploded. The explosion's epicenter lay in the back corner, on a raised black platform that glistened in what little light made it in past Gavin.

A wet, gurgling sound pulsed arhythmically from that corner. On the platform, restrained by bedding twisted about him while in the throes of agony, the mortal shell of the Gamorrean named Tolra somehow clung to life. Gavin could see where the flesh had split, allowing leg and arm bones to protrude. The skin itself had thinned to a green-grey translucency and hung in ragged ribbons from ribs and fingers.

The Gamorrean seemed to sense Gavin's presence, because he turned to look at him. With a thick sucking sound, like cold grease being slathered over machine gears, the skull turned toward him while the fleshy sac encompassing it did not. The Gamorrean's horns and tusks gashed his own skin, then the thick muscles on the creature's neck snapped, leaving the massive skull to loll unnaturally in a puddle of viscous tissue.

A chill settled over Gavin. Though he knew Tolra was dead and that the disease had long since eaten away any trace of sapience, he nodded toward the Gamorrean. "You saved them. You did it. May the Force be with you."

Shivering, he turned and walked from the room. He sat down outside and stripped the filmplast covering off his boots, then tossed them back through the darkened doorway. He didn't bother to look up when a shadow fell over him. "He's dead."

Asyr crouched down beside him. "The clean team will get here shortly. Are you all right?"

Gavin thought a moment before he answered. "I will be, and I think that scares me."

"No reason it should."

"I think there is." He jerked a thumb toward the hovel. "There is a Gamorrean in there who has been turned into a mass of jelly. The disease killed him, but it did so in a way that didn't let him die until he could experience every fragment of pain possible. There's nothing left to him, but he was still breathing when I went in there. He was so tough, he probably lasted longer than a week in the end stages of the disease."

The Bothan stroked Gavin's cheek. "He fought the disease. That's good."

"Sure, but the fact that we can find something noble in this seems twisted." He shook his head. "I've seen more death in my time with Rogue Squadron than I have ever seen before, but nothing was so hideous as this. A year ago I would have run screaming. Now I just clean my boots and wait for guys with sterilizer units to show up. I'm changing and I'm not sure I like it."

Asyr smiled gently at him. "It's called maturing, Gavin, and not everyone likes it. Now me, I think you're maturing very well."

Gavin half-coughed a laugh. "Thanks, but I still have to wonder if it's right that we can see something like that and just continue on."

"We continue on, my dear, because we must." Asyr's voice developed an edge. "The Gamorrean, he summoned up the strength to lock others out and protect them. That was good. You and I, though, have a different mission. This disease doesn't appear to affect our species, so we have volunteered to help out during this public health crisis, but that is not our primary purpose here. Our mission is to fly our X-wings, to locate and destroy the kind of monsters who would do this kind of thing to others. Doing that requires all the maturity we can muster."

"I know." He rubbed a hand along her spine, then looked over to where Emtrey was conversing with an Emdeeoh and two men carrying portable plasma-incinerator units. The droid would take samples; then the men would burn everything in the hovel, including the first five millimeters of ferrocrete, to a white ash that would be vacuumed up and disposed of safely.

Gavin let Asyr help him to his feet. "You're right, of course. I hope we can accomplish our mission. If we don't, I'm afraid we'll have to take Coruscant down to bedrock, and I don't think even that will erase the scourge of the Empire from the galaxy."

I THINK EVEN STORMTROOPERS would find my men terrifyingly efficient. From the dark security of the grav-car's interior, Kirtan Loor watched as four Special Intelligence operatives clad in civilian garb approached the building's door. As huge and imposing as they were, they moved with a lethal fluidity their armor normally hid. Almost casually, one of them placed a thermite boring charge on the door lock and set it, then accepted a blaster carbine from a compatriot and flattened himself against the building's wall.

A red light blinked three times on the thermite charge, then a smoke-shrouded gout of white fire burst to hissing life. The harsh light transformed the shadowed Imperial Center street into a chiaroscuro landscape burned clean of imperfections but still full of menace. One of the operatives punched a hooked prybar through the center of the fire and yanked the door open, then his three compatriots dashed through.

The blue backlight of stun-fire strobed momentarily through the doorway and gaps in the window shading. Loor waited for a moment, then saw two more flashes. A human figure appeared in the doorway and nodded in his direction, then retreated into the shadows of the building's interior.

Loor opened the grav-car's door and emerged. He gathered a cloak about himself and pulled the hood up to conceal his face from incidental observation. He strode forward purposefully, but he imagined himself a pale imitation of Darth Vader. Tall and skeletally slender, with dark hair, he had been told he resembled a young Grand Moff Tarkin. While that comparison had been one he had used to his advantage, he would have preferred to inspire Vaderian terror in those with whom he dealt.

He squeezed past the two operatives at the doorway and stepped over the drooling Ithorian lying in the center of the antechamber. Beyond it, through a short corridor and past a third operative, he arrived in a room that resembled a rodent nest more than it did a human dwelling. It stank of mildew and old, musty sweat, though the occupant's new terror added piquant elements to the room's stale bouquet.

Loor looked down at the small, balding man pinned to the stained mattress by the muzzle of a blaster. "Your surroundings are so miserable, I am almost moved to pity you, Nartlo, but then, pity is wasted on the dead, isn't it?"

"What are you talking about?" The man's brown eyes bulged with terror. "I don't know you. What did I do?"

"True, you do not know me, but you have brokered some cure for friends of mine. It has been selling at a high price, but they tell me that you have told them the market has crashed. At the same time they noted that the supply of cure you returned to them had gone from 95 percent purity to 75 percent purity." Loor shook his head slowly, mournfully. "My friends feel you have lied to and cheated them."

"No, no, I didn't do that." Nartlo tried to claw his way into a sitting position, but the operative beside the makeshift bed kept him rooted in one spot. "I drew off some of the bacta as a sample, but a deal went bad and I lost it. I didn't figure they'd believe I lost it, so I tried to cover up what I'd done. I'm sorry."

"And stupid if you expect me to believe a story that was ancient when the Old Republic was born." Loor let anger into his voice and won a groan from his victim. Because of the surveillance he had on Nartlo, Loor did know that the story was not wholly false. Some of the bacta had been lost when a deal went sour, but only *some*. The rest of the missing cure had been donated to an alien pleasure house for the employees' own use. Nartlo had spent a week basking in their considerable gratitude. "Tell me we won't find a Rodian concubine's suckermarks on your back if we strip off your shirt."

Nartlo accompanied his curling up into a fetal ball with a low moan. "I owed some favors."

"You *gained* some favors, more than you owed." Loor took a step closer to the bed, forcing Nartlo to crane his neck back to look up at him. "Now you owe *me* favors."

"Anything you want, anything."

"Good." Loor turned to the right and nodded at the operative menacing the small man. The operative withdrew a step and Nartlo coughed as the pressure eased on his rib cage. "You told my friends that the market for cure had crashed. Explain."

"The Rebels picked up a lot of cure. I don't know when or where, but it was recent and was really very quiet. Rogue Squadron was involved, though, I know that much. I've been selling some of your cure to people who do business with people who work for people in the Provisional Council, see. They've been buying to be able to keep themselves and their supporters healthy—no matter the plague doesn't seem to affect them."

Loor smiled within the dark sanctum of his hood. The New Republic government had put into place programs that were designed to be fair to the victims of the Krytos virus. The scarcity of bacta meant virtually all of the public supply went to individuals who were infected, with the goal being to save their lives. By curing them, public health officials could limit the spread of the disease. Others, mostly those from uninfected populations, argued that a prophylactic use of bacta to prevent the spread to new populations would be best. Public health officials argued that there was no proof pre-exposure bacta therapy could prevent someone from becoming infected with the virus, but that did nothing to stem the desire to get bacta and use it as preventative medicine.

Nartlo swiped at spittle flecking the corners of his mouth. "Seems there's going to be enough now so the provos think they won't need their own supply."

Loor frowned. "Impossible. It would take a decade of bacta cartel production to satisfy the demand here."

"Could be, sir, could be, but right now the word is out that the New Republic's government has things under control."

"It's a lie, of course, but a good one." Loor slowly sank down onto his haunches, letting his cloak pool around him. "You believe this bacta supply exists?"

"I think some does, sir, yes, sir."

"You will learn about it. All about it."

Nartlo's eyes grew large again. "I don't know as I can, sir. Security is tight."

"You owe me, little man." Loor's growl cowed Nartlo. "You will go to your contacts and this time offer to buy cure at a good price."

"What if they don't want to sell?"

"Tell them that they will find exposure of their previous black market bacta dealings rather painful and embarrassing. If that is insufficient, perhaps making an example of one or more of them would be persuasive. I can and will do that." Loor nodded toward the operative to his right. "Blasters have more than just a stun setting on them, you know."

Nartlo licked at dry lips with a dry tongue. "Yes, sir, I know."

"Good. I want to know how much they have, how long they think their supply will last. I need to estimate when the price will climb again."

"I can understand that, sir."

And with that information I can begin to project how large a facility they would need to store it and how best to destroy it. Loor began to smile. *I could even just spread the rumor that they have more than enough bacta to cure everyone, then reveal the true amount they have in their stores. The gap between what is hoped for and what is real should create a lot of unrest. That is a suitable fall-back plan, and one which I can pursue while seeking out and destroying the containment facility.*

"And, Nartlo, you will try to find out whatever you can about their storage, transport, and distribution network. If I do go buying more bacta as a hedge against shortage, I would prefer to go directly to the source. I would like to cut out the middlemen, no offense intended."

"No, sir, none taken."

"Good, good. I'm glad we understand each other." Loor straightened up again. "I will be interested in hearing what you can find out."

Nartlo nodded enthusiastically. "You can count on me."

"I *am* counting on you. See to it that you do not fail me."

"Yes, sir." The small man shivered. "But, sir, I was wondering . . ."

"Yes?"

"How do I . . ."

Loor laughed in as sinister a manner as he could manage. "We will find you. Have something for me in two days."

"But that's not enough time."

"But it is all the time you have, Nartlo." Loor turned and swept from the room. The operatives crowded behind him and the two at the door preceded him to his grav-car. Loor climbed into the back, one of them got behind the controls, and the other three disappeared into the night. "Drive."

Inertial forces pushed Loor back into the car's plush upholstery. He began composing the report he would send off to Ysanne Isard. The fact that the Rebellion had gotten its hands on a new supply of bacta would not please her. She had wanted the demand for bacta to bankrupt the Rebellion, but Rogue Squadron's capture of more bacta meant it was not nearly as pricey for the Rebels as Iceheart desired. The only way to counteract that bit of luck was to locate and destroy the bacta store, which was exactly what he intended to do.

The problem is that no matter how quickly I resolve this matter, it will not be quick enough for her. It occurred to him that her messages to him suffered little reduction in their venom, despite having to be recorded and transmitted instead of being delivered in person. He would have thought that the distance between them would have insulated him from her criticisms, but it had not. She seemed to have a preternatural ability to point up to him errors he had made, no matter how slight, and that kept him constantly off balance.

He realized that if he told her he was having some of his people train for a strike on the bacta facility before he knew what that mission would take, she would point out that he was wasting time and resources. He decided he would put men into training for smaller missions that could serve as diversions or that would, at the very least, provide the training framework upon which the bacta strike mission could be built. Iceheart might maintain that he was wasting resources that could be better used to locate the bacta facility in the first place. But trying to argue that stormtroopers could be used as spies was not the sort of blunder Isard would make.

The grav-car broke free of sub-urban roadway and shot up

into the night sky. Countless towers flashed past, each lit as brilliantly as the fire of the thermite charge, but not nearly as harshly. He wondered how many of the people and aliens living in those towers were rejoicing over the secret word that their worries about the Krytos virus would soon be over. *Many. Too many.*

Loor let his own laughter become a parody of the sound he imagined echoing through those towers. It struck him that laughter and sobbing were really not that different, and decided that he would do his best to see to it that others gained firsthand knowledge of this insight.

Before they die of the virus for which I will destroy the cure.

11

ADMIRAL ACKBAR SAT back in his Council chair and tried to pull serenity from the cool mist drifting down over him. Grand Moff Tarkin, in one of his more expansive moods, had once described politics to him as "soft warfare, the elegant duel of lightsabers instead of the thunder of turbo-lasers." Tarkin, with that description, had given no evidence of finding political fights frustrating because of the posturing and the treacherous riptide shifts of allegiances.

Or the inability to come to grips with problems in a direct manner. Ackbar had endured more reports on microeconomic fluctuations on planets he'd never heard of than any sapient creature could be expected to stand in one lifetime. Slowly, in working through the reports, Borsk Fey'lya and Sian Tevv were moving toward the matter that had been bruited about on the Provisional Council's staff level.

Glancing over at the Bothan councilor, Ackbar could see a feral gleam in Fey'lya's violet eyes. *The Bothans thrive on this soft warfare.* Ackbar had already recognized in Fey'lya a drive to lead or, when he had been outmaneuvered, a desire to vault out in front to where the leaders stood so he was placed among them. Ackbar had seen similar tactics among warriors who sought promotion, but true warfare tended to deal with such ambition in a most lethal fashion.

Mon Mothma nodded toward the Elom councilor. "Thank you, Verrinnefra, for bringing us up to date on the economies of our newest worlds. Next on the agenda is the matter of bacta. Borsk, you have a point to make?"

The cream-furred Bothan stood opposite Ackbar. "The recent mission which has liberated a supply of bacta and brought it here to Coruscant is, of course, a great victory for us and a great boon to the people here. For that we owe much thanks and praise to Admiral Ackbar and his staff. Their success also brings with it some burdens, not the least of which is the need to take precautions to prevent Warlord Zsinj from exacting retribution from us."

Ackbar leaned forward. "Forgive me the interruption, Councilor Fey'lya, but it strikes me that you are asking us to deal with the undertow before the wave has crested."

"Excuse me?"

Princess Leia smiled. "I believe the Admiral is pointing out that the supply of bacta brings with it far more pressing problems than a possible attack by Warlord Zsinj."

"More correctly, Princess, I meant to say that because an attack by Warlord Zsinj has always been possible, both before and after our strike, there have long been plans in place to deal with such. I am more than willing to review those plans, but I think the core problem with bacta needs to be addressed more quickly than the surface issue of Zsinj. Trouble is a vast ocean, and for us, bacta distribution is the issue lurking in the depths."

The Bothan's fur rippled. "There is indeed much to discuss on the matter of bacta distribution. With the supply we now have, I think it should be possible to create centers for preventative therapy to stop the spread of the virus. My people tell me that an hour's mist therapy per week should be sufficient to destroy the virus before it has a chance to incubate. Creating centers that would allow that much treatment would go a long way toward quelling the fear that has gripped this world."

Leia frowned. "I've seen no such reports concerning mist therapy. The review of the data we captured from General Derricote's lab does not show evidence of any testing in that regard. In fact, the only data the Imperials had on the Krytos virus showed massive amounts of bacta would be required to cure patients—having the effect of draining our supplies of bacta. There is no reason to suppose creating the centers you advocate would do anything but waste more bacta."

"Ah, Leia, I would have expected more compassion from you." Fey'lya glanced down at her. "If it were humans who were dropping dead of this plague, you would be the first to advocate creation of these centers."

Leia's dark eyes flashed coldly. "And you think I do not support your plan because it would save non-humans?"

"I would like to think better of you, but I know you have various constituencies to worry about. Like Admiral Ackbar, you would like to see some of the bacta reserved for use by our military. I understand this, for saving the lives of our valiant warriors is certainly commendable. I fear, however, your hedge against the unseen means there are countless individuals who might sicken and die and never get a chance to enter the military and fight for their freedom."

Doman Beruss raised a hand. "I think, Councilor Fey'lya, you do Princess Leia and every other human member of the Council a disservice by even hinting that opposition to your plan is based on an anti-alien bias."

"Ah, but even you are prey to it, Councilor Beruss. You refer to us as 'alien' and the Princess called us 'non-human.' Why are we defined by you and in comparison to you? Humanity certainly has contributed much to the Rebellion, but it did so because the Empire had done all it could to suppress and subjugate the species it saw as harmful and aberrant. Humans—being those who learned their trade at the hands of our Imperial masters—were the only people capable of taking a leadership role in the actual Rebellion. The rest of us contributed as we could, and made great contributions—contributions that led to the successful conclusion of the major campaigns in the Rebellion.

"I do not accuse you of being wholly unfeeling, but I think your perspective in this matter is compromised." Fey'lya smoothed the fur on the top of his head. "I believe the matter of bacta distribution is one that should be decided by those of us whose people are prey to the virus."

Ackbar rose from his chair and slapped a hand against the table top. "In that case, Councilor Fey'lya, you will also be required to recuse yourself from any decisions in this matter."

"What?"

"There is no known case of any Bothan being afflicted with the disease." *I have no doubt Iceheart wanted you Bothans to survive so you could help split the Alliance.* "Sullustans and Shistavanens have been infected, leaving open the very real possibility that Wookiees could find themselves susceptible to the virus. Quarren have died from it, leaving the Mon Calamari population vulnerable. I have heard of no Elom who have become ill, but Twi'lek, Gamorrean, and Trandoshan populations have, so the possibility of the disease jumping to the Elom is not out of the question."

The Bothan's fur rose on head and shoulders, but Ackbar ignored the signs of Fey'lya's anger. "Moreover, from a public health standpoint, your plan of therapy centers is more of a risk than it is a help. The facilities you suggest would call for vast numbers of people congregating in an environment where contact with infectious fluids is not difficult to imagine. And, even if there were studies to show bacta mist did kill the virus, using it carelessly promotes the chance of a bacta-resistant strain of the virus being passed among people who believe they are being protected from it. If such a strain does appear, we will be powerless to stop the plague from destroying the galaxy."

The Bothan kept his voice low. "What, pray do tell, would you suggest, then?"

"First and foremost, we secure the water supply. We have evidence to suggest the virus was introduced into the planetary water supply, and for all we know, there are pockets of virus frozen in the glaciers just waiting to be melted before they become virulent again. Second, we continue the intensive therapy to control and cure those populations we know are infected. It is important to note here, I think, that human medtechs have been tireless in caring for victims of the virus. Their immunity to the disease certainly means they have less to fear than others, but that immunity in no way makes it incumbent upon them to help out the way they have."

Ackbar held a hand up. "Third and final, we need to deal with the black market. The rumors of a supply of bacta arriving on Coruscant have depressed the prices, but estimates of how much we got from Zsinj are grossly high. When the truth comes out, prices will begin to rise, and selling off portions of the supply will become very attractive. If we don't have our supply depleted through profiteering, we stand a good chance of buying enough time to obtain more bacta from Thyferra and solving our problem once and for all. If not, we will find ourselves bankrupt and dying of the virus."

The Bothan opened his hands. "So you think we should just continue to proceed in the manner in which we have gone about things so far?"

"No, by no means." Ackbar looked around the room and then up at the misting system. "We argue here whether bacta-mist therapy has any value, yet we have a system installed here to protect us. All of us, including the humans, know affluent members of our populations have purchased bacta on the black market to use in their own preventative therapy. And, I have no doubt, people have come to you since the news of our victory has leaked out, asking you to procure bacta for them. While I know none of us would agree to such a thing, the perception that we might, and that there is special treatment for some selected folks going on, is one that will heighten the panic our people are feeling."

Sian Tevv sniffed. "This virus is more than panic, Ackbar. It is real and deadly."

"Agreed, but our actions make it deadlier still. If one person believes there is no hope for himself, that there will be no cure when he needs it, he might not seek treatment. A day's delay not only can cost him his life, but can infect his family and friends. The fact is that if we project the image that says the virus can and will be defeated, everyone will do what they can to defeat it."

Leia smiled. "It's the same morale-building technique that kept us going during the dark days after Derra IV and Hoth."

The black-furred Wookiee councilor's bark flowed into a murmur, and Leia's gold protocol droid translated. "Ambassador Kerrithrarr suggests treating the virus as an enemy against which everyone is enlisted. With discipline and direction the spread can be minimized."

Ackbar nodded at the Wookiee. "An apt analogy."

Borsk Fey'lya's eyes narrowed. "A military model might well be sufficient to deal with the virus, but do you suggest we use it to curtail black market trading? Having storm-troopers breaking into private homes to deprive people of bacta supplies will hardly endear us to our people."

Mon Mothma shook her head. "No such thing is advocated. General Cracken is devoting a certain amount of his energy to this problem, and is working to put the New Republic Security Force together. The NRSF will replace the old Imperial Sector Ranger force, and is meant to be a law enforcement and counter-insurgency force. It will be some time before the force will be ready to administer all that needs to be dealt with here, but we have an offer for dealing with our law enforcement needs in the interim."

Mon Mothma used her comlink. "Please send Vorru in."

Ackbar saw the hackles go up on Fey'lya and felt his own

flesh crawl. The doors to the chamber opened, and through them walked a small human with a thick head of white hair. From his size, which was not that big, even for a human, he could have easily been dismissed as benign, yet a warrior's instinct told Ackbar that was just an image Vorru sought to project.

He'd met the man once before, when Fliry Vorru, then an Imperial Moff, had been a guest of Tarkin. The two men were physical opposites, but so alike in temperament and spirit that Ackbar had wished they would turn on each other and destroy one another. That didn't happen, though circumstances soon conspired to get Vorru sentenced to Kessel, where he had remained until he had been freed and returned to Coruscant as part of the Rebel operation to take the planet.

Vorru looked up and Ackbar read pure cunning in his dark eyes. "I thank you for seeing me, esteemed Councilors. I thank you for my freedom. I find myself in a position to repay the debt I owe you."

Leia's head came up. "You don't consider your part in the liberation of Coruscant to have canceled that debt?"

"If the truth be told, Princess Leia, I do not." Vorru stiffened formally, then bowed his head. "The liberation of the planet would have been accomplished more smoothly and efficiently if not for the treacherous behavior of one of my lieutenants. While I did not know Zekka Thyne was working for Imperial Intelligence agents, I must accept responsibility for his actions. In effect, the liberation proceeded without my help, so my debt to you remains."

A pained expression passed over his face. "You brought me here in the hope that I could revive Black Sun and turn it into a force that would aid the effort to take Coruscant from the Empire. I did what I could, but the fact is that the Imperial effort to expunge the remnants of Xizor's organization were as ruthlessly efficient as only Darth Vader's vengeance could be. What little of the leadership remained was destroyed in internecine battling. When I arrived here there was a paucity of leadership and an insufficient amount of time to once again establish control over the various factions present on Coruscant. Durga the Hutt and others resist unification, so Black Sun is effectively dead."

Ackbar sat back in his chair. "I would have expected more regret in your voice at that pronouncement."

Vorru shrugged. "Black Sun was Xizor's dream, not mine."

Fey'lya folded his arms across his chest and remained standing. "And your dream is . . . ?"

"Freedom, the same as your dream." Vorru smiled. "The Empire treated criminals the same way it treated you Rebels. With the Empire's grip broken, you Rebels have become the New Republic and have gained legitimacy. The criminals who have long been repressed by the Empire are not all evil, but many have been trapped in a cycle of lawlessness precisely because they knew they could expect no mercy from the Empire. While they were not Rebels, they were no less victims of Imperial repression.

"To bring things to the point quickly, we no longer wish to be treated as criminals. We want a chance to gain legitimacy and lead normal lives. For this we realize we need to offer you something of value, and so we shall. We know the ways of the black market. We know how to disrupt it and break it. We know the ways of criminals and how to disrupt their activities. We know the underworld of Coruscant and we know how to bring to justice those you want to punish."

Doman Beruss stared at Vorru. "You want us to make you the Commissioner of the Coruscant Constabulary?"

"I do not think you that foolish, Doman Beruss. I knew your father and mother and I know you cannot be easily deceived." A smile came readily to Vorru's face—a smile Ackbar did not trust. "What I want is for my people to be allowed to administer the law in the underworld here. Your Security Force will have more than enough to do with the areas of Coruscant where you can project power. We already have various off-world populations forming their own militias and civil defense corps, so why not tolerate a similar force created out of my people?"

Mon Mothma arched an eyebrow at Vorru. "Very few others have as colorful a history as you do, Fliry Vorru."

"But some of those who have equally notorious backgrounds are continuing in service to the government, though the leadership and philosophy have changed."

Ackbar slowly nodded. The realities of governing a vast panoply of worlds necessitated using the Imperial governmental apparatus to maintain communication and order. While a wholesale replacement of the bureaucracy would have been ideal, the fact was that, just as the Rebel military had relied on people with Imperial training, so the government was being forced to rely on clerks and administrators who had faithfully served the Empire until it fell. While most of these people had an allegiance to their jobs and not to the government, the tacit clemency granted to them in return for continuing to work did not sit well with many of the Rebels.

Fliry Vorru presented an interesting case. He *had* directly contributed to the winning of Coruscant. While he underplayed his contribution, Vorru could easily have turned Rogue Squadron over to the Imperials, preventing the Rebel conquest of the planet. His support, despite the betrayal of subordinates, had facilitated the Rebel victory, making him a valuable ally.

And his request of us is an ally's request for trust. Ackbar half-closed his eyes. Vorru's request also made sense from a purely pragmatic position. While Cracken's law enforcement organization would soon be functioning fully, it would never have been as effective in the underworld as Vorru would be. The Palpatine Counter-insurgency Front, black marketeering, and a dozen other problems needed attention on Coruscant, and yet Cracken still needed to attend to intelligence matters involving Warlord Zsinj *and* Ysanne Isard, wherever she was.

Vorru opened his hands. "The question I place before you is this: will you grant me and my people the trust we have earned?"

Leia's eyes hardened. "The Empire was a common enemy we had between us, hence our alliance. In acting against them you *have* earned trust, but I suspect you see the account more fully than we do."

"This is true, Leia, but Vorru's point is well taken." Mon Mothma pressed her hands gently against the table top. "The fight against the Empire is truly what bound the Alliance together. We must build on that basic level of trust if we expect the Republic to thrive. As long as Fliry Vorru's people are willing to abide by the conduct standards we set for our law enforcement and militia forces, they will remain within the bounds of our trust. If they step outside those guidelines, they will be outside their lawful duty and will be dealt with in a suitable manner."

"You will find me a most able and loyal servant in this matter, Mon Mothma."

"So I trust, Fliry Vorru."

"So we must *all* trust," Ackbar murmured.

Something dark flashed through Vorru's eyes as he turned toward the Mon Calamari. "I would have thought you above veiled threats, Admiral Ackbar."

"I *am* above them." Ackbar's mouth dropped open in a Mon Calamari grin. "I merely meant that we must take your word concerning your loyalty because your previous masters are all dead, and the greatest of them through our efforts. If you choose to read a threat in *that* set of facts, I cannot stop you from doing so."

"But if I get out of hand you will destroy me?"

"You have earned trust." Ackbar leaned forward and gave Vorru a wall-eyed stare. "Spend it unwisely and I will do what I must to settle your account."

12

A LL THE WHILE in the back of the grav-cab, Wedge tried to puzzle out what Mirax had found on the *Pulsar Skate* that could threaten the Alliance. With anyone else Wedge would have made an allowance for hyperbole, but Mirax had never been prone to melodrama. *In fact, she tends to see issues and emergencies rather clearly.*

Wedge shivered. Once before the Ashern rebels of Thyferra had inserted a virus into bacta shipments that induced an allergy to bacta in those who were treated with it. This, in effect, left them without treatment for a whole host of ills. If Mirax possessed evidence that the batch of bacta stolen from Zsinj had been similarly contaminated, not only would it doom millions of people to die from the Krytos virus, but the withdrawal of the bacta from the health services system on Coruscant would spark riots that would kill many more people.

That would surely rip the Alliance apart. Non-humans would say that the bacta was being hoarded for use by humans in case the Krytos virus jumped species and began to kill them. Humans would also be blamed if non-humans were hurt or killed by the contaminated bacta, and any attempt to blame the contamination on the Ashern rebels would be decried as false and part of a human conspiracy, since it was well known that the Zaltin and Xucphra combines were run by humans.

Let it be anything else but bad bacta.

Wedge had the droid flying the cab let him off three blocks and two levels from the hangar where Mirax kept the *Pulsar Skate*. While he wanted to get there as quickly as possible, the urgency in her voice kindled a desire for caution in him. He'd learned a lot from Mirax's father, Booster Terrik, about the need for caution, especially at those times when events seemed to be moving too fast to allow any delay. Wedge regretted the lack of a sidearm, but he did have a comlink and took a moment to preset it to the squadron's emergency frequency.

He forced himself to slow down as he wandered toward the hangar. He stopped to look at the holographic displays set in shop windows or to read the latest news as it sped past on the omnipresent news-scrolls. With each stop he looked around and tried to spot anyone paying over much attention to his presence. He saw no signs he was being followed, but took the added precaution of wandering into a tapcaf, going out through the lower level, then coming back up and heading to the hangar.

At the door Wedge announced himself. The computer got a good voiceprint match, then opened the door. Wedge stepped through into the security lock area. After the door closed behind him, another door in front of him opened up and allowed him into the hangar itself.

A smile slowly spread across his face as he looked at the *Pulsar Skate*. The modified *Baudo*-class yacht had the overall shape of a broad-bladed dagger. The twin engines at the aft formed an abbreviated hilt. The broadest parts of the blade curved down to form gentle wings that swept up to a rounded prow. The ship very much did resemble the Corellian deep-sea skate for which it was named. It had sailed through a lot of parsecs between the time its hull was first welded and its current presence on Coruscant.

He quickly crossed the darkened hangar floor and made his way up the loading ramp. At the top of the gangway he nodded to Liat Tsayv. The Sullustan returned the nod without comment, and raised the muzzle of his blaster carbine enough so Wedge could pass unmenaced. The normally voluble Sullustan's grim silence gave Wedge a measure of how serious Mirax thought the situation was and filled him with a sense of dread.

He made his way past the galley and crew lounge to the hold. The hatch stood open, and through it he could see Mirax sitting on a duraplast crate. She looked well, though she still wore her brown hair in a long braid that she doubled up and fastened at the back of her head. She'd started wearing her hair that way since Corran's death and Wedge remembered her having done the same thing when her father had first been sent away to Kessel. *That's Mirax being serious and remote, walling her feelings off so she doesn't have to deal with the pain.*

A single red light provided all the illumination for the hold, yet it did little more than illuminate a two-meter-wide globe within which Mirax sat. Everything else remained in shadow, yet from the way Mirax looked out into the darkness, Wedge could tell something alive lurked there.

A cold chill shot down his spine, and all manner of irrational thoughts exploded in his brain. He paused in the hatchway and stared out into the blackness, trying to see what captivated Mirax's attention. He thought he saw red light glint off a rounded black dome, which he translated into Darth Vader's helmet. *No, he's dead. It can't be him again.*

Wedge smiled at Mirax. "I'm here. How are you doing?"

"I'm holding it together, Wedge, really." Her tone matched the hopeful nature of her words, giving Wedge reason to feel slightly relieved. "Thanks for getting here so fast. I don't know who else could help me with this, but it turns out you were their choice anyway."

Mirax gestured off into the darkest part of the hold. "Wedge Antilles, this is Qlaern Hirf, a Vratix native of Thyferra and a proud member of the Ashern Circle."

"The honor is ours, Commander Antilles." The voice from the shadows came deep and deliberate. Wedge heard his name pronounced with respectful precision; the hard sounds—the C in Wedge's title and the *t* in his name—were slightly abbreviated, as if snapped instead of spoken. Ooryl Qrygg, the squadron's Gand, produced similar sounds when he spoke, though even bringing to mind the image of the exoskeletoned pilot did not fully prepare Wedge for his first sight of the Vratix.

Qlaern moved from the shadows and into the circle of light slowly and benignly. The insectoid creature's head featured two bulging compound eyes, and Wedge realized it was light reflected from one of these that his imagination had transformed into Vader's headgear. The Vratix's bent antennae dangled over its triangular face, and its curved mandibles remained pressed one against the other.

The Vratix's stalk-like neck broadened into a cylindrical thorax and abdomen. The first of three pairs of limbs, which hung from the point where the neck joined the thorax, consisted of two trifold arms that ended in three long, delicate fingers and a thicker thumb, and sprouted stout hook-claws from the middle arm segment. The second and third sets of limbs were legs, yet they were mismatched. The middle legs connected with the body below what would have been the ribs on a human. Longer and far more powerfully built than the other pair of legs, their configuration led Wedge to imagine the Vratix capable of great leaps and savage kicks in combat. The last pair of limbs were certainly more than vestigial, serving as they did to keep the Vratix's abdomen from dragging on the ground, but they reminded Wedge of little more than the landing gear on an X-wing: useful to have when you need them, but built to be tucked away when work had to be done.

The Vratix body appeared to have a uniformly grey color to it, but Wedge put that down to the lack of light in the hold. The claws on its forearms were black, but with lighter flecks, which led Wedge to believe the black color was cosmetically applied, not something native to the creature itself.

"I am pleased to meet you, Qlaern Hirf." Wedge smiled and extended a hand toward the Vratix.

Qlaern's hand came in toward Wedge's, then moved past it and came up. The Vratix brushed its fingers over Wedge's face. The creature's flesh, which Wedge expected to be cold and hard like armor, was dry and warm. While he could feel the solidity of the exoskeleton beneath it, the scaly texture of the skin covering the Vratix somehow made the creature seem less alien to Wedge.

Mirax reached out and brushed a hand over the flesh of Qlaern's right foreknee. "The Vratix find both sound and vision to be deceptive senses. As Qlaern reports it, both sight and sound are things that are of the past the moment you perceive them. Only touch reports information that is concurrent with the gathering."

"Interesting perspective." Wedge shifted his hand around to grip the Vratix's arm above the curved spikes. "Qlaern, you are the Ashern agent who tipped us to the presence of the bacta that Zsinj had captured?"

"We are responsible for that occurrence." Qlaern tilted his head to the right and then the left. "We would have preferred to transfer the bacta directly to you, but this was not possible. Our affluence is not such that we could present our gift in the manner we wished."

Wedge frowned. "I am not certain I understand what you are saying."

Mirax scooted over on the crate. "Sit down, Wedge. This gets complicated."

Wedge sat beside her. "Am I going to like this?"

"Parts of it, sure." Mirax smiled weakly at him. "At least, I think you will."

Qlaern spread his forelegs slightly to bring his face down to their level. "You know of our world."

"Some. Thyferra is a world in the Polith system, quite temperate in nature and an excellent world for agriculture. Thyferra is where bacta is produced and distributed by Zaltin and

Xucphra, the two corporations that have a monopoly on the bacta trade. The corporations are decidedly feudal in nature, with humans de facto governing a world where the Vratix are the majority."

The Vratix's head bobbed on the end of its neck. "Good. Not as much as she who is Mirax knows, but good."

"Please, tell me what I do not know."

"We have insufficient time for that, we think." Qlaern's head craned back as a sibilant hiss issued from its mouth.

Wedge looked at Mirax. "Sarcasm? A laugh?"

"I think so."

"Forgive us, but so many times we find humans say things they do not mean."

"Ah, then tell me what you believe I need to know."

"Much better." The Vratix settled a hand on Wedge's knee. "The healing properties of bacta were discovered during the days of the Old Republic. It was apparent to all that bacta was a miracle cure for many ailments and infirmities. The corporations which now control Thyferra and bacta made narrow profits, but made them on a wider range of sales. They set up many satellite manufacturing centers, all under license, all with Vratix verachen overseeing the final processes no matter where they took place. The thought then was to beat competition by producing better bacta for less than anyone else could."

"You mean there once was competition for the bacta market?"

"For more time than there has not been, but all of it before you were born. The Clone Wars made one thing abundantly clear—a supply of bacta could heal even the most grievously wounded soldiers and render them receptive to mechanical replacement limbs. This meant they could return to combat, saving the military the cost of training new warriors. As a pilot you know how much expense goes into training, so the saving is clear."

"And I know many a pilot, myself included, who owes his life to bacta therapy."

ROGUE SQUADRON: THE KRYTOS TRAP   103

"So it is." Qlaern nodded solemnly. "The Emperor decided that the only group that should have a guaranteed supply of bacta was his military. He systematically suppressed small manufacturers of bacta in favor of Zaltin and Xucphra. They realized greater profits by letting the marketplace set the price and utilized Imperial soldiers to wipe out independent growers and to round up all the verachen to return them to Thyferra."

Wedge frowned. "Twice now you have used the word 'verachen.'"

"We are verachen." Qlaern tapped his free hand against his thorax. "Bacta is an organic product made through the blending of alazhi with kavam. Kavam is itself a compound made of other ingredients. Alazhi, because it is grown, comes in various potencies depending upon location, soil content, rainfall, and even spontaneous mutation. Verachen oversee the proper combination of these components into the bacta. Each lot has a minimum potency, but sometimes the bacta will be most potent and work extremely well. Such is the batch we have presented to you as our gift."

"Gift?" Wedge placed his hand atop Qlaern's hand. "Please do not think me dense, but there are some things you say as if you expect me to already understand them."

"Forgive us. We have been foolish."

"That's partially my fault, Wedge." Mirax added her hand to the pile on Wedge's knee. "The Vratix are not exactly a hive mind, but there does appear to be surface thought exchange among Vratix who spend a lot of time in close proximity to one another. The reason 'verachen' is plural is that while Qlaern here might be the supervisor in charge of a batch process, Qlaern will have subordinates who act almost as remotes, reporting back and receiving orders on a subsensory level of some sort. Qlaern may have been under the impression you and I similarly shared thoughts."

"So you know what he's talking about?"

"I think so—and, actually, Qlaern is not a *he* per se. The Vratix can both father and bear young, depending upon stages in their life cycle, which I guess is rather long." She inclined her head toward the Vratix. "When it speaks of the Clone Wars, it's speaking from life experience."

"Huh?" Wedge smiled. "So, will you clear up this gift thing for me?"

"Sure, if you don't mind, Qlaern."

"We are grateful for your aid."

Mirax drew in a deep breath. "The Vratix have made you a gift of the bacta and all that entails."

"Why me?"

Qlaern's antennae twitched. "Your fame has made you known to us. You are known as a fair and wise man who values loyalty. This we value as well."

Wedge's eyes narrowed. "I appreciate that, but I still don't understand. What's in this for the Vratix?"

The Vratix inclined its head toward Mirax. "This you must explain, for you will do it better than we will."

Mirax nodded, then took another deep breath. "The Vratix are giving this bacta to you because they want you, Wedge Antilles, to represent them before the Provisional Council. They want to join the New Republic."

"What?" Wedge's surprise at being asked to represent the Vratix immediately faded beneath a sense of disaster. Thyferra was the sole supplier of bacta, but the world had steadfastly remained neutral in the civil war. Everyone believed that this was so they could gouge both the Empire and the Alliance, thus enriching themselves while the war raged. To keep Thyferra happy, the Alliance had even inducted two of its human residents—one from a Zaltin family and the other from a Xucphra family—into Rogue Squadron. Bror Jace, the pilot representing the Zaltin corporation, had been killed fighting against the Empire. Erisi Dlarit, the other Thyferran, still flew with the squadron, and viewed the Ashern as murdering terrorist monsters.

And there's the problem. If the New Republic granted the Ashern any sort of status, the Thyferran government would react harshly and swiftly. Any hope of getting bacta from the cartel—no matter how successful Erisi's backdoor efforts in that regard might be—would die quickly and horribly. If the bacta supply dried up, the Krytos virus would ravage Coruscant and, quite likely, spread to other worlds and kill billions of individuals.

If I refuse the request . . . then what? Wedge looked up at Qlaern. "The bacta you made available to us, there's nothing wrong with it, is there? We're not in a situation where you have to mix something else in for it to be effective, such that if I refuse your request, the bacta will be useless or harmful, are we?"

Qlaern's mandibles clicked open and shut again. "There was once a case where verachen fouled a batch of bacta. The reasons for that action were sound. The results of that action were unacceptable. The Vratix ask for your help, but cannot do so at the expense of your people. The bacta, it is a gift to you. So is this verachen."

"What?"

"We have come here to Coruscant because we know you cannot jeopardize your people by taking up our cause. As verachen we have ways and means to mix up more than just bacta, or to make bacta more effective. We are here to learn of this Krytos virus and to stop it."

"But this virus could kill you."

Qlaern shrugged. "Great risk is necessary to defeat great evil. You know this."

Wedge slowly smiled. "That I do. Your offer impresses me, but I cannot act alone in this. I have people to whom I must speak."

Mirax raised an eyebrow. "Not the Council, right?"

"No, not the Council, not right off. I only really have one choice: General Cracken. If word of Qlaern's presence gets out, or Erisi catches wind of the Vratix working with us, Thyferra will hear about it quickly and we'll be stuck. Cracken can provide security and whatever resources Qlaern will need to do the job."

Mirax smiled. "And it might distract him from persecuting Tycho."

"It might do that, indeed."

The Vratix hissed sharply. "It is a beneficent balm that soothes more than one wound."

"Agreed." Wedge stood and clapped the Vratix on both shoulders. "I'm glad you're here, Qlaern Hirf, because there're plenty of wounds to be found, and decidedly little soothing going on. If you can do anything—anything more than you've already done—to stop the Krytos virus, I'll gladly represent you before the Council and, if need be, even take your case to Thyferra itself."

13

A JOLT RAN THROUGH Nawara Ven and traveled out to the tips of his lekku, making them twitch. He immediately blushed, bluing the shadows on his grey cheeks and beneath his eyes. *If I do not have more control than this, Tycho is lost.* He pulled his braintails back so they dangled beneath the level of the defense table. *No reason to let the opposition read involuntary motion as a sign of my nervousness.*

His nervousness would not be denied, however. The trial was being held—*staged* was the term he preferred to use—in the old Imperial Justice Court. High vaulted ceilings had been covered with polished black marble panels streaked with white, giving the whole room the feeling of actually being on a high promontory and open to the night sky. The black marble had also been used to build up the High Bench at which the Tribunal would sit, rather ominously; it reminded Nawara of the Imperial Palace's towering edifice.

Below the ceiling level, stainless steel, molded ferrocrete, and duraplast castings completed the court's design. While the forms meshed perfectly with the stone shapes, the rest of the room seemed artificial and not a little sterile. *This room does not seem conducive to compassion.* Nawara looked around at the upper gallery and the seats in the court, which were packed with individuals slavering for justice.

Justice, in this case, means they want my client shot into the sun. Admiral Ackbar had acquiesced to Nawara's request that the trial not be sent out in real-time holo. While it could have been argued that news of the trial had already done as much damage to Tycho's reputation as it would be possible to do, broadcasting the trial could easily serve to further inflame public sentiment and cause trouble. Nawara had already been questioned about defending a *human*, and that sort of thing would only get worse if everyone in the galaxy was able to watch the trial unfold.

The discussion about broadcasting the trial had been the subject of an executive session of the Provisional Council. Borsk Fey'lya had tried to argue that justice conducted in the shadows was just a continuation of Imperial policy. Nawara had countered that a publicly broadcast trial abandoned any pretense of justice and became a sporting event where a man's life hung in the balance. He argued that *how* the Republic conducted the trial was as important as the outcome, because any perception of injustice, no matter how slight, would get magnified and form the core for discontent and dissent.

And they agreed with Ackbar to keep things limited to news summaries. It's not much, but it's something. He shook his head. *Now if I blow it, at least folks won't know it until later.*

Across from him, Commander Halla Ettyk rose from her place at the prosecution table. Athletically trim and tall, Ettyk cut a very commanding figure with just a hint of lean menace to her. She wore her black hair gathered back into a thick braid—somewhat reminiscent of Princess Leia's current hairstyle—providing Nawara an unobstructed view of her strong-jawed profile. Fire filled her brown eyes as she glanced at him, then turned her attention toward the tribunal.

"If it please the court, we will call our first witness."

Ackbar nodded. "Please, Commander."

"The Prosecution calls Lieutenant Pash Cracken to the stand."

Nawara hit a couple of keys on his datapad, calling up the deposition Pash had given him earlier. He let his eyes track over the Rylothean script, but did so only to cover his surprise at Ettyk's choice of lead witness. He had fully expected her to start with Iella Wessiri or General Cracken to establish a connection between Tycho and Imperial Intelligence. Instead, by calling Pash first, she appeared to want to firmly set up Tycho's having the motive, means, and opportunity for killing Corran, then work backward into the larger treason picture.

I should have seen that coming. Since the great public hue and cry about the case had pushed the treason angle, that was the vector he'd expected Ettyk to take in presenting her case. He'd thought she'd establish the treason, then show that Corran's murder was necessitated to cover the treason. By coming at it the other way around and establishing the murder, she got treason by implication, and all the evidence she presented after that just went to bolster a fact she had previously proved.

"This pitches our defense into the Bright Lands," muttered Nawara.

Tycho leaned over toward him as Pash stepped into the witness box and was sworn in. "What do you mean?"

"There is ample circumstantial evidence to show you killed Corran. Emtrey could convince a jury of droid-haters that you certainly *could* have killed Corran. I could baffle a jury by pointing out how many others could have done the job, but the Tribunal is going to be tough." Nawara narrowed his pink eyes. "I had hoped we'd have to fight over treason first, since it's a weaker charge, but we'll have to deal with this first."

Tycho gave Nawara a confident smile. "You'll get me out of this."

"I will."

Ettyk moved out from behind the prosecution table with the supple ease of a taopari stalking prey. "Lieutenant Cracken, your service record has already been appended to the transcripts of this trial, so I will not ask for a recitation of your numerous citations and awards won in service to the Alliance. I would, however, like you to think back to the events that led up to the night when Coruscant fell to our forces. Can you do that?"

"Yes." Pash nodded and a lock of red hair curled down over his forehead.

"Good." Ettyk gave him a polite smile. "Where were you at that time?"

"Here, on Coruscant."

"And you were present on Coruscant as part of an assignment given to Rogue Squadron?"

"Yes."

"Did that assignment include orders that posted Captain Celchu to Coruscant?"

Pash shook his head. "I only know *my* orders for the assignment, Commander. My orders contained nothing that referred to Captain Celchu."

"So, at the time you left your base to travel to Coruscant, you expected Captain Celchu to be where?"

"Objection!" Nawara stood. "The question is irrelevant *and* the prosecution has provided no foundation to show the witness could answer it."

Admiral Ackbar nodded slowly. "Sustained on the relevance grounds. Lieutenant Cracken's expectations are immaterial, Commander Ettyk."

"Yes, Admiral."

"And you, Counselor Ven, need not stack objections. We'll take them as they come in, shall we?"

Nawara nodded. "I appreciate the court's admonition and I shall remember it." He returned to his seat and forced himself to breathe slowly. *You aren't going to win this case with the first witness. Be careful but not so eager.*

"Lieutenant Cracken, there came a point during the operation here on Coruscant in which the squadron's personnel were drawn together, correct?"

"Yes."

"And Captain Celchu was not among those people, correct?"

"He was not there, no."

"But there was news of him, was there not?"

Pash leaned back in the witness chair. "Yes."

"One report was that an attack by Warlord Zsinj on the base at Noquivzor had hit Rogue Squadron's staff hard and that Tycho Celchu was among the missing."

"Yes."

"Who delivered that report?"

"Commander Antilles."

"After hearing that report, you believed what about Captain Celchu?"

Pash glanced down at his hands. "I thought he was dead. He was listed as 'missing in action,' but you learn that really means 'dead, and we don't have enough pieces left to fill a thimble, so we can't prove it.' I expected we'd get confirmation of his death fairly quickly."

Ettyk gathered her hands at the small of her back. "There was another story told about Captain Celchu, yes?"

"Yes."

"Who told that story?"

"Lieutenant Horn."

"What did Lieutenant Horn say about Captain Celchu?"

"Objection, hearsay."

"Exception, Admiral: The statement Lieutenant Cracken will relate was told against Lieutenant Horn's best interest."

"What?" Nawara Ven's jaw dropped open. "How is what Corran said about the defendant going to be against Corran's best interest?"

Ettyk smiled. "Lieutenant Horn prided himself on his observational skills, and when he related the story of what he had seen, he made it into a self-depreciating tale. Given his position of authority in the squadron, this was against his best interest."

"Admiral, that is a gross misuse of the hearsay exception."

"You won't be able to keep the story out—Commander Antilles filed it as part of a report concerning the operation here on Coruscant."

Nawara's lip curled back in a snarl and gave Ettyk a view of his sharpened teeth. "If you want to bring that story in, by all means, lay the proper foundation and call your witnesses in order." *You may indeed succeed in bringing this stuff in, but I'm going to make you work for it.*

Admiral Ackbar leaned over and consulted with General Madine for a moment, then straightened up and nodded. "The objection is overruled."

Nawara felt his lekku twitch. "Admiral, this leaves me grounds for an appeal."

"It may indeed, Counselor Ven, but the ruling stands." Ackbar pointed toward the witness. "Lieutenant Cracken, you will tell the court what Corran Horn said, as best as you can remember."

Pash nodded as a frown gathered on his face. "Corran said he'd seen Tycho on Coruscant on the same day Warlord Zsinj hit Noquivzor."

"And what did he say Captain Celchu had been doing when he saw him?"

"Talking with someone in a cantina."

"Who was he speaking with?"

"Objection. The question calls for a conclusion based on facts not in evidence."

"Please, Commander, rephrase your question."

"Yes, Admiral." Ettyk glanced back at Nawara for a moment, then looked over at Pash. "Whom did Lieutenant Horn *say* he saw in conversation with Captain Celchu?"

"He said it was Kirtan Loor, but—"

"That's quite enough, Lieutenant, thank you."

"But—"

Admiral Ackbar looked down from the bench at Pash. "I'm

certain Counselor Ven will allow you to finish your answer under cross-examination."

"Yes, sir."

"Now, Lieutenant, I want you to recall when it was that you saw Captain Celchu after the report of his death."

"Three weeks ago. He showed up and saved us from stormies trying to kill us."

"Did his presence cause you to reevaluate Lieutenant Horn's story?"

"No, I don't think so."

"No?" Ettyk's expression sharpened. "You had been told Captain Celchu was dead, then you saw him again. You learned he had, *in fact*, been on Coruscant at the time Horn said he'd seen him. Did that not give you cause to wonder about what Horn had seen?"

"Things were very busy at the time. Desperate. I was given orders. I didn't think about things I didn't have to think about."

"Not even a bit? Not even when your orders included taking precautions to keep a traitor in your midst from getting information out to Imperial sources?"

"That was normal for a covert op."

"But you had to wonder if there wasn't really a traitor in your midst, correct?"

"No."

"No?" Ettyk's head came up. "You're a friend of Captain Celchu's, aren't you?"

Pash hesitated. "I'm in his squadron. I know him. I know what he's done. He's saved my life."

"And you think you owe him something?"

"I said he saved my life."

"And you don't want to be testifying here against him, do you?"

"No." The response came emphatic and strong.

"And, in fact, I had to compel your testimony with a subpoena, didn't I?"

"Yes."

The prosecutor looked up at the Tribunal. "I'd like permission to treat this witness as hostile."

Nawara winced. "Not good."

"Why not?" Tycho asked in a whisper.

"In direct testimony the questions are supposed to be open and nonleading. On cross-examination you get to lead the witness toward the answers you want." Nawara scratched at his throat. "A witness who is forced to answer questions always leaves the impression he's covering something up, so it makes even innocent things seem condemning. Pash is trying to do my job for me, but he's just making it tougher."

Ackbar waved a hand toward Ettyk. "Permission is granted to treat Lieutenant Cracken as hostile."

"Thank you, Admiral." Ettyk smiled. "Now you're a smart man, Lieutenant Cracken. You attended the Imperial Military Academy under a false identity your father created for you, correct?"

"Yes."

"And the operation that took you to Coruscant involved your arriving under a false identity, correct?"

"Yes."

"So you have some understanding of what it takes to operate covertly in a hostile environment, just as any spy would, correct?"

"Yes."

"It would be natural for a smart man like you to use what you had learned to try to check and see if you could detect any signs of a spy in your midst, correct?"

"It would seem that way."

"It really was that way, wasn't it, Lieutenant?" Halla Ettyk opened her hands. "You certainly found yourself evaluating people and trying to decide how much you could trust them, yes?"

Pash's frown deepened. "Yes."

"And Captain Celchu figured high on your list of suspect individuals, didn't he?"

"On a scale of one to infinity he ranked about a five."

"But that was higher than anyone else there, correct?"

"You're making it sound wrong."

"I move for the answer to be stricken as nonresponsive."

"So ordered." Ackbar again looked down at Pash. "Just answer the questions, Lieutenant."

"The ranking you gave Captain Celchu was higher than anyone else's ranking, wasn't it, Lieutenant?"

Pash nodded reluctantly. "Yes."

"Thank you. Now, on the night, two weeks ago, you were preparing to fly a mission that would aid in our conquest of Coruscant."

"Yes."

"What was that mission?"

"Five of us were going to fly cover for the rest of the squadron as they tried to bring the planetary shields down."

"To do that you needed fighters, correct?"

"Yes."

"And you had them?"

"Yes."

"Where did they come from?"

Pash took in a deep breath and exhaled slowly. "Captain Celchu had purchased them during his time here on Coruscant."

"And he had even flown a mission here, correct?"

"Yes, the mission where he saved us."

Ettyk turned back to the prosecution table and studied the datapad. Iella Wessiri came around to face her. "That night you witnessed a conversation between Captain Celchu and Corran Horn, did you not?"

"I did. I wasn't a party to the conversation, though."

"But you did overhear it?" Ettyk turned and spitted the witness with a forthright stare.

The pilot hung his head. "Yes."

"Did you hear Captain Celchu tell Lieutenant Horn that he had checked over the fighter Horn would be using?"

"Yes."

"And did you hear Lieutenant Horn threaten to work to expose Captain Celchu's treason once he returned from the mission?"

"Yes." Fatigue dragged at the red-haired man's reply.

The prosecutor smiled. "And what was Captain Celchu's response to that threat?"

"He said he had nothing to fear from Corran's investigation."

"As if he knew there would be no investigation?"

Nawara stood quickly. "Objection! It calls for speculation and is inflammatory."

"Sustained."

Ettyk turned and nodded to Nawara. "Your witness."

Nawara hesitated for a second. The evidence Halla Ettyk had laid out so far came as no surprise and was circumstantial. All she had gotten from Pash was that he had seen Tycho and Corran exchange some harsh words. That would go to motive, and some of the comments did cover opportunity to fix Corran's fighter, but without the Headhunter there was no evidence of tampering.

All he could accomplish on cross-examination would be to ask Pash to recount Tycho's explanation for the meeting where Corran saw him talking to Kirtan Loor. Tycho had explained he'd been speaking to a Duros trader, Lai Nootka, not Kirtan Loor. Nawara knew Ettyk would object to Pash's repetition of Tycho's explanation on hearsay grounds. Without being able to call Lai Nootka—or putting Tycho on the stand—there was no way to get at that whole subject.

Unless I called Kirtan Loor and he denied ever meeting Tycho! He put the chances of that happening at something just under the chances of the Emperor showing up and granting the Rebels one and all an Imperial pardon.

"Counselor Ven?"

Nawara looked up at Admiral Ackbar. "Sorry, sir. I have no questions of this witness at this time." The Twi'lek resumed his seat.

"Very well. Next witness, Commander Ettyk."

Ettyk stood once again. "The state calls Erisi Dlarit to the stand."

14

CORRAN HORN FELT as clumsy as the Trandoshan dragging him through the interrogation center's corridor. The injection an Emdee droid had given him back in his isolation cell had already begun to take hold. He had it in his mind that at least part of the concoction used was *skirtopanol* and that was not good. The one time he'd been under its influence, back during an exercise at the Corellian Security Force Academy, he confessed to all sorts of minor transgressions from his childhood. That would have been merely comical, but one of his father's cronies was overseeing the interrogation seminar and supplied his father with the text of his confession.

I don't think Iceheart will . . . When he started he'd had a full thought there, but the very image of Ysanne Isard that sprang into his mind killed things. Corran knew enough to know the drugs were working the way they were supposed to. He started to moan from fear and frustration, which earned him a backhanded cuff from his guard.

The blow and the dry-rot scent of the Trandoshan combined with his fear to bring memories rushing full-blown and terrible back into his mind. He saw little holographic images hovering in the air before him. Three figures, two men and a female Quarren, sat at a table in the darkened corner of a tapcaf. The two men—one of them his father—were deep in conversation. His father showed his agitation in the way he poked a finger at the smaller man and the color rising in his face.

Into the picture walked a Trandoshan bounty hunter wearing a bulky dust-cloak thrown over his shoulders. The lizard-man strode past the table and on up toward Corran until his green, scaly face eclipsed sight of Corran's father. The Trandoshan, Bossk, stepped back, slapping a power pack into the blaster carbine he'd produced from beneath the cloak. He spun slowly and sprayed red blaster bolts back and forth over the trio at the table.

The Quarren all but exploded into a black mist. Corran's father caught two shots high in the chest, slamming him against the back of the booth. As he slid from sight, the little man to whom he had been speaking tried to dive for cover. Unfortunately for him, the Trandoshan's fire blasted the table into flaming splinters and half-melted metal and still hit him. The little man took three bolts in the torso and a fourth that blew the back of his head off.

Corran saw himself in the scene. He saw no transition, no arrival. He just was there, kneeling in the blood, surrounded by burning bits of table. He held his father's body in his arms. He wiped the Quarren ichor from his father's face with a borrowed rag, all the while willing his father to open his eyes and announce he would be fine.

The two blackened holes in his father's chest stared up at him. At first they reminded him of a viper's fang marks, then they blinked. One became an icy blue and the other a volcanic red. The world blurred for a moment, then all the colors flowed together and became solid white, as they did when he was in hyperspace.

Then he reverted and found himself standing before Ysanne Isard in a predominately white room.

She frowned. "It fascinates me how all of our interrogation

sessions with you end up coming back to your father's death. There are countless psychiatric advocates who would find your preoccupation with your father's death to be grand justification for adherence to disciplines as useless as Jedi training. I do not."

Corran blinked his eyes. He couldn't recall going from the corridor to the interrogation chamber, nor being bound to the man-form that held him upright. The straps at his shoulders, and across his chest, waist, wrists, and ankles all pinched and chafed in such a way that he knew he'd been in restraints for quite some time. He couldn't remember anything but seeing his father die again, yet his throat felt raw enough that he knew he had to have been speaking or shouting *or screaming*.

Isard turned, presenting him her profile, and nodded to unseen minions beyond a mirrored wall. "What I have learned so far is a great deal of gossip that might be suitable for embarrassing the Corellian Diktat, but *that* sort of information is hardly in short supply. You have not ensconced yourself highly enough in the councils of the Rebellion to be of use to me—at least, I do not believe you have. It is entirely possible you have managed to resist interrogation in certain areas."

Corran shook his head. "You got the wrong guy."

"Then I will just have to make you into the right guy, won't I?" Her eyes narrowed with irritation as she faced him again. "Had Gil Bastra not sent you to the outlier worlds, you would have become part and parcel of the Rebellion. You would have found yourself in General Cracken's confidence and I would have found you very useful in that regard. Then again, it *is* possible that he set you in Rogue Squadron so you could watch Tycho Celchu and uncover his ties to me."

"No."

"No? Cracken must have done that. You *were* his agent, yes?"

Corran shook his head adamantly. "No. I wasn't a spy for Cracken."

"Were I inclined to believe anything, I might be inclined to believe you in this case. Unfortunately I need proof." She stepped aside as the Trandoshan wheeled in a device that bristled with probes and danced with the colorful illumination of an ever-changing light array. The probes had been fitted on a concave surface that could easily close over him and the rack to which he was bound. Corran caught the stink of ozone as the Trandoshan brought the device closer. He didn't like the fact that he heard a click down at his feet when the lizard-man finally nudged the device into place.

Isard smiled in a manner that made Corran want to shrivel up and die. "This is a variant on a design Darth Vader created to torture, among others, Han Solo at Bespin. As you know, humans have a number of different types of neural receptors. This device is designed to stimulate three of them—the original only worked on the pain receptors. I have found that adding stimulation for the heat and cold receptors is most effective in getting what I want out of those I interrogate."

Corran wanted to snap off some quip, but fatigue and anxiety prevented him from mustering the required concentration.

"So, now we begin, Lieutenant Horn. Just tell me what I want to know. . . ."

". . . AND I WON'T have to ask the court to let me treat you like a hostile witness."

Iella Wessiri almost felt sorry for Erisi Dlarit as Halla Ettyk tried to coax cooperation out of her. In going over the depositions before the trial opened, Iella and Halla had agreed that members of Rogue Squadron would be hostile and resistant to anything that made them speak against Tycho Celchu. Halla had decided, therefore, to bring them up first and get them out of the way before she brought in the investigators and other witnesses who could attest to Tycho's involvement with the Empire. Halla had pointed out that Nawara Ven would probably end up calling all the Rogues back to the stand, but by the time he did that, their positive affirmations about Tycho would sound hollow and unsupported to the Tribunal.

"Flight Officer Dlarit, how did you come to be on Coruscant two weeks ago?"

Erisi brought her chin up and her blue eyes flashed defiantly. "Corran Horn and I were inserted into Coruscant under the guise of being a Kuati *telbun* and his mistress. For the entire journey to Coruscant and the subsequent week, we were together almost constantly. We were good friends and talked a great deal."

Halla Ettyk nodded. "So you were confidants?"

"We shared confidences, yes." The black-haired woman smiled politely. "It is difficult to keep secrets when you are living in such close proximity with someone."

"And Corran Horn felt free to discuss things with you?"

"Objection: relevance."

Iella glanced over at Nawara Ven. The twitching of his braintails betrayed some nervousness, but the Twi'lek was objecting at all the places Halla had predicted he would. *She said he had talent. She didn't think he could win the case, and his decision not to cross-examine Cracken wasn't what Halla had anticipated.*

Halla looked up at Admiral Ackbar. "This is foundational, Admiral. She was living with Corran Horn for a considerable portion of the last part of his life. I would suggest this would qualify her to give opinions on his demeanor."

"Overruled."

Erisi frowned briefly. "We discussed many things rather openly and frankly."

"How would you characterize the conditions under which you spent time with Lieutenant Horn?"

The Thyferran pilot shrugged. "I saw him in combat, during which he was calm and a leader. A hero. I saw him in regular circumstances as well. He could be funny and compassionate and, well, attractive. I saw him in all different ways and situations."

"On the night Coruscant fell, how would you characterize him?"

"Anxious and agitated."

"And what was the source of his irritation?"

Erisi chewed her lower lip for a moment. "Corran said . . ."

"Objection." Nawara Ven stood. "This is hearsay."

Halla Ettyk took a step forward. "I would ask for an excited outburst exception, your honor. She has already testified that Horn was anxious and agitated."

The Twi'lek stepped up beside Halla. "My learned colleague certainly understands that being agitated and saying something in no way makes it subject to the excited outburst exception."

"Sustained."

Nawara smiled slightly as he returned to his bench, but Halla's expression just darkened. "Very well. Flight Officer Dlarit, did you speak with Lieutenant Horn before you took off on the mission that evening?"

"Yes."

"You stated he seemed anxious and agitated. Did you find his state of mind unusual?"

"Objection, counsel is leading the witness."

"Rephrase the question, Commander."

"Flight Officer Dlarit, how did Lieutenant Horn's state of mind strike you at the time?"

Erisi tugged at a wisp of hair behind her left ear. "Anxiety I could understand. We were all anxious to get going and to see if the mission would succeed or not."

"And his agitation?"

"That wasn't like Corran."

"Had you seen or heard anything that, in your mind, explained his agitation?"

The witness hesitated. "I saw Corran speaking with Captain Celchu. I couldn't hear what they were saying, but I saw them speaking together. Then Corran came over and spoke with me."

"And you concluded?"

"Something in their conversation had set Corran off."

Iella glanced down at the datapad on the prosecution table. Halla had gotten out of Erisi all she expected the witness to admit—testimony showing Corran to be out of sorts as a result of his conversation with Captain Celchu. When they had deposed Erisi they had learned the nature of her conversation with Corran. While Halla would have loved to get that testimony in, hearsay prevented it. The excited outburst exception wasn't something she had expected to succeed.

Halla smiled at Nawara. "Your witness."

The Twi'lek stood. "Flight Officer Dlarit, how long was it between the time you reported speaking to Corran and the previous time you had spoken to him?"

"An hour."

"Now, you just testified that you saw Corran speak with Captain Celchu. Did you see Lieutenant Horn speak with anyone else before speaking with Captain Celchu?"

"No."

Nawara's head came up as if her answer surprised him. "You didn't see Lieutenant Horn speak with Mirax Terrik?"

Erisi shrugged her shoulders. "I suppose I did. I saw them standing near each other and saw her run off, but I don't recall any conversation."

"But you do concede that they may have spoken to each other?"

"Yes."

"So, as nearly as you know, Lieutenant Horn might have had multiple conversations that could have set him off?"

"I suppose so." Erisi blinked a couple of times. "That could be it."

The Twi'lek bowed his head. "Thank you, Flight Officer, that's all I have for you."

———

CORRAN FELT LIKE a block of burning ice caught in a lightning storm. His flesh felt on fire while his bones seemed chilled to absolute zero. Every pain receptor in his body strobed on and off on a near-constant basis. The pain would start at his feet and move up in a wave, or descend on him like a rain shower, or pummel him with randomly delivered jolts.

He would have welcomed death but for the horror of spending eternity with the memory of such pain so fresh.

He heard a hiss, and the rack retracted from what he had taken to calling the Inducer. Corran hung limp from the restraining straps and welcomed the constant, unrelenting, unshifting pain the straps caused as they sank into his flesh. Sweat poured down over his face and stung fiercely where he'd managed to bite through his lower lip, but even that sensation was a relief from what he had just been through.

Ysanne Isard entered the interrogation chamber and waved the Trandoshan out. "I would find you fascinating if you knew more, Horn." She glanced at the mirrored panel on the wall. "Your tolerance for pain is remarkable."

Corran would have shrugged, but every ounce of energy in his body had been exhausted in screaming answers to the questions fired at him during the session. He couldn't remember what he had said. He recalled that in those few moments of lucidity which he could touch between pulses of agony, he had tried to focus on the cold or heat. Locking into those sensations had seemed to dull the pain somehow. Now, in the absence of pain, he doubted that observation was correct, but it had been a sanctuary into which he had retreated, and that was a very small victory.

She posted her fists on her hips. "You present a problem for me. You don't know enough to be useful, and your position within the Rebellion is so low that you are hardly vital. If I return you to them, they will likely treat you much as they are treating Celchu now. You won't have even the freedom he had before his arrest. This does not incline me to send you back.

"On the other hand, you would be perfect to mold into my own avenger. Your resistance to pain will make your rehabilitation into a right-thinking Imperial time-consuming, but not impossible. Your core discomfort with the unlawful nature of the Rebellion is a foundation on which I can build you anew into the tool I need. I can form an Avenger Squadron around you that will go after and destroy Rogue Squadron. Using a Rogue to destroy Rogues, that would be delicious."

Corran summoned strength from reserves he didn't know he had and smiled. "You won't live long enough to see me turn on my friends."

"Good, anger directed at me, excellent." She politely applauded him. "Hate me all you want. I'll turn your hatred for me into hatred for those who haven't saved you from me. You won't be the first broken that way, and you'll not be the last."

"I won't break."

"Ah, but you will. They all do." She nodded solemnly as the rack hissed and slowly lowered him toward the Inducer. "And when you break, I will put you back together again, and in gratitude you will do all I ask, without question or regard for loyalties you once held dear."

15

IT WAS PROBABLY in a place like this that Rogue Squadron plotted the conquest of Imperial Center. Kirtan Loor ducked his head beneath a series of moist, moldy pipes and followed his guide deeper into the rusted-out bowels of Imperial Center. Loor had been driven deeper into the planet-wide city than he thought possible, then had gone several kilometers farther through a hot, wet labyrinth that had him imagining he'd passed through the core of the world and was now working his way up and out the other side.

The Special Intelligence operative leading him through the maze cut to the left and through an oval opening hacked through the wall of the access tunnel. The opening seemed, at first glance, as if it was chopped through the wall; but when Loor grabbed its edges as he climbed through the hole, the striations he felt made him wonder if it hadn't been *nibbled* out of the ferrocrete. *Unless I can find a way to use it, I don't want to know what chewed this hole.*

The low, wide area into which Loor stepped stank of rust, stagnant water, and mildew. The few standing puddles had an oily slick on them that phosphoresced slightly. The weak light supplemented the temporary floodlights the operatives had arranged to display their motley collection of airspeeders. All in all the tableau was unremarkable and unlikely to attract attention from anyone save a truly desperate airspeeder thief.

And wouldn't he be surprised at what he got.

The dented and dinged airspeeders, which were of a variety of years and makes, had been carefully worked over by the operatives and transformed into a half-dozen flying bombs. The hollow spaces in the chassis had been filled with explosives. Designed to be flown by remote from a companion airspeeder, they would be driven like proton torpedoes into the various bacta storage facilities around the world.

An operative came walking over to Loor, unable to keep a smirk from his square face. "As you can see, we are prepared to go at any time. We have completed our initial electronic sweep of the target sites and have found them negative for counter-remote tactics or equipment."

"Very good." The Empire had long ago perfected precautionary measures to take against bombs that might be set to detonate by remote. The easiest of these was to broadcast strong signals on a variety of comlink frequencies of the sort used by Rebel terrorists to detonate such bombs, causing a premature detonation while the bombs were still in the attackers' keeping. Broadcasting from patrolling airspeeders in hostile areas had even detonated explosives in bomb factories that Intelligence had suspected existed, but had not been able to pinpoint for a more surgical strike. The harm done to innocents in the area when the bombs went off had been seen as just punishment for the failure of the people to report the Rebels working in their area.

Although they had been unable to detect similar counter-remote tactics in the bacta storage areas, Loor's people had decided against detonating the bombs by remote. Getting an airspeeder into position and leaving it there long enough for the setup team to get away provided a window for discovery and deactivation. Even though that window would be small, it was felt to be too risky; they intended to hit a number of sites in rapid succession, and if the Rebel forces discovered one bomb and sent out a warning, it would make hitting the others far more difficult. Moreover, the fact that they could not detect anti-remote equipment in their reconnaissance sweeps could have been explained by nothing more sinister than someone forgetting to turn the devices on that day.

The plan they had hit on was actually fairly simple. Commercial speeder-ferry vehicles were not an uncommon sight on Imperial Center, hauling broken air- and land-speeders to repair shops. Using a tractor beam and a simple remote-slave hookup, repair techs regularly flew speeders throughout the city. Using a speeder-ferry to haul a vehicle to the right area, then having someone fly it by remote into the building, was seen as a clean way to deliver the bombs. Since the remote-slave hookup was in common use by these sorts of vehicles, it couldn't be jammed without causing dozens of legitimate disasters, so Loor knew their delivery method was safe from interference.

Contact detonators had been rigged in the various panels and bumpers on each vehicle. The explosives would be triggered when the detonators were compressed with the force of an airspeeder slamming into a building. While a head-on collision with another airspeeder at significant velocity could cause the bomb to go off, the chances of that happening were relatively small. Regardless, the amount of explosives packed into the vehicles meant that any explosion in the general vicinity of the target would do substantial damage and, if not destroy the store of bacta, at least make its distribution difficult.

The operative looked up at Loor expectantly. "When will we be given the signal to go?"

Loor looked at his wrist chronometer. "Rumor has it that Mon Mothma is going to announce the particulars of the bacta distribution plan approved by the Provisional Council in fourteen hours or so. I am debating whether we should use these vehicles to punctuate her speech, or let public anticipation build for a day or so before striking."

Loor kept his tone light, as if the decision to be made was of little consequence. He preferred going off sooner rather than waiting, but he was fairly certain that Ysanne Isard would want him to wait. So far he had gotten no word back from her on this plan—*or on any of my plans.* This meant the decision was truly up to him, but he knew it didn't have to be made until an hour or two before the assault would take place.

The Intelligence agent frowned. "Contact me on a secure frequency three hours before the scheduled start of Mon Mothma's speech. Assume the operation will go off during her speech. When you call me, I will either cancel the assault and reschedule, or let you go. If you do not reach me, you are on."

"Very good, sir." The operative waved a hand toward the airspeeders. "If you care to inspect our handiwork?"

Loor shook his head. "You have ever been efficient before, Captain. I see no reason to doubt your preparedness now."

"Thank you."

"Of course." Loor smiled slowly. "And, speaking of efficiency, your people dealt with Nartlo, yes?"

"As you ordered, sir."

"Excellent."

"Yes, sir. I'll have someone conduct you back now, sir."

The operative waved another of his plainly clothed men over and Loor followed that operative out through another exit from the underground bunker. Loor found this route less odious, and the use of a series of turbolifts meant it took less time to get back into more hospitable regions of the city. After taking leave of the operative, Loor worked his way up and through the city. He constantly checked his surroundings and back-trail for sign of pursuit, but found none.

The prospect of destroying the Rebels' bacta supply pleased him, but not for the reasons most Rebels would ascribe to him. He took no delight in the fact that the destruction of the bacta would cause the deaths of millions, even billions. As odd as it seemed, even to him, their lives meant nothing. Since he did not know them, they were numbers, and Kirtan Loor had never been one to be terribly emotional about numbers.

Destroying the bacta would be a victory in the war he was waging against the Rebellion. He and his people were outnumbered, out-gunned, and under-resourced, but they were winning. So far they had struck when and where they wished. Just the fact that they were able to assemble an armada of bombs on Imperial Center without detection was a triumph in their battle against General Cracken and his forces.

Oddly enough, Loor realized that he was playing a game to sudden death, and it was more likely to be his death than that of his foes. Still, he now understood the secret thrill that kept the Rebels going. They had been the insects repeatedly stinging the bumbling giant that was the Empire. Yes, the giant had swatted them and, in some cases, had hurt them badly, but it could never kill all of them. The defiance they showed the Empire now burned in his veins, and while it did not make him think he was immortal or unstoppable, it did drive him with a desire to do more and more to torment his enemy.

He also knew that his efforts would not reestablish the Empire. That was not the goal Ysanne Isard had in mind when she set him up on Imperial Center as the leader of a pro-Palpatine movement. What he was doing would weaken the Rebellion and allow other forces to tear it apart. Whether those other forces included a warlord like Zsinj blasting his way into Imperial Center and taking it over, or the product of some other scheme Iceheart was undoubtedly planning, did not matter. Isard wanted to destroy the Rebellion, and that was the goal he intended to help her reach.

He smiled. He had been given a great responsibility, and his success would create a power vacuum at the heart of the Empire. Isard maintained her goal was *not* the resurrection of the Empire, but the destruction of the Rebellion; still, it seemed obvious to him that the recreation of the Empire was a natural consequence of eliminating the Rebellion. When the Rebellion collapsed, *if* he did things well, he would be in position to help restore the Empire. While he knew better than to make himself a direct rival to Iceheart, he also knew she wouldn't live forever.

Nor will I, but if I live longer *than she does, the Emperor's throne might well be open to me.* Loor smiled and sniffed proudly, but the scent of the city's lower reaches tarnished his fantasy. He glanced down at his feet and saw a glistening fungoid residue that seemed to shift colors as he watched it. Immediately desirous of returning to his eyrie and washing away the stink of Imperial Center's darker reaches, he fished a comlink out of his pocket and called for one of his guards to meet him with his airspeeder.

Loor did his best to scrape the goo off his shoes against the side of a building, but it clung tenaciously. He chuckled to himself, thinking of it as true *Rebel scum.* He made no headway in his battle with it and wondered if a lightsaber would be able to damage it. He'd concluded it would not by the time his airspeeder slid up to the curb and the rear gull's-wing door swung up.

Loor started into the passenger compartment, then caught himself. Inside, nestled in the corner, a smallish, white-haired man pointed a blaster pistol at him. "Sorry, wrong speeder. My mistake."

"No mistake. Get in." The man sighed. "Get in or my other people will shove you in."

Given no choice, Loor entered the vehicle and folded himself into one of the jumpseats. The door closed behind him, leaving the two of them alone in the speeder's darkened interior. Loor raised his hands and clutched the safety straps. "Is there any purpose in my putting these on, Moff Vorru?"

Fliry Vorru nodded his head graciously. "Very good, Agent Loor. Yes, by all means, strap yourself in. I do not anticipate this being a rough ride, but things can get turbulent here on Imperial Center."

"So I have noticed."

"I'm certain you have." Vorru set the blaster pistol on the seat beside him, then tugged at the grey cuffs on his midnight-blue jacket. "And I'm no longer a moff, merely a colonel in the Imperial Center People's Militia."

"Natty uniform. I'm sure it will show you off at your best when you hold a news conference and announce my capture." Loor tried to force a smile on his face, but it hardly seemed worth the effort. "Quite the coup for you."

"Indeed, it could be." Vorru yawned in an exaggerated fashion. "The question remains as to whether or not that is necessary."

"Excuse me?"

"You present me with a problem, Agent Loor. Your Palpatine Counter-insurgency Front is one of the reasons my militia was created. As long as you are a threat, the Provisional Council needs me. Without you, all we can do is go after petty black marketeers and other criminals."

"All of whom you currently control anyway."

"You overestimate my abilities."

Loor raised an eyebrow. "Do I? You found me quickly enough."

Vorru shrugged. "More by happenstance than anything else. I was in the process of consolidating my hold on the black market in bacta and had Nartlo under observation, since he had a source I could not isolate. My people had your people under observation when they visited him last night. We continued watching and were led to this vehicle. Your people are good at disguising themselves—by the way, the blond hair and goatee really do distance your appearance from that of Tarkin. Changing the appearance of a vehicle is not as simple."

The little man smiled. "I had no idea who we had found until we checked the records on this vehicle. The registration is utterly benign and ordinary, with no sign of slicing on the data-file at all. That indicated to me that the registration had made it into the computers through legitimate means, and *that* meant Imperial Intelligence. Since you had turned Zekka Thyne against me, I had made it my business to learn about you then, surprise, surprise, here you are."

"I hope I don't disappoint you."

"It's possible, but we'll see." Vorru frowned. "Normally I'd not have picked you up so early, but Nartlo indicated that he'd given you the locations of the Republic's bacta repositories. I immediately became suspicious—he maintained you were just a bacta dealer, but those containment centers just ache to be hit by the PCF. I tried to determine if Nartlo was lying to me, but you had anticipated I'd do that."

Loor smiled. "You used *skirtopanol* on him."

"Yes, and the convulsions were rather hideous."

"Convulsions? Hmmm. We gave him a supply of *lotiramine* and told him it would prevent him from getting the Krytos virus. I included strict dosing instructions. If he went into convulsions he must have taken four times the recommended amount."

"Some people assume that if one pill is good, more is better."

"He died?"

"Cerebral hemorrhage."

"He was useful, which is why we didn't just kill him outright. The *lotiramine* would have made interrogation difficult for the Rebels, and some of the information he had about my operation would have had them haring off in all sorts of wrong directions."

Vorru nodded. "Though he claimed no knowledge of a planned assault on the bacta stores, that *is* what you are planning, yes?"

Loor looked around the passenger compartment. "I would have thought General Cracken would resort to more professional methods of interrogation."

"He would, *and will*, if you do not choose to cooperate with me." Vorru crossed his legs and plucked at the crease in his slacks. "If I don't get answers from you, I will tell Cracken I have uncovered a plot to assault the current centers. He'll put precautions into place that will prevent your success while moving the bacta to new locations. You will lose and I will win."

"And you have a plan that will result in some other outcome?"

Vorru smiled. "You will now be working for me. You will hit targets I give you and you will hit them when I want them hit. I am not unsympathetic to your war against the Rebellion, I just wish to kill yet one more mynock with a single laser-blast."

Of course, it should have been obvious. Loor nodded. "You would do what Prince Xizor could not."

"Xizor relied too much on his personal abilities and not enough on the ability to read others."

"Having made Black Sun over into the People's Militia, you'll be in position to assume power if the Rebellion falters."

"But I have no desire to see the Rebellion fail. I just want to see the Rebellion's *leadership* fail. Manipulate the Bothans and appease them, frustrate the Alderaanians until they alienate the other humans with their constant reminders of how their world was martyred for the Rebellion, let the black market bankrupt the Republic so someone who has monetary reserves can come in and bail things out—"

"That being you."

"Of course." Vorru nodded. "Ysanne Isard may have injected the Krytos virus into Imperial Center, but the Rebels injected a more deadly virus into Imperial Center before that: *me.* They saw me as someone who could be a brake on the predations of the underworld here, but they forgot the Emperor himself had seen me as a rival for power once upon a time. What they forgot, I never have. Now the Emperor is dead and I am here on his world.

"The question for you, Agent Loor, is this: how do you want to destroy the Rebellion? Do you want to blast it apart, or distract it until it, too, sickens and dies? What you will find growing up in its place, I can assure you, will be to your liking."

The Intelligence agent pressed his lips together in a thin line. *My refusal to go along will mean my death, so my choice is obvious. And, as with Ysanne Isard, Fliry Vorru will not live forever.*

Loor nodded slowly. "What do you want?"

"I want you to hit only one of the six repositories at this time—the one just south of the Senate district. My people have already managed to steal most of that supply anyway, so your attack will cover our tracks and leave us to profit from the spike in black market pricing. I will give you other targets as we go along to further my aims."

"Consider it done. Tonight, during Mon Mothma's speech?"

Vorru's face blossomed in a broad smile. "Ah, you have a taste for irony. Splendid. I think our alliance will be most profitable for the both of us. I anticipate doing business with you, Agent Loor, will be an ongoing pleasure."

16

IELLA WESSIRI SMILED at Diric as she settled into the witness chair. Diric was in the court for the first time and actually looked excited by the crush of people. The bailiffs had let him sit right behind the prosecution table because that put him in close proximity to where she sat when she wasn't on the stand.

The ashen hue of Diric's flesh betrayed his fatigue, but the trial had piqued his interest. If not for the fire that put into his brown eyes, she would have remained adamantly against his attending the trial. She felt the trial had to be on the Palpatine Counter-insurgency Front's list of targets, and she didn't want Diric exposed to their violence. The sheer savagery of their strike at a bacta containment facility the previous night had left her shaken and, secretly, pleased to have Diric where she could see him.

Halla Ettyk stood. "Iella Wessiri, could you please tell the court about your personal employment history over the last eight years?"

"I joined the Corellian Security Force just about a standard year before the Emperor dissolved the Senate. I worked there for six years, moving up into the Smuggling Interdiction division, where I partnered for two years with Corran Horn. Approximately two years ago Corran, Gil Bastra, my husband Diric, and I all fled Corellia before our division's Imperial Liaison officer, Kirtan Loor, could trump up charges and arrest us. From Corellia Diric and I came to Coruscant and remained in hiding for a year. We had enough money that we didn't need jobs, so I did nothing during that first year here. Subsequent to my husband's disappearance, about a year ago, I joined the Alliance organization here on Coruscant and aided Rogue Squadron in bringing the shields down. Since then, for the past two weeks, I've been assigned to your office as chief investigator on this case."

The prosecutor nodded. "So, you worked with Corran Horn for two years."

"I *partnered* with him for two years."

"Describe what you mean by partnering."

Iella shrugged slightly. "It's akin to being married to someone in that you have to trust them completely. Your life is in your partner's hands in dangerous situations. The only way you can build up that level of trust is by getting to know one another. The job means you're together a great deal—in any given week you could easily see more of your partner than you do your own family. Some partners get to know each other so well that they almost get this Gotal-sense of being able to read each other's moods and react in situations without a word being spoken."

"Describe for us, please, your relationship with Corran Horn."

"We were close, very close. About six months after I started working with him, Corran's father was murdered. That event crushed Corran and I helped him through it. He'd been an only child and his mother had died previously, so he felt alone. The fact that Kirtan Loor freed his father's murderer had Corran burning for vengeance, but Loor's Imperial ties meant Corran couldn't do anything, and that frustrated him. Gil and I worked at calming him down, and he came around. The point is that when you help someone through such a difficult time, you get to see his heart and get to know him very well."

Halla Ettyk glanced at her datapad. "How well did you know Kirtan Loor?"

"He became our Imperial Liaison about a year before I was partnered up with Corran. I found him to be aloof and distant. We didn't socialize—he made no effort to get to know the rest of us after work and didn't socialize during office celebrations. He seemed to delight in frustrating investigations. In the three years I worked in the same office with him, I got to know him well enough to avoid him as much as possible."

"Did you become good at avoiding him?"

"Yes. He's fairly easy to spot, especially because of his height, and if he became too obnoxious, I could always retreat to the female officers' refresher station and he'd not follow me."

"You mention his height. How would you characterize his appearance overall?"

"Rather distinctive." Iella brushed her light brown hair away from the side of her neck. "He prided himself on looking like a younger, taller Grand Moff Tarkin, and he wasn't far wrong in that. He definitely stood out in a crowd."

"Would you say Corran Horn knew Kirtan Loor as well as you did?"

"Objection, counsel is leading the witness."

"Sustained. Rephrase the question, Commander."

"Yes, Admiral. How well could you say Corran Horn knew Kirtan Loor?"

"Objection. That calls for speculation."

"I'll allow it. Overruled." Admiral Ackbar nodded toward Iella. "You may answer the question."

"I'd say Corran knew Loor as well as I did. Corran seemed to know where Loor would be before Loor did, and he programmed Whistler to give him a sign if Loor was around and he'd not noticed yet."

"Thank you." Again Ettyk checked her datapad. "Please describe for us the kinds of materials you have reviewed during your investigation."

Iella started ticking things off on her fingers. "I have interviewed witnesses, I have listened to comlink recordings and read transcripts of same, I have looked at physical evidence and reviewed reports prepared by forensics concerning same, and I've reviewed the file evidence available."

"What sorts of things are in that file evidence?"

"Reports by Commander Antilles, Lieutenant Horn, and Captain Celchu about their time here on Coruscant."

Halla hit two buttons on her datapad. "I've now downloaded into the court's evidentiary computer a report by Lieutenant Corran Horn that I would like entered into evidence as People's exhibit 34. You have reviewed this report?"

"I have."

"What does it say concerning Kirtan Loor?"

Iella looked straight at Halla Ettyk. "In it Lieutenant Horn reports that he saw Captain Celchu in conversation with Kirtan Loor at a cantina called the Headquarters."

"Based on your experience as Corran's partner, how would you characterize the nature of this report?"

"Typical Corran: concise, to the point, and unequivocal in his statement of facts."

"And, based on your experience, how would you characterize Corran's identification of Kirtan Loor?"

"He was absolutely certain he'd seen Captain Celchu talking with Loor."

Ettyk smiled. "So there was nothing in the report, nothing in your experience that would lead you to question Lieutenant Horn's identification of Kirtan Loor?"

Iella hesitated. "Actually, there is one little detail about which I do have a question."

Surprise flashed across Halla's face, but she smothered it quickly. "Move to strike as nonresponsive, your Honor."

The Mon Calamari's barbels twitched beneath an open

mouth. "No, Commander, you asked one more question than you should have, and now you have to live with the consequences. Do you have anything else for this witness?"

"At this time, no sir, but I reserve the right to recall her."

"Understood. Your witness, Counselor Ven."

Iella straightened up in the witness box and tried to calm herself, but she felt her guts begin to knot up as the Twi'lek stood. Her heart started pounding a bit faster. She'd never liked being cross-examined, and she expected no mercy from Nawara Ven, especially after Halla made her mistake.

"Agent Wessiri, in your time with the Corellian Security Force, have you ever performed an investigation into a matter of treason?"

"No, but I have worked murder cases before."

"I know. You've worked many murder cases, haven't you?"

"Yes."

"And some have been easier to investigate than this one, haven't they?"

Iella nodded. "Yes." Though Nawara Ven kept his voice low and his demeanor easy, she didn't like the way he started nibbling in around the edges. He was projecting an aura of calm control, running the trial, and she knew that was bad. Once he got into a rhythm and she started moving along with him, he could turn and surprise her, and get admissions out of her that would give the wrong impression to the Tribunal.

"How long would you say the average murder investigation you worked lasted?"

"You'd have to be more specific."

"How long before an arrest?"

Iella shrugged. "Less than a week. If you don't have a suspect in custody by that time the trail can get very cold."

"The investigation itself, though, might go on longer than that, correct?"

"Sure."

"Because there are details to check, lab reports to read and analyze, witnesses to depose, more facts to be checked, and the like, correct?"

"Yes."

The Twi'lek smiled. "That takes a long time to do, doesn't it?"

"That depends."

"Say you want to do it right."

"I *always* want to do it right."

"Of course, but haste can make for sloppy work, can't it?"

"Yes."

"So a hasty investigation is potentially a sloppy one?"

"Yes."

Nawara Ven nodded. "So would you characterize two weeks from murder to trial as fast, in your experience?"

Iella nodded reluctantly. "It's faster than most trials."

"Have you ever been involved in a case that went to trial as quickly as this?"

She shook her head. "No."

The Twi'lek looked back at the datapad on his table. Iella saw lights flicker across the front panel on Whistler, then Nawara nodded and looped a braintail back over his shoulder. "I want to call your attention to People's 34. How long after the incident described was the report made?"

Iella glanced at the small datapad monitor in the corner of the witness box. "There is a two-week gap between the incident and the filing of the report."

"Now, in your experience as Corran Horn's partner, would you say he was usually prompt in filing his reports?"

"Yes." Iella glared at Whistler. "But sometimes there were delays, and the two weeks you mention were fairly busy."

"Is that the only reason, being busy, that you believe Lieutenant Horn delayed filing his report?"

"Objection, calls for speculation."

"Counselor Ven is asking the witness what she believes, not what she thinks the victim thought. I'll allow it. Overruled."

"Because we believed Captain Celchu was dead on Noquivzor, there seemed no way the report could be true, so there would have been no reason to file it." Iella leaned forward in her seat. "However, the minute Corran learned Captain Celchu was alive, he made that report."

"I understand that." The Twi'lek flashed her a smile full of pointy teeth. "In your time as his partner, had you ever known Corran Horn to make a mistake?"

"He was only human."

Ven's expression darkened. "Perhaps you can expand on that answer for those of us who are *not* human."

Iella blushed and glanced down at the floor. *What a thing to say, especially here and now!* "I mean, yes, he did make mistakes."

"Thank you. Now, you alluded to something in the report that left a question in your mind about the veracity of Lieutenant Horn's identification of Kirtan Loor. What was that?"

Her stomach folded in on itself. "Corran describes Loor as wearing a hooded cloak and following Captain Celchu out the back of the cantina as Corran entered it. Corran recognized Loor from his height and his gait, but he never actually saw his face."

"And as good as Corran was, you think that his making an identification without seeing the individual's face leaves room for him to be mistaken?"

"Yes."

The Twi'lek nodded. "Thank you for your candor. Nothing further."

Ackbar looked at the prosecutor. "Redirect?"

"No, Admiral."

The Mon Calamari nodded down at Iella. "You are excused, Agent Wessiri. I am going to recess the court at this time. The Provisional Council is meeting to discuss a number of problems and I must be there. I may, in fact, recess the trial for a week. I assume, from the question you asked earlier, Counselor Ven, you would not mind having the extra time for investigation of the case?"

Iella, returning to her place at the prosecution bench, watched Nawara's grey profile as he nodded. "I welcome the time to continue to prepare my defense."

"Commander Ettyk, you have no objections to a delay?"

"No, sir."

"Very good, court stands adjourned for one week."

IELLA ENTERED HALLA ETTYK'S OFFICE. "Diric's in the outer office, lying down. I hope you don't mind. The crush of people leaving the court was a bit much, but the bailiffs didn't seem to want to let him catch his breath. In fact, they weren't too interested in letting me bring him along with me here to the office."

The black-haired prosecutor shook her head. "Not a problem, but get him a special visitor's identification badge."

Iella frowned as she slipped into a nerfhide chair in front of Halla's transparisteel desk. "What's going on?"

Halla set a comlink down on her desk. "I just heard from Admiral Ackbar's aide, Commander Sirlul. The reason for the abrupt adjournment was more than a routine meeting of the Provisional Council. It appears, in the wake of the PCF assault on that bacta storage site, we've had a bomb threat here. They aren't sure who made the threat or how real it is, but they want a week to reinforce the courthouse complex."

"I see."

Halla nodded solemnly. "Just as well—it gives me a week to shore up my case."

Iella winced. "I'm sorry for what I said in there. I don't want to have Corran's killer get off, but—"

"Not your fault. Admiral Ackbar was right—I asked one more question than I should have. I tried to make sure there was no question that Corran had been right, and I was too smart for my own good." She shrugged. "At least nothing got said about the Duros that Captain Celchu says he was meeting with that night. Right now the Tribunal just knows that Corran might have been mistaken about his identification. If the Duros is brought in, they'll be free to wonder how much Kirtan Loor in a cloak looks like a Duros in a cloak."

Iella's eyes narrowed. "We all knew Celchu claimed he met a Duros that night."

"So it seems, but all those stories get traced back to Celchu himself, so anyone else bringing it up gets it stricken because of the hearsay rule. The only way that comes in is if Tycho takes the stand."

"What if the Duros testifies?"

"What's the likelihood of that happening? There's no evidence Lai Nootka ever was on Coruscant, as nearly as we can tell. Moreover, there was some history between Corran and Nootka—Corran got him out of an Imperial prison on Garqi, wherever that is. Why would Nootka run from the man who saved his life?"

Iella opened her hands. "Maybe he was just following Tycho."

"Fine. Let's assume that meeting was as innocent as Tycho has tried to make it out to be. It *doesn't* make the least little bit of difference. The bribe data alone is enough to show he was working for the Empire. Corran *believed* Tycho had met with Kirtan Loor; his threat to dig into Tycho's background because of that belief is our motive for the murder."

"But why kill Corran when you can show he's wrong about the meeting just by producing Lai Nootka?" Iella frowned. "Tycho always seemed confident of his innocence, which meant he either had Nootka where he could deliver him, blowing apart the foundation of Corran's threatened investigation, or—"

"Or he could be innocent?" Halla shook her head. "Don't plot a course into that black hole."

"But that black hole might be the truth."

"Sure, but we're not the triers of fact in this case, the Tribunal members are. We just have to present to them the best case we can muster, and the defense has to knock it apart." Halla's brown eyes narrowed. "You're not going to start in on me about wanting to make sure your partner's killer really is caught, because I'll tell you we've got him beyond a reasonable doubt."

Iella shrugged. "And if I don't want to be reasonable?"

Halla winced, then sat back in her white high-backed chair. "Idealists should not be in this business, you know."

"And your point is?"

"The Duros thing has bothered me, too. I can grant that Tycho might have pulled that name from Corran's file just to annoy him, but that would be very risky for him to do. The trail Tycho has left has shown him to be *very* careful, so I don't see him throwing out that sort of taunt. Therefore I can imagine that he really *did* meet with Lai Nootka. And if that's true, I have to wonder about our inability to find Nootka or any record of his presence here on Coruscant."

"So even though you believe Tycho was working for the Empire, you think Nootka's disappearance may be evidence of someone making sure Tycho's perfidy is obvious?" Iella frowned. "Who? Why?"

"Good, obstruction-of-justice questions to answer." Halla sighed. "You want to find Nootka, right?"

"If you don't mind."

Halla sat forward and fingered a small black wafer of silicon. "Do it. And take this—it's a code chip that will let you bring your airspeeder into the upper-level security garage. You can take the turbolift down to the court from there. It'll save Diric from having to go in and out with the courtroom crowds from now on."

Iella accepted it from her and smiled. "Things are just going to continue getting crazier, aren't they?"

"I'm afraid so." Halla visibly shivered. "I'm very much afraid so."

17

Aɪᴅᴇᴅ ʙʏ ᴛʜᴇ Tʀᴀɴᴅᴏsʜᴀɴ's healthy shove, Corran flew through the darkened doorway. Unable to see anything, he curled himself into a ball and hoped he didn't land on his head. He smashed his shins into something hard, then bounced down onto his right shoulder before continuing his roll. He hit more things, most of which cried out, and all of which gave way, then came to an abrupt stop against something very solid.

Corran opened his eyes and in the dim light made out the smiling, bearded face of a positively huge man. He'd come to rest against the man's shin and thigh—clearly the man had dropped to one knee to stop Corran's tumble through the room. Back along his flight path Corran heard the muttered curses of people he'd knocked down.

The bearded man stood and dragged Corran to his feet. "Quite the entrance."

"I had help in making it." Corran plucked at the shoulders of his tan canvas tunic and tried to settle it in place. The bulky garment extended all the way to his knees. The sleeves ran to mid-forearm, but that was because the shoulder seam started well below the curve of his deltoids. Naked beneath it, Corran felt a little uncomfortable. He knew that was part of the psychological war waged by Isard on him and the other prisoners—deny them human clothing and you deny them a little piece of their humanity.

The big man nodded. "The Trandoshan doesn't like anyone. I'm Urlor Sette." He offered Corran his hand. Sette was missing the last two fingers of his right hand but didn't seem bashful or embarrassed about it.

Corran met the man's firm grip with a solid one of his own. "Corran Horn."

"Glad to make your acquaintance." Sette pointed off to the left. "Come on, I'll take you to the Old Man." The big man's voice carried with it equal measures of respect and affection, reminding Corran of how he'd often called Gil Bastra "the Old Man."

Must be the nominal leader among the prisoners here. Corran realized that his being thrust into the general Lusankya population could have been another ploy by Isard to get him to reveal information he'd not given up during interrogation. Because he did not have a clear memory of what he had actually said while being chemically debriefed, he didn't know what she might be looking to confirm or uncover. *For all I know, this is an elaborate charade. I will have to be on my guard.*

Urlor led Corran out of the area near the doorway and deeper into the cell complex. It appeared to have been ground and drilled out of solid rock. Thick dust coated the floor and hung in Urlor's wake like ground-covering fog. The irregular rock walls and ceiling had pockets of luminous lichen clinging to them. Their lime-green light gave the dust an eerie glow, and greyed out the flesh of those standing about.

Corran followed Urlor into a side chamber with an entrance low enough that even he had to duck his head. Beyond the threshold the big man straightened up and moved aside. On the opposite side of the circular room, barely six meters from the entrance, an older, white-haired and bearded man sat up and hung his legs over the edge of a hammock braided together from darkened strips of tunic canvas. Corran immediately had a vague sense that he'd seen the man before, or a holograph of him, but if so, it was a long time ago, and he couldn't place him.

"Sir, this is Corran Horn. They just delivered him to us."

The older man stood and straightened his tunic, then peered closely at Corran. He felt as if under the scrutiny of his first drill instructor at the Corellian Security Force Academy. The effect was not wholly unpleasant in that it reinforced the leadership role into which the old man had been cast. "Come here, son, let me see you close up."

Corran closed the gap between them and felt Urlor drop in behind him, ready to prevent him from doing any harm to the old man. "I'm with Rogue Squadron, a lieutenant."

"You have the look of a pilot about you—size, anyway. You've got a good leader in Antilles—assuming Skywalker's not back in charge there."

"No sir, he isn't. Wedge Antilles is still in charge, and is a commander now."

The older man nodded, then squinted at Corran's face. "You're from Corellia?"

"Yes, sir."

"Did I know your grandfather?"

Corran shrugged. "His name is Rostek Horn. He was with CorSec."

The old man shook his head and straightened up again. "No, I was thinking of someone else, from the Clone Wars. I don't recall Rostek Horn, though I might have met him once or twice. It's possible."

Though the man qualified his statement, Corran felt he was being polite instead of indecisive. Although his age had given him white hair and wrinkled skin, clearly the man's mental faculties were not suffering from the ravages of age. The old man knew exactly who it was he thought Corran looked like, and he also knew that he'd never met Corran's grandfather. That clarity of mind impressed Corran, as did the mannerly qualification of his firmly voiced denial.

The old man extended his hand to Corran. "My name's Jan." His dark eyes flicked up toward Urlor. "Despite what *he* will tell you, there's no rank here. That was for when we were people. Now we're just here."

"Pleased to meet you, sir." Corran shook the man's hand and found his grip firm even though his hands were a bit bony.

Jan sat back in the hammock. "You say Antilles has finally accepted a promotion?"

"Yes, sir."

"He always seemed level-headed. Good officer material. And who's commanding the fleet?"

Corran hesitated. "I'm not sure how much of that you want me to discuss, sir."

A smile spread across Jan's face. "Very good, my boy. If you're in here it's because Isard has sucked you dry like the spider she is, but caution is good." He glanced down. "It's just that some of us have been in here since Yavin and, well, we wonder about how the war is going. We've had others through here who have told us a lot. We know, for example, that the Emperor is dead and with him another Death Star. And we know about the Ssi-ruuk. But news has been pretty spare in the last year and a half—you're the first military man who's not an Imp who has ended up here for about that long. The few civilians who've been here have been interesting, but their knowledge of how the Rebellion is going has been filtered through Imp news sources."

Urlor landed a hand heavily on Corran's right shoulder. "Imps would have us believe Rogue Squadron is dead and gone. Died at a place called Borleias."

"Sure, in some Imp's lum dream." Corran turned, slipping from beneath Urlor's grip, so he could see both men at the same time. "Rogue Squadron did get hit hard at Borleias, but that was more the product of bad intel going in than it was anything the Imps actually did to us. The fact is, though, that inside a month after we got bloodied, we were back and took Borleias away from the Imps. And, from there, we staged for the invasion of Coruscant."

His smile grew broad as pride swelled inside him. "Rogue Squadron went into Coruscant and managed to bring the shields down. I don't remember much, but I know our fleet arrived and I was evacuated by Isard as she fled the planet, so I have to figure the New Republic now rules Coruscant. It's ours."

"It is yours because *we* gave it to you."

Corran looked to his right, toward the doorway, and saw an obese man squeezing his way through it. The tunic, which was black like the man's thinning hair, could barely contain the man's bulk. Anger filled the man's brown eyes for a second, then melted away as he straightened up and tugged at the hem of his sleeves. "You inherited a sick world, a dying world."

Jan bowed his head in the heavy man's direction. "This is General Evir Derricote, late of Imperial service. He is the ranking Imperial here among us."

Corran immediately realized that a secondary reason for the lack of titles among the Rebel prisoners was to allow them to further differentiate themselves from the Imps in Lusankya. "I'm Corran, and I was at Borleias."

"Then you saw me smash the little invasion fleet you sent against me."

"Yeah, I did, and I lost friends at that battle." Corran balled a fist and arced it toward Derricote's bullet head, but it never landed. Urlor lunged forward, grabbed the collar of Corran's tunic, and hauled him backward. Corran's feet left the floor and the canvas rasped against the flesh of his armpits as the big man held him up. "Hey! That hurts!"

Urlor kept his voice even. "There's a rule—if we beat up on Imps, the staff here beats up on the Old Man."

What I almost did. Corran's mouth hung open as if to give the twisting sensation in his stomach a chance to escape. He nodded once and Urlor put him back down. Corran turned to Jan and bowed his head. "I won't let it happen again."

"Spirit is good, Corran, very good." Jan coughed lightly into his hand. "The general here was the one who told us of Rogue Squadron's defeat at Borleias. He left out your apparent return and victory."

Derricote sniffed. "Had I still been on Borleias there would have been more Rebel blood shed."

"Not likely. We pinpointed the power generator at the Alderaan Biotics facility and severed the conduit that sent the auxiliary power to your shield generators and ion cannons. A handful of TIEs survived our second raid, and those pilots surrendered when they flew home and found their base in our hands." Corran shrugged. "And as for Coruscant, the fact that you use the word 'inherit' to describe what we did, well, it means that the world is ours now. It might be sick, but it's better off in our hands than it ever was in yours."

"I doubt the dying think that."

"I doubt the dying blame the Rebels for their problems."

Derricote shrugged, and a shiver ran through the layer of fat around his middle. "It does not matter to me who they blame. When the histories are written, this shall be but a momentary disturbance in the Empire's epic."

Jan rocked to his feet. "That will be up to the historians to determine, won't it, General?"

"When I get out and put together my memoirs, you will fare well, Jan." Derricote ducked his head and slid his body back out through the doorway. He paused halfway through, and Corran thought for a moment he might have been stuck, but the fat man turned to look at Jan again. "Before I forget what I came here for, a batch is ready."

"Thank you. I'll have Urlor organize a party to help you decant it." Jan nodded at Urlor and the large man stooped to force Derricote from the doorway, then followed him out. The older man smiled. "The general is a recent addition to our population, but he has proved himself useful in that he's good with biotics. He's managed to ferment a relatively mild ale here, providing us with a forbidden pleasure that many of us had forgotten."

"You trust him and drink it?"

Jan shrugged. "He drinks enough of it that if it were lethal, he'd have long since been dead. Despite being proud of his Imperial service, he seems somewhat perplexed by his imprisonment here. He thought he had fulfilled the parameters of a project for Iceheart, but she disagreed and he's here."

Corran nodded. "I can understand his confusion. I don't know why I'm here either."

"It may be temporary. We get a lot of transients who are transferred out in bulk. Traffic into and out of Lusankya seems to be relatively rare."

"That's not good news. If this place is truly a backwater planet, the chances of our being found by the Alliance are tiny."

Jan fingered the knots in the braided canvas cord that gathered his hair into a ponytail. "I've been here for, as nearly as I can determine, seven years, and no one has found me yet." His laugh came warm and natural, not tinged with the sort of madness Corran had heard in Derricote's laugh. "There's always tomorrow."

"Right." Corran sighed and looked around the small chamber. "Urlor's acquainted me with one rule. Are there others?"

"We do what we're told when we're told to do it. Rations are not great but are not starvation fare, either. Produce is seasonal but not so peculiar as to let us pinpoint where we are. I think there's an agrocombine maintained to supply us, though none of us down here ever see it. We assume there are lower grade prisoners who are used to maintain it, but we're in the deepest level, which has the highest security. At least that's where we think we are. Could be there's something more stringent, but I've not seen it."

"What do they have us do?"

"Hard labor make-work." The old man sighed. "Big rocks are made into little rocks, little rocks are made into gravel, and gravel is moved from one point to another. It is painfully and mind-numbingly boring, designed to crush hope and make the days meld one into another. It drives some of the men insane."

Corran lowered his voice. "Anyone ever escape?"

"Not quite that insane, son."

"No one has tried?"

"Few have tried, no one has made it."

"To your knowledge."

Jan's mouth opened, then he shut it and nodded. "To my knowledge—you are correct. At any rate, no one has made it since I've been here."

Corran frowned. "Those who have tried, they get brought back here?"

"Parts of them, anyway." The old man pointed vaguely off deeper into the caverns. "The Imps have a chamber where they keep the skulls and other relics of their dead. We smuggle ours into the mines where we work and bury them."

"So escape is impossible?"

Jan winked at him as he dropped his voice into a conspiratorial whisper. "I never said impossible, I just said it hadn't been done successfully."

Corran laughed quietly. "I'm with Rogue Squadron. Impossible is our stock in trade, and success is what we deliver."

Jan slapped him on the shoulder. "Now I'm thinking it's a pity I didn't know your grandfather. With a grandson like you, I'm sure we would have gotten along famously."

"I have a feeling you're right, sir." Corran nodded solemnly. "And being his grandson, I'm going to do everything I can to get out of and off of this rock."

The old man smiled. "From the moment I saw you, Corran Horn, I somehow expected nothing less."

18

WEDGE FELT MORE trapped by wearing a dress uniform and being in the witness box than he ever had in action against the Empire. He didn't see Halla Ettyk as a simulacrum of Ysanne Isard or an enemy warrior with whom he would be doing combat. The pleasant expression on her face belied either of those descriptions. Moreover, Wedge knew he had entered her arena—for him to think about defeating her here was as foolish as for her to imagine she could best him in a dogfight.

This is all about survival—mine and Tycho's survival.

The prosecutor looked up from her datapad. "Commander Antilles, how did you come to be on Coruscant before our forces had taken possession of it?"

"My squadron and I were inserted into Coruscant in a pathfinder capacity. We were here to evaluate the world from a number of points of view to determine if, how, and when the Alliance might want to attempt to take it."

"I see. What was the security classification on this operation?"

"The highest. If it had been known that we were coming or that we were here, we would have been dead."

Halla nodded sagely. "In preparation for sending your squadron out, what role did Captain Celchu play?"

Wedge shook his head. "He played no part."

"Why not?"

"Objection." Nawara stood at the defense table. "Calls for a conclusion."

"It goes to the witness's state of mind, Admiral."

Admiral Ackbar shook his head. "Counselor Ven, please do not object to questions calling for answers that Captain Celchu's commanding officer should know. Overruled. You may answer the question, Commander."

Wedge nodded. "Captain Celchu was seen as a security risk by General Cracken, so he was not involved in the preparation for the mission."

"Then how did Captain Celchu end up on Coruscant?"

This is not going to sound good. Wedge sighed. "I do not like covert missions. The things you don't know always seem to be the things that get you into trouble. If any of our people got picked up on the mission, it would be logical for the Imps to conclude there were more of us present, and hunt us down. I wanted someone on Coruscant whom I could trust to get me out of difficult situations."

"So you chose someone that Alliance Intelligence did not trust."

"I chose Tycho for a number of very good reasons, Commander Ettyk. He had been to Coruscant before and knew his way around."

"But he was captured on Coruscant, correct?"

"Yes."

"And imprisoned in a place the Empire uses to create covert operatives, correct?"

"So I have been told."

Halla smiled slightly and gave him a slight nod. Wedge felt it was the sort of salute one pilot might toss another for a good shot—the sort of salute that came with the promise of destruction on the next pass. A wave of heat washed over him and he

wanted to loosen the collar of his dark green jacket. *Can't.
Don't want to let her know she's beginning to get to me.*

"Commander Antilles, why did you feel you needed your
own person operating independently on Coruscant?"

"If things went bad and some or all of General Cracken's
operation here on Coruscant was uncovered, we would be in
dire straits."

"Did you have a reason to suppose there *was* a chance the
operation would be compromised?"

"I'm not certain I understand the question."

"What reasons did you have to fear your operation might be
compromised to Imperial Intelligence?"

"There is always a risk of such betrayal with any covert operation. Certainly the fact that we were going to be on Coruscant had to suggest that was a possibility."

"And you knew, as you just told us, that Captain Celchu had
been captured on Coruscant, so that was certainly in your
mind, yes?"

Wedge frowned. *Where is she going with this?* "Yes."

"And there were other incidents involving Rogue Squadron
where betrayal had been previously mentioned, correct?"

"I am not certain I understand what you mean by that."

"Please characterize for the court the first mission to Borleias."

"It was an unmitigated disaster. I lost people, the Alliance
lost people, and we didn't take the planet."

Halla glanced down at her datapad. "And there was an investigation conducted upon your return to determine if your
mission had been betrayed to the enemy, was there not?"

"Yes, but Tycho was never implicated, never under suspicion."

"I know—still, your mission to Coruscant was staging from
Noquivzor, which was where the mission to Borleias staged
from, was it not?"

"Yes."

"So the spectre of a chance that whoever might have betrayed your first mission to Borleias could betray your mission to Coruscant certainly existed, did it not?"

"Yes."

"Hence your precaution."

"Yes."

"And yet you would tell us that you had no cause to suspect Captain Celchu of collusion with the enemy?"

Wedge blinked as Halla shifted her aim to a new target. "I had no reasons to suspect Tycho of anything."

The prosecutor's head came up. "You did not find the circumstances of Bror Jace's death the least bit suspicious?"

"Excuse me?"

Halla folded her arms across her chest. "I believe, Commander Antilles, you were present in the courtroom for the testimony of Captain Uwlla Iillor in regard to the mission to capture Bror Jace. At the time of his death did you not consider the possibility that news of his travel to Thyferra had been leaked to the Empire?"

"No."

"Not at all?"

"Well, not in any substantive way, and certainly not with Tycho being the source of the leak."

Halla narrowed her eyes. "Who obtained the permissions and filed the flight plan for Bror Jace's trip to Thyferra?"

"Tycho did, by *my* order."

"Did you approve the flight plan?"

Wedge hesitated as he felt pressure building up in himself. "No."

"Did you *know* the flight plan?"

"No."

"To the best of your knowledge, did anyone in your squadron outside of Captain Celchu and Bror Jace know that flight plan?"

Wedge's hands pulsed into fists. "No."

"Captain Iillor testified that her ship, the *Black Asp*, had been given specific orders as to where to go and when to be there to encounter Bror Jace. How could they have gotten that information, do you think?"

"A spy, I suppose. I don't know. Espionage is not really my stock in trade."

"So you would have a difficult time determining if someone was a spy or not?"

Wedge glanced down. "You're good at twisting my words, Commander. I know Tycho wasn't working for the Empire."

Halla's eyes narrowed. "You may have felt that, Commander Antilles, but tell me truthfully, when Corran Horn told you he'd seen Captain Celchu speaking to an Imperial Intelligence operative, tell me you didn't wonder, just for a heartbeat, if everything General Cracken and others had said about Tycho Celchu wasn't true."

Wedge closed his eyes. When Corran had come to him on Coruscant and reported what he had seen, Wedge had been unable to cover his shock. *I said to him, "That's impossible, Corran." I followed up with the explanation about Warlord Zsinj having attacked Noquivzor, but the first thing out of my mouth had been a denial of what I feared might be true. Just for a second I allowed myself to accept what he said, I refused to let myself* believe *what he had said, but I knew I could not* prove *his statement to be absolutely false.*

The leader of Rogue Squadron nodded and refrained from looking over at Tycho. "Yes, for a heartbeat, I did allow myself to consider what Lieutenant Horn said. I rejected it just that quickly."

"On what grounds?"

"I knew Tycho wasn't a spy."

Halla raised an eyebrow. "You didn't know Zekka Thyne was working for the Empire, did you?"

"No, but I never truly trusted him."

"Your opinion of him and his treacherous nature was based on what?"

"His history and . . ." Wedge caught himself.

"And?"

"His demeanor when I saw him."

Halla Ettyk opened her hands. "Were there no other factors in your forming your opinion of Thyne?"

Ven stood. "Objection, relevancy, your Honor."

Admiral Ackbar looked down at the prosecutor. "Commander, this does seem a bit far afield from where you started."

"It is relevant, your Honor. I'm closing in on my point."

"Proceed, but be aware I will strike this line of inquiry if you don't bring us to that point quickly."

"Yes, sir."

"The objection is overruled."

Ettyk nodded toward Wedge. "Commander, were there no other factors in your forming your opinion of Thyne?"

"Not really."

"Lieutenant Horn's opinion of Thyne was not important to you?"

"It was, and it was a factor, though Thyne's hostility to Corran was more indicative of trouble than anything else."

"But you felt your observations of Thyne justified Horn's opinion of the man?"

"Yes."

"So, when Thyne turned out to be an Imperial plant you had not detected, but whom Horn had warned you about, didn't you have to reconsider Captain Celchu's position in regard to what Horn thought about him?"

Wedge shook his head. "To be honest, Commander, there was so much happening at the time Thyne was revealed to be a traitor, that I could only consider one thing: getting my mission done. We had just received word that we had to bring the shields down so our fleet could invade. Mind you, Tycho passed that message to me. If he were an Imperial plant, he could have withheld that information and set a trap for our fleet."

"So then, Commander Antilles, you are *not* of the opinion that the Empire gave us this world, infected as it is with the Krytos virus, to destroy us?"

"I have no idea, Commander Ettyk, what was in the mind of Ysanne Isard at the time we took Coruscant."

"I see." Halla Ettyk took a datadisk from Iella Wessiri and exchanged it for one in her datapad. "But you do not discount that possibility, correct?"

"I cannot discount it."

"And you cannot discount the possibility that Captain Celchu was working for the Empire in helping give Coruscant to the New Republic."

"Yes I can." Wedge nodded solemnly. "I know Tycho. I know he's not a spy. I trust him."

"And you trusted Zekka Thyne until proved wrong about him, didn't you, Commander?"

"No, that's not the way it was."

"Perhaps not to you, Commander, but it was to one man." Halla Ettyk shrugged casually. "Corran Horn. And now he's dead."

Outside the courtroom, Wedge slumped against the cold stone wall. *Nawara tried to rehabilitate me as a witness, but the damage was done, I wanted to be in there and help Tycho, but I didn't.* He hammered a fist against the wall. "Sithspawn!"

He straightened up immediately as a woman closed to within inches of him. She held up a comlink and nodded to a holocam-carrying Ithorian. "This is Zaree Lolvanci, Kuati First Holo-News, and I'm standing here with Alliance hero, Commander Wedge Antilles. How does it feel, Commander, to know that your testimony is what will convict Captain Celchu?"

Before Wedge could gather his wits enough to answer, a body sliced between the holojournalist and him. Wedge felt a strong grip on his upper arm and heard a firm voice reply to the question in his place. "Commander Antilles's only interest in this matter is seeing justice done. He has every confidence that his faith in Captain Celchu will be vindicated when the defense presents its case. Until then, any speculation on the outcome would be premature and possibly prejudicial. And he has no further comment."

Wedge let Diric Wessiri guide him past the Ithorian and on through a security checkpoint, where two guards stopped the reporter and her holographer. Diric steered him to a bench and sat beside him. "Odious people, the holoshills, aren't they, Commander Antilles?"

"They don't make a very good first impression . . ."

"No, but it tends to last." The older man smiled at him. "How are you holding up?"

Wedge nodded. "I think I will be able to recover. Just need some time." He regarded the slender man closely. Though his flesh still seemed a bit ashen, spirit and fortitude shone in his eyes. "Thank you for saving me."

"I am glad I was able to help." Diric gave him a smile that appeared artificial only in that it looked as if Diric had to consciously work at remembering how to smile. "Iella was afraid something like that would happen. She sent me after you."

"I'd have thought she was happy with the turn of events. Commander Ettyk ate me alive."

"No, she wasn't happy." Diric patted a tunic pocket. "I have a pass that can take us up to the secure parking area. We can get in my airspeeder and leave here. Iella said she would be willing to join us later for dinner, if you wish."

"I doubt I would be very good company." Wedge glanced back toward the courtroom. "I wanted to end Tycho's persecution with my testimony, and all I did was leave the impression that even I think he was a spy."

"Not at all." Diric tapped Wedge's thigh with a finger. "First of all, the Tribunal judges know you and know how difficult that was for you. All Commander Ettyk really did was establish that Tycho was on Coruscant at your request and that the possibility of betrayal was in your mind."

"Sure, but she also made it sound like I wouldn't know who was a spy and who wasn't."

"Why would you?"

"What?"

Diric opened his hands. "As you said, ferreting out spies is not what you do. No one expects you to have been able to spot him as a spy if he was, and you certainly couldn't if he wasn't. And, between you and me, I don't think he is a spy."

"Thanks."

"None necessary. I've had a number of conversations with Captain Celchu in jail and I find him thoroughly likable. If he's a spy, well, then all of us are suspects." Diric held a hand up. "I would also like to point out that I have attended many trials in my time, and you did no worse on the stand than many people I have seen. You see your performance as hideous because you were hoping to put the state's case away with one telling shot. Unfortunately the case against Tycho isn't a Death Star. It isn't going to go away that easily. Nawara Ven knows what he's doing, though, and he'll do a good job."

Wedge stared down at his hands. "I'd like to believe you, but I feel the way I did at Yavin, when Luke told me to pull up out of the trench on the Death Star. Luke was right, there wasn't anything else I could do, but to abandon the effort at that point, it just didn't feel right."

"I understand that, but Luke Skywalker was correct and the Death Star was destroyed."

"Yes, but Biggs Darklighter died. If I'd stayed in there, maybe—"

"Maybe he would have lived and you would have died?" Diric shook his head ruefully. "And you probably think that if you had been flying the night Coruscant was taken, Corran would still live?"

I hadn't thought about it, but, yes, that notion has been bouncing around in the back of my mind. "It's not that I have a death wish, you know."

"I know that very well, Wedge. I have seen this survivor's guilt in Iella, in Corran and his father, and in others." He pressed a hand to his own chest. "Even I have known it. We all have friends and acquaintances who meet with what we see as an untimely death. With me, because I do nothing, I wonder why it wasn't me who died. I wonder what I have done to survive. With you and others who actively oppose evil, you wonder what it is that you could have done to prevent another person's death. Those questions have no answers—at least none outside the philosophical realm. For me they are a point of departure for thought, but for you and my wife they are just sources of frustration and regret.

"This is why, of course, my wife is working so hard to uncover who caused Corran's death. That's the only way she will be able to defeat the frustration and assuage her feelings of guilt. She hated what you were put through on the stand, because you are her friend, but her loyalty to Corran demanded she sit through it and help Commander Ettyk, if need be." Diric shook his head. "Fortunately she did not have to help. You two are enough alike that I imagine you can see how much that would have hurt her."

"Yeah, I can see it." Wedge rubbed at his temples with both hands. "And I can understand the frustration. I have to wonder if there was a way to prevent Corran's death."

"Undoubtedly there was, Wedge, but it was not open to you. *If* Captain Celchu was a spy, then General Cracken and Winter and Iella all missed the signs of it."

"But Corran didn't."

Diric's smile returned more naturally. "As much as I valued Corran as a friend, he was not always right."

"So Whistler has indicated."

"And no one knew him better." Diric patted him on the leg. "Maintain your faith in your friend. He deserves it."

"Again, thank you."

"No thanks are necessary. So, would you like me to take you somewhere? We can eat or drink and Iella can join us."

Wedge thought for a moment, then shook his head. "There should be another two hours of testimony today, shouldn't there?"

"Yes. Winter was called after you were."

Watching Winter testify has got to be hard on Iella. They were even closer than Iella and I became, and with Winter and Tycho being together . . . "Iella will need you there, because Winter's testimony is going to be tougher on her than mine."

"But you shouldn't be alone right now."

"I won't be." Wedge jerked a thumb toward the east. "I'm going to go down a level, then over to the Galactic Museum via the walkway. I'll spend some time in the Criminal Gallery, visiting old friends, then I'll come back here when court is adjourned for the day and take you up on your offer. I have a feeling that when today is over, Iella isn't going to want to be alone either. No matter how this turns out, I do consider her a friend, and I want to make sure she has no reason to doubt that at all."

19

G AVIN SHIFTED HIS shoulders uneasily and tugged at the cuffs of his dress jacket. *I feel about as comfortable here as Commander Antilles did on the witness stand.*

Asyr slipped her arm through his as the tether-lift stopped and the doors opened. "It's not going to be that bad, Gavin. Liska Dan'kre, our hostess, is an old friend of mine. We schooled together before I went off to the Academy."

"If she's hiring a skyhook for this party, she must be filthy rich."

Asyr purred contentedly. "Rich, yes, but you'll find nothing filthy about her." She led Gavin from the lift box onto the entry platform which overlooked the whole of the skyhook's disk. "Impressive, isn't it?"

"Yeah." The circular skyhook actually formed a bowl with several pathways spiraling down through forested depths to a central courtyard. A kilometer in diameter, the floating garden flew high over the mountain district of Coruscant. Off to the northeast, beyond the Manarai Mountains, Gavin saw the top of the Imperial Palace. "I can't believe I'm here."

Asyr looked up at him, puzzlement riding openly on her face. "What's wrong?"

Where to begin? "Nothing, really, I suppose. It's just that, well, on Tatooine we had no skyhooks. They weren't deemed safe enough—one good dust storm blows up out of the nastier regions and it would pull one of these skyhooks from the sky."

The Bothan patted his hand. "The repulsorlift generators are more than sufficient for keeping this skyhook aloft. Don't worry about that."

"Then there's the jungle." He gave her a weak smile. "You weren't with us on one of our duty stations, but it looked a lot like this. I got shot there. My stomach is already acting up because of it."

Asyr rubbed her hand over the faint trace of a scar on his belly. "I've seen what the bacta left you for a souvenir, remember, love?"

Gavin blushed. "Yeah."

"And I think you're not nervous about that as much as you're nervous about being here among my people." She raised a finger and pressed it to his lips to forestall a comment. "I know you're not bigoted—if you were you'd not be here—but you've even said yourself that most of your life has been spent among humans. It's not unusual to be anxious when outnumbered—I feel it whenever we go to places where humans predominate."

Gavin's shoulders sagged a centimeter or two. "I should have realized . . . I'm sorry."

"Don't be." Asyr smiled broadly. "Come on, let's make an impression on my friends."

Gavin brought his head up and smiled. "As you wish, Asyr, so shall it be."

Together they descended from the entry platform and started off on a path that took a long, looping spiral down to the central courtyard. The guests at the party were mostly Bothans, and all of them stared at the couple as they walked past. Gavin knew that had to be because of the high-necked, sleeveless gown Asyr wore. Woven of iridescent blue and purple thread, the color shifted and shimmered with her every movement. The garment clung tight to her slender body, but the fact that the skirts had been slit from ankle to high on her thigh meant she was not hampered while walking. She'd loosely draped a simple blue stole, woven from the metallic thread used in her dress, across her back and through her elbows, completing the outfit.

Other Bothan females wore similar gowns, but none so well. Though he was not wholly adept at reading Bothan body language and facial expressions, the rippling of fur on necks and shoulders of those they passed by told him that Asyr's gown was making quite an impression indeed. Gavin thought he looked pretty sharp in his Rogue Squadron uniform, but he was a black hole compared with a supernova, and quite content with that role.

As they reached the courtyard, a lithe female Bothan with black and tan markings excused herself from a circle of individuals who were listening to Borsk Fey'lya holding forth on something. She wore a gown similar in design to Asyr's, though it had been made of cloth of gold and had been accented with jet beadwork in the form of stripes. She beamed broadly as she approached them. "Asyr Sei'lar, you are a vision!"

Asyr gave her friend a big hug. "Thank you for the invitation, Liska."

Liska pulled back and looked up at Gavin. "And you are Asyr's friend."

Gavin executed a semiformal bow. "Gavin Darklighter of Rogue Squadron, pleased to make your acquaintance." He took her hand in his and shook it gently.

Liska sighed contentedly, then smiled at Asyr. "So mannerly, no wonder you find him so attractive. How did you meet him?"

Asyr hesitated for a moment. "I was part of an operation in Invisec before the liberation. We met then."

Gavin smiled. "She was trying to get me executed as an example to the Imps."

"You always did play a little rough, Asyr."

Asyr shrugged. "Luckily he had Nawara Ven defending him, so the execution was delayed. Imps showed up, Gavin saved my life and I his in the ensuing firefight. Not much more to tell than that."

"Quite the first date, Asyr. It's a wonder he dared go out with you again." Liska linked her arm through Asyr's. "You never seemed to get into this sort of trouble when I've been there to keep you safe."

"True enough."

Liska looked up at Gavin. "I'm going to steal her away for a moment or two, just to get caught up. You don't mind, do you?"

Gavin gave her a big smile and shook his head. "Not at all— seeing you again is all she's talked about since the invitation came. I'll just find myself something to drink."

Asyr reached out and gave his right hand a squeeze. "Won't be but a minute."

"Have fun." Gavin watched Liska lead her away, then looked around, surveying his surroundings. Knots of individuals— almost exclusively Bothans—dominated the landscape. About the only place they were not predominant was at one bar where a couple of humans, two Ithorians, and a handful of other non-Bothan individuals seemed to have taken up residence. Gavin drifted off in that direction, keeping his strides even and his head up even though something in his belly made him want to hurry over there.

He looked at the bartender. "Lomin-ale, please."

A short, balding man smiled over at him. "You should drink the expensive stuff—the Bothans are paying for it."

"Perhaps, but I *like* lomin-ale." Gavin accepted the frothy green glass of ale, sipped, then licked the foam off his upper lip. The ale was good, though not nearly cold enough for his tastes. *Bothans don't seem to like particularly cold drinks, so that's not a big surprise, I guess.*

The shorter man offered Gavin his hand. "Herrit Gordon, Ministry of State."

"Gavin Darklighter, Rogue Squadron."

Herrit shook his hand firmly. "Glad to meet you. I did a tour of duty with the Diplomatic Corps on Bothawui, so they felt they had to invite me." He pointed off toward a woman who looked positively dowdy amid a circle of Bothan females. "That's my wife, Tatavan. She learned to speak Bothan, so she's quite popular among the Bothans."

"A useful skill, I have no doubt. I only know a few words." Gavin sipped his ale again. "I came with Asyr Sei'lar. She's a friend of Liska Dan'kre."

"I know the family. I liaised with her father on Bothawui. Minor nobles, but they have a thriving trade business to support them, so they wield a bit more power than might be imagined by their place in the formal hierarchy."

"Powerful, really?"

"She was able to bring you, wasn't she?"

Gavin frowned and drank again, killing the need for an immediate reply. *I know she didn't bring me as a trophy—she told me that much and I believe her.* "You make it sound as if she's trying to annoy some of the folks here."

"Not the impression I meant to make, I'm afraid. Asyr is something of a renegade. She went to school with Liska and some of the others."

"I know. She told me."

"I'm sure she did. That school, however, was meant to prepare her for a life as a trader or in a governmental position. Without her family's permission she transmitted an application to the Bothan Martial Academy and was accepted. She did very well there, and her family is very proud of her accomplishments, but they wonder when she will abandon what they see as adventurism and get a real career."

Gavin's smile returned to his face. "I doubt that will happen very soon. Asyr seems very at home in the squadron."

"Don't underestimate the pull of the Bothan family structure. Their families are very tightly bound together."

"Nothing wrong with that."

Herrit nodded, then looked toward his wife and paled. Gavin followed his gaze and saw a trio of male Bothans approaching them. The leader stood as tall as Gavin, though he did not have Gavin's bulk. Creamy white fur and golden eyes contrasted with the black uniform he wore. His subordinates wore similar uniforms, but their fur was a motley riot of orange and black.

The lead Bothan stopped right in front of Gavin, but did not offer a hand in greeting. "I am Karka Kre'fey, grandson of General Laryn Kre'fey. You were with Rogue Squadron at Borleias?"

"I was." Setting his ale on the bar, Gavin aped Karka's stance by grasping his hands together at the small of his back. "Is there something I can do for you?"

"Reports on the assault suggest my grandfather was poorly prepared for the assault and made foolish decisions in the battle."

"And?"

The Bothan's golden eyes burned with anger. "I would know if you feel these reports are correct."

Gavin ignored the gasp from Herrit. "In my opinion, they are."

Karka's open-handed slap arrived with no warning and caught Gavin over the left cheek, snapping his head around. Gavin staggered back a step, but the bar kept him from going down. He grabbed onto it with his hands, then straightened up slowly. He wanted to shake his head to kill the ringing in his ears, but he stopped himself and instead looked Karka hard in the eyes.

"I understand your being upset over your grandfather's death."

"I am upset because you have besmirched his honor."

"Be that as it may, don't slap me again."

"Or?"

Herrit stepped forward. "Please, let's not have an altercation here."

Gavin reached out and grabbed Herrit by the back of the

neck. He directed the diplomat back to his place at the bar. "We're not going to have a fight, sir."

Karka's lip curled back in a snarl. "You have sullied the honor of the Kre'fey family. I challenge you to a duel."

Gavin shook his head slowly. "No."

"You refuse to accept?"

"I will not fight you."

"Then you are a coward."

Gavin laughed aloud. Just a year previous he would have leaped on Karka and done his best to pummel him, but his time with Rogue Squadron had changed him so that was not an option. *Actually, it is an option, but not one I'm compelled to choose.* In the last year Wedge and Corran and even Tycho had impressed upon him the fact that what others thought and said didn't matter—it was the person inside and what he thought of himself that mattered. *That's what allows Tycho to endure everything he's going through. He's got a quiet kind of courage that doesn't require boasts and defenses because it's the courage that kicks in when it's really needed.*

While part of him still wanted to know the satisfaction of using his fist to disassociate Karka's teeth from their sockets, another part of him reveled in his freedom to ignore the challenge. Because he would not allow himself to be aroused by the Bothan's taunts, those taunts had no power. They became pitiful in their efforts, and transparent. *And ignoring them hurts Karka more than any physical damage I could inflict upon him.*

Gavin met Karka's molten stare. "Call me a coward if you wish, I don't care. You are not my enemy. My enemy is the Empire and its remnants. Maybe you can't see that. Your grandfather *could*. Strikes me that you honor his memory more by continuing his crusade than in trying to hide mistakes he may have made." He extended his right hand toward the Bothan.

Karka stared at it as if it were a snake, then snarled and spun on his heel. His subordinates fell into step with him, prompting a sigh of relief from Herrit as they departed.

The bartender plopped a fresh lomin-ale on the bar for Gavin. "To your health, sir."

Herrit clinked his lum mug against the glass. "You handled that well. Sorry I got in your way."

"No blood, no report." Gavin worked his jaw around and heard it pop. "I'll be feeling that tomorrow."

Asyr appeared at his side. "What happened?"

Gavin shrugged. "Nothing, really."

Herrit smiled. "Just a couple of boys getting some exercise."

Asyr looked up at Gavin. "Exercise?"

He smiled and nodded. "Yeah. I gave that maturity you were talking about a workout. Felt pretty good, too."

"If you want to leave, we can."

Gavin shook his head. "No, stay and see your friends. Have fun. I don't think there's going to be any more excitement tonight."

THE FACT THAT Borsk Fey'lya was nowhere to be seen heartened Admiral Ackbar greatly as he entered Mon Mothma's living quarters. The presence of General Cracken confirmed that the reason he had been summoned was business, but that everything would be conducted informally. Whatever action needed to be referred to the Provisional Council would be in its own good time.

Had he thought Mon Mothma possessed a Bothan's sense of subtlety, he would have assumed the way her apartments had been redecorated were designed to encourage a sense of well-being in him. Diaphanous blue and green drapes rippled gently in front of the windows—the movement being caused by the air conditioning, though it did suggest the windows behind the drapes were open. The carpeting had a rich aquamarine hue to it, and the tile pattern used to decorate the lower half of the wall had a nautical motif. The upper part of the wall matched the carpet in color, but the recessed oscillating lights in the ceiling gently picked up and sparkled from the rainbow pinpoints worked into the paint.

Even the furnishings were more to his liking than most. Painted in greens, browns, and blues, they had an organic and flowing shape to them. They lacked the pure symmetry that most humans seemed to prefer. The table in the center of the room, for example, could have been water that had been poured out on the ground, frozen, and then placed atop legs. The lack of sharp edges and jagged corners somehow drained tension from the room, and Ackbar felt himself relaxing.

Mon Mothma smiled in warm welcome. "I thank you for coming so quickly after I sent for you. I know the trial is your primary concern and is occupying much of your time."

"The trial is indeed a concern of mine, but I consider it a cove, when my real concern is the ocean of security for the New Republic." Ackbar opened his hands. "I must compliment you on the decor—I find it most pleasing. You grew up in one of Chandrila's port cities, did you not?"

"Yes, my mother was the governor there. I learned to love the Silver Sea. I find that making my home over in the image of where I lived in better times is good for my sanity."

"You have done a wonderful job." Ackbar looked around the room again. "It is a pity to bring the discussion of difficult times into such a beautiful place."

"There are always compromises that become necessary." Mon Mothma waved Ackbar to a floating chair fashioned after a fan of blue seaweed. She seated herself in a similar chair, and General Cracken joined them by dragging over a green coral chair. "There are some things that have come up that could require Council activity, but I think it would be better to present them to the Council as *fait accompli*."

Ackbar's barbels twitched. "Insulating the Council from a backlash?"

"And preventing the chance for people to profit from what we are going to be doing, materially or politically." Mon Mothma sighed heavily. "There are times I can see glimmers of what made the Emperor decide to dissolve the Senate. I reject that course of action, but I can certainly feel its allure. I especially hate it when action that is necessary is delayed so various individuals can set themselves up to reap the benefits of doing what they have no choice but to do. Not the way it was when we had to deal directly with the Empire."

"I have ridden the crest of that wave myself, Mon Mothma. Being a rebellion was much more simple than being a government." Ackbar settled back into his chair and folded his hands into his lap. "What is it you would have of me?"

Mon Mothma looked at General Cracken. "You might want to give the Admiral some of the background on this."

Cracken nodded. "Though the pro-Palpatine terrorists last struck ten days ago, that attack has had a chilling effect on our bacta distribution efforts. The Krytos virus is beginning to spread a bit more quickly than we projected when we got the bacta from Warlord Zsinj. People are balancing their fear of the disease against their fear of being at ground zero of a terrorist attack. Black market prices for bacta are beginning to climb again because, in effect, the PCF attack has made our bacta off-limits to a lot of people. The demand for bacta from other sources is thus increasing, and so are the prices."

Ackbar gave Cracken a wall-eyed stare. "Vorru and his militia have not been able to crack down on the black marketeers?"

"Vorru claims his people are concentrating on keeping the PCF under wraps. They're reacting to every rumor they get and, though we have not released this information to the public, they *have* uncovered a couple of bombs that our people think were created by the PCF. I do not for a minute think Vorru is playing everything entirely straight, but his people are maintaining order in a sector we had no chance of controlling."

"And how does this concern me?"

Mon Mothma nodded. "General Cracken has been in charge of some ultra-secret researches into the Krytos virus. Details of them have been kept even from me, but their continuation requires a quantity of ryll."

The Mon Calamari pressed his hands together. "And that will require an expedition to Ryloth."

"Precisely. Aside from getting the ryll, I think this will be an excellent opportunity for us to open some diplomatic channels with the Twi'leks, even if it is only at a very low level."

"And you will want Counselor Ven to go."

"Yes." Mon Mothma smiled. "All of Rogue Squadron, in fact. Commander Antilles made quite an impression there several years ago, and the contribution of Nawara Ven to the taking of Coruscant has attracted a lot of attention on Ryloth. This notoriety will add weight to our negotiating position."

"So you need me to delay the trial *and* release Rogue Squadron to this duty."

The leader of the New Republic narrowed her eyes. "Is there a problem with this? Surely you can find a reason to grant a continuance in the case."

Ackbar's mouth dropped open in a silent laugh. "Find *a* reason? I could find a school of them, Chief Councilor. I applaud General Cracken's ability to uncover so much so quickly about Captain Celchu's involvement with the Empire—the pace of discovery is remarkable. The trial is moving with such alacrity that there is no way the defense has adequate time to prepare. Counselor Ven is doing his best, but this is clearly the most difficult assignment he's been given since joining Rogue Squadron."

"So this is not a problem?"

"No, though I suppose the continuance cannot be granted on the grounds that Rogue Squadron is going off on a secret mission to Ryloth?" When silence met his question, Ackbar opened his mouth in a smile. "I was being facetious. It was a joke."

Cracken laughed, but Mon Mothma just smiled. "Forgive me, my friend, but as General Cracken will attest, I have not heard many things that make me laugh of late."

"I understand." Ackbar sat forward. "I will, of course, clear Rogue Squadron for the mission. Will you be wanting Erisi Dlarit to fly that mission?"

"I should think so. Is there a reason we would not want her on it?"

Ackbar shrugged. "Since she is involved in pushing the Xucphra corporation to sell us a great deal of bacta, I would think putting her in jeopardy on a mission would be contra-indicated."

Mon Mothma looked at her Intelligence director. "Is she in danger on this run, General?"

Cracken frowned. "We anticipate no trouble."

Ackbar blinked his eyes. "And if the mission is betrayed to the PCF?"

"We have the Imperial spy, don't we? Isn't that why Captain Celchu is on trial?"

"Yes, Chief Councilor." Cracken's dark eyes sharpened. "What the Admiral is suggesting is that we cannot be certain Captain Celchu was the *only* spy in service to the Empire. The potential for betrayal does exist here *and* on the Ryloth side of things. While sending her out might endanger her, holding her back might be taken incorrectly by officials on Thyferra, dooming that deal."

"But if she dies, that could also hurt us." Mon Mothma shook her head. "The lack of clear-cut decisions is what makes this job so difficult. The Thyferrans seem to set great store by Erisi Dlarit's flying with Rogue Squadron. I suppose we will have to let her go."

Ackbar nodded. "I concur. That is the tide on which you should sail."

"And you, General Cracken," Mon Mothma said, "will have to make certain security around this mission is not breached. We cannot afford to have the mission disrupted, nor can we af-ford to lose Erisi Dlarit."

"Of this, I am aware." General Cracken nodded solemnly. "I understand the gravity of the situation. If there is a leak, we'll find it—find it and eliminate it. The New Republic can afford for us to do nothing less."

20

"I AM FAIRLY CERTAIN, Colonel Vorru, that I do not like this turn of events at all." Kirtan Loor peered down at the smaller man but clearly did not have quite the intimidating effect on him that Loor wanted. "I invited you here to inform you of my plan as a *courtesy*, not to allow you to veto it."

Fliry Vorru shrugged. "Ah, but I *have* vetoed it."

No! "No! I cannot allow this." Loor's hands balled into fists. "My agreement with you was to let you select domestic targets that help weaken the New Republic's government. I have abided by your decisions in any case where the target was of that sort. This is not one of those cases."

Loor stalked around his darkened office, flitting like a moth around the circle of light that anointed Fliry Vorru and made his white hair shine brilliantly. "The destruction of Rogue Squadron has been a priority with me since well before they took Imperial Center, and now, *now* they are within my grasp. I have a squadron of X-wings here on Imperial Center that I will use to attack Rogue Squadron's base and destroy them on the ground. It will be perfect and will allow me to finish a mission that has taken far too long to complete."

Vorru leaned back in Loor's tall chair and put his booted feet up on the surface of the desk, scattering a stack of datacards. "What were once your priorities do not matter to me. I deem this attack too risky. Cracken will suspect I leaked information about Rogue Squadron's impending mission to you."

"No, no he won't." Loor's fingers itched to be punching data up on his datapad—*or to be strangling you, Vorru.* "I uncovered evidence of a run to Ryloth based on fluctuations in the secondary ryll-derivatives black market. I traced it back to a woman in the medical corps who's been making extra money producing her own brand of patent medicine. It's mostly lum, with ryll and a drop or two of bacta in it—useless, of course, but she's begun to raise the price. It's assumed that when Rogue Squadron brings the ryll back to Coruscant, its effectiveness against the virus will be touted and her medicine will be in high demand. I can give her to you and you can point her out as the leak."

"Suggesting that a quack producing a folk remedy led you to Rogue Squadron is what will get me implicated."

"Nonsense." Loor slapped his hands against his hips in frustration. "You know as well as I do that Ryloth is as dark a den of *iniquity* as exists this side of Varl. The Twi'leks have not supported the Rebellion in any great numbers, so the most prominent Twi'lek in the New Republic is Nawara Ven. The Republic has to use him as their negotiator and, lo and behold, the prosecution asks for and gets a continuance of the case. That leaves plenty of time for Rogue Squadron to make the trip to Ryloth and back. The only obvious assumption is that they're going to make the trip."

Loor shook his head. "I've known *where* Rogue Squadron has been stationed for a while now. This is my opportunity to hit them right at a time when the failure of their mission will severely hurt the New Republic."

"Your reasoning is flawless, Agent Loor, but that concerns me not at all." Vorru's dark eyes glittered. "I even find your devotion toward the elimination of Rogue Squadron admirable.

However, your taking action against Rogue Squadron does not suit me at this time; therefore you cannot launch your assault."

"And if I choose to ignore your *advice*?"

Vorru twisted his head slightly sideways. "Do you really want to test me, Kirtan Loor?"

Loor hesitated, losing his chance to snap back a defiant answer. Anyone else asking that question would have filled the words with impending doom, but Vorru asked it in an easy tone, as if asking a child if she were certain she wanted to do something that was obviously dangerous. His expression, his posture, bore no obvious menace, and yet Loor found himself more fearful of Vorru than he would be of a buzzadder coiled and ready to strike in his place.

"Testing you would get neither of us anywhere."

"I always thought you were more than reasonable." Vorru swung his feet off the desk and swiveled the chair around so he could stand. He withdrew a datacard from inside his militia tunic and tossed it on the desk. "You and your people have been good and have done nothing of import for nearly two weeks. I have found you a new target."

Loor exchanged places with Vorru, spun the chair around, and dropped into it. He pulled himself around to face the desk and saw Vorru's shadowed form standing opposite him. Loor shoved the datacard into his datapad, punched up a directory, then opened the file labeled "target.die." The architectural renderings of a building showing stress points filled the small screen.

The Intelligence agent looked up. "It's small. I don't see bacta storage areas or barracks facilities. What is it?"

"A school."

"School?" Loor frowned. "You mean a training academy?"

"No, a school. For children."

"Children of the Rebel leadership?"

"Hardly. They've been too busy to breed." Vorru shook his head quickly. "This is just a normal school, with normal children—some aliens, but mostly human."

"Why?"

"Why? Because the students are drawn from the local population."

Loor's frown deepened, and confusion made his voice tenuous. "No, why hit a school?"

"Come now, Agent Loor, you didn't expect to get great results without inflicting great pain, did you?" Vorru laughed lightly. "You probably thought you could cling to some shred of honor. By hitting factories and military facilities and places where adults congregated, you could put fear into them. By hitting bacta distribution centers, you could make parents concerned about the welfare of their children, but it would be the Krytos virus that killed the children, not you. Is that it?"

"I . . . perhaps . . ."

"Perhaps nothing, *that* is *exactly* what you were thinking. And because of it, your efforts would have been for naught." Vorru leaned forward, supporting his body on both arms. The light from above hid his eyes in black triangles. "Threaten a child and you will unite the parents against you. *Kill* a child and those who have lost it will retreat in mourning. Those around them will feel their pain and likewise look to their own families. They will keep their children close and out of schools. This will shatter the Rebellion's ability to indoctrinate the young. It also makes the Rebellion look unforgivably weak. People will demand things be done and it will be left to me to do them."

And one of the things you shall do is use me as a scapegoat for your evil. The illusion of control over his own situation evaporated in a heartbeat. To Loor his future was clear: He would carry out more and more heinous missions for Colonel Vorru; then, eventually, Vorru would betray him. He would remain alive and free until Vorru had no further use for him, then he would be broken and displayed as proof of Vorru's virtue.

It struck Loor as almost comical that he could see Vorru's desire to strike at a school as *evil*, yet his desire to hit Rogue Squadron was nothing more than duty. The difference, ultimately, was that the strike at Rogue Squadron would advance the cause of the Empire, while the strike at the school would only strengthen Vorru's position. *We are not as far apart as I would like to think, but neither are we as close as Vorru sees us.*

Nor am I as stupid as he thinks I am. Loor hit a button on the datapad and read the list of materials needed to undertake the operation. "When?"

"A week. There will have been no news of the trial in that time, so this will really attract attention."

Loor's head came up. "Will you need me to sacrifice some of my men to your militia?"

"Not immediately." A shadowed smile spread across the small man's face. "I have several troublesome individuals who need to die in an airspeeder explosion. The chemical composition of the explosives will match those in the school bombing. That will send Cracken's people off in a direction I want and leave you free to operate."

"Will you be selecting another target for us?"

Vorru straightened up, retreating into shadow. "No. Just go ahead and pick out a half-dozen targets you want to hit and I'll pick one or two from your list. I'll use them as tests for my subordinates to see if they can figure out how we can profit from these things. Competition will keep them sharp."

"I would imagine."

"I'm certain you would, Agent Loor." Vorru sketched a mock salute. "I look forward to the results of your handiwork."

WEDGE LOOKED AROUND the lab set deep in the bowels of the Imperial Palace complex. "So this is where the Krytos virus was developed?"

General Cracken nodded. "You noticed, when you came in, that the place is kept under negative pressure. If the seals are breached, air flows *in*, not out. It precludes the possibility of pathogens getting out."

Wedge frowned. "But I thought the Krytos virus could not be spread by air, only by fluid contact—in drinking water or when someone came in contact with bodily fluid from an infected person."

"That's absolutely true, but in this lab they were manufacturing a virus that had never existed before. They wanted something that would mutate relatively quickly so it could spread between species. With that sort of thing the chance of a spontaneous mutation that would let it become airborne and still remain infectious is one that must be guarded against." Cracken led him on through a throng of white-coated lab assistants to a back room where Qlaem was using its hands to enter information into a datapad. A number of droids worked in and around the room, apparently orchestrated by a Verpine droid that looked much like a metal avatar of the Vratix.

Qlaern drew its hands back to its thorax as Wedge entered the room. "Commander Antilles, we are pleased to see you." The Vratix's right hand came out and gently brushed Wedge's cheek.

Wedge stroked the Vratix's arm in return. "The honor is mine. You know, I expect, that my squadron will be leading the expedition to Ryloth."

"Yes, of this we are aware. We also know that Mirax will be traveling with you."

"Right." The trip to Ryloth from Imperial Center would take five days, and that was a bit long to be trapped in the cockpit of an X-wing. Ten of the squadron's X-wings would be loaded aboard a modified Rebel Transport, the *Courage of Sullust*. Wedge would travel with Mirax in the *Pulsar Skate*, with his X-wing ensconced in the cargo bay that would, if things went as planned, be filled with ryll for the return trip. The X-wings would fly escort out of Ryloth; then they would be loaded aboard another transport after the first leg of the journey, for the rest of the trip to Coruscant.

Airen Cracken patted the Vratix on the shoulder. "As you asked, I have brought Commander Antilles. You have something to tell him?"

"Yes, of course." Qlaern rested both hands on Wedge's

shoulders. "We have analyzed the virus and various medicinal preparations. Ryll will have some effect against the virus. Its efficacy varies widely. We have been pursuing the reason for this. We have been advised that ryll is classified in a number of different grades by the Twi'leks. Most of the ryll available off Ryloth is of the lowest grade."

"They don't export the best, I can understand that."

"Good. The rarest grade of ryll is known as ryll *kor*. It makes up approximately three percent of all ryll. The compound contains in it trace elements that appear to work against the virus, but exactly how and why we are not certain. We need as much ryll kor as we can get."

Wedge nodded and patted the backs of the Vratix's hands. "How will I know it?"

"The ryll kor tastes . . ." Qlaern stopped. "You would not be able to differentiate the taste, we think."

"Probably not."

"Kor absorbs light except in the ultraviolet range."

Wedge glanced at Cracken. "Meaning?"

"It looks black, like charcoal, except to someone who can see in the UV range." Cracken smiled. "I have some gear that will be able to sort kor from ryll that's dyed black. You might check, though, perhaps your Gand can see in the ultraviolet range."

Wouldn't surprise me. He doesn't breathe or sleep and can regenerate severed limbs. "I'll ask Ooryl if he can help me in that capacity." He looked back at Qlaern. "I'll get you your kor."

"Do that, Wedge Antilles, and we shall cure the disease."

And then I'll be bound by my promise to represent you to the Provisional Council. Wedge smiled and brought Qlaern's right hand up to feel his face. "We'll be back before you know it, I promise. And you know I keep my promises."

21

CORRAN HORN SHUFFLED along in line with the other prisoners. He affected the dull-eyed, hopeless stare most of them displayed for their guards. He moved when told to move and stopped when told to stop. In no way should any of the guards in stormtrooper armor conducting them to the mines have noticed anything out of the ordinary about him. To them he should have appeared to be just like all the other prisoners being herded to the mines.

He hoped against hope the facade he put forward fooled them, because as dull and soporific as he might seem on the outside, he was seething and anxious on the inside. After only a week in the general population he had decided to make his first stab at escape. He had briefly discussed his plan with Jan and found the man's insights useful, but he had ignored Jan's entreaties to put off his attempt.

The prospect of being killed in his first try did daunt Corran, but not as much as he thought it should have. He had a hunch that he wouldn't be killed if he was captured. He knew that was foolish, and that he had no factual basis for making that judgment, but it felt right. During his career with CorSec, and as a pilot with Rogue Squadron, he'd gone with gut feelings before, and won more times than he'd lost.

Although he did not have any facts to support his feelings about escape, he did have some circumstantial evidence that made him optimistic. First and foremost was the fact that he wasn't dead yet. He couldn't imagine Ysanne Isard keeping him or anyone else around unless they were useful. As long as he did not prove to be more of a bother than he was worth to Iceheart and her plans, he'd be kept alive.

Second, and it was a rather bizarre fact, was the method of return for the unsuccessful escapees. Most of them came back as fire-blackened skeletons, or parts thereof. The only way to match them up with the people who had escaped would be through genetic testing. Since that was unavailable to the prisoners, they had to assume the bodies were, in fact, those of the escapees. However, since confirmation was impossible, Isard could have simply picked a prisoner out of the less secure prison levels, and had him burned beyond recognition and dumped in the high security area. As long as she could identify *who* had escaped, returning a close match would be pretty easy, and the high-security prisoners would be left imagining escape was impossible.

Third and finally, Corran saw that Jan really did care for the men under his control. His fear for Corran's safety was genuine, and not based in any fear of retribution against himself. As the leader of the Rebel contingent, Jan felt responsible for the other Alliance prisoners. He'd seen enough people die in the fight against the Empire that he wanted to prevent people from throwing their lives away needlessly. He clearly believed that some day, that day being sooner rather than later, the Alliance would find them and free them, and he wanted as many of his people alive on that day as possible.

As wonderful as Jan's care and concern was, it also tortured the older man. Corran could clearly see Ysanne Isard's fine hand in that. By letting Jan take responsibility for all the Rebel prisoners, she created dozens and dozens of avenues to attack him. With each one of them who went away or died, a little piece of Jan died. How he had endured that much pain for so long Corran could not imagine, but he hoped, by taking responsibility for himself, he could ease the burden on Jan's shoulders.

Seventy paces from the cave mouth they passed the opening to the latrine. The fixtures in it were rudimentary, but did include a water spigot so a minimum of hygiene could be observed. Thirty paces beyond it, about halfway to the mine complex, the line of prisoners passed through a barred gateway that was locked closed at night. Corran thought its presence was unnecessary, since the Imps had placed infrared detection units at both ends of the corridors. *Then again, those units aren't really that hard to defeat, especially if the people monitoring them are as alert as the guards marching through the dust with us.*

A full 203 paces from the mouth of the cavern complex, Corran passed through what had once been a ship's hatchway and into the prisoners' workstation. Rumor among the prisoners had it that Lusankya dated from before the Clone Wars and incorporated parts from various ships that had been blasted to pieces in a naval action beyond the atmosphere. The scavenged hatch and the condition of the old, worn tools did suggest a certain amount of antiquity to the facility, but that conclusion came so easily that Corran was disinclined to trust it. *If that's what Isard wants us to think about her* Lusankya, *then I don't want to think it.*

Beyond the hatch they proceeded down a steep grade to a long rectangular cavern that had five tunnels shooting off it like fingers off the palm of a hand. All the fingers ended in doors that were cobbled together from ship bulkhead panels and held closed by chains and locks. The tunnels were big enough to allow a small mining droid to pass through them, but the doors were always shut when the prisoners came into the room, so Corran never saw the droids digging out the ore they processed.

At the far end of the chamber from the entryway sat several

piles of huge boulders. Men would work on them with heavy sledgehammers, bit by bit breaking them down into smaller rocks. Other prisoners would carry those smaller rocks to the middle of the chamber, where more prisoners would smash them with smaller sledges. Yet more prisoners with shovels and screens would sift the debris, pitching back the larger stones. The resulting gravel would then be hauled in buckets to a conveyor belt that carried the gravel up and away. At the top of the conveyor belt the gravel disappeared through a heavy steel grate.

No one knew much about what lay beyond the grate. They knew air was blowing out of it because they could see a fair amount of dust blown back into the air around the conveyor belt. Most of the prisoners assumed the belt led to a blast furnace where the gravel was melted down, or a mixing container where it was being made into ferrocrete. Corran argued that it was just as likely that the gravel was being dumped into hovertrucks and taken out to pave walkways in some Moff's garden, and if that was true, the grate was all that stood between them and freedom.

All of the prisoners knew what they were doing was simply make-work, but the Imps had taken the precautions necessary to prevent work stoppages. The conveyor belt's workings had been sunk into the ground so the prisoners couldn't get access to the motor and sabotage it. Steel fibers had been woven into the length of the belt to keep it strong and had been tightened so virtually no slack appeared in the belt on its return trip to the depths of the mine's floor. A railing had even been set up to prevent prisoners from accidentally falling onto the belt or getting caught in the mechanism.

Corran dumped his bucket of gravel into the maw of the container bolted on the conveyor belt. Humming away loudly, the belt started the gravel on its twenty-meter journey to the grate. Corran watched it go for a second, then allowed the next man in line to bump him out of the way.

Heading back to where Urlor was shoveling gravel into buckets, Corran took a quick inventory of the guards watching over them. A full squad of men in stormtrooper armor guarded them, providing one trooper for every ten of the eighty prisoners in the work detail. Six of the troopers carried blaster carbines. The other two crewed an E-Web set up just inside the hatchway, making any attempt to rush out of the mine suicidal. The sharp slope up which the prisoners would have to charge would slow them enough that the two-man heavy blaster would cut them all down. Though none of the guards were as big as stormtroopers, nor seemed as well disciplined as the Empire's shock troops, even they would have been enough to quell a prisoner revolt.

Urlor tossed a shovelful of gravel toward Corran's bucket but missed with half of it. "Don't do this, Corran." He kept his voice low enough that the rattling *chuff* of gravel pouring through a screen hid it from outsiders. "Wait. Learn more."

"This *is* learning." He winked at the bigger man. "Guards have their blasters selected for stun."

Jan looked over from the end of the screen he was holding. "You'll risk your life on the flick of a thumb?"

Corran tapped himself on the chest. "Rogue Squadron, remember."

"Corellian, more like." Jan shook his head. "None of you have any respect for odds."

"Why respect what you have to beat?" Corran gave each of them a nod. "Trust me, I have to make this run."

Urlor dumped a final shovel's-worth in the bucket. "May the Force be with you."

"Thanks." Corran, letting the bucket dangle down between his legs, started the awkward, hunched-over Rybet-walk back toward the conveyor belt. His plan was simple: he'd dump his bucket, then hop over the railing and ride the belt up to the grate. Up there, at least as viewed from the work floor, there appeared to be enough shadowed space to conceal him. If he could then get down through the grate, or find a hidden passageway out, he'd be free.

"You there."

Corran looked over at the guard pointing at him. "Me?"

"Come here."

Why me? Corran shuffled over toward the man. "Sir?"

"Don't question me, prisoner." The guard, clad in the lighter weight scout version of the armor, loomed over him. "You're new and need a lesson."

Without warning the guard brought the blaster carbine up and around in a one-handed backhand stroke that caught Corran over the right ear. Stars exploded before his eyes and the clank of metal on skull started a fierce ringing in his ears. A flange on the barrel cut his ear and split his scalp, while the force of the blow spun Corran around to the left.

Pain overrode panic. As Corran whirled he held on tight to the bucket, brought it up, and let it fly when his tormentor came into view again. The gravel-filled container smashed into the guard's faceplate. The man's head snapped back as the blow knocked him from his feet. He stumbled backward as the bucket flew on comet-like, spraying out a gravel tail.

Corran's vision cleared and seconds seemed to take hours to pass. The guard's carbine, the muzzle glistening with his blood, hung in the air. Corran knew he could snatch it before it hit the ground and burn down the two closest guards in a heartbeat. Half the guards in the detail would have been accounted for. Getting the rest would be difficult, but the other prisoners could swarm them. They'd take the guards' weapons and . . .

And die trying to clear the E-Web. Or die trying to fight our way out of the belly of this prison. All of them will die, and their deaths will be on my head, if I grab that gun.

He heard the whine of a blaster and saw something blue shoot past him. All the prisoners dove for the floor. They shrank into a huddled carpet of dirty arms and legs, ducking their heads to avoid recognition, yet peeking out to see what would happen.

All of them went down save for one.

Jan.

Eyes filled with horror and pride, he nodded to Corran.

Corran, understanding, nodded back.

The stun-bolt caught Corran square in the middle of his chest. It did to his nervous system what an ion-bolt did to a machine. In one instant every nerve in Corran's body fired, instantly wracking him with pain, burning him up, shaking, crushing, and freezing him. All of his muscles contracted, bowing his back, grinding his teeth, and kicking him up into the air with a little hop. His limp body's impact on the ground probably hurt, but his nervous system couldn't route reports to his brain properly, so he really didn't know how he felt.

Except it's not good.

He saw Jan crouching over him. "I'll see they get you help."

Corran wanted to nod, wanted to blink, wanted to do something to let Jan know he heard him, but he couldn't. About half the time he'd been hit with a stun-bolt before—in training exercises and a couple of times with CorSec in the field—he'd lost consciousness. The times he hadn't, he'd wished he had, because the feeling of helplessness created by being trapped inside a body that didn't work was worse than any pain.

The medical team called for by the guards arrived rather quickly, bringing with them a repulsorlift stretcher. After they loaded their unconscious comrade on it, they reluctantly draped Corran over the man's legs, leaving Corran's head dangling and his hands and feet scraping along the ground as they hauled the two individuals out of the mine.

Staring down at the floor, he couldn't see much on the trip out. The medtechs wrestled the stretcher into a lift, and the one to the right of the door, at the foot of the stretcher, punched a button and started the box ascending. Corran heard three tones, which he took to mean they had ascended three floors, then the lift stopped and the medtechs again struggled to get the stretcher out of the lift.

They floated Corran on through corridors that appeared much more modern and maintained, if floor tile was any indication, than the rest of the facility. Finally they brought the stretcher to a stop in a place where he caught the familiar scent of bacta, and unceremoniously dumped him to the floor. He rolled onto his left side, his cheek pressed against the cold flooring.

He caught snatches of the conversation between the medtechs and the Emdee droid that would be caring for the guard, but the ringing in his right ear made it difficult for him to catch everything. Moreover, he wasn't certain he could trust any sensory inputs, because what he was hearing through his left ear was simply impossible.

Starting from above his head and continuing on down toward his feet, he heard the dopplered sound of stormtroopers—*real*, well-disciplined stormtroopers—marching along. That was not remarkable in and of itself except in that if they had been there, they'd have been marching over him, and as messed up as he was, he was fairly certain he'd have noticed that. The only other alternative was that they were in a room below him, marching on the ceiling, and what that meant was, at that time, well and truly beyond his ability to comprehend.

22

WEDGE THUMBED HIS COMLINK ON. "What do you need, Mirax?"

"Coming up on the Kala'uun Starport, Wedge. I thought you might like to be up here on the bridge as we come in. It's quite the sight."

"On my way." He glanced around the cargo hold and nodded at his R5 unit. "Hang on, Mynock, we're almost there. Keep a scanner on these crates for me, will you?"

The cylinder-headed droid beeped affirmatively. The R5 unit then exchanged some softer tones with the *Pulsar Skate*'s Verpine maintenance droid.

No, they can't be talking about me. Wedge laughed at his flash of paranoia and stepped out of the hold. The doors crunched shut behind him. Letting a hand trail along the corridor's ceiling, he made his way along the spine of the ship to the bridge. He thought he might have been imagining things, but heat from the atmosphere already appeared to be bleeding in through the ship's hull. *Scant wonder there are Twi'leks that think of Tatooine as a suitable place to flee to during the hot season here.*

He stepped down into the bridge and dropped into a seat behind Mirax. "I'd forgotten how impressive this is."

The tortured surface of Ryloth spread out before them like the shards of a shattered earthenware vase. Black basalt mountains thrust up into a dusky red sky. Centermost in their view of the planet stood a massive mountain with a huge tunnel cored into the interior at its base. The smaller holes dotting the face of the mountain would have appeared to be natural openings except for the regularity with which they were arranged.

Because the planet rotated on its axis once per year, the same side of Ryloth always faced the sun. Kala'uun existed near the terminus line—where day and night met—making it one of the cooler sunside locations. Because of Ryloth's elliptical orbit, the planet did have seasons, though most humans could not tell the difference between summer and the cool season since both were unbearably hot.

"Yeah, impressive and impressively treacherous. Liat, watch the crosswinds as we enter the tunnel."

The Sullustan pilot chittered angrily at her.

"I know you can't miss the rocks out there, I just want to make sure *we* miss the rocks." Mirax smiled. "No heat storm activity today, it seems, but the currents can still be tricky."

"Right."

Liat Tevv took the *Pulsar Skate* down into the canyon that led to the tunnel. Harsh winds had smoothed the stone to the consistency of polished glass in some spots, and had torn away huge dagger-like slabs in others. Smaller areas of damage to the rocks—some graced with a splash of paint or metallic debris—gave mute testimony to the need for care in negotiating the approach to Kala'uun.

The *Pulsar Skate* slipped into the approach tunnel with plenty of room to spare on all sides. Liat flicked on the ship's external running lights and floods, filling the dark tunnel with jagged shadows. Up ahead a massive portcullis slowly rose into the tunnel's ceiling. As they flew past it Wedge guessed it was at least thirty meters thick and would require a lot of pounding before it admitted unwanted visitors.

Mirax glanced back at him. "Ever get the feeling that the portcullis is as much for keeping folks in as it is for keeping them out?"

"Only when I'm on the inside of it." Three years had passed since his first and last trip to Kala'uun, when he and the rest of Rogue Squadron had arrived unbidden and in pursuit of a Twi'lek. The circumstances of this trip were certainly more favorable. Even so, just to make certain there were no grudges being borne against him, he'd put Emtrey's scavenging abilities to good use and had him round up a plethora of gifts for the Twi'leks.

Mirax nodded. "Kala'uun is the one place my father figures he didn't make out like a bandit. The Twi'leks are tough negotiators."

"I hope that skill holds for Nawara's efforts on behalf of Tycho."

Mirax's brown eyes narrowed. "I hope so, too, I think. I know you believe Tycho had nothing to do with Corran's death, but I can't be so sure. I wish I could, really, because Tycho helped me save Corran at Borleias."

"Don't forget that Tycho saved me and the rest of the Squadron on Coruscant."

"I've not forgotten that, but while he was saving you, Corran and I were saving each other from the Empire and the traitor in Fliry Vorru's organization." She patted Wedge on the knee. "We've been over this a dozen times and I'm getting better about it, I really am. I don't cry nearly as much right now as I did."

Wedge tipped her face up with his left hand and brushed a tear from her cheek with his thumb. "Hey, being sad doesn't reflect badly on you at all."

"Thanks." Mirax sniffed a little. "It's just that it seems so ridiculous sometimes. We'd not even dated. We didn't know each other that well. For his death to hurt this much we should have been a lot closer."

"That's the trick of it, Mirax, you *were* a lot closer than you imagine. The two of you shared a lot of the same qualities." Wedge smiled. "Your father and Corran's father were mortal enemies. Why? Because they were a lot alike, too. Both of you had strong relationships with your fathers, which is reflected in how you turned out. Under different circumstances old Booster and Hal Horn probably could have been friends. You and Corran became friends because you met under those different circumstances."

She frowned for a moment. "You are probably right. I could also help myself get over this, I think, if I could just finally accept the fact that Corran's dead. Listening to the comlink call when he went in, that was pretty nasty, but we never found a body. I know it's stupid to make anything of that, what with the building coming down on him and all, but my father always said that if you don't see a body, don't count on someone being dead. He did once—"

"And it cost him his eye. I remember the story." Wedge laughed lightly. "*Now* I remember it. That explains a lot."

"What do you mean?"

"Biggs, Porkins, Corran, my parents—I never saw their dead bodies. Partly because of your father's story, I suspect, and just human stubbornness, I find myself sometimes expecting to see them walk into my office."

Mirax's face brightened. "Or you think you see them walking along in a crowd. You catch a glimpse of them." She glanced down. "Part of me thinks that we see them because we don't truly believe they're dead. Maybe the barrier that separates the living from the dead is permeable as long as there is someone who doesn't accept death. Sithspawn, listen to me. I'm talking like a glitbiter."

"That's not a problem, Mirax, I understand." Wedge leaned forward and kissed her on the forehead. "And I don't think your theory is all that wrong. I don't imagine we can bring people back to life by hoping, but letting their memories live on inside us is not a bad thing to do at all."

The Sullustan cheebled something at Mirax, prompting her to spin around in her command chair. She hit several switches above her head, then punched a button on the console. "Landing gear deployed, repulsorlift drives engaged. Kill thrust and set her down gently."

Liat's melodic grumble accompanied the delicate thunder of the *Pulsar Skate*'s landing. Mirax slapped a button on the command console and Wedge immediately felt a rush of warm air as the ship's gangway lowered itself. Mirax nodded toward the aft and the opening. "After you, Commander Antilles."

"Thank you, Captain Terrik."

Mirax smiled. "By the way, I think you look slicker than a Hutt's slime trail in that native garb."

"Thanks." Since the mission was diplomatic in nature, Rogue Squadron had been supplied with clothes like those their counterparts on Ryloth would wear. Because of the planet's oppressive heat, the natives tended to wear loose, bulky, hooded cloaks over their other garments. The nature of the clothes they wore beneath the cloaks depended upon their occupation. Twi'lek warriors tended to be clad in a loincloth, wrapped leggings to the knee, fingerless gloves, and a highly decorative bandoleer that did still serve a martial function. Their cloaks also tended to be abbreviated, as if their whole costume was meant to show they were tough enough to endure even the harshest of conditions on the planet.

Wedge's attire varied only slightly from that Twi'lek warriors wore. His brown boots came up to his knees and beige trousers had been tucked into them. To that he added an emerald green loincloth and a bandoleer of the same color. All of his battle ribbons and awards had been embroidered on the bandoleer, starting with two Death Star representations at his right shoulder and ending with a symbol representing Coruscant near his left hip. The crests of the Alliance and Rogue Squadron stood side by side over his heart. His cloak was a darker green than his bandoleer and had been lined with a shiny red fabric that formed two red wings when he folded the cloak back behind his shoulders.

He descended the gangway and looked up. Kala'uun Starport occupied a colossal cavern which had been hollowed out of the heart of the mountain that sheltered it. Above his head lay level upon level of Twi'lek clan warrens, comprising the living quarters and work areas of over 100,000 Twi'leks. He could only guess at what the warrens looked like—according to Nawara, few were the non-Twi'leks who ever saw them, and those individuals were people a clan had acknowledged as a friend.

The *Courage of Sullust* had landed off the *Skate*'s starboard wing. Nawara Ven disembarked and came walking over toward Wedge. They wore similar clothes, though Nawara's loincloth, bandoleer, and cloak were all a deep shade of purple. His cloak had been lined with a grey that was slightly darker than his skin tone. "Are you ready, Commander?"

Wedge nodded. "Lead the way."

Nawara did, and Wedge followed a step behind him and one to his left. "It looks like our welcoming party. Is the Shak clan still the Head-clan here?"

One of Nawara's braintails ran back along his spine. The tip of it jerked up and down in what Wedge had been told was the Twi'lek equivalent of a nod. "Koh'shak is still the master of the starport. It would appear, from the colors of the individual next to him, that someone from the Olan clan has chosen to greet us as well."

"Cazne'olan, perhaps?"

Nawara shrugged. "Possibly. I don't know him. The Olan clan and mine do not mix much—no animosity, just little association with each other. His presence here could be good or could be very bad."

Wedge smiled, stepping up beside Nawara as they both stopped before their hosts. Nawara Ven bowed deeply, bringing both his braintails down to dangle limp by his knees. Wedge aped his bow, then opened his hands and pressed their backs against his thighs. The gesture was slightly awkward but was meant to symbolize exactly what the limp braintails did: a lack of negative feelings and thoughts about the people in front of him. Without braintails he had to rely on the universally peaceful symbolism of an empty, open hand to make his intent clear.

Wedge and Nawara straightened up at the same time, then their hosts bowed to them. Scarlet cloth swathed the corpulent Koh'shak. The gold badges of his office and clan held his outer cloak closed at his throat, though his round middle poked through the central opening. Wedge got an eyeful of Koh'shak's red robe and a wide cloth of gold sash pressed into the double duty of containing his girth and supporting a pair of Sevari flashpistols.

Cazne'olan would have seemed thickset except by comparison with Koh'shak. His black cloak covered a bright yellow robe and blue sash. The gold office and clan badges he wore were smaller than Koh'shak's, but the craftsmanship on them seemed more delicate and less overpowering. Cazne'olan held his bow for a second longer than Koh'shak, but straightened up with less effort.

The heavier Twi'lek opened black-taloned hands. "In the name of Kala'uun's Clans, I bid you welcome, Nawar'aven."

"In the name of my clan, I am pleased to be accepted at Kala'uun." Nawara turned to his left. "I am pleased to present to the Clans of Kala'uun my commanding officer. . . ."

Cazne'olan stepped forward between Nawara and Koh'shak, extending his hand to Wedge. "Nawar'aven, you have no need to introduce Wedgan'tilles to us. We remember him from his last adventure on our world."

Wedge smiled and shook Cazne'olan's hand. "Good to see you again."

"And you." Cazne'olan took a step back and paused for a second before his headtails began to twitch up and down. "You have done much and learned much in the time since we have seen each other. Not the least of which is learning how to dress."

Nawara glanced over at Wedge. "Commander, I did not realize—"

"No reason you should have Nawar . . . ," Wedge hitched a moment. The way the Twi'leks ran Nawara's name together, he couldn't be certain exactly what Nawara's clan name was. *When in doubt, go with indigenous custom.* ". . . Nawar'aven. It was an adventure the squadron had well before you joined it. Suffice it to say it was resolved to the satisfaction of all interested parties."

"It was indeed, Wedgan'tilles." Koh'shak stretched the last syllable of Wedge's name into a whole sibilant phrase of its own. "And now you are come here seeking satisfaction of another kind."

"Quite true, Koh'shak." Wedge half-turned and pointed back at the two Alliance ships. "We have for you some wondrous things drawn from the various worlds of the New Republic." As he turned back to face the starport's master, he noticed Nawara and Cazne'olan speaking to each other in low tones, with their braintaiis convulsing wildly.

Koh'shak closed his pinkish eyes and settled interlaced fingers over the bulge in his middle. "I am certain what you have brought will be impressive. Shall we begin our negotiations?"

His offer seemed a bit abrupt to Wedge, and the surprised look on Nawara's face indicated he also thought something was amiss. *What's going on here?*

Before Wedge could venture a reply, Nawara gently grabbed Wedge's right forearm. "While the Commander applauds your alacrity in seeing to his needs, we have been traveling for days to get here. He chooses to invoke *twi'janii.*"

Koh'shak's eyes popped open with the speed Wedge would have expected if the starport master had felt a gun being jammed against a spine. "I welcome Wedgan'tilles and would have granted him *twi'janii* without reservation if I felt he did not find our climate oppressive."

"Open your eyes yet wider, Koh'shak." Cazne'olan gestured toward Wedge. "He is a warrior in truth as well as dress. Even in the hot season he would not be discomfitted."

"Your courtesy in reminding me of that is appreciated, Cazne'olan." Koh'shak's words came out light and even, but the violent twitching of his braintails seemed to belie the benign tone of the reply. "Wedgan'tilles, you and your people are to consider yourselves our guests. We will see to your pleasure, then to our business."

"You are most kind," Wedge said, believing Koh'shak to be anything but. *I don't know what he has in mind as* our *pleasure, but I'm certain* his *will be business, and I don't anticipate that being much fun at all.*

23

ELBOWS PLANTED ON either side of the dataterminal's keyboard, Iella leaned forward and rubbed her hands over her face. The jolt of excitement she had expected had come, but it faded far too quickly. Fatigue and an unfocused fear flooded through her in its wake. She could feel herself beginning to slow down, but she refused to surrender.

No, no giving up now. I won this one. She pressed her fingers against her eyelids. *I think.*

She had begun her quest to locate the Duros captain, Lai Nootka, in a most organized and methodical way. She pulled as much as she could about him from Imperial and Alliance sources and compiled a profile of him based on that information. The most complete Imperial record came from a planet named Garqi where Nootka and his crew had been imprisoned for several months on charges of smuggling for the Alliance. Nootka's presence on the planet had been well documented, and the Prefect Barris, Nootka's Imperial adversary, had paid dearly for his brush with the Alliance.

Garqi was where Corran met Nootka.

Alliance files were far more generous in the amount of information they provided. Nootka had indeed moved shipments for the Alliance, but he acted on their behalf only when it suited him. He didn't appear to have firm ties to the Alliance—not even as firm as those Mirax Terrik had. Nootka's distance from the Alliance, yet willingness to work with it, certainly put him in a grey area that might have been why Tycho chose to trade with him.

Iella's inquiries then went off in several directions at the same time. She started a search for any records pertaining to any of the aliases and various ship identification codes she could find for the *Star's Delight*. She was less interested in the Alliance material than she was the Imperial records, but she did note that Nootka had not been off on missions for the Alliance at the time Tycho said he met with him on Coruscant.

She also dug deeper into the person who was Lai Nootka himself. The Duros were a race of tall, slender, blue-skinned beings whose facial expressions seemed, to most humans, to be entirely dour. They remained aloof, and it was often said that they lacked noses because they were disinclined to stick their noses into business that did not concern them. Most Duros remained neutral concerning the Rebellion, but a few brave individuals like Lai Nootka dared trade with the Rebels. Only in this did Lai Nootka appear to be different from the majority of his people, which made researching him much easier.

Iella's greatest triumph was in locating the series of young-adult Duros novels from which Nootka drew inspiration for his various aliases and the new names of his ship. He had mixed and matched first and family names of characters to create aliases for himself, and then for each alias, gave his ship a name that was not associated with the corresponding characters in the books; but everything had indeed come from that pool of names. When none of the aliases she already had for him turned up an Imperial record, she tried inventing additional aliases, using the process she imagined Nootka himself had used to create his new identities. She started pumping these possible aliases through the Imperial computer and hoping for the best.

The computer had reported back a lot of misses, but finally she got a hit. Just four days before Tycho's meeting with Lai Nootka, a modified CorelliSpace Gymsnor-3 freighter named *Novachild* entered the Coruscant system. A Duros named Hes Glillto had been listed as the captain of record. No departure for that ship or captain had been recorded, but this didn't surprise Iella. The one record providing the information about his arrival was in a duty log filed by Lieutenant Virar Needa of Orbital Solar Energy Transfer Satellite 1127 *after* Coruscant had fallen to the Alliance and *after* Tycho Celchu had been taken into custody.

Though officially part of their duty, OSETS officers seldom maintained or filed such logs, but from what she could see Needa had been obsessive about it. The log had data concerning incoming and outgoing ships that traveled in-system during Needa's watches on the station. The lack of a departure record for *Novachild* could have meant nothing more sinister than that the ship had left while Needa was sleeping, but Iella felt in her gut that was unlikely.

She sat back in her chair and looked at the data on the screen again. The fact that no other Imperial records mentioned the *Novachild* or Hes Glillto told Iella the records had been deliberately purged. *And anyone with the access needed to purge those records could easily manufacture and enter the data that shows Tycho was in Imperial Intelligence's pay. Or, Tycho himself could have doctored things to make it look as if he had been framed.*

Iella slowly shook her head. The information she had was intriguing but essentially useless. She could not prove Lai Nootka and Hes Glillto were the same person. The *Novachild*'s arrival put it on Coruscant a couple of days before the meeting Corran had witnessed, but she couldn't exclude the possibility that the ship had departed before the date of the meeting. Unless she could definitively place Nootka on Coruscant at that time, she couldn't prove Tycho was telling the truth.

And I'm not so sure I want to do that. She sighed. Diric had told her about some of the conversations he'd had with Tycho. He was more convinced than ever of Tycho's innocence, and his opinion *did* carry a lot of weight in her mind. Even so, if Tycho *had* caused Corran's death, Iella didn't want him to be able to get away with it. *I owe Corran that much.*

A familiar hoot brought her back to the present and sparked a smile on her face. "Whistler!"

The small green and white R2 beeped happily. Behind him, tottling along, came Rogue Squadron's black, clamshell-headed M-3PO unit. "Good morning, Mistress."

"Morning?" Iella glanced at the Chronographie readout at the top of her datapad's screen. "I don't believe it. I've been here eight hours. Diric will kill me."

Emtrey's head canted to the left. "I would hope not, Mistress Iella. That would be a crime and—"

"I was speaking metaphorically, Emtrey, not literally." Iella frowned at the droid. "I meant that he would be upset with me."

"Ah, I see."

Iella patted Whistler gently on his domed head. "So what are you two doing here in the computer center?"

Whistler warbled nonchalantly.

"We can so tell her, Whistler." Emtrey's head righted itself and thrust forward, giving Iella a good view of the gold eyes burning in the hollow of his face. "You do want the *truth* to triumph, don't you?"

Iella nodded slowly. "Every day it seems I'm hearing less and less of it. What have you got?"

Emtrey pointed toward her dataterminal's I/O port. "Whistler, hook in there and show her what we found."

Whistler squawked rudely—a sound Iella recognized as one she'd often heard the droid use to chasten Corran. Her throat thickened as melancholy tried to suck the life out of her, but she shook her head. She looked up at Emtrey and forced words out past the lump in her throat. "What have you been doing?"

"We have finished the tasks Master Ven set for us before he

left with the others, so we started going over transcripts and noticed an underlying assumption everyone seems to have made concerning the conquest of Coruscant."

"And that is?"

"It is assumed that Ysanne Isard *let* us have the world because she *wanted* us to have it, infected as it was with the Krytos virus. The stresses possessing it has put on the Alliance certainly are great, and the assumption is probably valid, but there is no straight-line correlation between her desire to let us have the planet and actions taken in the final days."

"I'm not certain, at this hour, I follow what you're saying." Iella rubbed at her burning eyes with her left hand. "Can you break it down and be more specific?"

"Certainly." Emtrey glanced down at the R2 unit. "Show her the current disease case grid."

Whistler chirped happily. The data on the terminal's screen vanished beneath a graph that plotted incidences of sickness over time in red. A thick blood-red line quickly blossomed into a triangle with a steep hypotenuse, then leveled out into a rectangle that began to flare upward again over the last ten days. The disease had spread quickly at first, but had plateaued—until recently.

Iella nodded. "The plateau indicates the period when the disease stopped spreading because bacta therapy managed to keep it under control."

"Exactly. The graph of fatalities has a similar profile."

"I can imagine. This is pretty horrible."

"True, Mistress. Whistler, now run the plus-six graph."

"Plus-six?"

"The projected disease report graph we would have seen if the planet had fallen to the Alliance just six days later than it did." The new graph exploded from the starting point and spiked quickly off the top of the screen. "Projected fatalities in this model are 85 percent of afflicted populations."

Iella's jaw dropped open. "Whole alien populations would have been wiped off Coruscant."

"Exactly. This model, when broken down by species, shows a complete depopulation of Gamorreans, Quarren, Twi'leks, Suilustans, and Trandoshans. The chances of the disease traveling off-world are incalculable, but the potential for galaxy-wide extermination of some species cannot be discounted."

She blinked and rubbed at her eyes again. "Why are the models so different?"

Silvery highlights flashed from the edges of Emtrey's black carapace as he raised his hands. "One reason is highly speculative. First, it seems that in boiling off a reservoir to create the storm that brought down the planet's shields, our efforts destroyed a large amount of the virus present in the planetary water system. Second, and far more germane to our discussion, is the abbreviated incubation period our arrival gave the disease. Had the Alliance arrived just a week later, we would already have had a wave of deaths and a whole new round of infections because of contact with bodily fluids from the victims and the virus in the water system."

Iella nodded slowly. "If we had been just a week later in liberating the planet, there would have been no way to save it. Non-human members of the Alliance would have fled, dooming their own populations. Without non-human support, the Alliance would have foundered."

"That seems probable, Mistress."

"Yeah." Iella's brown eyes tightened. "So the reason the Imps stopped our initial effort to shut down the shields was to keep us from taking over the world *too* soon. For Iceheart it wasn't a matter of *if* but *when* we'd take the world. And since Tycho's contribution to our efforts were what enabled us to bring the shields down *before* the time that would have been optimal for Iceheart, we can suppose he wasn't working for her."

Emtrey nodded and Whistler trumpeted triumphantly.

"Unless, of course, that's exactly what Iceheart wants us to think." Iella shook her head. "Not bad work, you two, but it's about as helpful as what I found on Lai Nootka. I can put someone who ought to be him flying something that ought to be his ship here about the time Tycho said he met with Nootka, but I can't prove it. I'd dearly like to believe Tycho is being framed, but I don't see a good reason why Isard would be devoting so many resources to getting someone who is really not that important."

Whistler reeled off a series of sharp bleats.

"Yes, I will tell her." Emtrey looked down at Iella. "Whistler says discrediting Tycho will discredit Rogue Squadron. If Tycho is convicted, Commander Antilles will be distracted. Tycho's conviction could also cause an inquiry into the events of the first assault on Borleias. He could be blamed for the disaster, absolving the Bothan General of his mistake, and that might make the Bothans feel they can grab for more power."

"I can follow that, but it's too risky a return for Iceheart to take an interest in it. There has to be something else."

"There is, Mistress Wessiri." Emtrey lowered his hands to near his hips. "Whistler says Ysanne Isard would do it because she's cruel."

That idea landed in Iella's gut and sat there like one of Hoth's frozen continents. "You know, Whistler, you may have something there. Toying with an innocent man like that is exactly what she would do, especially when it meant that the Alliance was dancing to a tune she called. Of course, that doesn't prove Tycho is innocent, but thwarting her is enough to make sure I keep digging until I learn what's really going on, one way or another."

24

CORRAN SCRATCHED AT HIS RIGHT EAR, flaking off some crusted flesh. "Yeah, I know it sounds as if I got hit harder than I did, but I'm convinced I'm right." He looked at Jan. "I think it's a good shot at getting out of here, or at least one that has to be explored."

"I agree."

Urlor shook his head. "Too far-fetched."

"Which is why I want to test my theory when we're down in the mine."

Urlor's massive left hand stroked his beard. "Will you give this foolishness up if your experiment fails?"

Jan raised an eyebrow and glanced at Corran. "Will you?"

Corran hesitated before answering. Though he had not blacked out, the Emdee droid had kept him in the infirmary overnight for observation—at least Corran assumed it was overnight, having had no way of judging the passage of time. Corran had gone over in his mind what had happened and came to two conclusions. The first, which no one doubted, was that the guard had singled him out because someone had mentioned his desire to escape. Though Corran hadn't mentioned it to anyone other than Jan and Urlor, the questions he had asked of the inmates would have been enough to alert even the most dense of individuals to his plans.

The second thing he had concluded, and had spent the last week attempting to convince Jan and Urlor was true, was that they were all upside down. The technology for creating and negating artificial and real gravity was ancient. Ships of all sizes and stripes could generate their own gravity. Reversing the gravity in the complex would lead any escapees to assume that by going up they'd be getting closer to the surface and freedom when, in fact, they'd be getting farther from it and killing their chances of escape. If Corran *had* heard troopers marching past, any escapee would run full on into at least one level occupied by soldiers. Even if he didn't get captured, by the time he realized what had happened, he'd have a long way to go just to get back to the prison level, much less go beyond it to freedom.

He shook his head. "No, I'll still go even if my experiment is unsuccessful. *I* have no doubt that I'm right—the experiment is just to convince *you* I'm right."

Urlor folded his arms across his chest. "Why do you care if we believe you?"

"If I'm right, you can come with me."

The big man held up his ruined right hand. "You'd find a cripple of little use to you. I've learned to become patient. I'll wait for you to come back."

"You're wrong there." Corran looked at Jan. "How about you?"

The older man sat silently on his billet for a moment, then shook his head rather firmly. "Forgive me. There is no way I can go, but I allowed myself to indulge in the fantasy."

"You're strong. You could make it."

"I appreciate your assessment of me, Corran, but it is overgenerous." Jan shrugged. "Besides, just as a desire to keep me safe prevents our people from harming our Imperial compatriots, so a desire to keep our people safe prevents me from joining you. If I escape, Iceheart will kill the lot of us. I'll remain here and keep them safe until you can bring help back."

Corran frowned. "So neither of you will go?"

"No." Urlor shook his head. "You'll be on your own." Unspoken in that sentence was the conviction there was no way to guarantee that the Imps didn't have spies among the Alliance prisoners.

And my traveling alone means that if I'm a spy, I won't be taking anyone else with me. "Don't worry, I'm no Tycho Celchu, nor will I let myself be betrayed by one another time."

Jan's eyes narrowed. "Tycho Celchu? He was here once for several months. They called him out one day and he vanished. Was he a traitor?"

"He's the reason I'm here. He gave the Imps override code data on a Headhunter I was flying. They took control and I'm here." Corran forced his balled fists open. "Isard told me Tycho is on trial for my murder, so justice does prevail."

Urlor scratched at his jaw. "Celchu was a sleeper, wasn't he?"

As much as Corran hated Tycho, that description sent a shiver down his spine. Within the prisoner population were individuals who were suffering severe shock from their interrogations. Most were ambulatory, but not much beyond that. In the brief time he'd been in the general population he'd seen one or two of them recover to a certain extent, but their attention spans and short-term memory were short and shot respectively. They *did* seem to get better, but only gradually.

"I believed he was, but that must have been an act. If you think about it, being a sleeper meant many people would speak in front of him. When he recovered he'd have folks trying to help him with his memory." Jan shook his head. "When he got to the point where he should have been better, they pulled him out and debriefed him. He had me fooled."

"He had a lot of people fooled, Wedge Antilles included." Corran nodded firmly. "He's not fooling folks any longer, though. Just goes to show the Empire doesn't win them all, not by a long shot. And if my experiment works, we'll give them one more loss to account for."

In some ways Wedge was surprised by his reaction to the display of hospitality Koh'shak put on for his benefit. He found it both barbaric and somehow naive. An area had been cleared near the Alliance ships. Opalescent glowstones—technological lamps designed to look like natural stones—had been brought out from homes and arranged in a circular pattern. While red and gold highlights played through them, the illumination they produced was coldly blue and white. It made the humans into pale ghosts and rendered the Twi'leks as cyanotic ice creatures.

Rogue Squadron and the ships' crews had been invited to the celebration. The visitors arrayed themselves in a circle that put them five meters from the outer edge of the glow-stone circle. Twi'leks from various clans interspersed themselves among the visitors, with one who spoke passable Basic acting as interpreter for two or three others. Wedge harbored no illusions about what was going on—his people were being interrogated, albeit politely. Their stories would be compared at Twi'lek councils, and decisions would be made about the future of Ryloth based on what the Twi'leks learned.

Servants passed around the outside of the circle, offering the visitors food, drink, and gifts. The musicians who had been assembled opposite him played a variety of string and wind instruments producing notes that ran up and down on a thirteen-note scale. Wedge found the music only marginally painful, while Liat Tsayv and Aril Nunb seemed to be moving in sync with notes he couldn't hear. Out behind the cold spectral light cast by the glowstones, life continued as usual in Kala'uun. People walking by gawked for a moment or two, and many braintails—or *lekku*, as Wedge had learned they were called in Rylothean—twitched with silent messages about the assembly.

Wedge didn't really have eyes for much of what was happening outside the visitors' circle, primarily because of what was going on at its heart. A lithe, petite Twi'lek female dancer spun and leaped through the air. Her tattooed lekku lashed out like whips, then whirled down and enfolded her like ivy. The tails of the loincloth she wore similarly clung to her body, sliding away as she whirled, to reveal silken flesh over taut and powerful muscles. She gave Wedge a pixie-wink, prompting a smile from him, then she twirled off to charm another of the visitors.

Cazne'olan draped a braintail over Wedge's shoulder. "Sienn'rha is the only positive thing Bib Fortuna ever accomplished. He stole her from her darkside family and meant to present her to Jabba the Hutt. In preparation for that he had her taught to dance as well as she does. She was saved from Jabba by your Lukesky'walker. She always dances wonderfully, but this night she approaches perfection because of the gratitude she feels to the Alliance."

"She is spectacular." Wedge could not deny that he found her dance exciting and even stimulating, but that bothered him just a bit. By seeing her as being so seductive and beautiful, and reacting to her on a physiological level, it was very easy for him to forget she was a living, thinking creature. That made it deceptively simple for him to see how the Imperials found objectifying and dehumanizing other races justifiable—*if they seem like animals or appeal to you on an animal level, clearly they are animals.*

Cazne'olan tapped him on the shoulder. "It would be possible for a private dance to be arranged for you, my friend."

"I appreciate the offer, but . . ."

Cazne'olan's voice dropped to a whisper. "Sienn'rha asked me to convey that suggestion to you, on her behalf. She is well aware of your history and considers you quite a hero."

"I see." Wedge considered for a moment all the offer implied and felt sorely tempted. Sienn'rha's sensuous beauty, from her full lips and dark eyes to her fluid and athletic grace, hinted at pleasures he'd not had time to enjoy for . . . *If I can't remember off the top of my head, it's been well and nigh too long. But is here and now, with Sienn'rha, the time to change that?*

Wedge smiled at Cazne'olan. "Convey to her my profound appreciation of her offer, and my sincere regret at having to refuse. Ultimately I am here as a representative of the Alliance. Perhaps some time when I am merely here as myself. . . ."

"She will understand, I think."

"I hope so." Wedge frowned for a moment. "I have a question to ask you about something you said a moment ago."

A lek twitched. "Ask."

"You pronounce my name as Wedgan'tilles and Nawara Ven's name as Nawar'aven, running them together. When you mentioned Bib Fortuna, you distinctly broke his name up. Why?"

Cazne'olan nodded slowly and let his lekku slip from Wedge's shoulder. "Bib Fortuna was a member of the Una clan. Because of his predations on his own people, he was cast out. The joining of personal and clan names is, among us, a sign of belonging. Breaking the names apart is a statement of the distance between that person and his people."

Wedge nodded. "How do you decide what a name will become? Nawara is a member of the Ven clan, but you make his surname into 'aven' when you pronounce it."

"And I know your surname is Antilles, but I break it in two."

"Exactly."

The Twi'lek laughed lightly. "Naming conventions are determined by a venerable set of rules—superstitions almost—that transform names into auspicious omens. Ven, for example, translates into Basic as 'silver.' Nawara would translate roughly as 'speaker' or 'tongue,' either of which suggests a gifted negotiator. However, if his name were pronounced as Nawara'ven, because of peculiarities in Rylothean, his name would mean 'tarnished silver.' By changing the pronunciation slightly we retain the correct meaning."

"I'm impressed." Wedge smiled openly. "So, what does my name mean, the way you pronounce it?"

The Twi'lek shrugged. "There is no good, direct translation of foreign names, but Wedgan'tilles comes close to 'slayer of stars.'"

"I like it."

"It is much to be preferred to the alternative suggested by the Basic pronunciation."

"Which is?"

"Difficult to translate."

"Give me a rough go at it."

Cazne'olan's braintails twitched sharply. "Being generous, it is 'One so foul he could induce vomiting in a rancor.'"

Wedge shuddered. "I prefer your pronunciation, I think."

A gentle vibration running through the ground forestalled further lessons about Twi'lek culture. He assumed the vibration was produced by the raising of the portcullis, so he looked off toward where the tunnel entered the Kala'uun cavern. Boiling up out of it, in three pairs, came a half-dozen Uglies. The X-wing fighter's distinctive S-foils jutted out from the sides of a TIE fighter's ball cockpit. The stabilizers had been fastened to a collar that surrounded the cockpit, and as the fighters maneuvered and cavorted in the air above the assembly, he saw the S-foils rotating around the cockpit, making the design similar in principle to that of the B-wing fighter in service with the Alliance.

Never seen those before. Must be a homegrown Twi'lek design. The S-foils collapsed into a single wing on either side of the cockpit, then landing skids extended from the bottom of the collar and the peculiar ships descended. They landed in a rough semicircle facing the Alliance ships, easily menacing all the visitors.

One of the cockpit hatches opened and a huge Twi'lek pilot emerged from the top of the sphere. He wore a black Imperial flight suit, but a scarlet loincloth and cloak had been added to make it seem closer to native warrior attire. His lekku had been tattooed with a variety of sinuous and serpentine shapes which Wedge supposed were Rylothean glyphs, but he could not even guess at their significance.

As the warrior strode over to the circle, the music died and the servants shrank back. Sienn'rha stopped her dance and retreated into Wedge's shadow. Wedge stood, with Cazne'olan on one side and the great, lumpish Koh'shak on the other. As the warrior came closer, Wedge saw he was positively huge, easily forty centimeters taller than Wedge and massing at least another thirty kilos. How he actually managed to jam himself into the TIE cockpit Wedge couldn't imagine.

The warrior stepped through a quickly widening gap in the circle, then stopped five meters from Wedge. "I am Tal'dira, first among Twi'lek warriors. You, the lekku-less who wears the clothes of a warrior, you are Wedge Antilles?"

Wedge did his best to ignore the faint retching sound Tal'dira made in the back of his throat as he pronounced Wedge's name. "I am Wedgan'tilles."

The Twi'lek warrior raised an eyebrow at Wedge's reply. "And you have come here for ryll?"

"I have come for ryll kor." Wedge's reply won a gasp from Koh'shak and a lekku-twitching from Tal'dira. "Is there a problem?"

"None, Wedge Antilles, if—" Tal'dira drew a pair of slender vibroblades from sheaths hidden in his bandoleer, "—you are willing to fight to prove you are a warrior. A warrior should deal with warriors. Win the fight and the kor shall be yours."

Wedge's stomach tightened and his heart began to pound. As a pilot, in his X-wing, he had no doubt at all that he'd be able to vape Tal'dira and his X-ball. *In a vibroblade fight, though* . . . As much as he would have preferred to avoid fighting, he knew he really didn't have any choice in the matter. The kor was vital to stopping the Krytos virus. *If I have to carve this Twi'lek behemoth up to get it, I will.*

He held out his right hand. "I will fight."

Tal'dira tossed him one of the vibroblades. "A warrior should deal with a warrior."

"My thoughts exactly."

The warrior's lekku writhed up and down once affirmatively. "Good."

Wedge flicked the blade on with his thumb. "Come on. I'm ready."

"You are, but your opponent isn't." Tal'dira looked around, studying each of the Rogues. They all wore Twi'lek warrior garb, and the disdainful expression on Tal'dira's face suggested he found something wrong with that. He openly appraised them, looking each of them up and down before passing from one to the next.

Will he pick one of them as my foe? Wedge felt his stomach begin to implode. *I know Twi'leks can be cruel. Is he going to force me to slay one of my own people because of some affront we've given him?*

Tal'dira looked back at Wedge. "I have made my choice. Prepare yourself."

Wedge nodded. "I'm still ready."

"Good." The warrior casually tossed the vibroblade to Koh'shak. "I choose you."

The starport master's eyes ballooned as he bounced the inert vibroblade from hand to hand. It slipped from his grasp and ricocheted off his stomach before tumbling toward the ground. The obese Twi'lek began to bend over, thick fingers wriggling slothfully in a vain attempt to catch the blade before it could hit the ground.

In one flowing motion that nearly shamed Sienn'rha's performance, Tal'dira swooped forward and plucked the blade out of the air. It hummed to life and with one deft cut, split the brooch holding Koh'shak's cloak closed. The garment puddled around Koh'shak's feet and a stiff-arm blow to the chest dropped the starport master on top of it.

Tal'dira grabbed one of Koh'shak's braintails and yanked none too gently on it, then pressed the vibroblade to the Twi'lek's throat. "Warriors should deal with warriors, Kohsh'ak! Wedgan'tilles came to us as a warrior, leading a

band of warriors, including our own Nawar'aven. You knew of
this mission to Ryloth but hid that knowledge from me so you
could profit from the gifts our visitors would bring. That is fitting conduct for a merchant, but not a warrior, Kohsh'ak!"

Tal'dira's delivered the altered pronunciation of the starport
master's name harshly, filling it with scorn. Wedge had no idea
of what it meant, but he was glad Tal'dira's anger wasn't directed at him.

Tal'dira released Koh'shak and turned the vibroblade off.
He resheathed it, then turned toward Wedge. "The blade you
possess is my gift to you, Wedgan'tilles. This kor you want will
be delivered to you, a gift between warriors. It is happily given
in the hopes it can heal those who have been touched by treachery and cowardly action. All I ask in return is your forgiveness
for this breach of etiquette."

Wedge turned his vibroblade off and tucked it into the top
of his right boot. "A warrior does not hold another warrior responsible for the actions of a merchant." He turned and pointed
to the Alliance ships with his left hand. "On those ships I have
gifts from my warriors to yours, offered in the spirit shared by
warriors."

Tal'dira clapped Wedge on both shoulders. "There is much
honor in you, Wedgan'tilles, and in your Rogue Squadron. I
will be most pleased if, while the merchants scurry about un-
loading and loading our ships, you will continue to join me in
Twi'janii." Looping a lekku over Wedge's shoulders, Tal'dira
pointed at the musicians. "Play for our guests, play the best you
ever have. You are playing for the pleasure of warriors now, and
nothing less than the best will do."

25

CORRAN'S MOUTH FELT like a desert, and it wasn't just because of the dust created by working the grater. He'd been planning his little experiment so he could test his theory about the prison's orientation for the last two days, and was fairly certain that what he had in mind would work perfectly. Despite his confidence, he'd hesitated, telling himself he'd wait for the rock that would work the best.

He'd found the rock on the grate. It had something of a clamshell shape—momentarily reminding him of Emtrey's head. It fit easily in his palm and would fly well. It had enough mass to it to make his throw possible, and yet had a narrow enough cross-section and dark enough color that it wouldn't easily be seen in the cavern.

His mouth was dry because the fear coiling in his belly was sucking all the moisture out of him. He couldn't think of what he had to be afraid of. His life couldn't get any worse. He was locked in the highest security prison the Empire had ever known. Most people had never even heard of Lusankya, and most of those who had thought it was a rumor. Even during his time on the Corellian Security Force he'd only heard passing references to it. Beyond believing that it existed and was not a good place, he'd known nothing about it.

Corran caught other prisoners in his work group looking at him, and in their expectant glances he found the source of his fear. *I'm afraid of being wrong and disappointing them.* Only Jan and Urlor knew what he intended to do, but a number of other prisoners had been recruited to stage the distraction that would allow him to act. They had figured out he was going to be doing something related to escape, but they had no clue what it was, nor did they expect to be told. Despite their ignorance, they were all enthused with the idea of helping him out. Hopes they had long since abandoned were being revived by his escape attempt.

Corran closed his fist around the stone. *This had better work.*

He looked over at Urlor who, in turn, nodded to two men working with the smaller sledgehammers. One of them brought his sledgehammer down on the ground hard, then loosened his grip so the tool cartwheeled away. The handle grazed another man, who screamed, clutched at his shin, and started hopping around madly, all the while swearing he was going to kill the clumsy oaf who let go of the hammer. The workers backed away from the careening hammer and the two men, then started shouting encouragement to them in hopes of goading them into a fight.

Corran retreated along with the others, then stopped when Urlor and a knot of three prisoners screened him from the guards. He looked at the rock, gave it a kiss, then hauled back and hurled it up toward the apex of the ceiling, thirty meters away. *Come on, come on!*

Corran's theory had been simple. *If* the prison was oriented upside-down, then gravity generators would be operating beneath his feet to keep him in place. The generators were clearly strong enough at this surface to hold him to it, but the farther he got from them, the weaker their grasp would be. If, in fact, the cavern's ceiling was actually closer to the core of the planet than where he stood, the planet's natural gravity would be strong there.

If that were true, if his theory was correct, the rock would hit and hold.

Down on his level the guards began shooting into the crowd. Stunned prisoners began to collapse in waves.

Up above, the stone clipped a stalactite. Deflected, it continued to travel upward, but now at an angle. As Corran watched, the stone seemed to slow and begin to stall.

All around him blue stun-bolts dropped prisoners. Two of the men screening him went down. Then Urlor twitched and fell to the ground. *Down* to the ground.

The stone fell *up*!

The stone rattled up in between two stalactites and nestled there safely. As it settled into place, two tiny points on it twinkled, and Corran imagined it *was* Emtrey's head and he'd just gotten confirmation of his theory from the droid. *I was right! There is a way to escape!*

The stun-bolt's blue agony played over Corran. Once again every nerve in his body fired, every muscle tightened, and every joint creaked. Wracked by pain, he collapsed with the others and rolled onto his back. The world swam in and out of focus and he knew, this time, he was going to black out. That should have filled him with dread, but when he could see clearly, Emtrey looked at him from afar.

And looking at the stone, he knew he was looking *down*, which meant things for him were definitely looking *up*.

Evir Derricote, slaving with the other Imperial prisoners at the far end of the cavern, turned to look at the commotion the Rebels were causing, but he did not hurry to do so. It would have been beneath him to let them think their squabbles were of interest to him. Affecting an air of nonchalance, he turned and watched them disinterestedly.

Then he saw Corran Horn.

222 MICHAEL A. STACKPOLE

The diminutive Rebel had irked him the first time they had met, then had compounded his error by gloating over his part in taking Borleias. As the Rebel reared back to throw something, Derricote almost called out a warning to the guards, but something forestalled him. He watched Corran make his throw and saw a small missile shoot up toward the ceiling.

Derricote lost it in the shadows above and began to wonder what Horn was up to. The rock he had thrown clearly was insufficient to dislodge a stalactite or trigger a collapse of the ceiling. As unwise and annoying as Horn had appeared to be, Derricote never would have classed him as suicidal, yet if he was successful in an effort to dislodge a big piece of rock, it would drop straight down on him and the carpet of stunned prisoners covering the cavern floor.

The Imperial General saw Horn go down. *The little fool will likely be hit by the rock he threw. Serves him right.* Derricote almost turned away, but stopped to see if his prediction would come true.

It did not.

He did not see the stone fall back to the earth.

This started General Derricote thinking. He prided himself on being intelligent. He had, after all, created the Krytos virus. It was not his fault that Ysanne Isard's expectations for it were unrealistic. He had done his best, but that was not good enough for her, so he ended up in her private prison, subject to her whims. *The whims that imprisoned me can also free me.*

Derricote could think of dozens of explanations for why the stone did not fall back to the cavern floor. The simplest explanation was that it had become lodged between stalactites. However, for that to happen, Horn would have to be incredibly lucky. He doubted the prisoners would have staged the sort of charade that shielded Horn's effort just so he could test his luck in a place that, ultimately, housed those who were utterly without luck.

One by one Derricote examined and discarded explanations for the rock remaining on the ceiling and, at last, hit upon the only one that seemed to make sense. *Iceheart has us standing on our heads. Any fool who tries to escape to the surface will just go deeper and deeper into her prison. Horn discovered this fact, tested his hypothesis, and has his result. And, just as obviously, he means to use it to escape.*

The general slowly smiled. He could easily let the guards know Horn was planning to escape, but doing that would make him nothing more than an informant. Informing was weak and would not be rewarded by Ysanne Isard. She wanted action. She wanted him to do something to atone for his failure. To please her he would have to act, because taking action was strong.

This Horn will bear watching. When he moves, I will be ready. Derricote tugged at the abbreviated sleeves of his tunic. *He will become the source of my redemption and I will once again know the glory of service to the Empire!*

26

"THANK YOU, ADMIRAL, I *do* have questions for Tsillin Wel."
Nawara Ven sorted through his set of datacards, then fed
one into his datapad. On the long journey to and from Ryloth
he'd read Wei's depositions and had formulated a series of
questions to ask her. There really was little to dispute in what
she had to say, but he needed to make certain the Tribunal understood the limitations of what she had testified to.

In direct testimony the Quarren had seemed a bit testy, and
Admiral Ackbar had admonished her to be cooperative. If
needed, Nawara knew he could exacerbate that natural Mon
Calamari-Quarren enmity and completely discredit her testimony in Ackbar's eyes. Generals Salm and Madine, on the
other hand, might react negatively if he provoked her.

Combat piloting is often much easier than this.

Nawara looped a lekku over his shoulder. "Agent Wei, according to your earlier testimony, you've been auditing Imperial
expenditures for years, is that correct?"

The Quarren's facial tentacles quivered. "I have said this,
yes."

"And the purpose for studying these expenditures was to estimate how much money the Empire was pouring into anti-Rebel activities, correct?"

"Yes."

"This means you were looking for evidence of expenses that were hidden—black projects, so to speak, that did not appear on any official Imperial budget."

The Quarren nodded. "Budgets for such things are regularly hidden within other programs. A terra-forming budget might, for example, have miscellaneous expenses linked to it that cover the cost of military development projects. Prior to our taking of Coruscant I would compare known expenses with the budget expenditures and create a picture of what the Empire was spending."

"I see." Nawara glanced down at his datapad. "Now, you have told the court that my client, Captain Celchu, was paid approximately fifteen million credits over the past two years. This would be the amount of time that has passed since his escape from Imperial custody. Is that a fair summarization of your testimony?"

The Quarren's turquoise eyes glinted wetly. "I indicated that fifteen million credits is all we have been able to uncover. The money is located in six different accounts. There could be more."

"But you are uncertain of that?"

"Counselor Ven, since the occupation of Coruscant I have been working night and day analyzing Intelligence accounts. There are literally millions of accounts. I feel fortunate to have uncovered the six we have found so far."

Nawara pressed his hands together. "But these six accounts are not the only accounts you have looked at, correct?"

"No, I have reviewed thousands of accounts myself, and my staff has reviewed nearly a million."

"So the accounts you have linked with my client are not remarkable?"

"I don't understand the question."

"Allow me to rephrase it." Nawara smiled. "How many Im-

perial agents have you found that have funds in numerous accounts?"

A translucent membrane nictitated up over Tsillin Wei's
eyes. "A few."

"A few what? Dozen? Hundred? Thousand?"

"Dozen."

"And how many of those individuals have six accounts?"

The Quarren shifted slightly in the witness chair. "So far,
none, but we have a great deal of work to do yet."

Nawara nodded. "Now, discovering the links between these
files and an agent is not easy work, is it?"

"No."

"Is one of the difficulties that Imperial Intelligence took
pains to make it difficult to locate the identities of their agents?"

"Yes."

"Do they encrypt data?"

"Yes."

"Do the encryption routines vary in difficulty depending
upon the value of the agent?"

"Objection." Halla Ettyk stood. "Calls for speculation on
the part of the witness."

"Admiral, Agent Wel is overseeing an Intelligence division
that has been at war with Imperial Intelligence for years. Clearly
she would be familiar with the degree of security the Empire
used to protect its assets and hide information."

"Overruled. You may answer the question as best you are
able."

Wei's facial tentacles rolled up and slowly unfurled. "Encryption does become more difficult the more valuable the
asset. The methods used to hide Captain Celchu's identity show
him to be of middling importance to the Empire."

Nawara smiled. "So you have uncovered other agents on the
same level of importance as him?"

"Dozens. Hundreds."

"And each of them had fifteen million credits paid out?"

The Quarren hesitated. "No."

"No? How much *were* they paid?"

"Thousands."

"So you're saying that while Captain Celchu was protected like an agent of little value, he was paid out of all proportion with his apparent worth to Imperial Intelligence?"

"That is one conclusion that could be drawn from the accounts."

"Is the other perhaps that he was set up to look like a valuable agent as part of a frame-up?"

"Objection. Speculation."

"Withdrawn." Nawara nodded to Commander Ettyk. "Agent Wei, how much money has Captain Celchu taken from his accounts?"

Wei's tentacles writhed. "None."

"To your knowledge, is there any evidence that Tycho Celchu knew the accounts existed?"

"No."

Perfect. "So these accounts could have been set up and made to look as if Captain Celchu was an Imperial agent without his knowledge, specifically to discredit him in a trial like this?"

"Yes."

Nawara let his smile blossom fully. "And in your experience, has Imperial Intelligence ever set up such accounts to attempt to make the Alliance think someone is an agent in their employ?"

The Quarren glanced down at her hands. "Yes. At least once."

"And who was that?"

Tsillin Wei glanced up at the bearded man sitting at Admiral Ackbar's left. "General Crix Madine. I found the accounts and also proved they were false."

"And you have diligently applied yourself to proving the accounts you have linked to Captain Celchu are false as well, correct?"

The Quarren shook her head. "That is not part of my job."

"So you just manufacture evidence for the state. Truth means nothing."

"Objection."

"Sustained." Admiral Ackbar looked down at Nawara. "You have made your point, Counselor Ven. There is nothing more you can gain on this line."

"Yes, Admiral." Nawara returned to the defense bench. "No further questions."

IN THE HOLDING CELL, Nawara rubbed some warmth back into the tip of his right lekku. "No, you're right, Captain, we did score points today. I think General Madine will question whether or not you're being paid off."

Tycho smiled over at him. "That's good, yes?"

"In a way, yes."

"What do you mean?"

Nawara shrugged. "The idea that you're an agent who was being paid by the Empire isn't supposed to impress the Tribunal—it's meant to impress the public. It's only one of three motives that would explain your actions. It does provide the prosecution with an embarrassment of riches. Greed is the easiest thing for most folks to understand, especially when you're talking that much in the way of credits."

Tycho's binders clicked against the edge of the table as he slid his hands from it and held them against his chest. "Corran's threatening to expose me is another motive. What's the last one?"

"Lusankya." Nawara opened his hands. "The Tribunal, at this point, has a choice. If they assume you betrayed the squadron because you were being paid or because you feared what Corran would uncover, they can convict you of murder and treason without any problem. Everyone will understand what happened and there won't be any messy details to deal with. If they decide, on the other hand, that you did what you did because of Imperial brainwashing at Lusankya, then they would be bound to find you innocent by reason of diminished sapience. In that case you'd be placed into a hospital and treated for your affliction, to be released whenever you are cured."

Tycho stared down at his hands. "Which could be never."

"That's *your* nightmare. *Their* nightmare is that some Emdee-oh droid with a Cognitive Matrix analysis package will unscramble your brain and declare you cured in a week or two. They'd have to let you go free, which would make the justice system seem impotent."

Tycho's head came up and the bright blue of his eyes surprised Nawara with its intensity. "What you're saying is that the sabacc cards have been programmed against me."

"It's worse than you know." Nawara jerked a thumb toward the exterior wall. "The day we got back from Ryloth, the Palpatine Counter-insurgency Front blew up a school. It's been thirty-six hours and they've still not found all the bodies. Some were vaporized in the explosion, unrecoverable—just like Corran's. Both humans and non died in the blast. Someone claiming responsibility said that such acts of terror would continue until the state's sham trial of you, an obviously innocent man, was ended and you were set free."

"What?" Tycho shook his head. "In court you showed that the Imps had planted the information to frame me, and now you're telling me that they're saying I've been framed? What's going on?"

"Your trial is divisive. The government is using it to show they, unlike the Empire, can handle things in an open manner. Imperial agents, on the other hand, are making it look like evidence is being trumped up against you. It makes humans think you're a sacrifice being offered up to keep the Alliance together. The non-human population already thinks you're guilty and somehow responsible for the Krytos virus—it doesn't matter that you had nothing to do with it."

Tycho leaned forward and slapped his hands on the table. "Nawara, you have to let me testify on my own behalf. I can convince them I'm innocent."

The Twi'lek sat back. "You've been talking to Diric again, haven't you?"

Tycho nodded. "He visited me while you and Wedge were gone. Aside from Winter, he was my only visitor. He says that talking to me has him convinced I'm innocent."

"That's great for him, but he was also an Imperial prisoner, so he feels a sense of kinship to you. Most other folks don't have that bond."

Tycho raised an eyebrow. "You endured Imperial discrimination against non-humans. Can you really say you *weren't* an Imperial prisoner?"

Nawara hesitated for a moment. The greatest thing for him about joining the Rebellion had been having the weight of oppression lifted from him. As a non-human he was treated as inconsequential by the Empire. Imperial magistrates would ignore him and his objections, or they would overrule him and threaten him with contempt for wasting the court's time by bringing up points of law. He knew that at any moment he could be gathered up in some Intelligence sweep and incarcerated for whatever was left of his life, and no one would know.

Fear was once a constant factor in his life. Then he joined the Alliance, and while he didn't fully leave fear behind, he was given control over it. Now, with the Empire in retreat, that same control had been extended to others. Even the most despised individuals in the Empire now knew freedom.

And still have a taste for revenge against their oppressors.

"Yes, I could say I, too, was their prisoner, Captain, but that doesn't matter. The fact is that if you testify, Commander Ettyk will destroy you on cross-examination."

"How?"

"She'll go back through your life and make it into a mockery of what it's been." Nawara's eyes narrowed to bloody crescents. "She'll point out that you volunteered for the Imperial Academy and were a successful TIE fighter pilot. She'll suggest you were so callous that you were speaking to your family and fiancée via the holonet at the precise moment Alderaan was destroyed—all because you had learned, being as you have always been an Imperial Intelligence agent, when your world's destruction would take place."

Tycho's jaw shot open. "But that's preposterous."

"You and I know it's preposterous, but there are countless people out there who would believe it. You've been to the Galactic Museum. You've seen how the exhibits about the Emperor twist facts into lies. It's no surprise that such twisting can take place. The fact is, though, that people believed the Emperor died at Endor destroying a *Rebel* Death Star. It will be very easy for those same people to believe the worst of you."

Nawara hooked a taloned hand over Tycho's binders. "You don't remember your time at Lusankya, but she will make your amnesia sound like lying. And she's good, very good. She'll have you saying things you don't want to say. Damage will be done and we won't be able to recover from it."

Tycho slumped back in his chair, dragging his hands into his lap. "We've really got nothing to prove my innocence, do we?"

"We have testimony about all you have done that is positive and good. Whistler and Emtrey came up with an analysis of the Krytos virus infection pattern and I can get experts up to show how your actions actually made it much milder than it could have been. And we're still looking for Lai Nootka."

"So you're telling me that we need a miracle?"

Nawara nodded. "I'd take one if you had one to offer, but then again, I wouldn't worry too much. Winning this trial is merely impossible, and we're Rogues. We'll get it done."

Tycho sighed. "Or die trying."

27

"Ah, Commander Antilles, welcome." Admiral Ackbar stood as the man entered his office. "I apologize for the short notice, but time rolls away as the tide."

"I came as quickly as I could, Admiral." Wedge gave the Mon Calamari a friendly smile. "It must be important."

"It is. You're the first person outside the Provisional Council to hear this." The Mon Calamari opened his mouth in the closest approximation of a human smile he could muster, hoping to put his visitor at ease. "The Xucphra faction on Thyferra has agreed to send us a substantial shipment of bacta. Your squadron—all of whom were called back to duty and are currently under a communications quarantine—will be sent out to meet the freighter convoy and bring it back here to Coruscant."

"I see." Wedge's face took on a suitably grim expression. "Aren't we a bit small to be protecting a convoy of, what, thirty ships?"

"Twenty, actually. Most are small ships, like the *Skate*. We have a few larger ones going, but our hauling resources have never been abundant." Ackbar's chin fringes wriggled. "We are having to rely on stealth and secrecy to safeguard the shipment—

and not by my choice. The whole matter of negotiations about all this bacta have become very delicate."

Wedge raised an eyebrow. "How so?"

"We never expected your visit to Ryloth would be kept secret, but the news of it traveled more quickly than we expected. Apparently the Thyferrans know we obtained ryll from Ryloth. Some of the Thyferrans wanted to cut us off from bacta completely, pointing to your trip as an attempt to circumvent them. Cooler heads prevailed, so we're getting this shipment, but it is barely sufficient to keep people alive. If the basic combinations with ryll work, we might double the effective strength of what we have, but that's still not going to be enough to effect a final cure of the Krytos virus."

Ackbar sighed as weariness washed over him. "While Xucphra officials are willing to send us the bacta to keep us paying them credits, they are very wary of advertising the fact that they're working with the New Republic. They only benefit from all this if they are able to sell bacta to all sides in the conflict. They want this convoy to appear to be a private enterprise—it was suggested that Mirax Terrik could take credit for it and profit from it. They will get the ships to our rendezvous point, then we take over. You'll ostensibly be on a training mission and offer the escort as a courtesy."

Wedge frowned. "Rogue Squadron is a high-profile outfit. We're bound to be watched. Why use us?"

"You have a Thyferran." The Mon Calamari's lip fringes twitched. "It has been suggested that having Erisi and Rogue Squadron present to guide the ships back here to Coruscant would prove to the Thyferrans that we appreciate the risks they are taking."

"Do I sense Borsk Fey'lya's furred hand in this?"

"You do, though he was not alone in it." *The Council meeting where this plan was floated seemed more difficult than any of the battles I've fought against the Empire.* "The possibility of having our bacta supply cut off is causing people to take whatever steps they can think of to appease the Thyferrans."

Wedge's eyes narrowed. "The big problem we have with the Thyferrans is that they could cut us off at any time."

"They have the monopoly, so they can do that. The fact that ryll kor might make bacta more effective against this virus does not diminish our need for bacta. Before the Empire aided the Xucphra and Zaltin corporations in monopolizing the bacta trade, we might have been able to find other sources of bacta. Now we have no choice but to trade with them. While we *could* manufacture our own bacta, the startup costs for a facility that could produce what we need would—well, I can't say it would bankrupt us, because the New Republic may already be over that line. And you didn't hear that from me."

"No, sir."

"So, Commander, you see our dilemma. We are dependent on the bacta cartel, yet our supply is shaky. Steps taken to secure our supply could anger the cartel—if those steps do not include them—or could anger our enemies enough that they strike at the cartel itself. Warlord Zsinj's *Iron Fist* could put a chill on convoy traffic and cause us significant trouble."

"But they would stop shipping him bacta, too."

"True, but his need for it is not as great or urgent as ours is."

"Point taken."

Ackbar shrugged. "As smugglers put it, we have all our spice in one freighter, and other solutions to the problem seem impossible. I know Rogue Squadron prides itself on doing the impossible, but I think this bacta problem is beyond even your capabilities."

"Perhaps, sir."

Wedge's curious reply seemed tinged with deception, but Ackbar found it hard to believe Wedge would be involved in plotting. *He has been spending a certain amount of time in General Cracken's company, and Cracken's reportage to the Provisional Council has been handled by subordinates of late, but to combine those things into a plot would be leaping to a conclusion of Borskean proportions. Even so, it does seem rather plausible.* "Do I take it you disagree with my assessment, Commander?"

Wedge's shoulders shifted uneasily. "I would have to say I think you're probably correct, sir, but Rogue Squadron has done many things in the past that were thought impossible."

Ackbar nodded. "You realize that anything you might do in this regard could have catastrophic results if the Thyferrans disapprove."

"If I were involved in anything, sir, that would be foremost in my mind."

"Very good." *Whatever you are doing, I wish you grand success.* "General Cracken will be briefing your people. May the Force be with you—in all you do."

Wedge smiled. "Thank you, sir."

Ackbar hesitated, then his eyes shrank to demi-lunes. "Be careful, Commander. Billions of lives hang in the balance. If something goes wrong, I doubt if even your status as the Conqueror of Coruscant will save you from becoming more reviled than Tycho Celchu."

28

KIRTAN LOOR STARED at the glowing holographic text hanging in the air in front of him and found himself poised between unbridled terror and unbound elation. The message offered him a way out from beneath Fliry Vorru's thumb, but only if he took steps that could easily anger Ysanne Isard. Doing that *could* destroy him. *But doing nothing clearly* will *destroy me*.

The text, after it had been decrypted and decoded, carried a simple yet explosive message. Twenty ships—New Republic and privately owned freighters—would be traveling from Thyferra with a shipment of bacta bound for Imperial Center. Rogue Squadron was to meet them in the Alderaan system—*as if all the bacta in the galaxy could heal* that *wound*—and guide them in on the return trip to Imperial Center. The message contained the times and coordinates, easily allowing for the interception of the convoy.

If he destroyed the convoy, he would advance the Imperial cause beyond even Ysanne Isard's wildest dreams. He had the means to do just that at his disposal. His earlier plans to substitute a look-alike group of fighters for Rogue Squadron and have them strafe the squadron's base required him to put together a full dozen X-wing fighters. They would be hawk-bats among granite slugs if he set them on the freighters. He was more than willing to do that, blasting every single freighter from the *Pulsar Skate* to the *Rebels' Pride* into free-floating atoms.

He had only one problem: he wasn't supposed to know what the message said.

Imperial spies in service to the Rebellion had been given a variety of ways to make contact with their superiors. Certain public terminals, for example, had special coding that routed messages along secure lines to specific destinations. A datadisk could be recorded and left in any number of blind-drops for pickup by agents. Face-to-face meetings could be and had been arranged, even with the highest profile agents around. Whatever was necessary to move information would be done.

The Rebels were not without countermeasures, and they were effective when they wanted to stop information from getting out. Fortunately Coruscant was still more of an Imperial world than it was a Rebel one. While Rebel computer code experts had gone through the planetary computer system and shut down many of the most obvious stealthways into it, they had not found them all. The Rebels would clearly have preferred to avoid using the Imperial computers at all, but running Coruscant without them was impossible, so compromises were made.

The Imperial agent in Rogue Squadron had resorted to one of the most simple stealthways in the system to get the message out. A coded message was created and saved as usual, then deleted. The command used to delete the message was a batch command, one commonly used to purge a month's worth of old messages at a time. When the computer asked for a date from which to begin the purge, the agent gave it the date and time, down to the second, the message had been created. The ending date for the purge was the same date and time.

The deletion routine in the system took that information and began special processing. A copy of the message was whisked away to a randomly chosen memory sector and there encrypted. At the original memory location where the message had been stored, zeroes were written to erase all traces of the message, then corrupted copies of other documents were written into its place. A scan of files would show documents and programs in the normal process of being overwritten.

No trace of the coded message was left in its original location. The agent was safe.

The encrypted message was transferred through a series of accounts and finally ended up on a datadisk that was dumped into a blind-drop. One of Loor's Special Intelligence operatives retrieved it and brought it to him. Loor himself decrypted and decoded it. He told himself he did so because messages from that agent had normally traveled directly to Ysanne Isard. The fact that he had ended up with a copy meant the normal channels of communication were closed and he wanted to make certain delays did not prevent action from being taken to capitalize on the information.

Had I forwarded it to Iceheart blindly I would not be caught in this trap. Because the rendezvous would take place in less than three days, there was an open question as to whether the message would reach Isard in time for her to do anything about it. Loor felt fairly confident she would act to destroy the convoy, and his own squadron had enough firepower to chew up the twenty-ship convoy with little problem. A pair of proton torpedoes would destroy most of the freighters, which meant a full dozen could die in the first pass. Another volley of torpedoes would cripple or kill the others, and the X-wings could follow up with lasers to finish off the survivors.

Probably not flashy enough for her, but if my X-wings were marked up to be Rogue Squadron ships—and the news-nets have been full of examples that making last-minute changes to match the paint jobs will be easy enough—I can sow more discord and distrust between the people and the Rebel government. Iceheart would like that.

The problem with doing just that, however, was that the operation did not help him eliminate Vorru as a threat. *If,* instead of destroying the convoy, he hijacked it to another system, he would have control of a very large shipment of a vital commodity. While Vorru had a solid lock on the bacta black market on Imperial Center, there were other worlds clamoring for the medicine. If he used his supply correctly he could enrich himself. He would betray Vorru to the Rebels—not to the government on Imperial Center, but to the constituent governments on the various Rebel homeworlds, thereby increasing distrust between them and the rulers on Imperial Center.

Or I can enrich myself, buy a world all my own, and put Boba Fett on retainer to slay my enemies. That thought brought a smile to Loor's face. *The list would not be long, but it would not be an easy one to complete. A fitting challenge for a man with his skills.*

Loor closed his eyes and gently massaged them beneath his eyelids. As satisfying as enriching himself would be, he realized he had to be very careful. Killing Vorru and Isard would provide him short-term pleasure, but he had to be looking at his long-term position. His first step was to guarantee his survival, his second to maximize his potential for power. Hijacking the bacta worked just as well to hurt the Rebellion as did destroying it, but it left him vulnerable to accusations by Isard that he wasn't devoting himself to his duty of destroying the Rebellion. She could easily see the hijacking as a move to make him independent of her, and she would not like that.

I can always argue that I wanted to get out from under Vorru's influence and nothing more. He doubted that such an argument would insulate him from her anger and retribution when she found out what he had done. And he knew she would find out—it was a question how much time he had until she did. If he could keep her in the dark for a month, either he would have gained enough power that he did not need to fear her, or *she will have had me killed.*

He realized once again that only by escaping her could he possibly survive. *This gives me no choice.*

He carefully began to compose a message. He told her of his intent to use the duplicate Rogue Squadron to "eliminate" the convoy. He would later argue that he would have said "destroy" if that's what he had meant to do. *Time being of the essence, I can't give her the whole plan, I can merely let her know I am dealing with the problem.*

He scanned his message, then prepared it for sending. He almost sent it immediately, then hesitated. *No, if I send it now, she could possibly countermand my orders. I'll give her a day's warning. By the time she considers what will happen, it will all be done.*

And Kirtan Loor would be one giant step closer to being free.

29

FOUR MINUTES TO REVERSION TO REALSPACE. Nawara Ven began a quick systems check on his X-wing. Lasers were powered up and linked for offside firing in pairs. He had six proton torpedoes, and had configured that weapon system to shoot them one at a time. Fuel was good; acceleration compensator was set .05 off full, giving him a feel for his position in space, and his life-support systems checked out—including the heated stockings into which he fit his lekku to protect them if he got blasted out of his cockpit.

He shivered. He'd been shot out of an X-wing during the first battle of Borleias. The concussion of ejecting had stunned him. He'd floated in space, helpless, in the midst of a roiling dogfight. Cold nibbled away at his fingers, toes, and lek-tips, while a little Chronographic indicator flashing on the inside of his helmet's evac-visor counted down the minutes until his air supply quit. Watching the seconds slip away, he'd felt time was moving a lot faster than it should have.

I knew I was going to die. He shook his head. *Then Captain Celchu showed up and saved me. He didn't have to do that. In fact, he was insane to do that. After he pulled me to safety, there was no way I could ever think he was an Imperial agent.*

A beep from his R5 unit marked 30 seconds to reversion. "Thanks. Even up my shields forward and back. I don't expect trouble, but I want to be ready."

The droid complied with the request and Nawara prepared himself for the rendezvous with the bacta convoy. Rogue Squadron's Two flight, led by Lieutenant Pash Cracken and including Gavin and Shiel as well as Nawara, was supposed to break off and head sunward to cover the tail end of the convoy. The last ship was to be the *Pulsar Skate*, so they'd form up on it. One flight, with Wedge in the lead, would take the head of the convoy, and Three flight, which was still one pilot short, was to orient itself toward any trouble.

Not that there should be any. The shards of Alderaan formed an asteroid field commonly known as the Graveyard. The majority of traffic into the sector came from Alderaanian expatriots returning to see the sun beneath which they were born one more time and to leave grave-gifts among the asteroids. Others came to plunder those grave-gifts, and some even claimed to have seen a massive armory ship named *Another Chance* among the planet's ruins—though Nawara thought that ship as much a legend as the fabled Katana fleet.

I wanted to ask Tycho if he wanted me to leave anything for him, but I wasn't allowed any contact with him after I was briefed. Nawara had recorded a message and saved it in the computer for Tycho in case he didn't make it back, but the mission was supposed to be little more than ceremonial. Aside from their timetable slipping by three quarters of an hour because of a fuel pump failure that delayed their takeoff, the mission had gone exactly as advertised. *But it's the ones that are supposed to be easy that hurt the most.*

The white tunnel through which his ship had been hurtling exploded into a million separate pinpricks of fire. Some of those pinpricks resolved themselves into distant stars, while others refused to shrink. Green darts stabbed into some of the brighter points in the system, then those points exploded. "Sithspawn!"

"S-foils into attack position." Wedge's voice came through the helmet comm unit strong and cool. "Twelve, get me a full scan of the sector. One and Two flights, on me."

Nawara reached up with his right hand and flicked the switch that split his stabilizer foils into the cross pattern that gave the fighter its name. Nudging his stick to port, he brought his fighter in on Pash's starboard flank with a fighter-length separating them. "I've got you, Five."

"Thanks, Six."

Aril Nunb broke into the comm channel with her report. "Caught a flash of something big heading out—a Super Star Destroyer. It's gone, but in system we have two dozen eyeballs, two lambs, and a Strike Cruiser designated *Termagant*."

"What about the freighters?"

"We just saw the last one explode."

Nawara's stomach folded in on itself. "Gone? They're all gone?"

"An Imperial SSD wouldn't leave much behind." Fear and revulsion filled Rhysati's voice, and Nawara could easily visualize the hard look in her hazel eyes. "We're going in, right, Rogue Leader?"

"Twelve, any sign of the *Skate*?"

"No, Commander."

"Nothing at all? No beacon?"

"There's no beacon from half the hulks I have on my scan." Aril's voice softened a bit. "A Super Star Destroyer has enough power to completely vape any of the ships in the convoy."

"Right, right." Wedge's voice trailed off and no one spoke to fill the void. "Blast it! All right, listen up. We're going in, and we're going in hot. The Strike Cruiser is our primary target. Proton torps, dual-fire. I want it down and out immediately."

Erisi's voice crackled through the comm unit. "That means the TIEs will have no way to get out of here."

The edge in Wedge's voice came through unadulterated. "Is that a problem?"

"Not for me, Lead."

Nawara keyed his comm unit. "What about the lambs?" The two *Lambda*-class shuttles carried weapons and could be tougher than TIEs to handle because they also sported shields.

"We give them one chance to run. After that, they can go away, too."

Aril again spoke. "I'm downloading tac-data to everyone. *Termagant* isn't straight Imp, it's allied with Zsinj."

"*Was* allied with Zsinj." Wedge's ship began to lengthen its lead over the others. "Come on, Rogues. Warlord Zsinj apparently wanted the Alliance's attention. Here's where we make him pay for that mistake."

Following Wedge, the squadron sped in toward Zsinj's forces and the convoy debris. The convoy had been ambushed out beyond the Graveyard and a bit below the system's orbital plane. Rogue Squadron had come in on the other side of the orbital plane. Because of this, and because of the way Zsinj's forces chose to orient themselves respective to the system, by flying down to them, Rogue Squadron was, from their perspective, flying in *up* at their bellies.

Nawara watched his tactical screen. Because the TIEs were making strafing runs on what were left of the freighters, they had no unit cohesion. With the enormous amount of debris in and around where they were flying, Nawara would have been surprised if they had any clue about Rogue Squadron's approach. *So the ambushers get ambushed. How fitting.*

With the flick of his thumb he brought his weapons-control over to proton torpedoes. Another touch of a button and he linked both launching tubes. Range to the *Termagant* stood at 4.5 kilometers. The X-wings closed fast as Wedge led them down and around the freighter debris field, then over and in at the Strike Cruiser. Nawara's head's-up display went from green to yellow as the cruiser filled his sights, then blazed red as his R5's keening wail announced he had a target lock.

"Rogues, launch *now!*"

On Wedge's command the squadron fired their proton torpedoes in near-perfect unison. Twenty-two torpedoes streaked in at the lozenge-shaped Strike Cruiser, coming up toward the ventral hull. The first couple detonated brilliantly white against the ship's shields, but the rest pushed on through. Several exploded against the hull, shredding and blackening armor plating, while still more burst inside the ship. Argent fire gushed from the ragged hole in the ship's hull, then geysered out of several smaller openings on the upper part of the ship.

The Strike Cruisers, as a class of ship, had been highly lauded because of their unique construction. Built around a central skeleton that bound the bridge to the engines, their other components were completely modular. A cruiser configured to carry troops could, after a short stay in some spaceyard, emerge a TIE carrier like *Termagant*. Strike Cruisers allowed the Empire to change the makeup of the Imperial fleet without building entirely new ships.

That strength is Termagant's *weakness.* As the torpedoes exploded inside the ship, the ship itself began to break apart. The prow drifted upward as if the ship had run into an invisible wall. Armored hull plates shattered where they had covered the seam between the bow and the starboard TIE hangar. The forward part of the hangar started twisting as it ripped free of the skeleton. The cruiser began to roll, then the whole front half of the ship spun off as the ship's waist evaporated in the inferno the torpedoes caused.

"The eyes of the Warlord are upon us," Gavin quipped. "TIEs inbound."

Nawara flipped back to his lasers and broke to port with Pash. Coming up over the top, they climbed toward the incoming eyeballs. He punched all power to his forward shield and prepared for a head-to-head pass. He dropped his crosshairs on the growing speck that was an approaching TIE starfighter. He watched the range close, then popped a quick shot off. A pair of laser-bolts glanced off the eyeball's port panel, imparting a spin to the ship. Nawara started to dive after it, but with his speed, he overshot it.

"I got the other half of it, Six."

"Thanks, Gavin." Nawara evened out his shields and pulled back up. Inverting his ship, he completed a big loop and followed the rest of squadron back into the fray. In the boiling cloud of fighters, friend and foe flashed past so quickly that it was impossible to account for everyone's position. Nawara knew a number of the other pilots in the squadron had a "situational awareness" that was superior to his own, but he figured this battle had to be taxing even them.

And if you take long enough to line up a shot . . . The hiss of lasers gnawing away at his aft shield completed his thought and sent a jolt through him. "I have one on my tail. I'm going to try to shake him."

Nawara hit the right rudder pedal, swinging the X-wing's aft to port. He kicked the ship up onto the starboard S-foil, then pulled the stick back and curled down into a corkscrew dive. He throttled back a bit, hoping his pursuer would overshoot him, but the aft scan showed the pilot pulling a twisting roll and dive that covered more distance, keeping him in behind Nawara.

The Twi'lek punched the throttle forward and enlarged the gap between them, then broke hard to port and started to climb again. *Maybe that will get rid of him.*

Lasers hissing on his aft shields again told him the tactic hadn't worked. Nawara rocked the X-wing back and forth and bounced it up and down, making it a tough target to hit, but the TIE pilot stayed with him.

I have to do something. Sweat formed on his upper lip and leaked in at the corners of his mouth, coating his tongue with the taste of copper. His lekku twitched in their fabric prisons. *Maybe if I run into the Graveyard . . .*

He started to pull up and head for the asteroids, when something behind him exploded. He glanced at his aft monitor and saw no TIE there. "Thanks."

"My pleasure, Six." Erisi seemed pleased with herself. "My wing would be distraught if you were hurt."

"I owe you, Four, for the both of us."

"Acknowledged, Six."

Aril Nunb's voice broke in on the comm channel. "Lambs are running."

"Thanks, Twelve, let them go." Wedge's voice lacked none of its earlier vehemence. "We've got plenty to do here."

Nawara brought his X-wing up and evened out the shields. Trailing Erisi back in toward the fight, he saw two or three TIEs explode. Another came shooting out of the dogfight, then barrel-rolled in on Erisi for a broadside shot at her.

"Four, break up!" Nawara snapped his fighter up on the port S-foil, then climbed. He swooped in on the eyeball, stayed with it as the pilot juked down, then hit his trigger. The first pair of laser-bolts only melted holes in the starboard solar panel, but the second hit the ball cockpit dead on. The TIE began to spin out of control, then exploded in a cloud of brilliant incandescent gas. Debris sparked off his forward shield as he flew past the outer edges of the fireball.

"Lead, Five here. The TIEs are breaking off. They're heading for the Graveyard."

"I copy, Five. Rogue Squadron, let them go."

"You can't be serious, Lead."

"I am, Gavin."

"But what they did—"

"Doesn't matter right now. They're dead and they know it. I don't want any of us getting dead. Regroup in your flights and stand by." A momentary squeal ended Wedge's transmission, telling Nawara that the commander was shifting over to a different comm unit frequency.

Nawara rolled his fighter and dove down to where Pash and the other two members of Two flight were orbiting. Peering out through his cockpit canopy, he got the first good look at the remains of the convoy. *If humans can bring themselves to do this to a convoy of ships hauling bacta, I am glad I'm not human.*

A few of the freighters were still recognizable as such. Hull compartments had been blown open by explosions. Bacta that had geysered out through the holes had flash-frozen into monuments to the terror the ships' crews must have felt. Fires burned deep in the hearts of several ships, consuming the last remnants of atmosphere. Pieces of other ships drifted through the area, slamming into one another, breaking up yet further to careen into other dead hulks.

The worst image Nawara saw was of one small ship—*one barely bigger than the* Skate—that appeared, from the prow to midships, to be intact. Back of that point the ship did not really exist—at least, nothing recognizable as a ship. Turbolaser fire had hit so fast that the latter half of the ship had been liquified. An amorphous blob of metal fringed with condensed metal mist, like the down from a silvery bird, trailed in the ship's wake.

The sheer violence of the attack that had destroyed that ship shook Nawara. The transparisteel cockpit panels on the ship had blown out. He realized the Super Star Destroyer's turbolasers would have superheated the atmosphere in the ship. The crew would have been cooked inside and out in the blink of an eye. *They would have been dead before they knew what had happened to them, but their last moments must have been full of terror because of the SSD's presence.*

Nawara keyed his comm unit. "Hypothetical question: you're part of a convoy with minimal arms and you come out of hyperspace in the shadow of a Super Star Destroyer and a Strike Cruiser that's deployed its TIEs. Do you provoke an attack?"

"Ooryl cannot see how anyone would be that suicidal."

"Right, so you'd surrender and tell the SSD that you're hauling bacta, which is currently very valuable." Nawara frowned. "It makes no sense for anyone to have killed the convoy."

"That's why to know Warlord Zsinj is to wonder about his sanity." Disgust filled Pash's voice. "He's definitely someone who needs a lot of killing."

"Count me in."

"Me, too."

A squeal came through the comm unit, then Wedge spoke. "I've just had word with the TIEs. They're giving up—they were uneasy with the mission and they don't like the fact that we showed up. They're going to recon the hangar sections of *Termagant* and see if they can reboard."

"Why, that hulk's not going anywhere. The engines are in the other half and it's headed for the Graveyard."

"I noticed, Four. They're going to check for survivors and try to pick up enough oxygen to survive for as long as they can. Pash, I want you to take Two flight out of here and make for Tatooine. It's about eight hours out, give or take. Gavin can guide you in to Mos Eisley. Refuel there and hire a freighter that can carry a dozen TIEs. Get it here and haul the pilots clear. I'm sure your father would like to debrief them, so you should probably bring them to Coruscant with you."

"As ordered. We fly cover for the freighter in case our friends have any ideas about trying to commandeer it?"

"Right, though I don't think you'll find much opposition."

"How so?"

"Scan the debris. There're a lot of TIE parts out there and—"

Nawara looked at the readout his R5 scrolled up his screen. "X-wing debris. But we didn't lose anyone."

"No, we didn't." Some of the anger drained from Wedge's voice. "Of course, that's not what Zsinj's people say. They say they already killed off Rogue Squadron, right here, defending the convoy the way it was supposed to. Then we arrived and showed them we were tougher to kill the second time around."

Nawara blinked. "But that makes no more sense than attacking the convoy in the first place."

"No it doesn't, but there's no time to try to figure it out now.

You get to Tatooine. We'll check for survivors here, then head back to Coruscant and report. See you there in a day or so." Wedge sighed. "If by then you come up with any brilliant thoughts on what's happened here, I know I, for one, will be more than willing to listen to them."

30

KIRTAN LOOR WOULD have been trembling with outrage, but the lethargy of despair had a higher priority. He knew his days were numbered, and he wouldn't have bet on double digits even if given the longest of odds. He freely assumed the only reason he still lived was because Ysanne Isard enjoyed the thought of him cowering in fear, dreading each new day.

Yet even facing certain death at her hands, Loor did greatly admire how Isard had gotten him *and* Warlord Zsinj *and* the New Republic in one simple set of maneuvers. Rogue Squadron would also have been caught in the trap had their operation not fallen behind schedule—*and if I had not been playing* my *game.*

Within 24 hours of the ambush at Alderaan, Zsinj had sent a message to Coruscant via what was left of the Imperial Holo-Net system, indicating he and his people had attacked the bacta convoy because, according to his sources, the bacta was tainted and would have exacerbated the Krytos virus problem. He further claimed that Rogue Squadron had been present, had indicated they knew the bacta was tainted, and had fully intended that it should be distributed on Coruscant to "get rid of the xeno-trash" the Empire had left behind. He said he had no choice but to destroy the convoy and Rogue Squadron, then beseeched people to overthrow the New Republic's government and flock to his banner.

The only problem with his message, which was broadcast worldwide, is that it followed by roughly six hours a report about the attack on the convoy. This attack report had been delivered by the government and included holographic images created by and with commentary from members of Rogue Squadron. Zsinj's claim that he had destroyed the unit were proved false, and helped make the rest of his comments appear likewise untrustworthy.

Loor shook his head. Ysanne Isard had clearly leaked to Zsinj the information about the convoy. His report that he was sending a Rogue Squadron of his own to eliminate the convoy clearly would have arrived too late for her to get it to Zsinj. Loor had only given her 16 hours' notice of what he was doing, yet the timing of Zsinj's message to Coruscant suggested strongly that it took him at least a day to make it to Alderaan from wherever the *Iron Fist* had been.

All of this meant the message that had been routed to Loor and warned of the squadron's mission had also, somehow, made its way to Isard. She had acted based on that original message, then got Loor's follow-up message later. The appearance of his Rogue Squadron meant that Zsinj didn't wait around for the genuine unit to put in an appearance—he just struck and destroyed them all. Rogue Squadron had embarrassed him in the past, and this was his chance to get back at them, which he truly believed he had. The tainted bacta story clearly was an afterthought to mollify those people who might be upset by his destruction of so much bacta.

The loss of the bacta *had* struck quite a blow to the hopes of people on Coruscant. Coupled with that was a report from a governmental accounting office that indicated there was less ryll available than previously thought. Several Provisional

Council members suggested it had been stolen, but statisticians showed how the shortage was actually an artifact of good distribution. The previous supply, which had been supposed to last for two months, was down to seven weeks because more was getting out to more people.

It struck Loor as amusing that the government was still fighting the Emperor's ghost; it was the Empire's doing that had prompted everyone to look for the truth behind government statements. The fact that the Republic might be telling its citizens everything there was to tell did not stop people from thinking there might be something more to the story. *Teaching trust is a long process; learning it is an even longer one.*

And Ysanne Isard has, in short order, learned she can no longer trust me.

Had he done nothing and simply relayed the message to her when he got it, her plot would have discredited Zsinj, resulted in the loss of the bacta, *and* caused the destruction of Rogue Squadron. While she had no proof that he intended to steal the bacta and use it for his own gain, he knew she didn't *need* proof to condemn him. She knew he was smart enough to see how powerful that bacta could have made him. If he had succeeded he would have amassed enough power to begin to play on her level.

Now he was just a failure.

And failures, as far as she is concerned, are worthless. She would discard him as soon as the optimal use for him arose. *Which means I must find something to do with myself before she does.*

Loor allowed himself to laugh and banish some of the fear. He had plans to make, *big* plans. *Plans for the future and plans to get me to the future.*

GAVIN DARKLIGHTER CLEARED his throat and rapped gently on the doorjamp of Commander Antilles's office. "Excuse me, sir."

Wedge looked up from his desk, a bit haggard and bleary-eyed. "What can I do for you, Gavin?"

"I'd like to speak to you if I might. In private, sir."

Wedge straightened up in his chair, then nodded and waved Gavin to the seat in front of the desk. A couple of keystrokes killed the holographic lists of numbers hanging in the air above Wedge's holopad. They looked like quartermaster reports to Gavin, but he couldn't be certain, since he was reading them from the back side of the hologram.

"What is it, Gavin?"

How to begin? Gavin seated himself, then looked down at his hands. "Ah, sir, we, the squadron that is, have been discussing the situation at Alderaan. It was really pretty bad. I mean, those of us in Two flight got to see it a second time when we went to get the TIE pilots, and the destruction seemed even worse than we'd thought."

Wedge nodded and rubbed his eyes. "I know. I helped edit and narrate the government's report on the ambush. Warlord Zsinj's *Iron Fist* did a first-class job of ripping the convoy up from one end to the other."

Gavin frowned. "When I talked to the others, they said you've been pretty quiet about all that—about Mirax dying and all. I mean, I didn't know her nearly as well as you did, of course. I got to know her on the run into Coruscant when we came in secret, and I liked her. Not romantically, you know—not that there was anything wrong with her, but even *I* could see she was interested in Corran. Anyway, I remember you coming to talk to me about Lujayne Forge when the Imps killed her, and how much it helped and I thought—"

"You thought it would help me to let my grief show?"

"Well, your best friends aren't here for you. Captain Celchu is in jail, Princess Leia has dropped out of sight, and you and Mirax were close, so . . ."

Wedge smiled and sighed, then leaned back in his chair. "I appreciate this, Gavin, more than you know. I guess, with Mirax, I'm still in shock. There was no trace of her or the *Pul-*

sar *Skate*, so part of me wants to believe she had an astrogation error and jumped someplace else, that she wasn't there at
all."

"I think we'd all like to believe that, sir."

"It's ridiculous, of course, but that's part of the reason I'm
not ready to let her go, you know." Wedge frowned. "It seems
as if everyone I know, all the friends I make, are getting ground
up by the Empire or some malignant little offshoot of it. Fighting against the Death Stars—well, someone dying there somehow had meaning. The convoy, though, they were just bringing
bacta to a sick world. Even though their deaths have catalyzed
the Provisional Council into making a decision concerning
Warlord Zsinj, their lives were wasted, and I guess I'm tired of
that sort of waste."

Gavin looked up. "We're going after Zsinj?"

Wedge tapped his datapad. "I was going over information
concerning our supplies for deployment against him. I don't
know many details, and couldn't tell you any of them if I did,
but this convoy hit has made Zsinj a big target. Admiral Ackbar wants this data rather quickly, so I really should get back to
it."

"If you say so, sir."

Wedge leaned forward on his elbows. "Look, Gavin, I appreciate your coming here and talking to me about Mirax. I
don't think I'm ready to go into this all the way right now, but
I'm coping. It hurts, but I'm coping."

Gavin nodded. "Yes, sir." *Walling it away just delays things.*
"If you ever decide you want someone to talk to—"

"You'll be the first person I call." Wedge smiled and sketched
Gavin a brief salute. "Go get yourself some rest—and that goes
for the rest of the squadron. If we're going to be going after
Zsinj, I want us ready to move as fast as possible."

BORSK FEY'LYA STOOD behind his desk and smoothed the creamy
fur around his face. "Please, Asyr Sei'lar, do come in. I am hon-

ored that Rogue Squadron's newest ace has time to visit with me."

The black-and-white-furred Bothan bowed her head respectfully, then stood at attention as the door closed behind her. "I am honored a member of the Provisional Council noticed me."

"Noticed you? My dear, you are quite impossible to refrain from noticing. Aside from your performance in the squadron, you were positively stunning at the Dan'kre party the other evening. Please, be seated. No need for formality here, is there?" Fey'lya remained standing until she had taken her seat. She moved with an ease and strength he recalled possessing in his youth. Though he was not that long past his physical peak, he could already see how much he had lost from when he was her age.

Borsk Fey'lya also realized that had he been her age again, he would have been lovestalking her. He found her quite attractive, freely acknowledging that the white blazes in her fur gave her a dangerous look. The fire in her violet eyes likewise threatened to seduce him, but with maturity—unlike humans—he had moved away from personal vanity. Whereas a man might take a mistress her age to prove his continued virility, for Fey'lya that choice would prove he had not yet sufficiently focused himself on what was truly important in life.

The pursuit of power.

"I wish to communicate to you, Asyr, the congratulations and adulation of the people of Bothawui. You are well on your way to taking your place in the constellations of Bothan heroes like the Martyrs and even your predecessor in Rogue Squadron, Peshk Vri'syk. You liberated Coruscant and now fly with the New Republic's most famous fighter squadron. Your parents are very proud of you, and other Bothan parents everywhere have virtually no reservations when it comes to their children choosing you as a role model."

"Thank you, Councilor." Asyr's violet eyes blinked. "I would think parents could find far better role models for their children than me."

"Perhaps, but I should not be concerned about your liaison with the human, Galen." Fey'lya purposely misidentified her lover and was rewarded by a flash of anger rippling the fur of her neck and head. "Xenophilia is not unknown among us, and your dalliance adds a hint of romance to your image. Your Galen seems very capable of handling himself in a wide variety of situations—case in point being the way he defused the Kre'fey problem. Moreover, you are quite discreet—admirably discreet, actually."

"His name is *Gavin*, Gavin *Darklighter*. His cousin was one of those who died destroying the *first* Death Star."

"And our Martyrs died to enable the Alliance to destroy the second Death Star. It is fitting that heirs to two heroic traditions should find comfort together." Fey'lya raised a hand to calm her. "Please, forgive me if this mention of your personal affairs angered you. I did not mean to cause you any discomfort. *I* fully understand the sort of bonds that can be forged between people who endure adversity together. Others are not so accepting of things they see as different."

"Thank you, Councilor." Asyr frowned heavily. "Some other members of the Bothan community here are positively *imperial* in their xenophobic attitudes."

"*That* is not good at all. If you will permit me, perhaps I can help you with this problem. I have ample opportunity to speak with various groups—Bothan and other—here and back on Bothawui. It does no one any good for you to be persecuted for things that really are beyond your control. I was young once. I know how hot one's blood can be. I will use my influence to get attitudes to change."

"That would be most kind."

"I'm glad to be of service." Fey'lya smiled. "In fact, I had hoped to be of service to you when I invited you here, but this was not the subject I wanted to address."

Asyr met his gaze unflinchingly. "Yes, sir?"

"You were part of the mission to Alderaan, as I recall, yes?"

"Yes. I flew wing for Commander Antilles. I got the kills I did because he hung back and covered me."

"I see." Fey'lya pressed his hands together, fingertip to fingertip. "The timing of your arrival in the Alderaan system has become a point of interest for those conspiratorially-minded individuals within the government and without. You were late and the convoy was destroyed."

The younger Bothan's eyes narrowed. "If we had been on time, we would have been destroyed, just like the convoy."

"Quite so, quite so, and it is a good thing you were delayed. Still, you realize that tests on the samples of bacta ice that were brought back to Coruscant do show the bacta to be tainted and spoiled—in accord with Warlord Zsinj's allegations."

"Forgive me, sir, but those samples were blown up, flash-boiled, and peppered with debris. That they show up contaminated and useless is really no surprise."

"Under normal circumstances I would agree with you."

"What do you find unusual about these circumstances?"

Fey'lya gave her an indulgent smile. "Clearly the convoy's timetable was leaked to Warlord Zsinj. Since the Xucphra faction on Thyferra has seen fit to send bacta to the New Republic, it is safe to assume it was the rival Zaltin faction that tipped Zsinj about the shipment. Even so, we cannot rule out the possibility that members of this government sabotaged the effort to bring bacta to Coruscant."

"You can't be serious. That would make Mon Mothma or others out to be monsters who had sunk to Ysanne Isard's level or below."

"Of course I don't believe that is the case, but the problem is that others *do* think it possible. I am afraid that *you* could become implicated in all this because of your membership in Rogue Squadron." He pressed his hands flat on his desk and leaned forward. "I want to insulate you from any possible disaster coming down the line."

"Disaster?"

"Rogue Squadron will be sent out with the task force being used to punish Warlord Zsinj. It could very well be that this Alderaan incident means certain superior officers in the military see Rogue Squadron as a problem. Committing you in an action that destroys the squadron would eliminate that problem. I'm not saying this is what will happen, of course, but it could and I would like to put some insurance in place that prevents this from coming to pass."

Asyr's head came up. "What kind of insurance?"

Fey'lya gestured toward her with opened hands. "I would like you to prepare a report that indicates the delay in Rogue Squadron's arrival was a product of *human* error."

"Such a report could be used to strengthen the conspiracy theory."

"*If* I were to use it in such a capacity, yes, it could, but I would never do that."

"*Never?*" Asyr raised an eyebrow. "You know the Bothan saying—'Never means the right opportunity has not yet arisen.'"

"Then I should amend my statement—I would never use it except if I deemed it necessary to curb human excesses. You know—and the Krytos virus is but one example—mankind's capacity for cruelty to its own is infinite. The human members of the Alliance have not turned on us or on Rogue Squadron, but that's not to say they will *never* do that." Fey'lya tapped his desktop with a talon. "You are a Bothan. You were born with obligations and responsibilities. Writing this report is just one of them."

Asyr nodded. "I understand, sir."

"Good. I'll want that report within 72 hours. Don't fail me."

"No, sir." Asyr rose from her chair and bowed her head to him. "I understand the price of failure, sir, and I have no intention of incurring that debt."

31

IT'S TOO EASY. Though everything was going absolutely according to his plan, Corran Horn felt some unmitigated disaster was lurking ahead of him. The Imps who hung out near the mouth of the cavern hadn't bothered to make comments as he and Urlor headed off down the dark corridor toward the latrines. They walked close together, letting the infrared images of their bodies merge into one, creating a single image for the IR monitors at either end of the corridor.

Once inside the latrine area, Corran had doffed his tunic and soaked it in the single sink, then pulled the clammy garment back on. He likewise soaked his head, then smiled up at Urlor through the water running down his face. "I'm set."

Urlor raised a bushy eyebrow.

Corran nodded. *Yes, I have to go. I have no choice.* Corran slapped him on the arm, then headed to the entrance. Urlor followed, patted him on the back, then walked back toward the billet cavern, weaving slightly from side to side to widen his IR image. *Thanks, my friend.*

Corran, still sodden, turned to the left and walked on toward the mine. He kept his pace slow and turned sideways to present a narrow profile to the IR monitor near the gate. He wasn't certain that this would really minimize his heat image, but it was worth a try. His wet hair and tunic would be more effective in that department. Urlor's efforts to present a big target farther up the corridor might also help eliminate him from notice.

Thirty paces beyond the latrines he reached the doublegate. In the darkness he groped along the flimsy metal surface for the lock and chain. His fingers gently brushed across the number pad on the lock, but he resisted the temptation to try random combinations. He didn't know if a failure would set off an alarm somewhere or not, but he did know that trying to figure out the right combination would take enough time to make him drier than a Tusken Raider. *Unless I got lucky, and no one is that lucky.*

From the lock to the opposite door Corran counted sixteen links and winced. Seventeen links had provided him a tight squeeze two nights previously. Corran gripped the gate-halves, pulled them as far apart as possible, then tucked his right shoulder through the opening. He exhaled as much as he could, worked a leg through, then pushed and pulled himself the rest of the way to the other side.

He squatted on the other side of the gate and rubbed at his chest. *Just as well none of the others wanted to try to get out. Aside from some of the older prisoners and a few of the sick ones, no one could have fit through there.* Staying low, he worked his way forward. When he reached the entrance to the mine corridor, he turned into it and allowed himself a quiet sigh.

I can't believe how stupid they've been. Corran realized his criticism of the guards was not fair, primarily because their lack of security seemed deficient only in light of his theory about the orientation of the prison itself. No prisoner in his right mind would attempt to escape and head deeper into the bowels of the planet. The laxity in securing the path to the mines served as a strong clue that the mines did not offer a way out—if they did, they would be more secure.

Security is predicated on two things: the odd orientation of the prison and *the fact that even if someone gets out of the prison, getting off whatever world we're on is by no means assured.* Corran shivered. *If we're in the depths of Hoth, or in the desert of Tatooine or on the back side of Kessel, this escape attempt will end quickly enough.*

Despite those inauspicious thoughts, which sparked new feelings of unease in him, Corran pushed on. He reached the hatchway leading into the caverns and found it open. *Well, perhaps I am lucky, just a bit.* He would have felt luckier if he had a light of his own, but the prisoners had no access to anything more technologically sophisticated than a shovel. To navigate through the darkness all he had to guide him was the faint glow from the amber ready-lights at the base of the floodlights they used when working in the mine. Corran had mentally mapped them the way an astronomer mapped constellations, and he knew exactly where to head to get to the gravel loader. Having oriented himself toward his goal, he stood straight and started to make his way down the slope.

Pain exploded across the middle of his back, numbing his legs. He pitched forward and tried to tuck into a ball, but his legs ignored him. He knew from the pain in his back and knees, as they alternately struck the stone slope in his tumble, that his spine hadn't been severed. While this was good news, it paled within the larger context of his having been attacked in the mines.

He hit bottom and skidded to a halt on his back. He could feel the burning tingle of sensation returning to his legs, but they felt like lead and had no strength in them. The poor footing provided by the gravel combined with the weakness in his legs to keep him down, which he saw as a distinct problem as a massive, bulky shadow eclipsed several of the amber lights. The orange glow, though very weak, clearly illuminated the edge of the upraised shovel the man held.

"Nothing personal, Horn, but you're my way out of here."

Derricote? "How did you get past the gate? You couldn't have squeezed through."

The shovel remained at the top of the arc for an overhead blow. "I have money hidden away, in numbered accounts. I bribed a guard for the combination to the gate lock, same as I bribe them for ingredients for my nectar."

Appeal to his vanity. Buy yourself time to be able to move. "Very clever, General."

"And too clever to let you recover. Good-bye . . ."

The shovel began to fall. Corran rolled to the left and felt the shovel bounce off his right shoulder. He expected another blow, but instead heard Derricote gurgle and the shovel clatter to the ground. Gravel hissed as the Imp's bulk twisted around into Corran's line of sight. He heard someone grunt, then the sound of a falling body, but Derricote's silhouette remained upright.

Reaching back with his right hand, Corran grabbed the shovel's shaft, twisted his grip, and whipped the metal end around. He caught the Imp in the back of his legs, upending him. Gravel sprayed Corran as Derricote hit the ground. Rolling up onto his knees, Corran smashed the shovel down on the man's stomach, and when Derricote's hands dropped to cover his belly, Corran caught him with a blow to the head.

Derricote went limp.

"Is he dead?"

Corran looked over to where the voice had come from. "Jan?"

"Yes."

"How?"

The older man came close enough that Corran could hear the wet rustle of his tunic. "I noticed Derricote wasn't around—he's too big not to see. Urlor told me you were off. I assumed he was informing on you, so I came to stop you. When I saw him standing over you, I had to do something."

Corran reached out to check Derricote for a carotid pulse

and found the braided cord Jan used to tie his hair back wrapped around the man's neck. He handed it back to Jan, then checked Derricote's pulse. "Weak and thready. I must have broken his skull."

"Leave him. They'll think he fell trying to escape. We can get back before they notice."

Corran shook his head. "Can't do it. If they find him here, they'll know we know Lusankya's secret. We'll never get out." He grabbed the upper part of Jan's right arm. "Come with me. We can drag the body off and deposit it somewhere. They'll never find it until we're long gone."

The older man laughed lightly. "Oh, they will notice my departure more quickly than anyone else's. I can't go for that reason."

"And because they'll kill the others."

"Yes."

"I'm going to come back for you, you know. Whenever I get clear, I'm going to have Wedge bring the squadron in and we'll get you out."

"I know that, son. I'm counting on it." Jan clapped him on the shoulders. "I might never have known your grandfather, but I'm certain he'd be proud of you. I am. May the Force be with you."

"And you, sir."

"I'll clear away signs of the struggle. If you drag Derricote with you, I'll give you a head start and then I'll report he's missing. They'll be searching for him, but they'll not be looking in the places where you could hide. We'll cover for you as long as possible, but anything more than twelve hours is optimistic."

"I copy, Jan." Corran got up and began to drag Derricote's body by one arm toward the gravel loader. Jan grabbed the Imp's other arm and helped. Together they hefted him up on the safety railing. Corran checked Derricote's neck for a pulse. "Nothing. He's gone."

"Someday, perhaps, no one else will need to die in service to the Empire."

"Agreed." They upended the man and let him fall. Though Corran couldn't see Derricote hit, he did hear a crunch.

"Again, Corran, may the Force be with you."

"Thanks. Until we meet again." Corran shook Jan's hand, then climbed the railing and slowly lowered himself into the darkness. He stepped on Derricote's body, then crouched and scuttled under the conveyor belt. Beneath the belt itself, where it fed back into the drive-engine compartment, Corran felt around the outline of a hole in the sheet steel lining the pit. He'd first seen it a week earlier when shoveling gravel out of the pit, and knew it was what he wanted in the way of an escape tunnel.

Now, if only Derricote will fit. Corran wrestled the fat man's body over to the 60-centimeter-wide hole and stuffed him through. He heard another muffled impact, then slipped into the hole himself. *This has got to work.*

Corran had previously noticed that there was no access panel for the drive-engine compartment. If the engine broke down, it had to be accessed from another point entirely, which meant there was another way into the compartment. Down inside it Corran found himself on a steel-grate catwalk. He crawled around, reconnoitering by touch. Finally, off to the left side of the compartment near an access hatch, he found a light switch and punched it on. One dim panel provided the illumination for the chamber. Corran quickly dragged Derricote over to the closed hatchway, then he turned the light off again.

He listened at the metal hatch but heard nothing. His mouth dry, his nostrils filled with gravel dust, Corran took hold of the hatch's internal handle and eased it back. The latch system squeaked just a bit and rasped some, too, all of which sounded to Corran like the sounds issuing from an Imperial torture chamber. Certain he had alerted all Imperial forces in the facility to his presence, Corran carefully opened the access hatch.

The rectangular room on the other side of the opening was empty. Corran let out his breath—not realizing until that point he had been holding it. Just to be on the safe side, before he entered the room himself, he dragged Derricote's body over and shoved it through the hatchway. *So far he's been a good point man.*

Derricote fell to the floor of the room, and Corran slid easily through the hatch after him. He closed the hatch behind him and dragged Derricote's body to the doorway. Beyond it lay a cylindrical corridor roughly three meters in diameter. A red stripe of tiles spiraled down through it, starting at the center of Corran's side and ending up on the ceiling fifteen feet away. *Decorations! And who says the Imps are all gloomy?*

Corran started off into the corridor and found himself stumbling to his left. To make matters worse, Derricote's body slid in the same direction. Waves of dizziness slammed through Corran as he tried to walk the corridor straight through. He finally lost his balance and fell, ending up with his spine pressed to the red line about a meter into the corridor.

Oddly enough, lying there felt normal, even though he could see he was lying firmly against one of the tunnel's side walls. He shook his head as if that would clear up the problem, then he let his head slip back and rest on the red tiles. *Of course! This has to be a transitional corridor. Gravity is directly oriented on the red strip. It takes you from upside-down to rightside-up.*

With reason thus injected back into his world, Corran scrambled to his feet and started hauling Derricote along. His shoulders ached from the exertion, but he had no intention of leaving the man behind. Finding a place where Derricote's body could be hidden, or allowed to fall from a height before being discovered, would provide the Imp searchers with what they wanted and buy Corran time to complete his escape. *As long as they're looking for a fat man, they won't be looking for me.*

At the far end of the tunnel Corran straightened up. The room he found himself in, though dimly lit, appeared to be a utility room. He saw panels dealing with climate control as well as electrical power and other conveniences he had so recently lived without. From the number of different zones on the climate control panel, he knew the facility beyond the door was fairly large. He listened at the fiberplast door, but heard nothing from beyond it.

He drew in a deep breath, then hit the door release and crouched in the shadows as the door cracked open. The doorway provided access to a fairly opulent hallway which reminded him, rather faintly, of images he'd seen of the Imperial Palace. *Great, I escape a prison to find myself in some Imperial Moff's palace. It's certainly better than the hole I just got out of, but getting out of here unnoticed is not going to be that easy.*

He shrugged. *But easy isn't the object of this exercise— escape is. Escape I will.*

32

NAWARA VEN TRACED a talon through the ring of moisture left behind on the table by his mug of lomin-ale. *I shouldn't be here. This is madness.* He drank more of the bitter and spicy ale. *This is insane.*

By rights he shouldn't have been anywhere near a tapcaf, much less a dim, smoke-choked place like the Hutt Haven. The prosecution had rested its case and had left Nawara in a serious bind. While the evidence presented had been, for a large part, circumstantial, it was a *mountain* of circumstance. He had character witnesses, but nothing to refute the basic facts upon which the prosecution was basing its case, which meant he ultimately had nothing.

Which is why I'm here. Two hours earlier he had received a message requesting the meeting. He would have ignored it, but it had been signed "Hes Glillto," the name Lai Nootka had assumed on his last trip to Coruscant. Whistler had gotten the name from Iella, and that had prompted the droid to flag the message when it came through to Nawara. Whistler also reported there was no way to trace it back to the sender—it had come through a public terminal.

It's not a good thing when a lawyer is given to meetings with mystery witnesses to bolster his case. If the person he was to meet was really Lai Nootka, the state's case against Tycho would fall apart faster than a Jawa-fixed droid. Nootka could prove he'd met with Tycho on the night Corran said he saw Tycho meeting with Kirtan Loor. Once that fact was established it showed Tycho had nothing to fear from Corran and, hence, had no reason to want him dead.

Of course, I've got no reason to suppose it will be Nootka. Probably will just be some glitbiter looking to make money in return for some rumor. Nawara raised his glass to finish it, but before he could swallow the liquid, he saw a tall, slender figure enter the tapcaf. The figure wore a hooded cloak that hid him entirely. *It's just the way Nootka appeared in Corran's description of him.* Nawara straightened up as the figure cut through the crowd, then slipped into the booth's other seat.

Nawara offered his hand. "Nawara Ven."

A pair of long-fingered human hands came out from beneath the cloak and pressed flat against the table. "I know who you are."

"And you're not Lai Nootka." Nawara's eyes narrowed. "Are you going to take me to him?"

"No. I would apologize for the deception, but I am not sorry. Lai Nootka will not be coming. He is dead."

"What? Can you prove that?"

"He's dead, and I cannot prove it." The man's voice came low but strong from within the shadowed hollow of the cloak's hood. "I can, however, prove your client was not meeting with Kirtan Loor on the night Corran Horn saw him."

Nawara's lekku writhed as disbelief flooded his voice. "You deceive me and then expect me to believe you? How can you prove that?"

The man tugged the hood back far enough to admit some light, and Nawara felt his heart ache. *He looks like the ghost of Grand Moff Tarkin.*

"I can prove it, Nawara Ven, because I am Kirtan Loor and I

was nowhere near Tycho Celchu that night. In fact, I have never met him."

"And you can verify where you were?"

"Yes. I have evidence enough to satisfy you." Loor smiled slowly. "And evidence about spies throughout the New Republic that will satisfy even General Cracken."

What! This is too good to be true. This can't be happening. Nawara's jaw shot open. "You're lying. You can't be who you say you are."

"I can and I am. I will testify on your client's behalf provided the New Republic is willing to offer me immunity from prosecution for any activity I have undertaken on behalf of the Empire. They will pay me a million credits, create a new identity for me, and get me off Coruscant. I will tell them everything they want to know, and then some. Every Imperial agent on Coruscant will be exposed. It is that simple."

"But . . ." Nawara's mind was reeling. The implications of what Loor had said were staggering. "How can we be sure . . . ?"

Loor grabbed Nawara's hand and impaled his own palm on one of Nawara's talons. A bead of blood bubbled up. Nawara heard the sound of cloth tearing, then saw Loor blot the blood with a strip torn out of his tunic. He tossed the bloodied cloth to Nawara, then tore another strip from his shirt and bound his hand.

"Take the cloth to Commander Ettyk. Have her duplicate my Imperial file, then run a DNA comparison between the duplicate and the sample. She must run it against a duplicate of the file—if she runs it against the file itself, others might discover you're checking me out. Once you're certain I am who I say I am, you will broker the deal for me. It is a take-it-or-leave-it deal, no negotiation. Once you have the deal made, you will hold a press conference. At one point during the conference, whenever you wish, you will say 'I am very confident, supremely confident, that we will win.' I don't think I've heard you say that so far in the proceedings, so that will be the signal."

"No, I don't think I've said that. I *know* I haven't felt it."

"When you give the signal, I will send you another message to arrange pickup. At that time you and Iella Wessiri will get me. I don't want to see anyone else, just you and her. You I have to trust, her I know well enough to trust. You can't betray me and she won't. Anyone else, anything fancy, and no one will benefit from my information. Got it?"

Nawara nodded slowly. "I understand."

"Good. You have five hours."

"Five hours! That's not much time, especially starting at midnight." Nawara frowned. He almost added that he couldn't call a press conference at two or three in the morning, but the media operated in a frenzied enough atmosphere that he could tell them to meet him on Kessel at noon and they'd find a way to be there. "I need more time."

"You don't have it." Loor nodded once and the hood slid forward to again hide his face. "I don't have it. This all happens on my timetable. If it doesn't, if there is trouble, a lot of people will be sorry. I can give freedom to your client and Coruscant to the New Republic, for which I am asking so little. See that it gets done."

33

CORRAN SQUEEZED HIMSELF back in the corner of the library's cabinet and waited. He decided it was just as well that he didn't have a chronometer, because he would have constantly been looking at it. It seemed as if he'd been hidden away for years, though he knew it had hardly been more than fifteen minutes. *I can only hope that some of the criminals I hunted felt like I do now while stormtroopers are hunting me.*

Corran had been able to make a basic scouting run on the facility where he found himself and had concluded two things. First, the utter lack of windows suggested that this facility was underground. Given the general taste for grand vistas and high towers he'd seen in Imperial architecture on Coruscant, this led him to believe that whatever the planet's surface looked like was not worth seeing. This, in turn, made him think the surface was inhospitable and, therefore, not a place he wanted to travel without proper equipment.

Second, he concluded there had to be a secret exit from the facility. Aside from the tunnel back to the prison, the only visible means of leaving was a lift that had a keypad and clearly required a code for operation. While he assumed the Moff who owned the place would have had the code for the lift, he couldn't imagine the Moff did not also have a private bolt-hole. Unfortunately his hurried survey of the area hadn't given him any obvious candidates for its location.

One thing he *had* found was a garbage disposal chute. He dragged Derricote's body to it and dumped it in. He distinctly heard a splash; then a disgusting odor wafted back up, so he closed the hatch. It was only when he realized that he didn't smell much better himself that he decided, if things got tight, he'd go through the chute and take his chances getting out that way.

The Imperial facility had a layout that was a lot like a TIE starfighter's cross-section. The lift, garbage chute, and utility area formed a central core through which ran a long corridor. It intersected two corridors at right angles, one at each end. All of the corridors had high ceilings and doors running off them every seven meters or so.

His first impression of opulence had not been diminished in his survey of the facility. The entire place had been decorated with golden-brown wooden panels and hand-carved trim. Not being often treated to the lifestyle of the rich, Corran couldn't identify the wood, but he was fairly certain the faint rose scent filling the air came from it. He made a mental note to ask Erisi what kind of wood it was, since he assumed she would know.

More impressive than the wooden furnishings were the huge xenoscapes that took up whole walls in some of the rooms. Some were filled with water and had brightly colored fish swimming through them. Others contained dense, foggy atmospheres or boggy environments in which things flapped and slithered. Each room had its own private xenoscape and while most of the creatures looked harmless, a couple looked positively lethal.

Despite getting frightened by the sudden appearances of several luminous beasts along the wall of a darkened room, Corran was glad for the xenoscapes' presence. Some specimens were large enough that lifeform scanning equipment might have trouble differentiating him from them, frustrating a search. In his experience that sort of equipment was most valuable in determining where lifeforms were *not*, so that searches could be confined to the places where they *were* found. He assumed that if searchers were forced to go over the level carefully, he could elude them in a deadly game of hide-and-seek.

But then, he'd not been counting on the methodical nature of stormtroopers and how they did their work. During his scouting run a squad of eight came up through the turbolift and immediately posted two men in the facility core. The remaining six broke up into two teams of three and proceeded to go through each wing room by room. Once they finished in a room they closed the doors and used a datapad to set the locks and seal the room.

He'd fled from them as carefully as he could, but they pushed on. Finally he'd found himself herded into what, in the golden glow of the large aquatic xenoscape along one wall, appeared to be a very nice library. The shelves on three walls were lined with box after box of datacards. Both desks in the room had tabletop datapads with holoplates that could provide a fully tri-dimensional data-scanning experience. The chairs all seemed comfortable, and had the room not been built on an immense Imperial scale, Corran could have considered it cozy.

It had its quirks, though. In stumbling about he stepped into a circular design on the floor. He would have thought it a continuation of the inlaid wooden pattern, but it felt cold and synthetic to his bare feet. He had barely stepped into it when a holographic image was projected down from the ceiling and filled the circle. Corran leaped back and raised his hands to protect himself.

Ten feet tall, an image of the Emperor stared down at him. The figure looked strong and almost majestic—not at all the image of the twisted, malignant man who had overthrown the Old Republic and created the Empire. The hooded and cloaked figure stood there, then slowly raised his hands toward the ceiling. They returned to his side, vanishing as the cloak slid closed, then the figure shrank to more human proportions and melted away through the circle.

That display so unnerved Corran that he immediately sought cover. He noticed a long low row of cabinets beneath the xenoscape. He opened one of the cabinet doors but found he couldn't see much inside. The space smelled cramped and close; it reeked of mildew and reminded him of the location Tycho had found for the Rogues to hide while they prepared to liberate Coruscant. Had there been another choice he would have taken it, but the crisp click of boots on the floor outside the door told him his time had run out.

He crawled over some small boxes and into the narrow space, then pulled the door closed. The cabinet had been compartmentalized—he found himself in a cubicle barely a meter high and wide, though it did extend back nearly two meters from the door. A thick metal crossbeam framework supported the weight of the transparisteel xenoscape above him and the water it contained. Fiberplast panels lined the compartment on all sides and felt as solid as rock as far as his buttocks and spine were concerned. He pulled himself through the crossbeams and into the compartment's back half. He arranged the boxes and canisters in the front of the cabinet to shield him, but he knew even a cursory look would reveal his presence.

I hope they have a nice place in the shrine down there for my head. Stomach acid burbled up into his throat, but he choked it back down and endured the burning. *Probably doesn't hurt as much as blaster-bolts will.* He tried to recall the pain from the times he'd gotten shot—at Talasea, and in the mines—but sensation seemed distant, and unrelated to what he knew he would be feeling in short order.

He heard muffled voices from the other side of the cabinet door. Clicks and hisses accompanied them. *What can they be discussing?* Despite the ache in his spine and the burning in his throat, Corran smiled. *Maybe one of them decided searching these cabinets is stupid because there's no way Derricote could be hiding in here.*

Then, through the soles of his feet, he felt a slight vibration shake the cabinet framing. *If searching the cabinets was what they were arguing about, my team lost, which means I've lost.* Another cabinet door closed, this one closer if judged by the strength of the vibration. Then he felt the quiver of a cabinet being opened, followed by a strong tremor when it was shut.

That's it. He's getting frustrated. No one is in the cabinets. No one can be in the cabinets. They're too small to hide anyone, much too small. Corran pulled his legs up to his chest and wrapped his hands around his knees. He actually heard the cabinet next to his open. A comlink clicked. He thought he heard the word, "Clear."

Then he definitely felt the cabinet slam shut.

Corran pressed himself back into the corner. *There's no one in here. There's nothing to see here. No one is hiding in here. It's all clear.*

The door opened.

There's no one here. This cabinet is empty.

A light flashed in. It started at the far end.

Empty, empty, empty. All clear.

The light swept across toward him.

What a waste of time searching this cabinet. It's empty. There's no one here.

The light snapped off before it hit his face. The stormtrooper helmet, which had taken on the proportions and ugliness of a Hutt's ghost in Corran's sight, pulled back. "It's empty. There's no one here."

Corran clutched his knees more tightly to prevent his heart from pounding its way out of his chest.

"Are you sure?"

Despair exploded in Corran. *What sort of an idiot would trap himself in these cabinets?!*

The door slammed shut and bounced back ajar when the magnetic latch failed to catch. Corran caught part of a heated exchange between stormtroopers. He missed the initial comment, but the sharp reply came through loud and clear.

"If he's stupid enough to try to escape, he's stupid enough to hide in those cabinets. Finish checking those last two cabinets, then seal the room. This level is clear, so we move up."

Corran heard the other cabinets open and close, but it was the thunder of a storm that had passed him by. He dared not relax, and bumped his head against the top of the cabinet when a stormtrooper reshut the door to his compartment. The burning in his lungs matched that in his throat, then he slowly exhaled and drew in a new breath. He wanted to jump out of the cabinet, escape its coffinlike confines, but he didn't know if the stormtroopers had left the room yet.

Again he waited. He knew he had gotten lucky, but he was able to convince himself that it wasn't just luck that had saved him. In his time with the Corellian Security Force he had participated in countless searches for suspects. There came a point where he knew, in his gut, that the suspect had fled and his attention flagged. From what one of the stormtroopers had said, he concluded the library was the last room to be searched on that level; if so, the stormtrooper checking the cabinets was probably bored out of his mind.

Because he was bored, he got sloppy. Corran smiled and started breathing more normally. *Good thing he had his helmet on, otherwise he would have been able to smell me.*

He waited a little longer, even beyond the point where he wanted to crawl out of his skin. He fought against the panic rising in his heart. *If I panic, I die. Cool. Calm. You've been in tighter situations before. Take it easy.* He concentrated on breathing and waited for his pulse rate to go down, then slipped from the cabinet.

He found himself alone in the library. The lights in the xenoscape provided him ample illumination to find his way around, but he still wasn't certain what he was looking for. He assumed it was too much to ask for any of the boxed datacard sets to contain plans that would allow him to escape the room. Still, he'd conducted enough searches of criminal strongholds to find it easy to imagine that one box of datacards might be a dummy that, when pulled out or tipped up on edge, would open the door to a secret hiding place or, better yet, the Moff's bolt-hole.

It would have to be something obscure—something no one would ever choose to look at on purpose. With that as his search parameter, he found a lot of choices. The sheer variety of datacard collections impressed him. But each box he tried contained the appropriate datacards. *At least I can improve my mind while trapped here. Given enough time, I could become the galaxy's expert in all sorts of things, including worlds I've never heard of, like this Corvis Minor.*

He pulled the slim box labeled *The Complete History of Corvis Minor* off the shelf and was disappointed when no secret door opened up. He was about to put it back when he noticed the weight didn't seem quite right. He opened the box and dumped a compact holdout blaster into his hand. *If a blaster is considered the complete history of Corvis Minor, I'm thinking it's not a vacation spot.*

He put the box away and checked the blaster's power pack. *A half-dozen shots. It probably won't get through stormtrooper armor, but it can make them dive for cover.*

Keeping the blaster in his hand, he continued his survey of the library. He found no more surprises and gave up hoping there was a history of Corvis *Major* that would contain something more substantial in terms of weaponry. *Like an X-wing.*

Frustrated by the lack of success of his search, he turned his attention to the datapads. He wasn't sure the computers would be much more help than the library's inventory had been, but he assumed he could get some basic information to help him out. Most dedicated datapads included basic information about their surroundings. Something as simple as a map showing the evacuation route in case of fire or rebel invasion would point him toward exits.

Provided I can get into the system. Had Whistler been with him, the droid could have sliced into the system with ease. While he did know a few things about codeslicing himself, he'd relied on Whistler's skills so much that he could only perform rudimentary assaults on a system. *If there's a password for gaining access to the system, I'm blocked right there.*

At the smaller of the desks he flicked the holopad on. He opened some of the drawers, looking for the sort of datacard that might contain password information, when a word appeared suspended above the holopad:

[INQUIRY]:

Corran's smile blossomed. Whoever had last used the datapad had finished by turning off the holopad instead of logging off the computer. This deep in a secret Imperial facility, the chances of an Alliance spy getting to *that* terminal were slender, and if the security procedure for getting access was laborious enough, merely shutting the holopad down could seem like a tempting, if unsecured, alternative to making the system secure. *Whatever the reason, I don't mind.*

Corran called up a system catalog and shifted to the Lusankya database. Hundreds of names scrolled past too fast for him to read, so at the next prompt he called up his own record. It seemed fairly complete and decidedly up-to-date on data about him since his joining Rogue Squadron. *Tycho's doing, no doubt.* He highlighted a datalink labeled *Lusankya* and saw a brief history of his stay in the prison. Comparing the date given for his arrival with the dateline on the bottom of the holographic image, he realized he'd been in captivity for six standard weeks. That was longer than he'd been able to count, but his interrogation had been full of lost and warped days.

He highlighted another datalink. Next to the legend "CStatus:" was the code "R1." Corran chose it and got a quick explanation floating above the desk.

R1: Resistant in primary phase.

Notes: The subject could not be induced to fire upon positive icons despite being subjected to their hostile intent in simulation. His resistance in the second round of testing occurred sooner than in the previous round. Subject is unsuitable for conversion.

Corran stared at the green words burning in the air above the desk. When he had thought about it, he had assumed the simulator flights he had taken were just part of an interrogative technique. The technique let him fly, which made him feel good. If things were done correctly, that good feeling could be transferred to the Imps, then he'd tell them what they wanted to know. He could imagine it working just that way with any number of folks—they'd be seduced into giving up information without realizing what they were doing.

Clearly that was not what Isard had been trying to do with him. *She was trying to make me over into a monster, just like Tycho. She wanted me to become a tool she could use against the Alliance.* He shivered and wished he could somehow open his skull and scrape the memories of what he endured from his brain.

His eyes narrowed. *Well, your conditioning didn't work. I'm not your tool. I'm your enemy, and when I get out of here, I'm going to hurt you.*

He got back to an inquiry prompt and called up Tycho Celchu's file. *Finally, I'll have proof!* Corran summoned up the Lusankya data and had highlighted the "CStatus" code before he really looked at the value listed there. *R1. No way. That was my code.* He called up the data and sat back, stunned.

R1: Resistant in primary phase.

Notes: Though the subject's initial response to Imperial icons was positive, this appeared to be an artifact of his years spent at the Imperial Academy. It did not last long. Subject aggressively attacked Imperial icons. When those icons were overlaid with Alliance datastreams, the contradiction caused the subject to become catatonic. Subject is unsuitable for conversion.

But that's not possible. Tycho's a spy. I know it! Anger tore through Corran and immolated his brain. He wanted to believe that Ysanne Isard had planted this information so he'd not believe Tycho was a spy, but she had no way of knowing he'd get where he was to see it. Besides, his having that knowledge would serve no purpose to her benefit. Even supposing Tycho were killed by the Republic and Corran were allowed to escape and point out that Tycho had been innocent: that would cause strife in the New Republic, but how much? Was it worth the elaborate charade of letting him escape?

Corran got up from the chair and began to pace around the room. Isard had fed his hatred of Tycho and supported his conviction that Tycho had been a spy. That made no sense. From his file she would have known that he'd have been far more tortured inside by being told that he'd been wrong, and that his mistake was the foundation for Tycho's treason and murder trial. His own sense of personal honor would have eaten him up inside when he realized an innocent man was going to be convicted of a crime because of his mistake.

Lost in his thoughts, he stepped into the circle in the middle of the floor. The Emperor descended upon him and Corran jumped back. He snarled up at the image and marched on through it. "Quite the mess you created with your Empire, you know."

Corran realized that Isard's actions made no sense to him because she was coming at things with an Imperial sense of ethics—ethics that frightened him. She fed his hatred of Tycho because it gave her a button to which she knew he would react. His hatred was unthinking, and she didn't want him thinking at all. *Once she got me reacting through emotions, she could manipulate me. The problem was that my feelings in favor of the other members of Rogue Squadron overrode my hatred for Tycho. And, maybe, just maybe, somewhere deep down I didn't doubt him.*

However, there is evidence of a spy being connected with Rogue Squadron. He returned to the datapad and punched in the names of all the personnel in the unit or support staff. They all came up blank. Feeling a bit frustrated, he called up Tycho's file again and read over the parts concerning his time at Lu-

sankya. The details were pretty much in keeping with what
Tycho had told him: he didn't remember much of his time
there, then he was transferred to Akrit'tar. The Lusankya file
made reference to his escape from that facility and included a
couple of notes about Tycho's life since then, but didn't include
much detail until data started flowing from the Rogue Squadron source.

Pacing again, Corran began to work things out in his mind.
If Tycho was not an Imperial spy, then he wouldn't have been
meeting with Kirtan Loor. As much as Corran was certain he
had seen Loor that night, he admitted that having seen the man
earlier in the day at the Imperial Palace had rattled him, and
could easily have made him misidentify a Duros in a hooded
cloak as Loor.

Bits and pieces of things began to drop into place for him.
By a simple process of elimination he narrowed down the list of
possible spies, and one name rose quickly to the top of the list.
*No doubt about it—but then, that's what I thought about
Tycho. I have to get clear of here and check some things out. I
can't afford to be wrong this time.*

He looked up as the Emperor towered above him. Corran
stepped back. "You know, the sheer ego it takes to plant your
image in your own facility is unbelievable. This display does
nothing but take up space." It struck him as another useless bit
of Imperial ostentation. Then it occurred to him that just as the
cabinets hid the structure that supported the xenoscape, the
holograph did do more than one thing.

It stops people from standing on this spot.

Corran stepped forward and oriented himself to face in the
same direction as the Emperor. The world hazed out slightly as
the hologram settled down over him, but out of the corner of
his left eye he caught the momentary red spark of a low-grade
spotting laser being shot at him. It flickered on and off a few
more times, then the Emperor's hologram collapsed around
him. As it did so, the circle shifted and began to descend beneath the level of the floor.

The cylindrical hole closed over the top of him, then a man-sized panel slid open in front of him. Through it he saw the entry portal to a luxurious private tunnel-shuttle. *Similar to what we used to move prisoners from the detention center to court on Corellia, though this is much, much nicer.*

The panel closed and the circular platform began to ascend again. Corran found himself once more in the library and smiled. He went to the datapad, got back to the prompt he'd found initially, then shut the holopad off. Picking up the hold-out blaster, he inserted himself again into the Emperor's image. The lift again took him down and he entered the tunnel-shuttle.

In the forward compartment he found a keypad and controls, but he had no idea how to program destinations. Up at the top he saw a red button marked "Return" and poised his hand above it. *I don't know where this will take me, or how long it will take for me to get there, but anywhere is better than here.* He hit the button and sat back in the hope he'd enjoy the ride.

34

*T*HAT'S IT, THEN. Loor smiled and killed the sound accompanying the holographic images of Nawara Ven's press conference. The Twi'lek had said the phrase. The New Republic would become Loor's new home. *It's just as well Corran Horn is dead—our being on the same side would have killed him anyway.*

Loor folded up a small transportable datapad and slipped it into his pocket. Once he left his office he would use a public access site to plug in and send the directions for his pickup to Nawara Ven. Sending it from his office would have been easier, but would have increased the probability that a copy of the message would fall into Isard's hands. Though he planned to be hidden well away by the Rebels by the time she discovered he was missing, he wanted as much time for his disappearance to take place as possible.

At his desk he copied files from his desktop datapad to a datacard. "Helvan, come here."

One of his Special Intelligence operative cell leaders entered his office. "Sir."

Loor held the datacard out to him. "There has just been an announcement concerning the Celchu trial that leads me to believe there will be a fair amount of attention centered on the proceedings today. We shall take advantage of that. These are the plans and authorization for a strike at the largest of the Republic's bacta storage areas, the one in Invisec."

"The one guarded by Vorru's militia?"

"Is there a problem with that?"

"No, sir, the target is no more secure than any other Rebel facility. It is just that we have refrained from hitting targets he is guarding so far. . . ."

"Indeed." Loor shrugged. "An oversight on my part. Vorru thought himself immune to our wrath. He learns now he was wrong."

A smile tried to squirm its way into the SIO man's face, but failed to do more than tug at the corners of his mouth. "Sir, when do we strike?"

"Court begins early in the morning. Time the strike to occur with the first witness. That gives you approximately five hours."

"It's done, sir."

"Very good, Helvan. You make me proud."

"Thank you, sir."

The SIO man turned and practically ran from the office. Loor would have laughed, but he feared that might have betrayed his true intentions. The attack he had designed would call for a strike force of thirty SI operatives—three cells' worth. He designated a bacta facility as the target because he knew Isard would approve of it and might set aside, even for a moment, her fears about him. He chose Vorru as a target both to strike at the man's vanity and so he could hurt the man personally before he sold him out to the Rebels. *Stick the vibroblade in and modulate the oscillation rate.*

Loor prepared the plans for transmission to Isard by adding a note stating he intended to personally supervise the operation, and then sent them. He shut down his datapad, then took one last look out the window of his sanctuary at the brilliant galaxy of synthetic stars below him. *There will be other towers and other chances to rise to such heights.*

On a whim he turned on all of his lights and left them burning like a beacon in the night as he abandoned his office and set out on the most dangerous mission he had ever undertaken.

RUBBING SLEEP FROM HER EYES, Iella Wessiri entered Halla Ettyk's office. "You look as haggard as I feel."

Halla looked up at her with bloodshot eyes. "You don't know the half of it. Nawara Ven called me just past midnight. I've spent two hours meeting with him and various Provo Council members. This is all madness."

"Why tractor-beam me into it?"

Halla smiled. "Because you've been the one who's harbored little doubts about Tycho Celchu's guilt. We've got a witness now who can confirm his innocence. We have to bring him in, and you're going to help Nawara do the job."

Iella blinked her eyes. "A witness? Lai Nootka came forward?"

"Nope." Halla sat back and mischievous light played through her brown eyes. "Someone who demanded your presence. Said he'd only trust you to bring him in."

Who could that be? Iella's eyes narrowed. "Give me a name."

"Can't. This office isn't secure enough." Halla pointed toward the office window and the drapes drawn over it. "Someone you knew well, once upon a time."

Iella frowned. *Drapes? Curtains?* Her jaw dropped open. *Kirtan Loor?* "It can't be."

"It is. Code name is Behemoth."

"Right." *He's the biggest Intelligence agent we've brought in so far.* "What's the drill?"

Halla yawned. "Sorry. Nawara just gave his little media conference so Behemoth knows the deal is set. Nawara will be coming here and will be waiting until Behemoth can get him a message about pickup. I've arranged for you to get an armored airspeeder. You'll take Behemoth to a safe house, Nawara Ven will depose him, then you'll pack him up and bring him here in time for court. We want him in and out fast—we're counting on secrecy because he should have enough information about Imperial ops that almost anyone could want him dead."

Iella nodded. "You're not afraid I'll kill him?"

"Not before he clears Celchu of Horn's murder, no, I'm not. Cracken will want him after that, but my only concern is his impact on this trial." Halla shrugged, then blew a lock of black hair from in front of her face. "I've already told you he cut an immunity deal, so the only justice that will be done in this case is getting Celchu off. You know how these deals work."

"Yeah, they stink worse than Hutt-sweat, but you give something to get something." Iella sighed. "Don't worry, I'll bring him in safely."

"Never was worried about it."

Iella pointed to the hololink on the office's other desk. "I need to speak with Diric."

Halla frowned. "Not a good idea."

"If I don't, he'll wait up. He always has, but he's really not that strong anymore."

"No details, right?"

"Right."

"Go ahead." Halla stood and smoothed the wrinkles in her skirt. "I'm going down the hall to brew up something hot, dark, and stimulating. Can I bring you some?"

"Please." Iella sat down at the desk and entered her home link number. She smiled reflexively when Diric answered. "It's me."

"So it is, and with a smile." Diric stifled a yawn with his hand. "Forgive me. How are you? Is there anything you need? I can run it over."

"No, no, I'm fine, really." She forced her smile to broaden. "I just called to let you know I'm not going to be coming back home this morning."

"Anything wrong?" Irritation washed over Diric's face. "No, can't be if you're smiling. Something good, then?"

"Work, work I can't tell you about. You'll find it fascinating when I can."

"I can't wait. Sounds as if you have a big day ahead of you." He glanced off to the side for a moment, then nodded. "I'll get some fruit and put it together with your lunch so you can snack on it if there is a break. Will that work?"

"That'll be perfect, darling." Iella touched the hololink's screen and caressed her husband's face. "It really *is* going to be a big day tomorrow. You'll see why I can't say anything."

"I understand. Thank you for letting me know you're safe. I can try to get back to sleep now."

"Please do, Diric. Get all the sleep you can—enough for both of us."

"I'll do my best." He smiled at her. "Be careful. I love you."

"I love you, too." Iella hit a button and broke the connection. She sat back and sighed deeply. *It's very strange to find myself having to safeguard a hated enemy so he can exonerate a man in the murder of a good friend. I'm not sure Corran would appreciate the irony of the situation, but I do know he wouldn't want an innocent man imprisoned for a crime he didn't commit. I think that's as close to peace of mind as I'm going to get out of this. I just hope it's enough when all is said and done.*

35

N EVER, IN ALL THE TIME he had secretly worked for Ysanne Isard, had he gotten a message that revealed her to being close to panic. The messages she had sent concerning the remnants of Rogue Squadron and the need for their elimination had been more controlled and confident. Even after the Alliance took Coruscant and she disappeared, her messages had revealed a core of confidence that her activities would bring about the destruction of the New Republic.

He had to admit that she had not been far wrong in her beliefs in that regard. The Krytos virus had created such a demand for bacta that the New Republic had all but bankrupted itself trying to meet the minimum demand for the lifesaving liquid. They had been desperate enough to strike a deal for ryll with the Twi'leks, a gamble that could have caused angry Thyferrans to cut off the bacta supply completely.

Confidence in the government had begun to erode because of the bacta crisis. Warlord Zsinj's predations on a bacta convoy had dealt the public's belief in the government a serious blow from which they would attempt to recover by sending a task force under Han Solo's leadership to kill Zsinj. In fact, however, the more insidious damage to the government had been done by the government itself with the Celchu trial. Originally Tycho Celchu had been held up as an example of the evil perpetrated by the Empire, but Nawara Ven's spirited defense had pointed out that the evidence against Celchu was circumstantial and probably manufactured. The obvious displeasure expressed by Rogue Squadron's cherished heroes at Celchu's trial helped underscore the weak foundation for the government's case.

He neither knew nor cared if Celchu was innocent. Isard was very capable of arranging it so an innocent man appeared to be guilty or vice versa. He did know she was using the trial to hurt the government, and her efforts clearly were succeeding—which is why the tenor of the note surprised him.

In addition to summoning him to a meeting place, the note directed him to dispatch teams of his people to various sites in the Imperial Palace and Senate Hill areas. They were to go armed and shoot on sight the individual whose file she'd appended to the message. Many of the locations would be all but impossible to get to at this hour: a forty-third floor foyer in the Imperial Palace, an unused area of the Galactic Museum, an old Imperial Senate subcommittee room. Moreover, it struck him that the only place she wasn't asking him to send his men was the Imperial Courthouse. Since she wanted everyone in place before court could open, and since the target apparently possessed information she didn't want revealed, he assumed she had the Courthouse covered herself.

Fliry Vorru frowned. *She should have gotten Loor to send people out to these other sites, too, not just the Courthouse.* He flicked on his datapad and called up the reports from the people he had monitoring the activities of Loor and his operatives. Of Loor there was no report within the last hour, when he left his tower. Loor had gotten much better at eluding surveillance over the past several weeks, but he always showed up again in places that made re-acquiring him painfully easy.

The reports on some of Loor's operatives, on the other hand, sparked Vorru's interest. Three teams, a full thirty individuals, had congregated at the warehouse facility Loor used to store his heavy weaponry. *That makes for a big operation, and I've given Loor no targets for such an operation.*

Fliry Vorru realized that one of *his* facilities was going to be the target of that operation. Isard's orders were scattering his troops so he couldn't defend against the assault. *It has to be coming against the bacta storage facility—that's the only target I control which she would see as valuable. She wants to take it down to hurt the Republic, but hitting any of the others would make as much sense. The only thing this gives her is a terrorist strike against me, which strengthens my cover and distances me from association with her.*

Ordering him to be in a meeting place at a specific time was meant to get him out of the bacta storage area so he'd not be killed. If she confided in him the reason she wanted him out, he'd refuse to do what she wanted, choosing instead to protect his bacta and the profits he could reap by selling the "wastage" that occurred with each shipment. *As well as the other loot I have stored there.*

Despite the fact that her summons was meant to save his life, he took little joy in it. If things went as they had previously, she would appear in hologram and berate him for what he had or had not done for her cause. She used the fact that she could betray him to the Rebels as a bludgeon, and he cringed suitably when she did so, which seemed to satisfy her need to see him under her control. As nervous as her message suggested she was, he expected quite a beating.

What she does not understand, what she has never understood, is that I don't fear her at all. The Emperor considered me a rival. She is nothing compared to him. I work for her because her goals and mine coincide. I can play her off against the Republic and benefit in the meantime.

Fliry Vorru smiled. He prepared orders dispatching militia

teams to the sites she wanted, though he reduced her request for a dozen people at each location to three. The rest he ordered summoned to his bacta storage facility. He planned to have them moving as much bacta and other loot as possible to the various storage facilities he had scattered all over Imperial Center.

When she wants to know why I evacuated my facility, I'll tell her the Alliance tipped me to a strike. And to make that seem true . . .

Vorru switched his comlink to a secure frequency and initiated a call. He allowed the sleepy individual on the opposite end of the link to awaken enough to understand Basic, then he spoke slowly and carefully. "Forgive the hour of this call, Councilor Fey'lya, but I knew not where else to turn. I have learned of an impending PCF strike at a bacta storage facility. If we act quickly, a great tragedy can be averted."

ALL WEDGE COULD see of Emtrey in the darkness was the droid's glowing gold eyes. "What is it, Emtrey?"

"Forgive the intrusion, Commander, but we have just gotten an urgent message from Admiral Ackbar. There are terrorists about and we have to stop them."

Wedge shook his head to clear it. "Terrorists here, in our area?"

"No, sir. They're going to hit a bacta storage site. You're to fly cover for our troops opposing them."

The bedsheet slid down around Wedge's waist as he pulled himself up and pressed his back against the headboard. "Call in the squadron."

"I have, sir. They're all coming in except for Master Ven. He's not answering his comlink."

"Keep trying. When you get him, I want to speak with him. Get to Zraii and start pre-flight on our X-wings. Tell him I want no fueling delays this time."

"Done, sir." Emtrey pointed at the datapad on the desk in

Wedge's room. "The primary briefing document has already been downloaded for your review."

Wedge smiled. "Thanks." He threw back the covers and stepped out of bed. "Caf, lots of it, for me and for the ready room. I have a feeling this mission is not one we can fly in our sleep."

36

A TONE BROUGHT CORRAN AWAKE. A jolt of fear ran through him when he couldn't recognize his surroundings. He knew he wasn't in Lusankya anymore, or at least he hoped that was the case, but the thought that his whole escape might have been some elaborate charade staged by Isard to break him down gnawed at his spirit.

He hauled himself off the very comfortable bantha-hide divan. He'd not intended to fall asleep, but the tunnel-shuttle's appointments were plush and seductive, especially in comparison with what he had endured in Lusankya. *This is more impressive than the Hotel Imperial.* The shuttle had a small refresher station which had allowed Corran to take his first shower since his capture. The Lusankya diet had not been very high in protein content, so his hair, beard, and fingernails had not grown much during his captivity; still, he could have used a shave. *Then again, in this tunic, I'm hardly presentable.* He laughed. *If it were* really *that luxurious, there would have been a closet with a full wardrobe on board.*

Holdout blaster in hand, Corran walked over to the egress hatch and opened it. Waiting for him was what looked like a private lift. The box, paneled with dark greel wood, was otherwise featureless. This made Corran a little apprehensive; without controls, he had to assume it was programmed to go to a specific place. *I don't know if I want to be there, but I suspect it will be better for me than* here. He entered the lift and the doors closed behind him.

The car ascended quickly and quietly. Corran shook the lees of sleep from his head. He squeezed himself into the corner of the car just left of the doors, out of direct line with the opening. Blaster in his right hand, he was ready to pivot on his left foot, duck low, and come out shooting if he had to.

The lift slowed, then stopped.

The doors opened whisper-quiet.

The musty scent of stale air rolled into the lift. Corran brought the neck of his tunic up over his nose, then dropped it again, realizing it smelled slightly worse than the chamber beyond the doorway. He peeked out quickly and beyond a gauzy wall of spider webs saw a grey room and shadowy figures scattered about it. He ducked back, then looked out again.

No one is moving. Aside from the spiders and whatever they snack on, there's nothing living in here.

He sliced the web-wall in half with his left hand, then stepped into the long, rectangular room. Dust billowed up around his feet and coated his soles. Slender, dust-laden web-strands hung down from the ceiling like vines in a forest. Some of them attached themselves to the figures in the room, as if etheric umbilical cords maintaining the figures in their twilight existence.

Corran had no idea where he was, but the taint of evil in the room threatened to overwhelm him. That surprised him because he saw no active threat and didn't feel directly menaced. The sensation reminded him of his days back in CorSec, when he entered the scene of a particularly violent massacre of spice runners who had angered Durga the Hutt. *It was all destruction, but not wanton—it was completely calculated and deliberate.*

The figures he saw were all statues and mannequins. As he approached the first one, a little light flashed on in the space before it and resolved into a hologram of the head and shoulders of a man. A voice from the base of the statue said, "Avan Post, Jedi Master from Chandrila, served with distinction in the Clone Wars."

Corran looked up at the head of the white marble statue to see if it matched the hologram, but the face on the statue had been destroyed. The stone had melted back to the level of the ears and streamed down over the figure's torso. Nothing else about the statue's shape enabled Corran to figure out if it was Post or not. *Then again, why would the hologram of Post be connected to this statue if it isn't him?*

Corran frowned. *And why remove his face?*

Corran moved deeper into the room. The muted illumination came from glowtiles set near floor level and enabled Corran to pick out two darkened doorways set into one of the longer walls, but he didn't feel compelled to head out and explore the area beyond them. He couldn't explain it, but he had a hunch there was something important in the room, something he had to find. While intellectually he knew running far and fast was the best thing for him, his father had always encouraged him to follow his hunches. *Doing that has kept me alive. No reason to change now, especially now.*

As he moved through the chamber it became obvious that the statues and display cases were all exhibits in some sort of museum. *A Jedi museum.* Everything pertained in one way or another to Jedi Knights and Masters, with the vast majority of them having served in the Clone Wars. *Just over forty years ago, all of these people were alive.*

Without fail, whether the representation was a static hologram with little mementos, or a life-size statue, or a mannequin dressed as the person it represented, the Jedi's image had been ruined. Some statues lay in pieces on the ground. Some of the mannequins had limbs missing or holes pounded through the torsos. All of them had been defaced—most literally, though some had only had their eyes carved out. He could not discern a pattern to the damage—beyond the fact that all the faces were maimed in one way or another—but Corran knew there was one, keyed to the mind of the person who had done it.

Discarding his prison tunic, Corran pulled some clothes from one of the broken dummies and got into them. The rough-spun brown trousers and pale pull-over tunic itched against his bare flesh and threatened to drive him crazy. *From what I remember of Jedi stories, a Jedi would have chosen such clothes just to force himself to learn to ignore the physical sensations distracting him—his clothes become an exercise in concentration.* He couldn't remember where he'd heard that—it had to have been from his grandfather or father, because the Jedi were extinct by the time Corran had learned they had existed, and people who wanted to avoid Imperial scrutiny didn't display much interest in the Jedi Knights of old.

Corran's hand went to his throat to touch the medallion he'd worn since he'd inherited it from his father—a medallion he'd left with Whistler for safekeeping before his mission to Coruscant. Mirax Terrik had identified it as a Jedi Credit, a medallion issued in limited numbers to mark a Corellian Jedi's elevation from Knight to Master. *I guess carrying it around was my father's way of covertly defying the Empire.*

Corran pulled on a Jedi's brown cloak and fastened it at his throat. He swirled it around himself, sending lint-nerfs scurrying across the floor and leaping from the top of a display case. A glint of gold in that case caught Corran's eye. He stepped closer and swept dust from the glass with his hands.

His mouth went dry. *That medallion, it's just like the one I wore, save for the way the eyes have been gouged out of it. Who is that?* Irritated that the holographic legend didn't play, Corran jiggled the case. A hologram began to glow, creating an image of a slender man hovering above the glass, about twenty centimeters high. A voice, starting low and slow, then speeding up into a soprano, accompanied the display. "Nejaa Halcyon, a Jedi Master from Corellia, died in the Clone Wars."

The light from the holographic projection bled below into a static hologram. It showed Halcyon standing with a boy. The Basic legend running down the edge of the image read, "Nejaa Halcyon and an apprentice." The projection snapped off and the hologram went dark, but it took Corran several seconds to become cognizant of that fact.

That boy. That was my father. . . . He'd seen holograms of his father as a child, and the boy in the image looked very much like Hal Horn had at that age. *He even looked a bit like me. But that can't be, can it?*

Corran frowned mightily. Mirax had told him that the commemorative medallions were given to family, friends, students, and Masters by the Knight who appeared on them. *If my father had been his apprentice, that would explain how he got the coin, but he never said anything about knowing a Jedi or training with him.* My grandfather *did, but he never mentioned this Halcyon. That hologram has to be wrong, I have to have seen it wrong.*

He jiggled the case again, but the projection did not return. He stepped back and up to it again without results. He jogged and then shook the case, but that only moved the medallion around and tipped over the hologram. *I need light to see who's really in that hologram.*

Swaddling his left fist in his Lusankya tunic, Corran hammered it against the display case. The glass shattered into hundreds of sparkling shards. Looking around nervously, waiting for some alarm system to start blaring, Corran shook the canvas wrap off his hand and cast it aside. He carefully plucked out the medallion and put it in his pocket. To it he added the hologram and would have walked over to one of the footlights to examine it, but the third memento of Nejaa Halcyon attracted his attention.

Shifting his blaster to his left hand, Corran reached into the case and pulled out a thirty-centimeter-long silvery cylinder. A concave dish capped it, a thickened knob served as the pommel, and a black button rode in a recessed niche precisely where his right thumb naturally rested. Pointing the cup away from himself, Corran hit the button.

A silvery white shaft of light just over a meter in length hissed to life. It hummed low and mournfully as its cold illumination turned all the Jedi images into ghosts. Corran twisted his wrist around, bringing the energy blade through a set of interlocked loops. The sound quickened slightly as the blade transformed a strand of webbing into a drifting tendril of smoke.

Corran turned, thinking to sweep the lightsaber blade through one of the mannequins, but stopped before he struck. *These images have endured enough abuse. I won't add to it.* He knew he was correct not to contribute to the further despoiling of the monuments. Moreover, there had seemed to be a subtle pressure, a hidden malevolence in the room, that encouraged and condoned the destruction.

Corran felt good defying it.

He hit the button under his thumb once to shut the blade off. It remained lit. Corran frowned for a moment, then hit the button twice in quick succession, and the blade vanished. *The double hit to turn it off guarantees it won't go down in combat if the button is hit accidentally.*

As shadows reconquered the room, Corran shivered. Trying to integrate this storehouse of Jedi memorabilia with Lusankya was enough to make his brain hurt. *I'd probably have a better chance of figuring out what all of this stuff is doing here if I had a clue as to where I was. It's good to have clothes and equipment, but somehow I doubt disguising myself as a Jedi Knight is a way to become less conspicuous in making my escape. And that's still my first priority—getting out of here.*

Corran smiled and let the lightsaber roll back and forth across the palm of his hand. "I bet you'll make a wonderful door opener."

Suddenly a short, sharp pop echoed through the complex of rooms. A shockwave started dust swirling through the room, centered on a doorway back along the wall to the right. *Sounds like someone else is finding novel ways to open doors. This room is too open, nowhere to hide.*

Three figures dressed in black moved into and through the doorway. They paused there and swept the room with the harsh white beams of the glowrods fixed to the barrels of their blaster carbines.

Having no other option, Corran froze in place. The lights flashed over him, lingering only as long as they had on the other unmoving figures in the room.

"Nothing here."

The tallest of them nodded. "Then we wait." His voice trailed off for a second. "Hey, there was something funny about one of the dummies over here."

He played his light over Corran again and his friends likewise brought their lights to bear on him. "This one's got a face."

"Yeah, I have a face and I'd like to keep it." Corran thumbed the lightsaber to life. "I hope that's not going to be a problem for anyone."

37

WEDGE WALKED OVER to the circular holopad sitting atop a pedestal in the center of the briefing room. "We've only got time to go through this once, so listen up." He hit a series of keys on the holopad, causing a holographic map of the Palace district and environs to spring to life. The whole scene rotated up 90 degrees to give the pilots a chance to look down through the network of towers, tunnels, and causeways which clogged that section of the city. Deep in the lower reaches of the display a red square pulsed with life.

"We have a report that the Palpatine Counter-insurgency Front is staging from this location for a strike on a bacta storage facility in Invisec. We're flying cover for a commando force that is going to go in. The fact is that these PCF folks are very dedicated to their jobs and are likely to scatter when our forces hit. We expect speeder bikes, swoops, and speeders to be heading out of there. Since they used an airspeeder bomb to hit an earlier site, we have to assume that any and all such vehicles are moving bombs. We're going to take them down."

Wedge pointed to the empty seat beside Pash Cracken. "Nawara isn't here because our strike is going to hit the PCF about the same time Nawara normally runs the gantlet of holojournalists. If he's not there on the day Tycho's defense is supposed to open, they might think something is going down and move too soon. Ooryl, you'll fly on Pash's wing. Normal assignments for everyone else."

Pash glanced up at Wedge. "If we're going to be hawking targets through the city, isn't there a good chance we'll lose some of them? There are places an X-wing might not fit, but a speeder bike will."

"Your father's getting us a tracking feed from the security office onboard the Emperor's skyhook, but there is a chance some might get away."

Erisi's hand went up. "There will be a lot of civilian traffic up. How badly are these guys wanted? How much collateral damage do we risk?"

Wedge winced. "If any of them get through to their target, a lot of people will die. Thousands, perhaps even hundreds of thousands. When we go in the municipal authorities will issue a sector-wide emergency grounding call. Anyone who ignores that call, especially after we start lighting the area up, is making a very big mistake. We don't want to shoot civilians, but if you have a positive ID on a target, take it. Shooting in the city isn't going to be real pretty, but letting a PCF terrorist get through is going to be worse."

Erisi nodded. "What if the PCF people go to ground with the civilians?"

"Then they won't be blowing up a bacta storage facility." Wedge grinned grimly. "We'll spot them and call in someone who can help neutralize them."

"Ooryl believes this is a must-win, no-win scenario."

You have that right. We're busting open a rat's nest and hoping to kill all of them before they can do damage when they escape. The chances of collateral damage are high, and while a Corellian usually doesn't have any use for odds, in this case I wish they were much lower against us. "There is no denying that the probable outcome of our exercise is the loss of some innocent folks on the ground or in a building. We have to be careful but thorough. I can't tell you to shoot with children on a causeway backstopping your shots. I'm just going to trust that you'll be smart enough to avoid finding yourself in that situation."

He sighed. "Your astrogation droids have the map of the Palace sector and Invisec. The bacta facility is protected and you'll get a warning tone if you enter the exclusion zone around it. If you find yourself there, get out. They'll take your target. Anything else?"

He looked around the room, but no one had any comments or questions. "Great. Hit the hangar and mount up. Fly your best out there. We might not be up against a Death Star, but this mission is still vital. And may the Force be with you. Dismissed."

The pilots started to file out. Wedge noticed Asyr give Gavin a quick kiss, then stroke his cheek with her left hand. She said something to Gavin that Wedge couldn't hear, then she turned toward him and held a hand up. "Commander, if you have a moment."

"Just a moment, Asyr."

Asyr nodded to Gavin and he departed. She approached Wedge and the fur on the back of her neck rippled up and down. "Do you recall a conversation we had six weeks ago? About my having to make a decision?"

Wedge nodded. "I told you there would come a point where you had to choose between the squadron and your allegiance to the Bothan Martial Intelligence."

"You said at the time that you trusted me, and wanted to continue to trust me."

"Right. And I told you that if you chose to leave the squadron, I'd respect your decision." Wedge shook his head. "Of course, if you're doing that right now, I might not respect your choice of timing."

Her violet eyes flashed coldly for a second as she looked up at him. "I want you to continue to respect my decisions *and* my timing. And I want you to continue to trust me." She dug into the pocket of her flightsuit and pulled out a datacard. "I was ordered to prepare a report about the bacta massacre at Alderaan. It was felt a document that suggested our delay in getting there might, in some way, have been deliberate and the result of human action. That datacard has the only copy of said report. If anything happens to me, you'll dispose of this correctly, I would hope."

Wedge nodded. "And if you survive, what will you do with the report then?"

"I'm a member of Rogue Squadron, Commander, which means I only take *orders* from my superior officers." Asyr smiled. "What I do with that report, sir, is whatever you tell me to do with that report."

"You're taking a big step, cutting yourself off from your people."

"I know that, and I know it won't be easy, but the squadron is my home now. You've only ever asked me to fight and fly and possibly die. That I'll do for people I can trust. Those who ask me to betray friends, well, they've shown they don't want me to be trustworthy, so they clearly aren't. Those facts don't make the choice any easier, just more imperative."

Wedge tucked the datacard away in a pocket, then clapped Asyr on the shoulders. "Glad you're with us and on my wing. I always like flying with someone I can trust."

38

T HOUGH IELLA'S EYES burned from fatigue, the adrenaline
pumping through her system had her hyper-alert. She ef-
fortlessly wove the armored airspeeder through the canyons
and chasms of Coruscant, slowly closing in on the Justice Court
building. Nawara Ven and Kirtan Loor sat in the back, the lawyer continuing to ask questions and Loor replying with haughty
disdain.

Seeing Loor again had been a shock for her. She recognized
him instantly, but not without difficulty. He had always been
lean and cadaverous, though now his flesh had greyed a bit and
tightened over his cheekbones and around his eyes. He played
himself up to be supremely confident, but his clipped answers
and terse comments clued her to his fear.

Iella had no doubt that if Corran had been with them at the
safehouse where they deposed Loor, Loor would have crumbled
like stale *ryshcate*. Corran had always had a way of zeroing in
on a suspect's weaknesses. He would figure out the thing about
which they were lying, then push and push on those points,
pounce on inconsistencies, then increase the pressure until the
suspect confessed.

Loor had resisted giving them a full confession. He produced a datacard on which, he said, he had encoded and encrypted complete dossiers on the Empire's operatives within the bureaucracy. He had also guaranteed them that on the stand he would reveal the identity of the traitor within Rogue Squadron. After that, provided the other details of his surrender deal were carried out, he would provide the key to the datacard's encryption routine.

"Fine," she'd said, "but can you give us Corran's murderer?"

Loor had smiled coldly. "The traitor set him up, and the traitor I will give you. Corran's murderer, on the other hand, was Ysanne Isard. Her you'll have to get yourself."

And get her I will, somehow. Iella checked the advanced scanning system on the airspeeder's console. The scanner compared the profiles of all the traffic it had encountered so far against everything it was detecting as the journey continued. Matches would indicate they were being followed, but nothing had passed the computer's standards for a threat. *Good. We're clear, so far.*

"Coming up on the parking facility. We're going into the secure level, then down into the Justice Court." She wanted to add that the next few seconds, as she slowed to enter the building, were the most vulnerable in the whole flight. A single proton torpedo or concussion missile could destroy the airspeeder in the blink of an eye. A timed or proximity warhead could be launched from anywhere and catch them.

The airspeeder slid into the darkened tunnel and slowed. Ahead a green holographic projection cycled through various alphabets. The words "Facility is Full" appeared in Basic above and below whatever language was being displayed in the middle. The green backlight illuminated a gate that barred further passage.

Iella hit a button on the console keypad, then punched in her security code. Instead of giving her a new security code to use in bringing Loor to court—the addition of which might have alerted Imperial agents to strange goings-on—Halla Ettyk had just locked everyone else out with code that made the lockout look like a computer glitch.

The gate retracted into the floor. "We're in."

Loor shifted in his seat in the back. "Does it bother you, Iella, to be shielding me this way?"

"No more now than it did the first time you asked the question, Loor." She moved the vehicle forward into the darkened parking area, and midway between the gate and the lift doors, she slung it around, swapping it end for end, so the nose pointed back out toward the exit. She let the speeder drift to a stop approximately twenty meters from the lift. "Does it bother you having to depend upon me?"

Loor shook his head. "Not at all, my dear. You have a facility for loyalty—I don't imagine you are wasting it on me—and to your mission you will be true. Your job is to deliver me to court, then watch me walk away, shedding my crimes like a Trandoshan shedding skin."

"Reminding me that you let the Trandoshan who murdered Corran's father go isn't the way to get me to feel good about helping you."

"No, I suppose it isn't." Loor sighed nonchalantly. "I'll have to trust you'll want Corran's betrayer more than you want me dead, won't I?"

"That you will." Iella cracked her door open and emerged from the speeder. She took a quick look around, saw nothing, then rapped on the top of the car. "Come on out. It's clear."

As the other two left the vehicle, Iella pulled out her blaster and checked the power cell. *Full charge, good.* "Let's go. We get to the lift, I input the code, we head down and through the prosecutor's office. Simple, swift, and no one will get hurt."

Loor pulled up the hood on his cloak. "After you."

Iella growled at him and moved toward the elevator, taking up a position on the right side of the group. She held her blaster in two hands, up by her face, with the barrel pointing toward the ferrocrete ceiling. As she walked toward the lift she kept looking about, backward, forward, and side to side, trying to pick up on any movement, anything out of the ordinary. Across from her, unarmed though he was, Nawara looked about vigilantly as well.

Between them, his cloak billowing out to inflate his silhouette to the size of his code name, Loor strode confidently. Though she could not see his face, his stance and stride indicated he was blithely amused by her caution. *The grant of immunity has made him feel invincible.*

Iella felt the slick caress of a strand of webbing brush against her right cheek. She swept it away with her left hand and heard it snap near her ear. That struck her as odd, then sinister, as she saw Nawara bat at a similar thread with one of his brain tails.

The lift doors, barely ten meters away, opened with little more than a whisper.

As THE LIFT DOORS PARTED, Loor felt his pulse quicken. Time slowed until nanoseconds took hours to pass. His emotions spiked, fear braiding itself together with triumph. The fear came from the realization that he might die, for surely an assassin or assassins lurked in the lift. *I could well be dead before those doors close again.*

The triumph that wove in with the fear came from the realization that Ysanne Isard saw him as enough of a threat to kill him. She had always dismissed him before, patronized him, used him, and threatened to discard him. Now she saw how truly powerful he was. The desperation that marked this attempt on his life gave full measure to her concern over what he could do to destroy her.

Loor began to smile. *In this you show me I have won!*

IELLA BEGAN TO turn toward the unlit box, her blaster coming down as she squared her stance. Something black moved within the lift, a shadow that resolved itself into the form of a man dashing forth, a blazing blaster held in each hand. "Die, Derricote, die!" he screamed.

Scarlet bolts of blaster energy burned toward the trio. One caught Nawara Ven on the right hip. It spun him around and flung him through the air.

Before the Twi'lek could hit the ground, a pair of blasterbolts lanced through Kirtan Loor's chest. The first, which drilled him high on the left side of his body, lifted him from his feet. The second struck him high in the abdomen and centered on his midline, driving him back and down. He landed beside Nawara Ven's tumbling body and slid halfway over to the airspeeder.

Years of training overrode conscious thought in Iella. As bolts began to track in her direction, she coolly triggered a double-burst that stopped the assassin's charge only a stride or two from the lift. The bolts stabbed deep into the man's gut, snapping him forward. Blaster-bolts from his guns traced parallel lines down the ferrocrete as he hunched over, dropped to his knees, then fell forward on his face. His blaster pistols clattered down beside him, abandoned as his hands clutched at his ruined belly.

Keeping her blaster on his form, she ran forward and kicked the pistols away. The assassin made a sound, a little moan, and it cut her legs out from under her. She sank to her knees beside him and rolled him onto his back. Even before she saw his face, the sounds he made and the feeling of his bony shoulders told her who he was. Intellect momentarily overrode emotion, providing her the clues she needed to confirm his identity, then it retreated as pain and despair exploded in her.

She pulled his head into her lap and brushed strands of hair from his face. "Why, Diric, why?"

"Lusankya."

Iella's breath caught in her throat. "No, no, that can't be."

"She broke me. She made me into one of her own. She had me placed in Derricote's lab to watch him." Diric winced fiercely, and his body went rigid for a moment. "She sent me to kill him before he could betray her. I had no choice. That wasn't him, though."

Iella shook her head. "No. It was Kirtan Loor."

Diric managed a weak smile. "Good. I never liked him." He reached a hand up toward her face, but it never got there. "I'm dying."

"No." She fished for a comlink in her pocket. "I'll get emergency medical droids here."

"No, Iella, no. Isard made me what others accuse Tycho of being. He isn't. She had me reporting on him, too. From what she did, I cannot be saved." His tongue wet thin lips. "I can't live in suspicion, as a puppet. It would make life too . . . boring."

"Diric, no, we can help you."

"It's over. I love you. She wanted me to kill you. I couldn't resist." He smiled weakly. "I could defy—the trigger that opened the lift was supposed to be linked to a bomb. I did what I could. So you could stop me from betraying myself by killing you." Pain contorted his face. "Thank you for freeing me."

With her hand, Iella smoothed the pain on his face into peace, then realized he'd slipped away. Her throat thick, her eyes welling with tears, she gently lowered his head to the ferrocrete floor and kissed him one last time.

KIRTAN LOOR LAY on the ferrocrete and could feel nothing. He knew this was not good. That he was dying was an inescapable conclusion and it outraged him. He tried to feed that outrage as much fuel as he could, but he simply ran out. The anger and fury in him collapsed in on itself, imploding into a black void that sucked the last bits of life from Kirtan Loor.

At the heart of that void existed one fact, the one true thing that had marked his entire life. Gil Bastra had seen it. Corran Horn and Iella Wessiri had seen it. Ysanne Isard had seen it. Loor had done all he could to combat it, but it was a defect that was inborn and immutable. *I make assumptions. I refuse to look beyond them for reality. I am defeated by them.*

He stared up at the ferrocrete ceiling, seeking in its haphazard patterns some cosmic truth, but the only truth he found ground away at him. *She did not send an assassin to kill* me, *she sent him to kill Derricote. I am dying in his place, for his crimes. Is there anything worse?*

For some reason the image of Corran Horn came to him. *Horn said there was nothing worse than dying alone.* He fought to dismiss that idea, but as darkness nibbled away at the corners of his sight, he allowed as how that, just once, Corran Horn had been right.

39

D ESPITE HIS FATIGUE, Wedge couldn't remember having felt better. Strapped into the cockpit of his X-wing, with Mynock behind him, Asyr on his starboard wing, and atmosphere below his fighter, Wedge felt as if the galaxy's reset button had been hit. His mission was clear: safeguard the forces making a run on an Imperial terrorist cell. He didn't know if this was all that was left of the Palpatine Counter-insurgency Front, or if this was just one tentacle of that foul kraken, but he had no doubts they'd destroy it.

Gone were the ambiguities that had been forced on him. Tycho's trial was political. The run to Ryloth and the convoy escort mission from Alderaan had both been political. Even the raid on Zsinj's space station had been political. While he realized the whole Rebellion had, in essence, been political, his role in it had been military. *The targets we were given were military, picked because of their military value, and the mission parameters were ones that could be fulfilled through a military effort.*

Wedge keyed his comm unit. "Hunter One, this is Rogue Lead. We are on-station."

"I copy, Rogue Lead. Stand by for tactical team directives."

"As ordered." Wedge glanced down at his scanner. The squadron had broken itself down into five pairs of fighters. Four of the pairs orbited the target district with 90 degrees of separation between their positions. The last pair, Erisi Dlarit and Rhysati Ynr, flew high cover up around the level of the skyhooks. The lower fighters were meant to assist the raid and pick up stragglers, while the high-orbit pair would cut off any PCF terrorists that made it out of the district and in toward their target.

"Rogue Lead, this is Hunter One. We are taking heavy fire from the western approach. Help is needed."

"I copy. On the way." Wedge hit a button on his console, shifting the comm unit to the squadron's tactical channel. "Rogue Two, did you get that?"

"I copied, Lead." Asyr's voice betrayed no nervousness. "After you."

"Five, you and Ten with the next call, then Seven's element, then Twelve's element."

"As ordered."

Wedge kicked his X-wing up on the port S-foil, then hit the left rudder and pointed the fighter's nose at the ground. He let the fighter succumb to gravity, then rolled it and prepared to glide out onto the target. The Justice Court building flashed past, then Wedge hauled back on the stick and leveled out. *Target is five kilometers out and coming up fast.*

Even in the distance he could see blaster fire spraying out to cover the approaches on the west side of the building. As he swooped in, he saw one smoking speeder-ferry slowly drifting down toward the unseen ground. Wedge flicked his lasers over to single fire and dropped the crosshairs on the focal point for the blaster fire. As range dropped to a kilometer, he tightened down on the trigger and feathered the left rudder pedal to keep his fire tracking on target.

The X-wing's four lasers fired in sequence, peppering the middle level of the building with a staccato hail of energy darts. They swept across the wide doorway, some of them scattering half-hidden individuals inside the warehouse. Other laser-bolts shredded one of the two E-Web Heavy Repeating Blasters just inside the doorway, killing the soldiers crewing the weapon.

Asyr's X-wing came in right behind Wedge's and repeated his strafing run. As she flew through the area, Wedge chopped his thrust back, hit his rudder, and turned his fighter around. He punched the throttle, killing his momentum, then cut his repulsorlift coils in. Asyr sailed on past him and pulled up to begin a loop, while Wedge goosed his X-wing forward and brought it up in line with the warehouse opening.

"They're running!" Wedge hit the trigger and scythed fire back and forth across the gaping warehouse entryway. Two laser-bolts caught a small airspeeder in the middle and aft, slicing it into three equal parts. The pieces flew across the open area and rebounded off a neighboring building, then tumbled into the urban canyon depths.

The rest of his shots missed the legion of targets because what he was trying to hit tended to be small and moving very fast. Speeder bikes with and without sidecars corkscrewed their way out and down or up to elude him. One airspeeder just sailed out and dropped like a freefalling Hutt, sinking out of sight before he could track it. Others banked hard and flew fast to escape, though from comm unit chatter, each of them had been tagged and had pursuit on its way.

An ugly green light strobed through the warehouse. Wedge nudged the X-wing forward, and saw boxy silhouettes, each supported on twin pillars, bobbing up and down in the warehouse. A shiver ran down his spine, then he keyed his comm unit. "Scout walkers, three of them, with two coming our way. I've got them."

Wedge flicked his weapon's-control over to proton torpedoes. His aiming reticle went from yellow to red as the targeting computer locked on. Mynock shrieked with a lock-tone and Wedge hit his trigger. A proton torpedo streaked out, crossing the fifty meters between the X-wing and the warehouse in the blink of an eye.

The proton torpedo caught the rightmost AT-ST in the outside leg, just below the upper joint. The torpedo sheared the leg off, and the impact spun the scout walker around. It crashed into the walker next to it, then rebounded and bounced to the ground. Ten meters behind it the proton torpedo exploded, detonating the walker's concussion grenade magazine.

The second walker, which had awkwardly skipped forward after being bumped, ended up being slightly off balance when the grenades went off. A burst of green light from deeper within the warehouse outlined the upright walker as the downed walker's good leg whipped around and caught it across the ankles. The standing walker staggered as the pilot tried to widen its stance and remain upright. His efforts almost paid off and the walker had begun to straighten up, when its left foot ran out of warehouse floor. The machine wavered for a moment, then slowly keeled over in an ungainly plunge toward the ground.

The green light, from the last AT-ST's twin blaster cannon, again lit the interior of the warehouse. *What is it shooting at?* In the time it took him to form that question in his mind, he also came up with the answer. *No, can't let that happen.*

He nudged the throttle forward and picked up some speed. Flying into the warehouse, Wedge got to see the AT-ST fire one last shot at the far wall, widening the breach. An airspeeder—heavily laden, judging from the way the aft end struck sparks as it slewed around the scout walker—shot in toward the hole. The remaining walker squared off to face him and protect the airspeeder.

The other vehicles were decoys! This one is the bomb. Wedge hit enough left rudder to track the airspeeder, then fired a proton torpedo. The projectile hit the ferrocrete decking and skipped off, rising quickly. Instead of passing between the AT-ST's legs, it slammed full into the cockpit. The explosion filled the end of the warehouse with a firestorm. A black cloud billowed up with red-gold flame-claws slashing their way clear of it, while pieces of debris and shrapnel ricocheted and bounced throughout the warehouse.

Swirling tendrils of smoke curled out through the hole, and Wedge knew instantly where the airspeeder had gone. He guided the X-wing straight for the center of the hole the scout walker had opened in the other side of the warehouse. He made it through with centimeters to spare on both sides, then cut the repulsorlift generators and dove.

"This is Rogue Leader. The warehouse is clear. I'm out the other side."

Hunter One sounded faintly amused. "We would have let you come back out this way, Rogue Leader."

"Thanks, Hunter One, but I'm in pursuit of the bomb." Deep below him he saw the airspeeder level off and head toward Invisec. "Let the bacta storehouse know it's incoming, and so am I. With luck, only one of us will get there."

40

"HE'S NOT THE FAT GUY," said one of the three men facing Corran.

"Doesn't matter. Kill him anyway."

Corran pulled his right arm back and whipped it forward, sidearming the lightsaber toward the trio. The blade spun through a flat arc. The men on either side of the grouping dove for cover, but the center man's eyes grew wide and glowed in the blade's icy light. He shot twice at the light-saber, but missed with both bolts.

The lightsaber's silver shaft scythed through his middle and dropped him in two parts to the ground. Two wet, meaty thumps swallowed the clatter of the blaster carbine against the floor. The glowrod attached to the barrel flared, then went out.

Corran dove to the left, rolled, and came up in a crouch. He tracked a moving cone of light and fired at its base. He heard no scream to indicate he had hit his target, then a spray of blaster-bolts from the right forced him to duck again. As he slipped back into the shadow of a statue, his two foes extinguished their glowrods, leaving the footlights as the only illumination in the larger room.

Two assumptions I can make: first, they have comlinks and are going to be coordinating their attack. Second, they can or have called for backup, which means they win the waiting game, I have to get out of here, and the only way to do that is by going out the way they came in. He glanced over at the doorway which the lightsaber's glow backlit. *They're moving out to surround me, so now's the best time to go.*

Corran bobbed up and down twice, using the lightsaber's light to silhouette the obstacles in his way. The path looked fairly clear. He reached into his pocket and ran his thumb over the ruined face of the Jedi medallion. *You're not the one I used for luck, but here's hoping there was some left in the dies when you were struck.*

He took off at a dead run, cutting around one statue and then a display case before heading toward the doorway. Little holograms flickered to life behind him, drawing attention first to themselves, then to him. The first few shots fired at him burned holes in his cloak, but then his assailants shifted their aim and raked the doorway with blasterfire—blasterfire that should have exploded his heart and reduced his lungs to cinders.

And it would have except that the Jedi cloak caught the corner of the display case. It yanked Corran from his feet, then the throat clasp snapped. With his momentum thus slackened but far from depleted, he flew through the doorway feet first, centimeters below the line of blasterfire. He hit hard on his right hip and cracked his right knee on the granite floor, then slid toward the middle of the room.

His right hand closed on the hilt of the lightsaber. He switched it off and scrambled back toward the doorway through which he had just flown. He hoped to find the dead man's blaster carbine, but as he settled his back against the wall beside the doorway he saw its outline two meters away on the wrong side of the opening. *Hopeless, Gotta get up, gotta run for the exit—wherever it is.* Even though he knew running was the only viable plan, the stiffening sensation in his knee and hip told him a weak limp was going to be the best he could manage. *And I'll get vaped for the effort, I'm dead.*

Then he felt something solid thump against the wall behind him. Even before he heard the click of a comlink, he twisted around and rose up on his left knee. Jamming the lightsaber's cup against the wall with his right hand, he flicked it on and raked it upward. It pulled free of the wall at the top of its arc, spitting and hissing as blood evaporated from the silvery shaft of light.

The bisected man on the other side of the wall fell across the doorway just as the third man, who had been approaching the doorway from the opposite side, opened fire. The dead man caught two bolts that would have killed Corran before the man shifted aim and started tracking the lightsaber's arc. One bolt singed the hair on the back of Corran's hand, but the rest passed by without hurting him.

Corran's left hand came up and he snapped off two shots toward the blaster carbine's muzzle flashes. Both hit. The third man crashed backward into a display case, then hung there at odd angles. In the footlight Corran could see his hands twitch once or twice, as if still working the trigger of the weapon that had fallen to the floor, then the man lay still.

Corran extinguished the lightsaber, then clipped it to his belt. He shifted the belt around so the weapon hung at his left hip and wouldn't bang against the bruised one. Pocketing his holdout blaster, he crawled over to the body of the first man he'd killed, loosened the chinstrap on the helmet and pulled it off. Inside it he found a comlink in a clip. He pulled it out and listened for a moment to see if other troopers were on the way, but the comlink remained silent.

He retrieved the second man's blaster carbine and turned on the glowrod. He played it over the dead men and frowned. Their black uniforms weren't any sort of Imperial uniform he'd ever seen before, and the men themselves were mismatched enough that he knew they weren't stormtroopers. *I've never seen a stormtrooper without a helmet on, but I can't see them looking quite this ordinary.* Still, the uniforms were paramilitary, so he assumed the three dead men were members of a local constabulary force. *Another time I'd have thought you were allies, but in CorSec we didn't shoot someone just because he wasn't the suspect we were looking for.*

Corran played the glowrod over the bottom of the comlink and adjusted the frequency. *Now to find out where we are.* While he had long detested the Empire, it did manage to do some things with a remarkable amount of efficiency. One of them was the establishment and maintenance of standard measures. On each world broadcast stations had been set up to provide the exact time, both local and in relation to Coruscant. By tuning into that signal he could find out where he was and what time it was. *It occurs to me I've not seen outside for a long time.*

He held the comlink near his ear and slowly limped over to the hole the trio had blown in the wall on the far side of the chamber. "Must be a real backwater planet if they only sent three guys to catch an escaped prisoner—even *if* they thought I was Derricote. I wonder if I can ever get off it?"

Over the comlink he heard a mechanical voice announce, "8 hours, 45 minutes, Coordinated Galactic Time."

"Great, I'm on a world that's set its clocks to Coruscant time, no matter what the local situation is." He hefted the blaster carbine, glanced at the power level indicator, then played the light out through the hole into the next room. Unlike the one he had found himself in, the room beyond the hole was clean and orderly. *Even better, there is an open doorway to the outside.*

He was about to step through the wall when two irreconcilable ideas collided in his brain. It was rather clear that he was inside some sort of storehouse filled with Jedi memorabilia. The mansion from which he had escaped had obviously been an Imperial Moff's retreat, but what Imperial Moff would risk his position by hoarding so much Jedi material? The only Moff who could do that would be a powerful one, and powerful Moffs weren't found on backwater worlds.

Actually, there were no *Moffs so powerful that they would have dared defy the Emperor and Vader by hoarding this stuff. Only the Emperor could have . . .* Corran's jaw dropped open. *And the clock here is set to Coruscant time . . .*

Corran slumped against the wall. *It can't be. I can't be on Coruscant. It makes no sense. I remember traveling on a ship. Then again, I was so doped up . . . Maybe I am on Coruscant and Isard just wanted me to think I wasn't on Coruscant.* He chuckled. *It would explain why no one ever found Lusankya—it was here all the time, which means she is, too.*

He glanced back at the dead men. *And she has enough pull with local authorities to have them out hunting Derricote. I may be out of her clutches, but I'm not free, yet.* He glanced at the comlink and thought about tuning in to the military frequencies Rogue Squadron used, but rejected that plan for two reasons. *I'm not going to have the right scrambler codes to let me hear and speak with them, and even if I did, there's the traitor to consider.*

He shook his head. *I need someone I can trust. It's a long shot, but it's the only one I have.* He set the comlink and opened a channel. "This is Corran Horn calling. I'm not dead—I only feel like it—and I could use some help returning to the land of the living."

41

WEDGE PULLED BACK on the X-wing's stick and leveled out approximately 300 meters behind and above the airspeeder. He had to trim his speed back because even though the X-wing could close fast, the airspeeder could turn faster within the close confines of the city. Part of Wedge knew racing speeder bikes through the forests of Endor was safer than doing what he was doing, but he had no choice. *That bomb has to be stopped.*

"Mynock, make sure you're getting a solid tracking feed on that airspeeder."

The astromech droid shrilled out a confirmation of that order. Wedge watched the tracking data get updated, then rolled up on the right stabilizer foil and dove. He cruised down below the speeder's line of flight, entering a large boulevard that sped him forward toward Invisec. *If I can head him off . . .* "Mynock, plot all his routes from here to the target."

The droid shrieked like wind howling off the S-foils.

Wedge wove his way through the undercity, cutting around buildings, over walkways, and through tunnels, all the while marveling at the intricate labyrinth that was Coruscant. Making his way in and out, up and over or around tested his skills as a pilot. While not much of the dawn's light penetrated that deeply in the city, he did have enough to navigate by, but only just barely.

A shiver ran down his spine. *Corran and the others were flying out here at night when we took Coruscant. I never really appreciated what they did until now.*

Mynock hooted at him. Wedge glanced down at his monitor and saw various schematics flash past. "Slower, Mynock, I'm flying here, too." Wedge marked the location of the airspeeder and compared it with the maps. As the air-speeder sank to his level and below it, something clicked in the back of his mind. *That's it. I've got them.*

"Give me the lowest route in you can find, Mynock." Wedge banked starboard, chopped his thrust back, and brought the repulsorlift coils online. He hovered and drifted forward, remaining just outside the corridor described by the map Mynock had brought up. As he watched he saw the airspeeder move onto the route and begin to follow it in.

Wedge smiled. *It struck sparks in the warehouse and dropped like a rock outside. It's still going down because it's carrying too much weight. The speeder-ferry that was going down when I first flew in must have been meant to haul this bomb to a point where it could head down in at the bacta store. Now they have to go low because they don't have enough power to go high.*

He switched his fire control over to lasers and linked all four to give him a quad burst. As he did so, the airspeeder cruised through the thoroughfare. Wedge picked his speed up and dropped straight in behind it. Someone in the speeder spotted him and started shooting at him with a blaster rifle, but the bolts harmlessly impacted on Wedge's forward shield. The pilot tried to make the airspeeder juke, but every sideslip and turn just brought the vehicle lower and lower.

And into Wedge's sights.

He hit the trigger and sent a quartet of scarlet laser-bolts to converge on the blocky vehicle. The lasers vaporized the roof and filled the passenger compartment with fire. The speeder began to fall faster, with the aft end sagging downward. Something exploded up front, starting the speeder into a backward somersault. Two more quad bursts from the X-wing reduced the large chunks of vehicle into mist and metal hail.

The vapor cloud—made up mostly of gaseous explosives—ignited in a flash, momentarily blinding Wedge and prompting a scream from Mynock. Wedge kept a light but steady hand on the stick and rode out the shockwave. The X-wing's shields held, saving the fighter from damage. As his vision cleared and he flew through the smoke, he saw no trace of the airspeeder.

He smiled. "See that, Mynock? That mission wasn't so tough."

The droid brayed in what Wedge took to be a vaguely triumphant manner.

"Rogue Leader here. The bomb is gone. Report."

"Three here, Lead. We are over the Manarai Mountain district and have big anomalies out to the southwest. I have TIEs coming in, at least one wing."

"I copy, Three. On my way." Wedge hauled back on the stick and jammed his throttle full forward. The X-wing rocketed straight up. "Confirm thirty-six TIEs, Three."

"Confirm thirty-six, Lead, eyeballs and squints. They're coming this way and there's something else out there." Rhysati sounded shaken. "My sensors aren't picking it up at all well."

"Standby, Three." Wedge punched his comm unit over to another opchannel. "Antilles here. What's down there to the southwest?"

"Palace district control here, Rogue Leader. We're not sure. Civilian side is reporting groundquakes and massive destruction. We're just turning a satellite in that direction. Data coming up—I'll give you the raw feed."

"I copy, control." Wedge looked at the scan splaying itself across his sensor monitor and felt his spirits sinking as low as Mynock's mournful whistle. "That can't be. It just can't be."

"You're getting what we're getting, Rogue Leader."

Wedge flicked the comm unit back to the squadron's tactical frequency. "Three and Four, get back here. Now."

"What's out there, Lead?"

Wedge shivered. "It's something that shouldn't be there, Three. IFF beacons report it's a Super Star Destroyer that goes by the name *Lusankya*."

42

ADMIRAL ACKBAR TOOK his seat at the high bench, with Generals Madine and Salm below and to the left and right respectively. He waited for the defendant and prosecutor to be seated, then he looked out over the sparsely populated courtroom. "Today's session will be abbreviated. Even the most simple voyage can be ended by an unanticipated wave, and the wave affecting us here was titanic in proportions."

He glanced down at Tycho Celchu and the two droids at the defense table. "Captain Celchu, your lawyer is not here because approximately an hour ago he was shot and seriously wounded in the parking facility on the upper floors of this building. The assassin has been killed, but we have sealed the building for security reasons nonetheless. Nawara Ven was shot while in the process of bringing to court a witness who had recently surfaced to provide proof of your innocence. The witness offered his testimony on your behalf in return for a new identity and repatriation to another world. He provided a datacard filled with encrypted information that backed his claims concerning you as well as claims concerning the Imperial espionage net here on Coruscant.

"Unfortunately the assassin who wounded Counselor Ven succeeded in killing this witness." Ackbar looked over toward where Airen Cracken sat on the prosecution side of the court. "General Cracken has assured me he has people working on the datacard to see if they can slice the information out, but there is no telling if or when they will succeed."

Tycho frowned. "Where does this leave me?"

Halla Ettyk stood. "Admiral, the prosecution would be amenable to a continuance until Counselor Ven has recovered."

"Granted." Admiral Ackbar raised a gavel. "If there is nothing more we will stand in recess until Counselor Ven is able to continue."

Tycho held a hand up. "Wait, please, isn't there something I can do? Isn't it possible for me to represent myself in his absence?"

"That has always been your right, Captain Celchu."

Halla looked over at Tycho. "The admiral is correct, but really there is nothing you can do."

"I can call and question a witness."

The prosecutor shook her head and pointed at her datapad. "Not really. I have before me the list of witnesses Counselor Ven said you were going to call. None of the members of Rogue Squadron are here and available. The Duros Lai Nootka is not here and, unfortunately, is probably dead. You have no witnesses."

Whistler tooted.

Emtrey's clamshell head came up. "Whistler says we *do* have a witness."

Halla frowned. "Who?"

Tycho stood. "I can testify on my own behalf."

"It would be a mistake to do so, Captain. I would rip you apart on cross."

The R2 unit blatted rudely.

Tycho patted Whistler on the dome. "I agree."

Emtrey canted his head to the side. "Ah, sir, Whistler was agreeing with Commander Ettyk. You're not his witness. Your testimony won't put this whole business to rest."

Halla shook her head. "The only witness who could do that is dead."

Whistler trumpeted loudly, whirling his head full around in a circle. The droid bounced excitedly and his tone became a piercing shriek.

Ackbar's gavel cracked once, sharply, jerking Emtrey to attention. "Tell Whistler to calm down or I'll have a restraining bolt put on him."

The little droid stopped and hummed mournfully.

"Now what was he talking about, Emtrey?"

Whistler answered.

Emtrey glanced sharply down at him and gave him a good clout on the dome. "Make sense, Whistler. They're waiting."

Whistler repeated his previous answer.

The 3PO unit raised its arms and looked up at Ackbar. "I am sorry, sir, but he makes no sense. The stress-circuits must have become polarized. He doesn't know what he's saying."

Ackbar sighed. "Answer my question. Who is he saying this witness is?"

Before Emtrey could answer, a man spoke from the court's open doorway. "Begging your pardon, Admiral, I think Whistler intends for *me* to be called as a witness."

Ackbar's barbels twitched. *From the black depths all manner of beasts can swim.* "This is impossible."

"It wasn't easy," Corran Horn smiled, "but as for impossible, Admiral, you know impossible is what Rogue Squadron does best of all."

43

WEDGE SNAPROLLED UP on the port S-foil, then pulled the stick back to the box over his breastbone. He rolled the X-wing into a dive, then came up and around to starboard in a horizontal loop that brought him back head-to-head with the pair of eyeballs that had been bucking his exhaust. He spitted one on his crosshairs and hit the trigger, filling it with coherent light. The cockpit instantly combusted, and, trailing thick black smoke, the TIE fighter corkscrewed down to slam into a ferrocrete tower.

The TIE's wingman tried to avenge his partner, but Wedge never gave him a chance. He hit the left rudder pedal, pulling the aft end of the X-wing off to the right. The maneuver skidded the fighter out of the TIE's line of flight and fire. The TIE pilot tried to match the stunt, but as he did so he brought his fighter's hexagonal solar panel perpendicular to the ship's flight-line. In the vacuum of space that move would have given him a good shot at Wedge, but in atmosphere, it made the TIE jump and begin to roll.

Wedge brought the X-wing up on its port stabilizers and dove after the TIE. Just as the pilot began to regain control, slowing his spin, Rogue Squadron's leader tightened up on his trigger. A quad burst of laserfire blasted the port solar panel off the fighter. The TIE began to tumble uncontrollably toward the ground, but before it could descend into the black bowels of Coruscant, it bounced off an aerial walkway and exploded.

Pulling back on his stick, Wedge nosed his fighter toward the sky. He wanted to feel some remorse for the pilots he'd just killed. He waited for concern to bubble up in him for the people who could have been hurt when those TIEs fell into the city below. He wanted something other than cold concentration filling him, but he didn't expect it to come. *Those thoughts and emotions are normal, but normal doesn't exist at this place and time.*

All around him TIEs and the X-wings of Rogue Squadron swooped and climbed, rolled, dove, and looped. Laserbolts, green and red, filled the air as if each fighter was a renegade cloud spitting abbreviated lightning bolts at its enemies. TIEs exploded with regularity, showering the cityscape with half-molten bits of metal and staining the sky with oily black streaks that were the mortal remains of their pilots.

As exciting and dramatic as the dogfight raging above the mountain district was, Wedge remained cold and in shock. Out there a white needle stabbed skyward. The *Lusankya*—a Super Star Destroyer eight kilometers in length—laid waste to the area beneath which it had lain buried for years. Green turbolaser bolts pounded the cityscape, freeing the ship from the ferrocrete and transparisteel prison in which it had laired.

Wedge knew Super Star Destroyers had only come into service after the Battle of Yavin, which meant the *Lusankya* had to have been created and hidden on Coruscant before the battle of Endor. *Unless the constructor droids just built it there, then built over it.* The idea that a hundred-square-kilometer area of the planet could have been razed and rebuilt to hide a Super Star Destroyer seemed beyond belief, especially with no one noticing the ship's insertion into the hole. *Could the Emperor's power through the dark side of the Force have been sufficient to compel thousands or millions of people to forget having seen the* Lusankya *being buried?*

As hideous as that idea seemed, Wedge hoped it was the truth. The likely alternative—that the Emperor had ordered the deaths of all the witnesses—seemed that much more horrible.

"Lead, you have a squint coming up from below."

"Thanks, Five." Wedge rolled to port, then dove into a looping roll that took him out and around the Interceptor's attack vector. He let his dive carry him down into the upper reaches of the city. Using control telemetry from a skyhook to keep track of the squint, he cut around one of the star-raking spires and came up at it on a nearly vertical run.

It started to roll to elude him, but a little left rudder kept his lasers tracking. Half the quad burst missed, shooting past the cockpit windscreen, but the other two bolts hit dead on. They cored through the Interceptor's starboard solar panel and pierced the cockpit. The squint continued its lazy roll, then tightened it into a spin that sped the ship in an ugly, squared-off tower.

Out to the south the *Lusankya*'s aft came free of the planet. The superstructure of the Super Star Destroyer and its general outline fit with what he remembered of Vader's *Executor* at Hoth and Endor, but the *Lusankya* hull appeared to be resting on a massive platform made up of hexagonal cells. It fit the bottom of the starship perfectly, with openings in the hexagonal field so weapons could fire down at targets below and TIE fighters could launch from the ship's belly.

Wedge frowned. *What is that? It reminds me of a Hutt's repulsor-lift couch, but the* Lusankya *is a warship, not a lounging crime boss.* Suddenly he realized his analogy wasn't that far off. *The* Lusankya *is built for space travel, not fighting its way free of a planet. That must be a lift-cradle designed to get it up and out of the hole in which it was entombed.*

With the prow stabbing up into the sky, the *Lusankya*'s thrusters ignited. Searing blue plasma vaporized huge chunks of cityscape beneath the ship's aft end. The destroyer began to move forward and upward out of the column of smoke that marked its birth. *A ship that boasts a crew of over a quarter of a million individuals must have killed ten times that many lifting off.*

The massive ship turned its attention on a skyhook floating off its starboard bow. Altering course slightly, the ship gave more of its turbolasers and ion cannons a chance to bear. A Super Star Destroyer possessed enough weaponry to reduce a city to rubble from an orbital assault. At point-blank range, the weaponless skyhook offered the gunners a deliciously easy target.

The turbolaser batteries in the bow started firing at the skyhook as they came into range, then the broadside assault shifted to other weapons as the ship slid past. The verdant laser-bolts came so fast and so close that whole sheets of energy seemed to pulse from the *Lusankya* to the skyhook. In seconds what had once been an elegant disk with an Ithorian jungle paradise at its heart became a melted demilune with a forest fire crashing into the mountain district's towers.

As the *Lusankya* picked up speed, the gunners shifted their aimpoints and began firing at the upper atmosphere. Their shots hit and splashed color into the lower of the two shield spheres encasing the planet. Created to stop starship assaults from without, they proved just as powerful against an attack from within. Even so, after twenty seconds of the *Lusankya*'s withering barrage, a hole opened in the lower shield.

The TIEs fighting Rogue Squadron turned and launched themselves on an intercept course for the Super Star Destroyer. Because they were not capable of entering hyper-space themselves, if they did not rendezvous with the *Lusankya*, they would be stuck on Coruscant. Those who weren't shot down would be taken prisoner. *And if my ship had done that much damage heading out, I'd not be expecting very gentle treatment at the hands of my enemies, either.*

"Mynock, give me the range to the *Lusankya*."

The droid centered an image of the *Lusankya* on Wedge's

monitor, and the rangefinder showed it to be 25 kilometers distant. *And it still looks that big.* A shiver ran down his spine.

"Rogues, form up on me. We have three minutes at speed before we're right on top of the SSD. Let's harvest those remaining TIEs before she gets a chance to recover them." Wedge waited a few seconds for the cries and shouts of assent to die down. "Remember, that thing is bristling with turbolasers, ion cannons, concussion missile launchers, and tractor beams. When I call, you break off your attacks. Got it?"

Wedge fed shield power into his engines, boosting his speed. He saw Asyr pull up on his starboard stabilizer foil. "No heroics, Flight Officer Sei'lar, I want to return that datacard to you."

"As ordered, Commander."

Wedge glanced at his monitor and then the TIE they were closing on fast. "I have your back. He's yours."

"Thank you, Commander." Asyr's X-wing pulled ahead, then sideslipped down and to port. She stayed below and behind the TIE fighter until she'd closed the range to within 250 meters, then she nosed her ship up into the eyeball's exhaust. The X-wing's lasers fired two dual offset bursts. The first grazed the inside of the port solar panel, burning two long streaks along it. The second pair of bolts stabbed in through the exhaust ports. The whole eyeball shuddered, then silvery fire jetted out through the forward cockpit canopy, killing the ship's momentum.

The dead TIE dropped from sight with the grace of a Hutt in freefall.

"Nice shooting, Deuce."

"Thanks, Lead."

Wedge glanced at the Chronographic readout on his monitor. "Two-point-five minutes to range. Mynock, give me a warning at thirty seconds."

The *Lusankya* continued to pour fire into the planetary shields while what little ground fire that came up at it splashed harmlessly on its shields. The midship and stern guns fought to keep the hole in the lower shield open while the bow guns blasted away at the upper shield. The ship's assault sent waves of Rodian green energy skittering along the underside of the shields. The shields held at first, then began to erode, and finally collapsed.

Cutting his stick to the right, Wedge followed Asyr through a banking turn that put her on a pair of TIEs. "I have the leader, Commander."

"I copy. I'll pick up the tail, Deuce." He widened the separation between them, then cut back hard to port as the TIEs broke and Asyr came around in a looping turn that slipped her in behind the lead TIE. She fired and melted off a third of the TIE's starboard solar panel.

"Break left, Deuce!"

Asyr rolled to port as the second TIE fired. Its first shots splashed harmlessly on the X-wing's aft shields, but the subsequent ones went wide. The eyeball rolled to follow Asyr, but as he leveled out he drifted straight into Wedge's sights. One burst of scarlet laserfire and the eyeball disintegrated into one long, flaming streak in the sky.

Mynock gave Wedge the 30-second warning tone. "Break off, Rogues. The rest are just running." It looked like a half-dozen of the TIEs had survived the battle. As a screening force they'd done their jobs and kept local fighters off the *Lusankya* while it emerged. *While it was trapped beneath the city I bet it couldn't power its shields up. Without them, a concentrated volley of proton torpedoes might have been able to breech the hull, disable that lift shell, or destroy the bridge.*

Wedge glanced at his sensor display. "Four, this is Rogue Leader. Break off pursuit."

"Just a couple seconds more."

"Four, break off, *now!*"

"I've almost got him, Lead."

"You're too close, Four. Break off immediately!"

Erisi's X-wing fired a quad burst that caught an Interceptor on the starboard solar panel and right side of the cockpit. Something at the rear of the craft exploded, then seconds later the whole Interceptor came apart. A huge golden-red ball blossomed in front of Erisi's X-wing, then imploded into black smoke as she flew through it.

"Report, Four."

"I got him, Lead."

"And got crisped. Get back here."

Fear injected itself into her voice. "Rudder's gone, stick's sluggish."

"Erisi, you're too close to the *Lusankya*. Get out of there." Wedge brought his X-wing around to the left in a long, orbiting loop. "Mynock, pull status data from her R5 unit, now." He keyed his comm unit. "Erisi, roll and dive. Gravity is your friend."

"As ordered. No, wait." A wail as frightening as any Mynock had ever made shot through the comm unit. "They have a tractor beam on me. I'm at full thrust, but I can't break loose. Help me, help me!"

Pulling back on the stick, Wedge came up and pointed the nose of his fighter at the *Lusankya*. The big ship hung like a sliver of ice stabbed deep into the morning sky. He thought he could see Erisi's X-wing as a little speck against the Super Star Destroyer's bulk, but a sheet of turbolaser fire heading back toward him eclipsed her.

Hugging the stick to his chest, Wedge brought the X-wing over the top and pointed it back toward the planet. "On me, Rogues. We're going home."

"But, Lead, we can't just leave her—"

"Enough, Gavin. That's a Super Star Destroyer. It's impossible to stop if it doesn't want to be stopped."

"But impossible is—"

"I know, Rogues, I know." Wedge glanced at his monitor and let the cold shiver running up his spine bleed into his voice. "Impossible is what Rogue Squadron does, but right now that would cost us too much for too little gain. Just because we can do the impossible doesn't mean we always win."

44

CORRAN HORN MUSTERED a smile in response to Admiral Ackbar's blinking expression of disbelief. "If someone is inclined to call me as a witness, I think I can shed some light on the murder charges against Captain Celchu."

The Mon Calamari's mouth opened and closed a couple of times, then he nodded toward the prosecution table. "Perhaps, Commander Ettyk, the prosecution would like to reopen its case?"

The dark-haired prosecutor nodded. "Thank you, sir. We call Corran Horn."

Corran limped his way up toward the front of the court. He placed his blaster carbine on the prosecution table, then turned and approached the defense table. He squatted down beside Whistler and wiped a speck of dust from his optical lens. "Thanks for guiding me in here, Whistler. Without you, I've been lost."

The droid hooted softly, then opened the storage compartment in his dome. Corran reached in and pulled out his own unblemished Jedi medallion and the gold chain from which it hung. Corran fastened it around his neck, then fished the ruined medallion from his pocket and put it into the storage compartment. "Not quite a fair trade, my friend, but I'll make it up to you."

Coming up from his crouch, Corran looked over at Tycho. He nodded and lowered his voice into a whisper. "I owe you an apology, a *huge* apology, and a debt I can never repay. All this is my fault, and I'm sorry I caused you to go through it."

"You're wrong, Corran." Tycho shook his head. "You were manipulated by the Empire. So was I, so was everyone here. I'll accept your apology, but I won't acknowledge your debt."

"I'll still pay it, or at least make a down payment on it."

Tycho smiled. "Getting the murder charge removed from the indictment is a good start."

"I can do much better. Watch me." Corran nodded, then dropped a hand on Emtrey's left shoulder. He bent in close to the droid's aural sensors and kept his voice low. "Emtrey, say nothing. Shut up. Shut up. Shut up."

The droid's head swiveled around to look at him. "Sir, I understood the first request. Quadruple redundancy in orders is hardly required in my case."

Fixed you, have they, Emtrey? That's it, then, the last piece falls into place. Corran straightened up and shot General Cracken a quick nod. Turning back toward the front of the courtroom, Corran bowed his head to the Tribunal. "My apologies to the court, but there were things that needed saying."

Ackbar nodded. "Understood."

General Salm frowned. "Lieutenant Horn, I have to ask, how did you get here?"

"I started, at least this morning, from the Museum next door. Big metal doors sealed the aerial tunnel between the buildings, but, well," he said, brandishing the lightsaber, "you'd be amazed how effective these things are in opening doors. Your security personnel were stationed at the more accessible entry points, so I made it here without any other trouble."

Salm frowned. "I appreciate the critique of our security, but I meant the question in a more general sense. You, ah, are dead."

Corran limped his way into the witness box. "I think you'll want me sworn before I answer that question. It won't make the answer any more believable, but it'll give you some peace of mind."

A bailiff swore Corran in and Halla Ettyk approached him cautiously, as if he were radioactive. "I hardly know where to begin. Perhaps you can tell the court what has transpired since you were reported dead."

"Sure." Corran took a deep breath, then started. "I'm certain General Cracken will debrief me, and some of what I have to say probably shouldn't be said in open court, but I'll try to keep it cogent and coherent."

Ackbar nodded down at him. "Your discretion is appreciated."

"Yes, sir." Corran smiled at the prosecutor. "To answer your question, Commander, I was captured by Imperial Intelligence and taken to Lusankya. Ysanne Isard wanted to do to me what she tried to do to Captain Celchu: make me into an agent who would do her bidding when and where she wanted."

Halla frowned. "You said she wanted to do to you 'what she tried to do to Captain Celchu.' Don't you mean she wanted to do to you what she *did* to Captain Celchu?"

Corran blushed. "I thought, for the longest time, that she *had* programmed Captain Celchu and that his lack of memory about Lusankya was a blind to keep his Imperial ties hidden. The fact is, however, that his amnesia about Lusankya is not uncommon among those who wash out of Isard's indoctrination program. Other prisoners at Lusankya remembered Captain Celchu as being a *sleeper*—their term for someone who is rendered catatonic by the indoctrination process. I didn't become a sleeper. Later I had a chance to access computer files about prisoners at Lusankya. I reviewed my own file and then I called up Captain Celchu's file. I wanted it as proof that he *was* one of Isard's creatures, but he had the same susceptibility rating I did, which is to say that he had no susceptibility to her techniques at all. As far as she was concerned, we were as dense as duracrete."

"But his file could have been altered and left there for you to discover it."

"Possible, but not likely for two reasons." Corran held up two fingers. "First, the datapad I used to access the files was in a secure area that provided me with access to a working blaster *and* the means to go from Lusankya to here. Given the precautions Isard took to hide the location of Lusankya when I went in, I doubt any prisoner was meant to have access to that area. Second, at the time I accessed the files, Isard had no way of knowing I was in a position to access them. She believed another prisoner had escaped, not me, so any ruse would have been designed to ensnare him, not me."

Halla hesitated, concentration sinking her brown eyes into shadow. "That notwithstanding, we have to take into consideration the possibility that you might have been turned and are here so that both you and Captain Celchu could be put into positions of trust in the future."

"True, but the fact is that once the shadow of suspicion was lifted from Tycho, I was able to eliminate him as possibly being the traitor in the unit. If he is taken out of the hologram, there is only one other logical candidate for that position."

Before Corran could reveal the traitor's identity, a soldier burst through the courtroom doors and ran over to General Cracken. He said something quickly and urgently to the Alliance Intelligence chief. Cracken shot to his feet and pointed at Corran. "Lieutenant Horn, I order you to say nothing more at this time. Admiral Ackbar, we need to use the adjoining jury room, now!"

Corran hesitated, then frowned. "I wasn't going to reveal any of your secrets, General."

"Horn, shut up. That's an order." Cracken walked across the courtroom to the door in the southeast corner. He opened it and swore. "This can't be happening."

Corran vaulted from the witness box and followed on Cracken's heels into the large, rectangular room. Transparisteel made up the room's entire southern wall, with a small doorway cut in the middle of it to allow access to a balcony. Cracken worked a set of controls on the wall, fading the sequestration opaquing of the transparisteel to nothingness. Corran looked out to the south and felt his heart sink into his bowels.

A colossal white wedge knifed its way into the sky. A fearsome broadside silhouetted a skyhook against a green background, then sent a smoking crescent crashing planetward. The ship—Corran knew it had to be a Super Star Destroyer because of the size—continued its upward flight and turned its weapons on the lower defense shield.

Corran found himself drifting through the doorway and onto the balcony with Admiral Ackbar and the others from the court. Above the city TIE fighters and X-wings tangled together in a complicated dance punctuated with fireballs and underscored with laser light. Corran couldn't get an accurate count on the X-wings, but he didn't see any of them go down. *That's gotta be Rogue Squadron up there.*

The Super Star Destroyer moved up through the first defense shield. The TIEs started to run back to the ship that had launched them and the X-wings flew on in close pursuit. Corran smiled as more TIEs exploded or augured into the planet, but that appeared as a minor bright spot in comparison to the damage the Imperial ship had done to the defense shields.

Corran frowned. "Where did that ship come from?"

Whistler popped a sensor dish from his dome and let it spin around a couple of times before keening cautiously. Emtrey's head jerked up and down, from the ship to Whistler and back again. "Sir, he says that ship's transponders report it to be the *Lusankya*!"

Corran's jaw dropped open. *The bulkhead doors closing off access to the gravel mine wasn't salvaged from a ship, it was part of a ship. The turbolifts, too, were part of the ship. Our whole complex must have been one tiny part of the ship with bulkheads trimmed out with stone. The mines were outside it, but we lived all snugged up in the belly of an Imperial Super Star Destroyer.*

Cracken held a comlink up by his ear. "The ship appears to have been buried beneath a portion of the cityscape southwest of the Manarai Mountains. It came up firing. Freeing itself it devastated over a hundred square kilometers. Millions are missing, presumed dead."

Corran pointed at the platform made of hexagons hugging the ship's hull. "What's that below it, some new type of armor?"

Whistler hooted sharply and Emtrey translated. "Whistler says it appears to be a massive collection of repulsorlift cells grafted together to float the ship free of Coruscant."

"Ah," said Cracken, "so that's what they did with the lift-coils. Well before Endor, we uncovered an Imperial operation to collect an incredible number of repulsorlift components. We feared they might be planning to produce some new planetary assault vehicles with them, but could never trace the shipments. Now we know where they went."

He looked over at Ackbar. "Can you stop it?"

"Most of the fleet is staging at . . . elsewhere in preparation for the operation against Zsinj—to hunt down *his* Super Star Destroyer. The rest of the fleet is on an assignment for you. Can you get them here?"

Cracken shook his head. "From Borleias? Not in time."

"The Golan stations don't have enough power to bring *Lusankya* down, but they can hurt it."

Emtrey's eyes dimmed. "We're defenseless."

General Crix Madine shook his head. "The *Lusankya* started inside our defense shields—the point assault forces usually see as a goal. The fact that the ship is headed *out* means escape, not conquest, is its goal."

A Quarren aide slipped through the crowd to Admiral Ackbar's side and handed him a comlink. The Mon Calamari flicked it on. "Ackbar here."

"Antilles here, Admiral. We've broken off our pursuit of the

TIEs and are returning to base to refuel and get ready to go out again."

Hearing Wedge's voice again sent a thrill through Corran. He smiled and saw Tycho mirror his expression. "Are you thinking what I'm thinking?"

Tycho nodded. "If I had Rogue Squadron on my tail, I'd be running, too, even in a Super Star Destroyer."

Ackbar gave them a wall-eyed stare. "I concur with your plan, Commander, but you needn't have informed me of it at this time."

"No sir, I know that." A cold edge crept into Wedge's voice. "The reason I called is to tell you to let Tycho go. He wasn't the traitor. I know who is and I can prove it."

"What?" Ackbar's mouth hung open. "Who?"

Corran smiled. "Erisi Dlarit."

"I was asking Commander Antilles."

"Who was that?" Wedge asked remotely. "How did he know?"

Cracken made a quick adjustment to his own comlink. "Commander, this is General Cracken. Use no more names on this opchan—it might not be secure."

Ackbar shook his head. "How do you know who the traitor is?"

Corran pointed at himself. "Are you asking me?"

"No. Commander Antilles, please answer me."

"Simple. Because of Horn's death I had a subroutine added to the unit's astromech droids allowing me to pull diagnostic data from them. She reported damage over the comm unit that her R5 didn't report. She claimed the *Lusankya* had a tractor beam on her and pulled her aboard against her will. Work back from there and it's obvious."

Corran nodded. "Right. She was in a position to forewarn the Imps about Bror Jace's return to Thyferra—and there was no love lost between them. I told her that when we'd taken Coruscant I was going to search out the traitor in our midst. She'd helped me check out my Headhunter so she knew the codes, the same as Captain Celchu. She comlinked the data to Isard and I was taken."

General Salm shook his head. "Why would she do that? Why work against us?"

Wedge provided an explanation. "The bacta cartels were formed under the Empire. She and her people might have figured their monopoly would end if the New Republic succeeded in destroying the Empire."

Tycho pointed toward the sky. "It's through the second shield and outbound."

Barely visible above them, the *Lusankya* exchanged fire with a Golan Space Defense Station. Gouts of green energy passed back and forth between them. The station's fire buckled the *Lusankya*'s shield, collapsing the energy sphere that had kept the big ship safe. Explosions played along the huge ship's hull, but in their light Corran saw the *Lusankya* begin to pull away from the station.

The Golan Station continued to blaze away at the Super Star Destroyer, causing more explosions, but they seemed to form a wall between the station and the ship itself. It took Corran a moment to realize what was happening.

"They jettisoned the lift-cradle, sacrificing it so they could escape."

Cracken nodded. "Nothing to lose by doing that—the *Lusankya* isn't going to be trapped on a planet again."

"But it will be trapped again." Corran nodded solemnly, recalling his promise to Jan to return and free him and the others. He glanced at Whistler. "Can you determine the damage to the *Lusankya*?"

Whistler blatted negatively and retracted his sensor dish.

Corran squinted but couldn't see the Super Star Destroyer anymore. "Gone to lightspeed. I wouldn't like to be where that ship ends its journey."

"Being where it started from was bad enough." Cracken shivered. "Isard was here all along, and now she's gone."

Halla Ettyk folded her arms across her chest. "I take it I

should assume the evidence against Captain Celchu was largely manufactured by her?"

"I'd say that's a safe bet." Corran nodded assuredly. "If Captain Celchu had been convicted and executed, she would have revealed the truth and made the New Republic look as bad as the Empire ever did. It probably wasn't the most brilliant of her plans, but it didn't take much effort, either."

He turned and looked at Airen Cracken. "After all, the General here knew Tycho wasn't the spy all along."

Halla blinked. "Excuse me, what?"

Cracken slowly smiled. "Not bad for a man who's been in prison for the past month and a half."

General Salm glowered at the Intelligence chief. "You mean you knew Tycho Celchu was not an Imperial agent and you let me put him through all sorts of difficulties?"

Cracken shook his head. "Horn's right, I knew he wasn't the spy in Rogue Squadron, but I did *not* know whether or not Celchu was an Imperial agent."

"General Cracken took precautions to guard against Tycho being a Lusankya-style agent." Corran patted Emtrey on the shoulder. "General Cracken had Emtrey assigned to Rogue Squadron to monitor Captain Celchu. Emtrey had some special circuitry and programming installed in him that transformed him into an invaluable tool for a spy. If Captain Celchu had used him in that manner, General Cracken would have known what was going on. For General Cracken to have done anything less would have been grossly irresponsible on his part.

"Because of Emtrey, General Cracken knew Captain Celchu had not been meeting with Kirtan Loor the night I saw him at the Headquarters. I suspect Captain Celchu's prosecution was allowed to go forward to lull the real spy into a false sense of security."

"And to distract Isard." Cracken smiled briefly. "She has always enjoyed these little games."

Halla stared at General Cracken. "But you made Captain

Celchu into a pariah. People were likening him to Prince Xizor and Darth Vader. What you did was unforgivable."

"No, it was precisely what had to be done." Cracken looked over at Tycho. "I needed to use you to find out who the spy in Rogue Squadron really was, true, but there was a side benefit to you in all this. The fact that Isard would set you up to be convicted and executed means that you were of no *greater* use to her. If you were one of her Lusankya agents, she would have framed someone else so you'd have been absolved of guilt and trusted with greater responsibilities. She would have fine-tuned you, not discarded you."

He turned back toward Halla Ettyk. "As for the negative image of Captain Celchu that has been created, I can undo what has been done."

"Never." Salm shook his head adamantly. "Impossible."

"Though I am not a member of Rogue Squadron, I think it is quite possible." Cracken opened his hands. "We have a public ceremony rewarding the efforts of Rogue Squadron for their operations on behalf of the Republic. We let it be known that Captain Celchu was aware of the deception concerning his trial. . . ."

Tycho smiled. "Things *did* seem arrayed rather well against me."

". . . And his rehabilitation will be complete." Cracken clasped his hands at the small of his back. "That is pretty much what I had intended all along the way. Lieutenant Horn's appearance here merely makes Captain Celchu's innocence that much more obvious."

Halla looked over at Admiral Ackbar. "Sir, on behalf of the New Republic Armed Forces, I withdraw all charges against Captain Tycho Celchu."

The Mon Calamari opened his mouth in a smile. "It is with great pleasure, Captain Celchu, that I say this case is dismissed. You are truly free to go."

45

WEDGE ANTILLES KEPT his face impassive as Mon Mothma stepped up to the podium at the front of the dais on which they stood. The ten days since the *Lusankya*'s escape from Coruscant had been grueling. Abandoned Palpatine Counter-insurgency Front cells had begun to strike out anywhere and everywhere. Rogue Squadron, reinforced by Corran and Tycho, had flown numerous pursuit and cover missions, which seriously curtailed the PCF's activity.

Cracken's efforts to slice Loor's datacard had proven fruitless until its existence had been mentioned during one of Corran's debriefings. Corran noted that when Loor was working as the Imperial Intelligence Liaison with the Corellian Security Force, he'd had a trick for creating his encryption keys: he had memorized one day's listings of the Imperial Stock Exchange and used stock listings and prices as his keys. Corran had Whistler give Cracken the date of the listing Loor had used and they quickly discovered he'd keyed the encryption with Xucphra's listing on that day. The information on the decrypted datacard included a list of PCF safehouses and warehouse facilities, which Rogue Squadron and Cracken's people quickly destroyed.

Diric Wessiri's funeral had been tougher on Wedge than any of the flight missions. He found himself going over everything Diric had ever said to him, searching for any clue that would have revealed Diric's compelled service to the Empire. Wedge couldn't get Diric's kind words after his testimony at the trial out of his head. *That much compassion should have earned him a different end.*

Iella barely managed to hold herself together, and Wedge thought only Corran's reappearance allowed her to avoid a total emotional collapse. She'd mourned her husband once, then she got him back and had to kill him. Corran, having known her and Diric both, was able to recall for her the Diric of old. The pleasant memories seemed to soften the horror of what had happened, but only just a little and only occasionally.

Bright lights flashed on as a dozen holocams began recording the New Republic's Chief Councilor. "Citizens of the New Republic, it is a great honor and privilege for me to be speaking to you from Coruscant—a Coruscant that is now safe and finally free of the Empire's direct and evil influence. I am here, now, in the facility that is home to Rogue Squadron. You all have heard of this legendary unit—its pilots have ever been in the thick of the war with the Empire. Rogue Squadron won for us the opportunity to rescue Coruscant from the Empire, and since then they have been the bulwark that has preserved us from Imperial predation.

"In recognition of their efforts to defend the New Republic, the Provisional Council has created and is awarding to the unit and its members a medal intended to be the highest award our government can bestow upon military personnel. It is the Coruscant Star of Valor. The citation itself reads, 'For service and bravery beyond the bounds of what can be asked of a citizen by a government, and a willful commitment to put the good of the many above their own personal welfare, the Provisional Council unanimously and joyfully awards to Rogue Squadron and its members, the Coruscant Star of Valor.'"

As Mon Mothma turned and looked back at him, Wedge

came forward and accepted a transparisteel plate into which the citation had been etched. A hologram of the medal itself had been embedded in the transparisteel above the words, and a ghostly hologram of the unit's members had been placed behind them.

Mon Mothma shook Wedge's hand. "Congratulations, Commander. You and your people deserve this even more than I probably know." She then stepped back and waved him toward the podium.

Wedge hesitated, then stepped up to the microphones. He had been warned he'd be asked to say something, and a number of people had made suggestions, but it was Admiral Ackbar's advice he decided to heed. *Be brief, he said, and remember all those who need to be remembered.*

"This citation is not just for those of us who stand here behind me, but really for all those who fought in Rogue Squadron. None of them would have balked at making the sacrifices we have. All of us—everyone in Rogue Squadron and in the Alliance itself—have risked all we are to defeat a government that took joy in the sorrow and terror of its citizens. Winning this award, taking possession of Coruscant, these things are not ends in and of themselves, but blazes marking the trail we must all tread if the galaxy is ever to be truly free."

Gentle applause from the dignitaries and guests gathered beyond the dais accompanied Wedge's retreat back into line with the other pilots. As Mon Mothma walked past him, she let her left hand brush against his arm. He glanced at her and she gave him a smile. *I guess I didn't do that badly.*

She resumed her place at the podium and began speaking again. "Of the events that have transpired over the last year, there are many rumors and far fewer facts. Those rumors could all be dispelled by having an exact chronology of events created, and perhaps, in another generation or two, such a chronology could be made public. While we were a covert force fighting against the Empire, there was no questioning the need for stealth and secrecy. It was what kept us alive and allowed us to fight on against the Empire. Because of this secrecy we have defeated them in battle after battle."

Mon Mothma nodded in the direction of the holocam to her right. "With the New Republic in possession of Coruscant, it might seem that the time for such secrecy is past, but it is not. The Empire is not yet dead, and the dozens of petty warlords tearing at it have already and will continue to study us for signs of weakness. Their drive to restore the Empire, with themselves in Palpatine's place, means we cannot reveal all of our secrets.

"We can, however, reveal some of them. Doing so is not only a vital necessity, for secrecy can breed arrogance and we have all seen where that can lead, but a pleasure. It provides me a chance to right a great wrong and prevent possible future tragedies."

She turned and pointed toward Tycho. "This is Captain Tycho Celchu, as loyal a son of Alderaan and the New Republic as ever lived. He willingly chose to subject himself to a surrendering of his basic freedoms in order to bring the Empire down. Because of suspicions about what the Empire might have done to him, it was felt he could not be trusted, yet this man refused to let those suspicions prevent him from doing all he could to destroy the Empire. On numerous occasions he put his own life in jeopardy, flying unarmed into combat zones to rescue pilots who otherwise would have died.

"Most recently you have all seen him on trial for treason and murder of other members of Rogue Squadron. This trial, as public and as ugly as it was, played a crucial part in an Intelligence operation to uncover Imperial agents within the New Republic. Despite being held up as an object of revulsion to the New Republic, Captain Celchu did not shirk his duty. He allowed himself to become such a target because it would mean that Imperial agents felt free to operate more openly while Captain Celchu was the subject of such fierce scrutiny. Imperial agents, in helping to manufacture evidence against Captain Celchu, revealed themselves to us."

Mon Mothma opened her arms. "Let there be no citizen of the New Republic who harbors suspicions about Tycho Celchu.

His devotion to the New Republic is unquestioned. His return to active service with Rogue Squadron is a joyous event for us, and an event that should be feared by those who would attack the New Republic." She initiated applause for Tycho and everyone else joined in, including Wedge once he tucked the unit citation beneath his left arm.

Tycho bowed his head toward Mon Mothma, but declined an invitation to speak with a curt shake of his head.

Mon Mothma nodded back at him, then resumed her place at the podium. "It is said of Rogue Squadron that doing the impossible is what they do best, and another member of the squadron has shown himself to be perhaps the best of the best at it. Is there anyone in the New Republic who has not heard of Corran Horn? He was the pilot who flew through the worst storm in Coruscant's recorded history to bring the defense shields down, only to be slain through the treachery of one of his comrades. It was a story that touched all of us because it spoke to the best in one individual and the worst in another. We mourned Corran Horn because his untimely death seemed yet one more tragedy caused by the Empire at a time when the Empire should have been decidedly less virulent.

"We know of Captain Celchu's innocence because of a number of things, greatest among them Corran Horn's return from the grave. He was *not* killed on the last day the Empire held Coruscant. He was captured instead. When Ysanne Isard could not break him and transform him into a puppet, he was placed in a prison where she intended him to live out the rest of his life. Though he had been told that a failed escape attempt would result in his death, Corran Horn risked his life to win his freedom. He alone has gotten away from Lusankya, and his escape precipitated Ysanne Isard's own departure from Coruscant."

Mon Mothma beckoned Corran forward, but he followed Tycho's lead, acknowledging her gesture with a slight bow and a smile. That smile remained on his face as he straightened up, though he did give Wedge a covert wink. Wedge nodded in return, pleased that both men were content with allowing the focus of the ceremony to remain on the squadron instead of shifting it to themselves.

"Citizens, Ysanne Isard's flight from Coruscant and her subsequent actions have given birth to more rumors than can be counted. It is true that with the resources available to her she did travel to Thyferra and support a revolution that put the Xucphra faction in charge of the bacta cartel. She does now rule there and has effective control over the output of the entire bacta cartel. Given that she introduced the Krytos virus to Coruscant and directed covert Imperial operations to destroy bacta storage facilities here on Coruscant, this would seem to place her in a most powerful position. Literally, it would appear that millions will live or die depending upon her whim."

Mon Mothma's voice took on a more serious tone. "Her action would have caused a crisis except for two things over which she had no control. One was a direct and unwitting result of her own haste in taking action against us. When she ordered the creation of the Krytos virus, she wanted a virus that would mutate quickly and spread between species easily. Her scientists complied with her orders, but they failed to take into account what would happen if the spread of the virus was hampered. The Krytos virus was very deadly—in fact, too deadly for her plan to succeed. Infected persons died fast—in many cases too fast to be able to spread the disease very far. An illness that kills too quickly runs itself out of hosts and dies along with them. Those individuals who lasted long enough to spread the virus did so only because, as the virus mutated, it became less virulent. Since it did not kill them so quickly, they had a chance to pass it on, but it was no longer as deadly a virus as Iceheart wanted it to be.

"This high rate of mutation also weakened the virus's defenses. Analysis of the virus allowed a Vratix verachen to be able to synthesize a specific medication to combat the virus by growing the alazhi component of bacta in a ryll-rich environment. The resulting product, known as rylca, is now being produced in a hidden location by the New Republic. More than enough to eradicate the virus will be available here well before our bacta supply runs out."

Mon Mothma glanced momentarily back toward Wedge and he saw the glimmerings of a smile on her face. "Rogue Squadron itself did not produce the rylca, but they provided support for the product and were instrumental in obtaining both the ryll and the bacta used to create the rylca. Qlaern Hirf is a Vratix verachen from Thyferra and is the creator of rylca. Equally instrumental in the success of this effort is the woman who transported the components for the rylca and rescued the Vratix from the most dire of circumstances, Mirax Terrik. You may have heard that Mirax was killed in the ambush at Alderaan, but it appears her long association with Rogue Squadron allowed her to do the impossible as well and return from that tragedy to help us deal with the Krytos virus."

The New Republic's Chief Councilor led the assembly in a round of applause for both Qlaern and Mirax. The Vratix seemed utterly nonplussed by the demonstration, but Mirax blushed fiercely. She gave Wedge a fearsome stare that he recognized by virtue of having seen it many times before, and he knew what it meant.

She's right, it is all my fault that she's being embarrassed by the attention, but I'm glad she's alive to be blushing. As nearly as Cracken and his Intelligence people could make out, Erisi had betrayed the bacta convoy to the Empire for two reasons. The first was to eliminate a lot of bacta, dashing hopes on Coruscant and driving the price yet higher. The second reason was to get Mirax killed, since her *Pulsar Skate* was one of the ships in the convoy. Mirax recalled Erisi threatening her if Mirax continued her relationship with Corran, and the destruction of the convoy offered Erisi a way to kill her rival for Corran's affections. Given that everyone thought Corran was dead at the time, the act was taken as a reflection of Erisi's vindictive and petty nature.

Then again, Isard might have told Erisi of Corran's survival and promised him to her as a reward for her continued loyalty.

Wedge shivered at that thought. *Luckily for Mirax, the* Pulsar Skate *didn't go along with the final convoy jump.* Mirax had instead shipped out to Borleias, where the captured Alderaan Biotics Facility was put to use synthesizing rylca. *The plan had been for it to appear as if Mirax had just stolen a portion of the bacta going to Coruscant—what smuggler could have resisted taking such a prize? She would have remained out of sight until the production of rylca could allow the New Republic the freedom to anger the bacta cartel by announcing their possession of a facility that could produce enough bacta-like products to break the cartel. The death of the convoy provided an even better cover for her operation, so she remained* dead *until an opportune moment to reveal the deception.*

Mon Mothma faced the holocams one last time. "Citizens of the New Republic, the last vestige of the Empire's evil has been rooted out of Coruscant. What was once an Empire is now just a collection of bitter people clutching at whatever power they can find to keep themselves apart from those they have hurt. What they do not realize, and the reason they are doomed to failure, is that all power in the galaxy comes from the free and willful investing of power by one person in another. Human and non-human, gendered or not, young, old, hale or infirm, we can only *give* power, we cannot take it. Stolen power evaporates and when it does, the empires that were built on it and of it collapse, never to rise again."

46

WEDGE FOUND IT mildly annoying that he was able to resist the generally festive atmosphere of the reception following the awards ceremony. Various guests mixed and mingled with members of the squadron while holocams made the most of every holo-op. The images would be distributed throughout the New Republic, winning a small measure of the unit's fame for the politicians and other celebrities present.

Though he was inclined to view such opportunism with a cynical eye, he didn't condemn it. The Rebellion had won. Hundreds and hundreds of worlds flocked to the New Republic's banner. The New Republic fleet was poised to go after Warlord Zsinj in a campaign that would strike fear into the hearts of all the other petty warlords in the galaxy. Even Ysanne Isard had to know her days were numbered, since there was no way the New Republic could let her remain in control of the bacta supply. With the installation of Fliry Vorru as Thyferra's Minister of Trade, bacta prices had already started to climb, making that situation one that could not be tolerated.

The reason the celebration failed to reach him went beyond his sense of mourning for Iella Wessiri. She had declined to accompany him to the reception, and he understood why. No one saw Diric as anything but one more of Iceheart's victims, but Iella clearly thought she should have been able to spot something, to have known Diric was under Iceheart's control. The obvious implication of that thinking was that if she had been more vigilant she never would have had to shoot him and the guilt over that act would be one with which she would wrestle for the rest of her life.

Ultimately Wedge's reservations about the celebration came from the past. He remembered well the celebration on Yavin 4 that followed the first Death Star's destruction. *Our joy was this transparent, this unguarded. Then we evacuated the base and began running from the Empire. I know it's stupid to associate a victory and celebration with impending disaster, but . . .*

Borsk Fey'lya cut through the milling crowd and nodded his head toward Wedge. "I wanted to congratulate you, Commander, on a game well played."

"I beg your pardon?"

The Bothan tapped claws against the barrel of his lomin-ale mug. "There was a report concerning Rogue Squadron's intervention at Alderaan. I understand it has been classified as 'Most Secret.'"

"Indeed it has." Wedge suppressed his desire to smile. "It struck me that the information about the situation at Alderaan could have compromised our rylca operation. I suggested that classifying the report that highly would be a good thing."

Borsk Fey'lya's creamy fur rippled up the back of his head. "Good for you."

"No, Councilor, good for *you.*" Wedge let his voice drop into a low growl. "You would have found the report less than satisfactory for your ends, which would have prompted you to try to destroy one of *my* people. I can assure you that would have caused problems."

"If you want to play at politics, Antilles, I would welcome you onto *my* battlefield."

"I don't want to *play* at anything, thank you. I didn't join the Rebellion to play." Wedge opened a hand and pointed to the various members of the squadron. "My job is to make certain my people do their jobs and stay alive. What I do isn't about me or garnering power, it's about people: my people and the people we defend by going after the Empire."

"And doubtless you see politics as some dirty enterprise beneath your notice."

Wedge arched an eyebrow at him. "And you can convince me otherwise?"

"You're intelligent enough, Commander Antilles, to convince yourself I'm right. You already know *everything* is political. You know, for example, that what you have done for the Rebellion has granted you power—power you might well wish to use to advance your own plans and desires. You have things that will require support to accomplish, and building a coalition of support is political."

Wedge's brown eyes narrowed. *I had hoped to advance the Vratix case for joining the New Republic, and I thought Isard's taking of Thyferra would make that job just that much easier. Is Borsk Fey'lya trying to suggest that something so obviously right and necessary might flounder because I'm not going to play his game?*

Anger began to build in Wedge, but before he could give it vent, he felt the weight of a hand on his right shoulder. His fury drained away as he turned from the Bothan and began to smile. "As stars live and die! I didn't think you'd be here, Luke."

The tow-headed Jedi Knight enfolded Wedge's hand in a firm grip, then he pulled Wedge forward into a backslapping hug. "I wouldn't have missed it for all the Tibanna gas on Bespin. I was a bit late because, quite frankly, the Jedi exhibits your man found in the Galactic Museum are, well, absorbing. I've been chasing all over trying to locate traces of other Jedi, then it turns out a repository of a lot of stuff is on the planet from which I've been basing my searches. While very little of it deals with training, there is a lot of material that lets me piece together some history."

"Corran mentioned he'd found quite a haul. He said it was rather macabre."

Luke Skywalker nodded solemnly as he stepped back from Wedge. "Once the Emperor isolated those rooms, they became his own private playground. As the Jedi in there were hunted down, the Emperor defaced their monuments. There's enough evil there to be palpable, but I think things can be set to rights again."

Borsk Fey'lya came around on Wedge's left side. "The Council is already discussing an appropriation to allow for the rehabilitation of those exhibits." The Bothan extended his hand to Luke. "Councilor Borsk Fey'lya, at your service."

At his own service. Wedge caught a mischievous glint in Luke's eyes, as if the Jedi Knight knew what he was thinking.

"It is an honor to meet you, Councilor. The efforts of your people in eliminating the second Death Star and in liberating Coruscant speak to the nobility in the Bothan spirit."

"You are most kind, Jedi Skywalker."

Wedge laughed. "That's just because you're not a womp rat scurrying down some canyon, Councilor."

"No chance of his being mistaken for that, Wedge."

"Ahem, thank you." Fey'lya smoothed the fur at the back of his head. "Jedi Skywalker, you have made strides in reestablishing the Jedi?"

"Some, though I hope for more." Luke shrugged almost imperceptibly. "Progress is seldom measured in great leaps except when viewed with hindsight."

"It is much the same with nation-building."

"So I can imagine." Luke nodded, then turned and extended his hand to the male half of the couple walking up. "Tycho, good to see you again, and now out from under suspicion."

Tycho shook his hand. "Thank you, Luke. I believe you know Winter?"

The Jedi Knight nodded and offered Winter his hand. "My sister's friend and confidant? We are well acquainted. It seems I speak with her more than I do Leia, especially with my sister off on her embassy to Hapes. How are you doing, Winter?"

"Much better, now that Tycho is free." Winter slipped her hand from Luke's and again held Tycho's hand. "I understand you are spending most of your time in the Museum."

"True. There is a wealth of material there." Luke looked over at Wedge. "I was hoping you'd introduce me to this Corran Horn."

"Gladly." Wedge looked around, caught Corran's eye, and waved him over. Corran headed in their direction with Mirax on his arm and Qlaern Hirf following them like a shadow. "Luke Skywalker, it is an honor to present to you Lieutenant Corran Horn, Mirax Terrik, and Qlaern Hirf. This is Luke Skywalker, Jedi Knight and founder of Rogue Squadron."

Corran smiled and shook Luke's hand. "I'm very pleased to meet you, sir. One of the first things Commander Antilles ever said to me was that I was 'no Luke Skywalker.' You set a very high standard for all of us to shoot for."

"Not my intention, but I'm not averse to being used as a motivational tool." Luke smiled, then shook Mirax's hand. "What you and Qlaern Hirf have done to save lives here on Coruscant is worthy of much praise and even more thanks."

Mirax shrugged. "I'm strictly transport, sir, Qlaern did the hard work."

Luke shot a glance back at Wedge. "A Corellian smuggler without an attitude?"

Wedge shrugged. "She's smarter than most."

Mirax laughed. "No profit in bragging, only working."

"Indeed." The Jedi held a hand up and brushed it along the Vratix's arm as Qlaern touched his face. "Our thanks to you for creating rylca."

"Verachen is what we are. Our joy is in our success."

"And your success will make many people very happy." Luke withdrew his arm—forestalling introductions to the rest of the squadron as they crowded around—and, for a moment, his dark cloak closed around his body. When his hands again emerged from beneath the garment, he extended a slender silver cylinder toward Corran. "This belongs to you, I believe."

"No, sir. I returned it to the Museum, and the Jedi Credit, too." Corran tapped his breastbone. "I borrowed them when escaping from there and returned them when everything calmed down."

"I know that, Lieutenant Horn." Luke's hand remained halfway between them with the lightsaber held loosely in his grip. "What I mean is that this lightsaber belongs to you. They're often passed down from one family member to another."

Corran frowned. "I think you're making a mistake here. That lightsaber belonged to a Jedi named Nejaa Halcyon. It should go to his family."

"So it shall." Luke advanced it toward him. "Nejaa Halcyon was your grandfather."

What? Luke's remark, spoken in a low, calm voice, surprised Wedge as much as it seemed to surprise Corran. "Corran, you never said anything about your grandfather being a Jedi Knight."

"He wasn't. My grandfather was Rostek Horn. He worked for the Corellian Security Force. He wasn't a Jedi. He once partnered with one—liaised with him so CorSec could work with the Jedi on things on Corellia—but that was it." Corran unfastened his tunic at the neck and pulled out the medallion he wore. He unclasped the gold chain and gathered the Jedi medallion in his right hand. "The Jedi on this medallion may have been his friend, but he wasn't my grandfather."

Luke's voice remained even. "Your father was Hal Horn?"

"Yes."

"And his given name was Valin Horn."

"Yes, but everyone called him Hal." Corran blinked. "You don't think that was a rhyme for part of his name, do you? You think that was short for Halcyon, right?"

"What I think, Corran, is that Nejaa Halcyon died in the Clone Wars, and his friend, Rostek Horn, was there to support Nejaa's widow and son through the tragedy. Rostek married your grandmother and adopted your father." Luke frowned momentarily. "When the Emperor began to hunt down the Jedi and kill them, Rostek Horn, given his position in CorSec, managed to change records so that Nejaa's family was hidden from Imperial scrutiny. You and I are alike in that we come from families with a strong Jedi tradition, yet neither of us were aware of our heritage until later."

Luke reached out and took Corran's right hand in his left. He pressed the lightsaber into it and closed Corran's fingers around the shaft. "You may want to consider finding this lightsaber a coincidence or luck, but there's no such thing. I'll have you know that of the other two-dozen lightsabers in those rooms, only three worked without recharging, and this one had lain in a case far longer than any of the others."

"You mean my grandfather wasn't my grandfather?"

"Oh, he was very much your grandfather. He accepted the responsibility for directing you and your father into the sort of life that would honor Nejaa Halcyon and insulate you from the dark side of the Force. It was a difficult and courageous thing for him to do, and clearly he did it well." Luke smiled. "In fact, he did it very well. So well, in fact, I have an offer to make you. For thirty generations the Jedi Knights safeguarded the galaxy, and the Emperor was only able to succeed in our absence. I am dedicating my life to reestablishing the Jedi Knights. I want you to join me. Come with me. Train and learn with me. Become a Jedi Knight."

Wedge felt something hollow open up inside his gut in the wake of the hushed gasps of the rest of the squadron. He instantly recognized the void—*I'm jealous!* That surprised him for a moment, then he realized how the emotion had been born. Luke had always been a special friend, but as he had grown into his heritage as a Jedi Knight, distance had formed between them. They still got along well and had a great time in each other's company, but Wedge's inability to understand what it was to be a Jedi also forced them apart. *Now someone who does not know him as well as I do, someone he barely knows at all, is being offered the chance to learn about a side of Luke I can never know.*

Corran lifted the lightsaber up in front of his face. "You want me to become a Jedi Knight?"

"Yes. Together we can make certain no more Emperors can rise up to enslave a galaxy. Everything you were raised to do within CorSec you will be able to do in the whole of the New Republic. The Empire is but one manifestation of the Force's dark side and we will stand as a buffer between it and good people everywhere."

Mirax hugged Corran's left arm. "A Jedi Knight. This is quite an honor."

Corran shook his head. "No."

Wedge nodded at him. "Oh, it *is* quite an honor, Corran, one I envy you."

"You're not hearing what I'm saying." Corran's head came up. "I realize it's an honor to be asked to train and become a Jedi Knight. Believe me I do, but my answer is no."

Borsk Fey'lya's jaw dropped open. "No?"

"No." Corran frowned. "I have things I have to do. Erisi and Iceheart have crimes to pay for."

Luke's cloak closed around him and his face became impassive. "Beware revenge, Corran. Such black emotions open the way to the dark side of the Force."

"This isn't about revenge." Corran shook his head and pain washed over his face. "It's about obligations I have to people. People who helped me, other prisoners were on the *Lusankya* when it blasted out of here. I promised them I'd come back for them. Well, we know where they are: Thyferra. It's time we go get them."

Wedge nodded. "We clearly cannot leave Ysanne Isard and Fliry Vorru in charge of the galaxy's bacta supply. We're producing rylca now and might be able to produce some bacta later, but that'll never be enough. We're going to have to go after Iceheart, and I'd prefer it to be sooner rather than later."

Borsk Fey'lya's fur rippled. "But, in fact, Commander Antilles, your quest will never take place."

"What?"

The Bothan clasped his hands together at his waist. "The Provisional Council will never sanction an operation against Thyferra. We have your orders to join the *Mon Remonda* and head out after Warlord Zsinj."

"Those orders were issued before Iceheart escaped with Erisi and Fliry Vorru. It was before she took Thyferra. We can't be expected to follow those orders." Wedge stared disbelieving at the Bothan Councilor. "That's not right."

"Oh, it is quite right, Commander. Remember, the people of Thyferra overthrew their own government and installed Ysanne Isard as their leader. This makes the revolution there nothing more than a case of internal political maneuvering."

A cold chill ran down Wedge's spine. "And the Provisional Council cannot allow itself or its agents to interfere in the internal politics of a world, because that would frighten off potential member states from joining the New Republic."

"It might even convince some others to leave and break the New Republic apart." Borsk Fey'lya glanced at Corran Horn. "You might as well accept the Jedi's offer because your unit can do nothing on Thyferra. Rogue Squadron has other duties now."

Corran arched an eyebrow at the Bothan. "Okay, I quit."

The fur on the back of Fey'lya's neck rose like a rocket. "You cannot. Antilles, talk sense into him."

Wedge snorted. "I've heard sense, and it's coming from him." Fey'lya's tone of voice had told Wedge there was no way he could advance the Vratix case before the Council. The Vratix were the backbone of the Ashern, the native independence movement on Thyferra and Isard's only opposition. His proposing that the Provisional Council back the Vratix and their claims to self-determination would meet with equal enthusiasm as any other idea about interfering with Thyferran internal politics. *I promised Qlaern I'd do what I could for its people, but the New Republic is preventing me from keeping that promise.*

Wedge rubbed a hand along his jaw. "I joined this Rebellion to fight the Empire's tyranny. Just because we have Coruscant doesn't mean it's ended. The New Republic might not be able to strike at Thyferra, but there are *Rebels* around who can." He smiled. "I quit, too."

Borsk Fey'lya turned to his left. "It would appear, Captain Celchu, that Rogue Squadron is now your command."

"I don't think so." Tycho shook his head. "It's been a long time since I've been a civillian. I'm out as well."

Corran's Gand wingman rested a hand on Corran's shoulder. "Ooryl resigns."

"Nawara and I are out," Rhysati Ynr chimed in.

Gavin smiled. "I quit, too."

Aril Nunb, Inyri Forge, and Riv Shiel all nodded in agreement. "We're out."

Asyr Sei'lar slipped in under Gavin's arm. "I resign."

Borsk Fey'lya stiffened. "You're a Bothan. You cannot."

"I'm a Rogue. It is done."

The Bothan councilor snarled. "You can't do this. You have no ships."

"Begging your pardon, Councilor, but I never signed my X-wing over to the Rebellion. I have a ship."

"Very well for you, Lieutenant Horn, but no one else does." Borsk Fey'lya's amethyst eyes burned with fury. "The rest of you have no resources for getting ships. One X-wing and some broken-down tramp freighter will take on a Super Star Destroyer?"

Mirax shot him a nasty glance. "The *Skate* isn't broken down. They need ships, I can find them."

"And pay for them with what?"

Tycho smiled. "As I recall, the New Republic made a great deal of noise about a number of bank accounts belonging to me with a significant amount of credits in them."

"That money was supplied by Isard to frame you."

"So much the better to use it against her, wouldn't you say?"

"This is insanity! You cannot do this." Borsk Fey'lya raked his fur back down into place. "Jedi Skywalker, convince them of their folly. They will fail if they try."

"As my master told me, there is no *try:* one can only *do* or *do not*," Luke nodded solemnly. "It seems, Wedge, those are your choices."

"No choice at all, Luke." Wedge smiled broadly. "We're, ah, we *were* Rogue Squadron. We *do*."

ACKNOWLEDGMENTS

The author would like to thank the following people for their various contributions to this book:

Janna Silverstein, Tom Dupree, and Ricia Mainhardt for getting me into this mess;

Sue Rostoni and Lucy Autrey Wilson for letting me get away with all they have in this universe;

Kevin J. Anderson, Timothy Zahn, Kathy Tyers, Bill Smith, Bill Slavicsek, Peter Schweighofer, Michael Kogge, and Dave Wolverton for the material they created and the advice they offered;

Lawrence Holland and Edward Kilham for the *X-Wing* and *TIE Fighter* computer games;

Chris Taylor for pointing out to me which ship Tycho was flying in *Star Wars VI: Return of the Jedi* and Gail Mihara for pointing out controversies I might want to avoid;

My parents, my sister Kerin, my brother Patrick and his wife Joy for their encouragement (and endless efforts to face my other books out on bookstore shelves);

Dennis L. McKiernan, Jennifer Roberson, and especially Elizabeth T. Danforth for listening to bits of this story as it was being written and enduring such abuse with smiles and a supportive manner.

Read on for an excerpt from

ROGUE SQUADRON:
THE BACTA WAR

BY MICHAEL A. STACKPOLE

1

SOMEHOW THE DEAD OF NIGHT amplified the lightsaber's hiss, allowing it to fill the room. The blade's silvery light frosted the furniture and gave birth to impenetrable shadows. The blade drifted back and forth, prompting the shadows to waver and shift as if fleeing from the light.

Much as criminals would flee from the light.

Corran Horn stared at the blade, finding the argent energy shaft neither harsh nor painful to his eyes. He lazily wove the blade through joined infinity loops, then, with the flick of his right wrist, snapped it up into a guard that protected him from forehead to waist. *Relic of a bygone era, it still can conjure up images and feelings.*

He hit the black button under his thumb twice, and the blade died, again plunging the room into darkness. The lightsaber did conjure up images and feelings in him, but Corran doubted they were at all the images and feelings commonly felt by most others on Coruscant. To everyone, including Corran, Luke Skywalker was a hero and was welcomed as heir to the Jedi tradition. His efforts at rebuilding the Jedi order were roundly applauded, and no one, save those who dreaded the return of law and order to the galaxy, wished Luke anything but the greatest success in his heroic quest.

As do I. Corran frowned. *Still, my decision has been made.*

He'd felt it the greatest of honors to be asked by Luke Skywalker to leave Rogue Squadron and train to become a Jedi. Skywalker had told him that his grandfather Nejaa Halcyon had been a Jedi Master who had been slain in the Clone Wars. The lightsaber Corran had discovered in the Galactic Museum had belonged to Nejaa and had been presented to Corran as his rightful inheritance. *Mine is the heritage of a Jedi Knight.*

But that was a heritage he had only heard of from Skywalker. He did not doubt the Jedi was telling the truth, but it was not the whole truth. *At least not the whole of the truth with which I grew up.*

Throughout his life Corran Horn had believed his grandfather was Rostek Horn, a valued and highly placed member of the Corellian Security Force. His father, Hal Horn, likewise was with CorSec. When it came time for Corran to choose a career, there was really no choice at all. He continued the Horn tradition of serving CorSec. His grandfather had always admitted to having known a Jedi who died in the Clone Wars, but that acquaintance had been given no more weight than having once met Imperial Moff Fliry Vorru or having visited Imperial Center, as Coruscant had been known under the Empire's rule.

Corran found it no great surprise that Rostek Horn and his father had downplayed their ties to Nejaa Halcyon. Halcyon had died in the Clone Wars; and Rostek had comforted, grown close with, and married Halcyon's widow. He also adopted Halcyon's son, Valin, who grew up as Hal Horn. When the Emperor began his extermination of the Jedi order, Rostek had used his position at CorSec to destroy all traces of the Halcyon family, insulating his wife and adopted son from investigation by Imperial authorities.

Since exhibiting any interest in the Jedi Knights could invite scrutiny and my family would be very vulnerable if its secret were discovered, I probably heard less about the Jedi Knights than most other kids my age. If not for various holodramas that painted the Jedi Knights as villains and later reminiscences by his grandfather about the Clone Wars, Corran would have known little or nothing about the Jedi. Like most other children, he found them vaguely romantic and much too sinister, but they were distant and remote while what his father and grandfather did was immediate and exciting.

He raised a hand and pressed it to the golden Jedi medallion he wore around his neck. It had been a keepsake his father had carried and Corran inherited after his father's death. Corran had taken it as a lucky charm of sorts, never realizing his father had kept it because it bore the image of his own father, Nejaa Halcyon. *Wearing it had been my father's way of honoring his father and defying the Empire. Likewise, I wore it to honor him, not realizing I was doing more through that act.*

Skywalker's explanation to him of what his relationship to Nejaa Halcyon was opened new vistas and opportunities for him. In joining CorSec he had chosen to dedicate his life to a mission that paralleled the Jedi mission: making the galaxy safe for others. As Luke had explained, by becoming a Jedi, Corran could do what he had always done but on a larger scale. That idea, that opportunity, was seductive, and clearly all of his squadron-mates had expected him to jump at it.

Corran smiled. *I thought Councilor Borsk Fey'lya was going to die when I turned down the offer. In many ways I wish he had.*

He shook his head, realizing that thought was unworthy of himself and really wasted on Borsk Fey'lya. Corran was certain that, on some level, the Bothan Councilor believed he—not Corran—was right and his actions were vital to sustain the New Republic. Re-creating the Jedi order would help provide a cohesive force to bind the Republic together and to drape it in the nostalgic mantle of the Old Republic. Just as having various members of nation-states placed in Rogue Squadron had helped pull the Republic together, having a Corellian become a new Jedi might influence the Diktat into treating the New Republic in a more hospitable manner.

Skywalker had asked him to, and Fey'lya had assumed he would, join the Jedi order, but that was because neither of them knew of or realized that his personal obligations and promises exerted more influence with him than any galactic cause. While Corran realized that doing the greatest good for the greatest number was probably better for everyone in the long run, he had short-term debts he wanted to repay, and time was of the essence in doing so.

The remnants of the Empire had captured, tortured, and imprisoned him at Lusankya, which he later came to realize was really a Super Star Destroyer buried beneath the surface of Coruscant. He had escaped from there—a feat never before successfully accomplished—but had gotten away only with the aid of other prisoners. He had vowed to them that he would return and liberate them, and he fully intended to keep his promise. The fact that they were imprisoned in the belly of the SSD that now orbited Thyferra made that task more difficult, but long odds against success had never stopped him before. *I'm a Corellian. What use have I for odds?*

His desire to save them had increased with a chance discovery that embarrassed him mightily when he made it. In Lusankya the Rebel prisoners had been led by an older man who simply called himself Jan. Since his escape, Corran had caught a holovision broadcast of a documentary on the heroes of the Rebel Alliance. First and foremost among them had been the general who led the defense of Yavin 4 and planned the destruction of the first Death Star, Jan Dodonna. The documentary said he'd been slain during the evacuation of Yavin 4, but Corran had no doubt Dodonna had been a prisoner on Lusankya. *If I hadn't thought him dead, I might have recognized him, too. How stupid of me.*

Dodonna's celebrity had nothing to do with Corran's desire to save him. Jan, like Urlor Sette and others, had helped him escape. They had risked their lives to give him a chance to get away. Leaving such brave people captives of someone like Ysanne Isard not only failed to reward their courage but repaid them by leaving them in severe jeopardy of death or worse— conversion into a covert Imperial agent under Isard's direction.

"Couldn't sleep?"

Corran started, then turned and smiled at the black-haired, dark-eyed woman standing in the bedroom doorway. "I guess not, Mirax. I'm sorry I woke you."

"You didn't wake me. Your *absence* awakened me." She wore a dark blue robe, belted at the waist with a pale yellow sash. Mirax raised a hand to hide a yawn then pointed at the silver cylinder in his right hand. "Regretting your decision?"

"Which one? Refusing to join the Jedi Knights or"—he smiled—"or hooking up with you?"

She raised an eyebrow. "I was thinking of the Jedi decision. If you have reservations about the other decision, I can relearn how to sleep alone."

He laughed. "I regret neither. Your father and my father may have been mortal enemies, but I can't imagine having a better friend than you."

"Or lover."

"Especially lover."

Mirax shrugged. "All you men who've just gotten out of prison say that."

Corran frowned for a moment. "I imagine you're right, but how you came by that information, I don't want to know."

Mirax blinked her eyes. "You know, I don't think I want to know that, either."

Corran laughed, then crossed the room and enfolded her in a warm hug. "After my escape, Tycho expressed his regrets concerning your death to me. He told me how Warlord Zsinj had ambushed a convoy at Alderaan and destroyed it, including your *Pulsar Skate*. Everything inside of me just collapsed. Losing you just ripped the emotional skeleton out of me."

"Now you know how I felt when I thought you'd been slain

here on Coruscant." She kissed his left ear, then settled her chin on his shoulder. "I hadn't realized how much you had become part of my life until you were gone. The hole the *Lusankya* created blasting her way out of Coruscant was nothing compared to the void I had inside. It wasn't a question of wanting to die, but of knowing my insides were dead and wondering when the rest of me would catch up."

"I had it luckier than you. When he got the chance, General Cracken pulled me aside and told me how you'd gone on a covert mission to Borleias to deliver ryll kor, bacta, and a Vratix *verachen*. Zsinj's ambush conveniently covered your disappearance so the Thyferrans didn't know what you were setting up on Borleias with their bacta."

"Yeah, they would not have liked it if it were known we were using the Alderaan Biotics facility there to make rylca and, eventually, enough bacta to dent their monopoly." Mirax shivered. "I would have preferred the original plan working, because as much as I didn't look forward to being reviled and hunted down for stealing bacta from the convoy, I would have rather endured that than having all those other people killed."

"Nothing you could do about that."

"Nor was there anything you could do about your fellow prisoners being whisked away by Isard when she escaped in the *Lusankya*." Mirax backed up a half-step and held Corran at arm's-length. "You do realize that, don't you?"

"Realize, yes. Accept, no. Tolerate, no way." Corran narrowed his green eyes, but the hint of a smile tugged at the corners of his mouth. "You know, if you keep hanging around with me, you're going to get into a lot of trouble."

"Trouble?" Mirax batted her brown eyes. "Whatever do you mean, Lieutenant Horn?"

"Well, I precipitated the mass resignation of the New Republic's most celebrated fighter squadron and vowed that we'd liberate Thyferra from Ysanne Isard's clutches. So far, toward that end, we have a squadron's worth of pilots, *my* X-wing, and if you're really in this with us, your freighter."

Mirax smiled. "Versus three Imperial Star Destroyers and a Super Star Destroyer, not to mention any sort of Thyferran military forces that might oppose us."

Corran nodded. "Right."

Mirax's grin broadened. "Okay, so get to the trouble part."

"Mirax, be serious."

"I am. You forget, dear heart, that it was an X-wing and a freighter that lit up the first Death Star."

"This is a little bit different."

"Not really." She reached out and tapped his forehead with a finger. "You and I, Wedge and Tycho, and everyone else knows what it takes to defeat the Empire. It's not a matter of equipment, but of having the heart to use that equipment. The Empire was broken because, for the good of the galaxy, it *had to be broken*. The Rebels were given no choice, and because of that, they pushed themselves further than the Imperials did. We know we *can* win and that we *must* win, and Isard's people know nothing of the kind."

"That's all well and good, Mirax, and I agree, but this is a massive undertaking. The sheer amount of equipment we'll need to pull this off is staggering."

"Agreed. I don't think this will be easy, but it *can* be done."

"I know." Corran massaged his eyes with his left hand. "Too many variables and not enough data available to begin to assign them values."

"And three hours before dawn isn't the time you should be wrestling with such things. As bright as you might be, Corran Horn, this is not an hour when you do your best work."

Corran raised an eyebrow. "I seem to recall you singing a different tune last evening about this time."

"At that time you weren't concerned with Ysanne Isard, you were concerned with me."

"Ah, and that makes the difference?"

"From my perspective, you bet." She took the lightsaber from his hand and set it atop his dresser. "And I think, if you're willing to work with me, I can share that perspective with you."

He kissed her on the tip of the nose. "It would be my pleasure."

"That, Lieutenant Horn, is just half the objective here."

"Forgive me." Following her toward the bed, he stepped over the silken puddle her robe made on the floor. "You know, I just got out of prison."

"For that I won't forgive you but perhaps"—she smiled up at him—"I will make some allowance for good behavior."

THE STAR WARS LEGENDS NOVELS TIMELINE

BEFORE THE REPUBLIC
37,000–25,000 YEARS BEFORE
STAR WARS: A NEW HOPE

c. 25,793 YEARS BEFORE *STAR WARS: A NEW HOPE*

Dawn of the Jedi: Into the Void

OLD REPUBLIC
5,000–67 YEARS BEFORE
STAR WARS: A NEW HOPE

Lost Tribe of the Sith: The Collected
Stories

3,954 YEARS BEFORE *STAR WARS: A NEW HOPE*

The Old Republic: Revan

3,650 YEARS BEFORE *STAR WARS: A NEW HOPE*

The Old Republic: Deceived
Red Harvest
The Old Republic: Fatal Alliance
The Old Republic: Annihilation

1,032 YEARS BEFORE *STAR WARS: A NEW HOPE*

Knight Errant
Darth Bane: Path of Destruction
Darth Bane: Rule of Two
Darth Bane: Dynasty of Evil

RISE OF THE EMPIRE
67–0 YEARS BEFORE
STAR WARS: A NEW HOPE

67 YEARS BEFORE *STAR WARS: A NEW HOPE*

Darth Plagueis

33 YEARS BEFORE *STAR WARS: A NEW HOPE*

Cloak of Deception
Darth Maul: Shadow Hunter
Maul: Lockdown

32 YEARS BEFORE *STAR WARS: A NEW HOPE*

STAR WARS: EPISODE I
THE PHANTOM MENACE

Rogue Planet
Outbound Flight
The Approaching Storm

22 YEARS BEFORE *STAR WARS: A NEW HOPE*

STAR WARS: EPISODE II
ATTACK OF THE CLONES

22–19 YEARS BEFORE *STAR WARS: A NEW HOPE*

STAR WARS: THE CLONE
WARS

The Clone Wars: Wild Space
The Clone Wars: No Prisoners

Clone Wars Gambit
Stealth
Siege

Republic Commando
Hard Contact
Triple Zero
True Colors
Order 66

Shatterpoint
The Cestus Deception
MedStar I: Battle Surgeons
MedStar II: Jedi Healer
Jedi Trial
Yoda: Dark Rendezvous
Labyrinth of Evil

19 YEARS BEFORE *STAR WARS: A NEW HOPE*

STAR WARS: EPISODE III
REVENGE OF THE SITH

Kenobi
Dark Lord: The Rise of Darth Vader
Imperial Commando 501st

Coruscant Nights
Jedi Twilight
Street of Shadows
Patterns of Force

The Last Jedi

10 YEARS BEFORE *STAR WARS: A NEW HOPE*

The Han Solo Trilogy
The Paradise Snare
The Hutt Gambit
Rebel Dawn

The Adventures of Lando Calrissian
The Force Unleashed
The Han Solo Adventures
Death Troopers
The Force Unleashed II

THE STAR WARS LEGENDS NOVELS TIMELINE

REBELLION
0–5 YEARS AFTER
STAR WARS: A NEW HOPE

Death Star
Shadow Games

0

STAR WARS: EPISODE IV
A NEW HOPE

Tales from the Mos Eisley Cantina
Tales from the Empire
Tales from the New Republic
Scoundrels
Allegiance
Choices of One
Honor Among Thieves
Galaxies: The Ruins of Dantooine
Splinter of the Mind's Eye
Razor's Edge

3 YEARS AFTER *STAR WARS: A NEW HOPE*

STAR WARS: EPISODE V
THE EMPIRE STRIKES BACK

Tales of the Bounty Hunters
Shadows of the Empire

4 YEARS AFTER *STAR WARS: A NEW HOPE*

STAR WARS: EPISODE VI
THE RETURN OF THE JEDI

Tales from Jabba's Palace

The Bounty Hunter Wars
  The Mandalorian Armor
  Slave Ship
  Hard Merchandise

The Truce at Bakura
Luke Skywalker and the Shadows of
  Mindor

NEW REPUBLIC
5–25 YEARS AFTER
STAR WARS: A NEW HOPE

X-Wing
  Rogue Squadron
  Wedge's Gamble
  The Krytos Trap
  The Bacta War
  Wraith Squadron
  Iron Fist
  Solo Command

The Courtship of Princess Leia
Tatooine Ghost

The Thrawn Trilogy
  Heir to the Empire
  Dark Force Rising
  The Last Command

X-Wing: Isard's Revenge

The Jedi Academy Trilogy
  Jedi Search
  Dark Apprentice
  Champions of the Force

I, Jedi
Children of the Jedi
Darksaber
Planet of Twilight
X-Wing: Starfighters of Adumar
The Crystal Star

The Black Fleet Crisis Trilogy
  Before the Storm
  Shield of Lies
  Tyrant's Test

The New Rebellion

The Corellian Trilogy
  Ambush at Corellia
  Assault at Selonia
  Showdown at Centerpoint

The Hand of Thrawn Duology
  Specter of the Past
  Vision of the Future

Scourge
Survivor's Quest

ABOUT THE AUTHOR

MICHAEL A. STACKPOLE is the *New York Times* bestselling author of more than fifty-five novels, including *I, Jedi* and *Rogue Squadron*. He's won awards in the realms of podcasting, game design, computer-game design, screenwriting, editing, graphic-novel writing, and novel writing. He lives in Arizona and frequently travels the United States attending conventions and teaching writing workshops.

michaelastackpole.com

Twitter: @MikeStackpole

ABOUT THE TYPE

This book was set in Sabon, a typeface designed by the well-known German typographer Jan Tschichold (1902–74). Sabon's design is based upon the original letter forms of sixteenth-century French type designer Claude Garamond and was created specifically to be used for three sources: foundry type for hand composition, Linotype, and Monotype. Tschichold named his typeface for the famous Frankfurt typefounder Jacques Sabon (c. 1520–80).

A long time ago in a galaxy far, far away. . . .

STAR WARS

Join up! Subscribe to our newsletter at ReadStarWars.com or find us on social.

StarWarsBooks

@DelReyStarWars

@DelReyStarWars